HUMANS ARE FULL OF SURPRISES . . .

Even though the human was now unarmed, its stance was not that of prey. He was actually *challenging* . . . .

Human and kzin confronted each other with a long stare. The kzin seemed to be focusing on the Hellflare tattoo. Maybe the warcat did understand its meaning.

The kzin screamed and leaped directly at Gambiel.

Gambiel lifted his left foot from the entangling vines, straightened his right leg and — hoping he wouldn't screw himself right down into the criss-crossed foliage — performed a perfect veronica around the swinging left paw. Its claws extended five centimeters outside the flashing orange blur. As the furred flank passed, Gambiel struck backhanded at the third skeletal nexus. He heard as much as felt the joint crack.

The kzin's scream rose an octave in pitch.

The warrior came back on attack with a feint. Gambiel ignored the stroke but still countered with a twisting punch. It found only air and a whisk of fur.

In two more exchanges, the kzin absorbed one painful blow, and Gambiel took a raking that opened his right arm and shoulder to the bone. As he was trying to press back the flap of flayed skin, he felt a jet of arterial blood. The fourth claw had struck higher on his neck than he thought.

The kzin, sensing imminent victory, prepared its last charge.

Gambiel then made the decision that had loomed over his entire life for so long. He would not step aside again. He met the cha⸻⸻⸻ with a ⸻⸻ whose perfect focus on th⸻⸻⸻⸻⸻⸻⸻⸻ne-half centimeter lon⸻⸻⸻⸻⸻⸻⸻⸻s blow cracked that sk⸻⸻⸻⸻⸻⸻⸻⸻t claws swung across hi⸻

MAN-KZIN WARS V

Created by

Larry Niven

with

Jerry Pournelle

S.M. Stirling

&

Thomas T. Thomas

MAN-KZIN WARS V

Copyright © 1992, by Larry Niven

A Baen Books Original

Baen Publishing Enterprises
P.O. Box 1403
Riverdale, NY 10471

ISBN: 0-671-72137-2

Cover art by Stephen Hickman

First Printing, October 1992

Printed in the United States of America

Distributed by Simon & Schuster
1230 Avenue of the Americas
New York, NY 10020

CONTENTS

IN THE HALL
OF THE
MOUNTAIN KING

●

Jerry Pournelle
S.M. Stirling

● Prologue

Durvash the tnuctipun knew he was dying. The thought did not bother him overmuch — he was a warrior of a peculiar and desperate kind and had never expected to survive the War — but the consciousness of failure was far worse than the wound along his side.

Breath rasped harsh between his fangs. Thin fringed lips drew back from them, flecked with purple blood from his injured airsac. Unbending will kept all fourteen digits splayed on the rough rock; the light gravity of this world helped, as well. Cold wind hooted down from the heights, plucking at him until he came to a crack that was deep enough for a leg and an arm; the long flexible fingers on both wound into irregularities, anchoring him. He turned his head back down into the valley and closed both visible-light eyes, opening the third in the center of his forehead and straining against the dark into the depths of the valley. Yes. Multiple heat-sources in the thrintun-size range, and there were no large endothermic animals on this world. Nothing but thrintun and their slaves and foodyeast in the oceans and huge bandersnatch worms to convert it into protein.

Light-headed, Durvash giggled at that. There *had* been bandersnatch on this world, until the supposedly nonsentient worms had all turned on their thrint masters one day. Just as the sunflowers that guarded Slaver estates had all focused their beams inward. A thousand other surprises had happened that day; two centuries before Durvash was born, at the beginning of the War. The Slavers had never suspected, never suspected that the tnuctipun engineers had devised a barrier against their telepathic hypnosis, never suspected that the tnuctipun fleet that vanished into space when the Slavers found their homeworld would return one day. Thrint were fewer now.

So are tnuctipun, he thought, sobering; it did not do to depend on Slaver stupidity anymore. Most of the very stupid ones had died early in the conflict, along with a dozen thrintun slave species. The survivors were desperate. The information he had weaseled out of the base on this world was proof of that.

Durvash continued scanning, straining his eye up into the lower electromagnetic spectra. Over a dozen thrintun were toiling up the slopes below him. They had slave trackers — a species of borderline sapience but very sensitive noses — and hand weapons, and a powered sled with limited flight capabilities. He drew his sidearm, a round ball of energy with a handle, and whispered to it. The tool writhed and settled into a pistol-shape; he spoke instructions and an aiming-grid opened out above it. The map of the valley showed geological fault lines, but he would have to be very careful.

A word marked a spot on the map. "Twenty nanoseconds," he said, and turned to jam his head against the rock and squeeze all three eyes shut. Holding the weapon behind him he pulled the trigger. It would fire only for the specified time, on the specified spot . . . whuump. *CRACK.* Hot air blasted at him, slamming him back and forth, until broken shards of bone in his thorax gnawed at the edges of his breathing-sac. Automatic reflex clamped his nostril shut and made him want to curl into a ball, but tnuctipun had evolved as arboreal carnivores on a world of *very* active geology. They had a well-founded instinct about hanging on tight when the ground shook. Then rock groaned all around him, loud enough almost to drown out the sound of a falling mountainside across the valley, megatons of mass avalanching down on the river and the thrint hunters.

Total matter-energy conversion is a very active thing, even if only for twenty nanoseconds in a limited space.

Instinct kept his digits clamped tight on rock and weapon. When he woke again, he thought it was night for a moment. Then he realized it was only blackness before his eyes, and the pain began. It came and went in waves, in time to the thundering in his resonator membranes; his neck hurt from the loudness of it. Durvash spat blood and phlegm and growled deep in his throat. He crawled up the rock, crawled and crawled until he left a broad dark smear on the stone, fresh trail for the thrint hunters that would follow. He almost missed the cover of his hidehole.

Opening it was more pain, the pain of full consciousness to tap out the code sequence. By the time he reached the end of the tunnel bored through the mountain and sank into the control chamber of the tiny spaceship, he was whimpering for his mother. He made it, though, and slapped a palm down on the controls. Medical sensors sedated him and began the process of healing as best they could; other machines activated remote eyes and prepared to lift off as soon as practical.

I made it, he knew, as pain lifted and darkness drifted down. Compensators whined as the ship lifted. *We can stop Suicide Night.*

Halfway around the planet a single unwinking eye looked down on a display. A hand like a three-fingered mechanical grab touched controls.

"Launch a Godfist at these coordinates," the thrint officer rasped, his tendrils clenched tight to his mouth in determination.

"Master —" the three-armed slave technician said in agitation. A Godfist was a heavy bombardment weapon, a small spaceship in itself with a high-level computer, and well-armed for self-defense. The warhead held nearly a kilogram of antimatter. After it landed there would be very little left of the continent.

OBEY, the thrint commanded. The Power clamped down brutally; the Slaver could feel the technician's acute desire to be elsewhere.

I wish I were elsewhere too, the thrint thought bitterly, watching the Godfist lift on the remote screens. *I wish I were at the racetrack or with a female. I wish I were small and back home with Mother.*

"What does it matter?" he said to the air. "We're all going to die anyway." In about twenty years; the garrison here was to withdraw and leave only the foodyeast-supervisor quite soon. Dubious if they would make it to the next thrint-held system, anyway. The Power was of little use in a space battle against shielded tnuctipun vessels. "At least this powerloss-sucking tnuctipun spy will die before us."

As it turned out, he was wrong.

• CHAPTER ONE

Mixed crowd tonight, Harold thought, as he watched Suuomalisen's broad and dissatisfied back push through the crowd and the beaded curtain over the entrance. Sweat stained the fat man's white linen suit, and a haze of smoke hung below the ceiling as the fresher system fought overstrain. The screened booths along the walls and the tables around the sunken dance-floor were crowded, figures writhing there to the musicomp's Meddlehoffer beat, a three-deep mob along the long brass-railed bar. Blue uniforms of the United Nations Space Navy, gray-green of the Free Wunderland forces, gaudy-glitzy dress of civilian hangers-on and the new civilian elite of ex-guerrillas and war profiteers grown rich on contracts and confiscated collabo properties. Drinking, eating, talking, doing business ranging from the romantic to the economic, or combinations; and most were smoking as well. Some of the xenosophont customers would be uncomfortable in the extreme; *Homo sapiens sapiens* is almost unique in its ability to tolerate tobacco.

Tough, he decided. Outside the holosign would be floating before the brick: *HAROLD'S TERRAN BAR: A WORLD ON ITS OWN*. Below that in lower-case print: *humans only*. The fat man had chosen to ignore that in his brief spell as quasi-owner, and Harold agreed with the decision. The sign had been a small raised finger to the kzinti during the occupation years; now that humans ruled the Alpha Centauri system again, anyone who could pay was welcome. There were even a depressed-looking pair of kzin in a booth off at the far corner, the hiss-spit-snarl of the Hero's Tongue coming faintly through their privacy screen. That was the only table not crowded, but quarter-ton felinoid carnivores did not make for brash intrusion.

But it's a human *hangout, and if the aliens don't like it, they can go elsewhere,* he decided.

"Glad to see the last of *him*, boss," the waitress said, laying a platter and a stein in front of him. "I'd rather work for a kzin."

"Good thing you didn't have to, then," Harold said, a grin creasing his basset-hound features between the jug ears. Suuomalisen had bought under the impression — correct — that Harold was on the run from the collaborationist government, right towards the end of the kzinti occupation. He had also been under the impression — false — that he was buying a controlling interest; in fact, the fine print had left real control with a consortium of employees. He had been glad to resell back to the original owner, and at a tasty profit for Harold.

Akvavit, beer chaser, and plate of grilled grumblies with dipping sauce called; he added a cigarette and decided the evening was nearly complete.

"*Completely* complete," he murmured, as his wife joined him; he stood and bowed over a hand.

"What's complete?" she said. Ingrid Schotter-Yarthkin was tall, Belter-slim; the strip-cut of her hair looked exotic above the evening gown she wore to oversee the backroom gambling operation.

"Life, sweetheart."

"At seventy-three?" she said; Wunderland years, slightly shorter than Terran. She had been only two years younger than he when they were growing up in the old Wunderland before the ratcat invasion. Now, time-dilation and interstellar cold sleep had left her less than half his biological age. "Middle-aged spread already?"

"I'm spreading myself thin, personally," Claude Montferrat-Palme said, sliding in to join them.

Harold grunted. The ex-policeman *was* thin, with the elongated build and mobile ears of a purebred Wunderland *Herrenmann*. He also wore the asymmetric beard favored by the old aristocracy.

"Seems sort of strange to be back to private life," Harold said musingly.

Claude shuddered. "Count it lucky we weren't put before a court," he said.

"Speak for yourself."

Claude winced slightly; he had been police chief of Munchen under the kzinti occupation. Resister before Wunderland surrendered to the invaders, then a genuine collaborator; someone had to hold society together, to get whatever was possible from the kzin. Earth was losing the war. But then—

Then Ingrid came back, with the Belter captain, and Claude's world came apart. His help to the resistance had been effective, and timely enough to save him from a firing squad. Not timely enough to save his job as police commissioner, of course. Harold was tarred with the edge of the same brush; anyone who made money under the occupation was suspect in these new puritanical days, as were the aristocrats who had perforce cooperated with the alien invaders. *There* was irony for you . . . especially considering how the commons had groveled to the kzin, and worked to keep their war factories going during the invasions of Sol System. Double irony for Harold, since he was a Herrenmann's bastard and so never really accepted by his father's kindred. That might have changed if folk knew exactly what Harold and Ingrid and that Sol-Belter Jonah Matthieson had *done* out in the Serpent Swarm.

It would be too an exaggeration to say that the three of them — well, they three plus Jonah Matthieson —

had won the war; but it wouldn't be too large an expansion of the truth to say that without them the war would have been lost.

"Heroes are not without honor," Claude said. "Save in their own countries. Perhaps we should write a book to tell our true story."

"Sure," Harold said. "That would really make that ARM bastard happy. Right now he's happy, but —"

Claude's knowing grin stopped him. "Yes, of course. No books." He shrugged. "So we know, but no one else does."

And at that General Early had been tempted to make all four of them vanish, no matter their service to the UN. There would have been no trials. Freedom or a quiet disappearance, and for some reason — perhaps Early really had some human emotions — they'd been turned loose with their memories more or less intact.

They all frowned; Harold thoughtfully, looking down at the wineglass he rolled between his palms.

"I don't like it," Ingrid said. "Oh, I don't miss the fame — more trouble than it's worth, we'd have to beat off publicity-seekers and vibrobrains with clubs. I don't like General Buford Early — remember, I worked for him back in Sol System" — Ingrid had escaped the original kzin attack on Alpha Centauri and made the twenty-year trip back to Sol in suspended animation — "and I don't like the ARM getting a foothold here. What did our ancestors come here *for*, if not to get away from them?"

Both men nodded agreement. In theory, the ARM were the technological police of the United Nations, charged with keeping track of new developments and controlling those that menaced social peace. That turned out to be *all* new technology, and the ARM had grown until it more-or-less set UN policy. For three centuries they had kept Sol System locked in pacifistic stasis, to the point where even the memory of conflict was fading and a minor scuffle got people sent to the psychists for "repair." That placid changelessness and the growing sameness of life in the overcrowded, over-regulated solar system had been a strong force behind the interstellar exodus.

The ARM had kept Solar humanity from making ready after the first kzinti warship attacked a human vessel, right up to the arrival of the First Fleet from conquered Alpha Centauri. The operators of the big launch-lasers on Mercury had had to virtually *mutiny* to fight back, even when the kzin battlecruisers started beaming asteroid habitats.

"*I* don't like the way Early's so cozy with the new government," Harold growled.

"In the long run, luck goes only to the efficient," Claude said, and the others nodded again, because it wasn't hard to guess his train of thought.

The war was ended by pure luck: the weird aliens who sold the faster-than-light spacedrive to the human colonists on We Made It had really won the war for Sol. The kzin Fifth Fleet would have crushed all resistance, if there had been time for it to launch from Alpha Centauri and cover the 4.3 light-years at .8 c. Chuut-Riit, the last kzin Governor, had been a strategic genius; even more rare in his species, he never attacked until he was *ready*. Fortunately for humanity, that Chuut-Riit hadn't lived to send that fleet.

It had been Buford Early's idea to send in an assassin team with the scoopship *Yamamoto*'s raid as a cover. Jonah, and Ingrid, and an intelligent ship that had gone insane. A mad scheme, one that shouldn't have worked, but it was all Earth could try — and it had worked. Was General Early a military genius, or incredibly lucky?

Now the hyperdrive would open the universe to Man. The problem was that it eliminated the moat of distance; the hyperwave, the communications version of the device, gave contact with Earth in mere hours.

Cultures grown alien in centuries of isolation were thrown together . . . and serious interstellar politics became possible once more, and ARM General Buford Early was right in the middle of it all.

"I thoroughly agree," Claude said. "He's got Markham under his thumb, and a number of others. It's already unwise to cross him."

"As Jonah found out," Ingrid sighed.

Harold felt a prickle of irritation. True, Ingrid had chosen him — when both Claude and the Sol-Belter were very much available — but he didn't like to be reminded of it. Even less he didn't want to be reminded that she and Jonah had been lovers as well as teammates. It hadn't helped that the younger man refused all help from them, later.

She shook her head. "Poor Jonah. He should not have been so . . . so brusque with General Early. Buford is older than the Long Peace, and he can be . . . uncivilized."

● CHAPTER TWO

Jonah Matthieson belched and settled his back against the granite of the plinth. The long sunset of Wunderland was well under way. Tall clouds hung hot-gold nearly to the zenith of the pale blue sky, where the dome of night was darkening. Along the western horizon bands of purple shaded down to crimson and salmon pink. War had done that, the *Yamamoto*'s raid two years ago pounding the northern pole with kinetic-energy missiles at near light speed, then the fighting with the Crashlander armada later, which had included a fair number of high-yield weapons on kzinti holdouts. There was a *lot* of dust in the atmosphere. Wunderland is a small planet, half Earth's diameter and much less dense, a super-Mars; the gravitational gradient was small, and the air extended proportionately farther out. Hence there was a lot of atmosphere for it to fill.

And a wonderful sunset for one mustered-out stingship pilot to sit and savor, particularly if he was drunk enough. Unfortunately the bottle was empty.

A sudden spasm of rage sent it flying, out to crash among the other debris along the front of the Ritterhaus. The ancient government house had been a last strongpoint for the kzinti garrison in Munchen. Scaffolding covered the front of the mellow stone, but the work went slowly while more essential repairs were attended to. Much Centauran industry had been converted to war production during the occupation, and what survived was now producing for the United Nations Space Navy and Wunderland's own growing forces.

Jonah lurched erect, mouth working against the foul taste, blinking gritty eyes. For a moment the sensation reminded him —

"Oh, Finagle, I hurt."

They had come from Earth, Jonah and Ingrid and the artificial intelligence ship *Catskinner,* and the ship's computer had found something that shouldn't have been there. A ship that had floated in the Belt for so long that it had accreted enough dust to become an asteroid. A ship held unchanging in stasis, unchanging for billions of years, until it was awakened. Not just the ship. The Master.

Jonah shuddered.

That had been one of the times the thrint's mind-control had slipped. It had been busy, keeping control of all the minds of the Free Wunderland flotilla, trying to find out what had gone on during the several billion years it had lain in timeless stasis.

Eyes blurring, burning, skin hanging loose and gray and old around the wrists of bleeding hands, speckled with ground-in dirt.

Thrint tended to forget to tell their slaves to remember personal maintenance; they were not a very bright species. What humans would call an IQ of 80 was about average for Thrintun, and Dnivtopun hadn't been a genius by Slaver standards. That had been almost the worst of the subconscious humiliation. The Master had been so *stupid* — and under the Power you couldn't help but try to change that, to rack your brains for helpful solutions. Help the Master!

Jonah had been the one to crack the problem of making a new amplifier helmet to increase the psionic powers of the revenant Slaver. *That* would have made Dnivtopun master of the Alpha Centauri system and every human and kzin living there. Made him ruler of a new Slaver empire, because there had been fertile thrint females and young in the ship, the ship encased in its stasis field and the asteroid that had accreted about it over the thousands of millennia.

He moaned and pressed the heels of his hands to his temples. Yes, he'd broken free for an instant at the end, enough to struggle with Markham. Ulf Reichstein-Markham, who had *liked* the telepathic hypnosis the Slaver imposed. The psychists had erased Markham's memories of that; now he was a hero, space-guerrilla kzin-killing Resistance fighter and stalwart of the Provisional Government. The psychists hadn't been nearly as thorough with Jonah Matthieson, one-time Terran Belter, ex-combat pilot in the UNSN, assassin of Chuut-Riit. They'd just given him a strong block about the secret aspects of the affair, and turned him loose. He was supposed to recover fully in time, too. Not soon enough to have his job back, of course. No one wanted an unstable combat pilot. They'd give him his rank, but he'd be a paper shuffler, a useless man in a useless job. So he'd asked to go home. Belter prospectors were slightly mad anyway. And he learned that a hyperdrive transport back to Sol was out of the question, and there wasn't even a place for him in cold sleep aboard a slowship. Shuffle paper or get lost. Of course they'd hinted there was one other possibility, one he'd hated even more than shuffling paper.

He'd been bitter about that. That had led to more trouble . . .

A man was walking by, with the brisk step of someone with a purpose and somewhere to go.

"Gut Herr, spare some money to feed a veteran?" Jonah asked. He despised himself each time he did this, but it was the price of the oblivion he craved.

"*Lieber Herr Gott*," the man's voice rasped. Wunderland was like that, conservative: they even swore by God instead of Finagle. It had been settled by North European plutocrats uneasy with the way Earth was heading under the UN and the ARM. "You again! This is the third time today!"

Startled, Jonah looked up. The face was unfamiliar,

clenched and hostile under a wide-brimmed straw hat. The man's suit was offensively white and clean, a linen bush-jacket. Some well-to-do outbacker in town on business.

"Sorry, sir," Jonah said, backing up slightly. "Honest — I didn't look at your face, just your hands and the money. Please, I won't hit on you again, I promise."

"Here." A solid gold-alloy coin, another Wunderlander anachronism. "And here, another. To keep your memory fresh. Do not bother me again, or the polezi I will call." Frowning: "How did a combat veteran come to this?"

Jonah ground the coins together in his fist, almost tempted to throw them after the retreating back of the spindly low-gravity. *Because the bloody ARM is punishing me!* he screamed mentally. *Because I spoke out!* Not anything treasonable, no secrets, no attempt to evade the blocks in his mind. Just the truth, that they were still holding back technological secrets — had even while Earth faced defeat at kzinti hands — that they were conspiring to put the whole human race back into stasis, the way they had in the three centuries of the Long Peace, before the kzinti came. That the ARM had secret links, secret organizations on all the human-settled worlds. *Buford Early, Prehistoric Man, has frozen me out.* The ARM general probably thought he was giving a gentle warning, tugging on his clandestine contacts until every regular employment was closed to Matthieson. So that Matthieson would come crawling back, eventually.

Early was at least two centuries old, probably more. Old enough to remember when military history was taught in the schools, not forbidden as pornography. Possibly old enough to have *fought* against other humans in a war. He was very patient . . . and he had hinted that Jonah would make a good recruit for the ARM, if he altered his attitudes. Perhaps even for something *more* secret than the ARM, the thing hinted at by the collaboration with the *oyabun* crimelords here in the Alpha Centauri system. Jonah had threatened to reveal that.

Go right ahead, Lieutenant, Buford had said, laughing. It creased his carved-ebony face, gave you some idea of how ancient he really was, how little was left of humanity in him. Laughter in the gravel voice: *It's been done before. Whole books published about it. Nobody believes the books, and then they somehow don't get reprinted or copied.*

"Finagle eat my eyes if I'll crawl to you, you bleeping tyrant," Jonah whispered softly to himself.

He looked down at the coins in his hand; a five-krona and a ten. Enough to eat on for a couple of weeks, if you didn't mind sleeping outside in the mild subtropical nights. Of course, that made it more likely someone would kick your head in and rob you, in the areas where they let vagrants settle. Another figure was crossing the square, a woman this time, in rough but serviceable overalls and a heavy strakkaker in a holster on one hip.

"Ma'am?" Jonah asked. "Spare some eating money for a veteran down on his luck?"

She stopped, looking him up and down shrewdly. Stocky and middle-aged, pushing seventy, with rims of black under her fingernails. Not one of the tall slim mobile-eared aristocrats of the Nineteen Families, the ones who had first settled Wunderland. A commoner, with a hint of a nasal accent to her Wunderlander that suggested the German-Balt-Dutch-Danish hybrid was not her native tongue.

"Pilot?" she said skeptically.

"I was, yes," Jonah said, bracing erect. He felt a slight prickle of surprise when she read off the unit and section tabs still woven into the grimy synthetic of his undersuit.

"Then you'll know systems... atmosphere training?"

"Of course."

"We'll see." The questions stabbed out, quick and knowledgeable. "All right," she said at last. "I won't give you a fennig for a handout, but I could have a job for you."

Hope was more painful than hunger or hangover. "Who do I have to kill?" he said.

She raised her brows, then showed teeth. "Ach, you joke. Good, spirit you have."

She held out a belt unit, and he laid a palm on it as hope flickered out. There would be a trace on it from the net, General Early would have seen to that. There had been other prospects.

"Hmm," she grunted. "Well, a good record would not have you squatting in the ruins, smelling . . . " She wrinkled her nose and seemed to consider. "Here." She pulled out a printer and keyed it, then handed him the sheet it extruded, together with a credit chip. "I am Heldja Eladsson, project manager for Skognara Minerals, a Suuomalisen company.

"If you show up at the listed address in two days, there will be work. I am short several hands; skilled labor is scarce, and my contract will not wait. The work is hard but the pay is good. There's enough money in the chip to keep you blind drunk for a week, if that's your problem. And enough for a backcountry kit, working clothes and such, if you want the job. Be there or not, as you please."

She turned on her heel and left. Alpha Centauri had set, but the eye-straining point source that was Beta was still aloft, and the moon.

"I won't spend the chip on booze," he said to himself. "But by Murphy's ghost, I'm going to celebrate with the coins that smug-faced farmer gave me."

The question of where to do it remained. Then his eyes narrowed defiantly. Somewhere to clean up first, then — yes, then he'd hit Harold's Terran Bar. It would be good to sit down and order. *Damned* if he would have taken Harold Yarthkin's charity, though. Not if he were starving.

The chances were he'd be the only Terran there, anyway.

● CHAPTER THREE

Minister the Honorable Ulf Reichstein-Markham regarded the Terran with suspicion. The office of the Minister for War of the Provisional Government was as austere as the man himself, a stark stone rectangle on the top floor of the Ritterhaus. Its only luxuries were size and the sweeping view of the Founder's Memorial and Hans-Jorge Square; for the rest it held a severely practical desk and retrieval system, a cot for occasional sleep, and a few knickknacks. The dried ear of a kzin warrior, a picture of Markham's mother — who had the same bleakly handsome, hatchet-faced Herrenmann looks with a steel-trap jaw — and a model of the *Nietzsche*, Markham's ship during most of his years as a leader of Resistance guerrillas in the Serpent Swarm, the asteroid belt around Alpha Centauri. Markham himself was a young man, only a little over thirty-five; blond asymmetric beard and wiry close-cropped hair, tall lean body held ramrod-tight in his plain gray uniform.

"Why, exactly, do you wish to block further renovation of the Munchen Scholarium?" he said, in his pedantic Wunderlander-flavored English. It held less of that guttural undertone than it had a year ago.

General Buford Early, UN Space Navy, lounged back in the chair and drew on his cheroot. He looked to be in late middle age, perhaps eighty or ninety, a thick-bodied black man with massive shoulders and arms and a rumpled blue undress uniform. The look was a finely crafted artifact.

"Duplication of effort," he said. "Earth and We Made It are producing technological innovations as quickly as interstellar industry can assimilate them — faster than the industries of Wunderland and the Serpent Swarm can assimilate them. Much cheaper to send data and high-end equipment directly here, now that we have the hyperdrive, and hyperwave communications. You're our forward base for the push into kzinti space; the war's going to last another couple of years at least, possibly a decade, depending on how many systems we have to take before the kzin cry uncle."

Markham's brow furrowed for a moment, then caught the meaning behind the unfamiliar idiom.

"The assault on Hssin went well," he pointed out.

That was the nearest kzin-held system, a dim red dwarf with a nonterrestrial planet; the assault that took the Alpha Centauri system had been mounted from there. UN superluminal warships and transports had ferried Wunderlander troops in for the attack. Early could read Markham's momentary, slightly dreamy expression well. *Schadenfreude*, sadistic delight in another's misfortune. Hammerblows from space, utterly unexpected, wrecking the ground defenses and what small warships were deployed at Hssin. Then the landing craft floating down on gravity polarizer drive, hunting through the shattered habitats and cracking them one by one. Hssin had unbreathable air, and it had been constructed as a maintenance base more than a fortress.

"True," Early nodded. "And that's just what Wunderlanders should concentrate their efforts on — direct military efforts. Times have changed; it doesn't take decades to travel between Sol and Alpha Centauri any more. With the Outsider's Gift" — the hyperdrive had been sold to the human colonists of We Made It by aliens so alien they made kzinti look familiar — "star systems don't have to be so self-sufficient anymore."

Markham's frown deepened. "Wunderland is an independent state and not signatory to the United Nations treaties," he pointed out acerbicly.

Early made a soothing gesture, spreading his hands. The fingers moved in a rhythmic pattern. Markham's eyes followed them, the pupils growing wider until they almost swallowed the last gray rim of the iris.

"You really don't care much about the Scholarium, do you?" the Terran said soothingly.

Markham nodded, his head moving slowly up and down as if pulled on a string.

"True. It vas of no use to us during the occupation, und now makes endless trouble about necessary measures." His accent had grown a little thicker.

"There are so many other calls on resources. And it really is politically troublesome."

Another nod. "Pressing for early elections. *Schweinerie!* What does nose-counting matter? Ve soldiers haf the understanding of Vunderland's problems. The riots against the Landholders must be put down! Too many of my colleagues prejudices against their social superiors haff."

"The alliance with the UN is important. We have to stand by our allies while the war is on, after all."

This time Markham seemed to frown slightly, his head jerking as if it tried to escape some confinement. Early moved his fingers again and again in the rhythmic dance, until the Wunderlander's face grew calm once more.

"True. For ze present."

"So you'll deny their application for additional funds."

"*Ja.*" Early snapped his fingers, and Markham started.

"And if you have no further matters to discuss, Herr General?" he said, impatiently keying the system on his desk.

"Thank you for your time, sir," Early replied, standing and saluting.

*   *   *

"You got what you wanted?" the man who called himself Shigehero Hirose said, as they walked out the guarded front entrance of the Ritterhaus.

The mosaic murals were under repair, their marble and iridescent glass tesserae still ripped and stained by the close-quarter fighting that had retaken the building. It would have been safer to use heavy weapons from a distance, but the Wunderlanders had been willing to pay in blood to keep the structure intact. Here the Founders had landed; here the Nineteen Families had taken the Oath. Early shook his head slightly at that; too much love of tradition and custom, even now; too much sense of connection to the past. The ARM would have to deal with that. That sort of thinking made people uncomfortably independent. Isolated anomic individuals were much easier to deal with, and also more likely to accept suitably slanted versions of past, present, and future.

There was still a slight scent of scorch in the lobby's air, and an even fainter one of old blood. The volunteer repair crews were cleaning each section by hand with vibrosweeps and soft brushes before they began adding new material.

"Most of what *we* wanted," Early said, with deliberate emphasis.

Hiroge was the *oyabun* of his clan, and a man of some weight on this planet. The organization had grown during the lawless occupation years, and they were putting their accumulated wealth and power into shrewd investments now. Nevertheless, he bowed his head slightly as he answered:

"We, of course. Still, did not your psychists plant sufficient key commands last year?"

"We had to be careful. Markham was unstable, of course" — no wonder, after the resurrected thrint had used him as an organic waldo mechanism for weeks on end — "and besides, he'd be no use if we altered his psyche too much. We were counting on his subconscious craving for an authority figure, but evidently that's not as vulnerable as we thought. And he's getting more and more steamed about the political situation here, the anti-aristocratic reaction. Ironic."

"Which in turn is favorable to us," Hirose said.

"Oh, in the long run, yes. Nothing more susceptible to secret manipulation than democracy."

He sighed; in many ways, the Long Peace back on Earth had been more restful. A successful end to the long clandestine struggle, with an official agency, the ARM, openly allowed to close down disrupting technology. There had been fierce struggles within the Brotherhood over releasing the hoarded knowledge, any of it, even in the face of the kzin invasion. Necessary, of course; but the hyperdrive was *another* complicating factor. Now the other colonized systems were no longer merely dumping-grounds for malcontents, safely insulated by unimaginable distance. They were only a hyperwave call away, and each one was a potentially destabilizing factor.

He sighed. Perhaps the struggle was futile . . . *Never.*

"There is another factor I'd like you to check into," he went on. "Montferrat and his friends, and Matthieson. They know entirely too much."

"An isolated group," Hirose said dismissively. "Matthieson is disintegrating, and alienated from the others."

"Perhaps; but knowledge is always dangerous. Why else do we spend most of our time suppressing it? And" — he paused — "there's a . . . *synchronicity* to that crew. They're the sort of people things happen around; threatening things."

"As you wish, Elder Brother," Hirose said.

"Indeed."

• CHAPTER FOUR

"My nose is dry," Large-Son of Chotrz-Shaa said, leaning forward to lap at the heated single-malt: *I'm worried.* "We are impoverished beyond hope."

His brother Spots-Son made a *meeow-ur* of sardonic amusement, and poured some cream from the pitcher into his saucer of Glen Rorksbergen. Thick Jersey mixed sluggishly with the hot amber fluid as he stirred it with an extended claw. Both the young kzin males were somewhat drunk, and neither was feeling cheerful in his cups.

"Which is why you order fifty-year whiskey and grouper," he said, gesturing at the table. The two-meter fish was a mess of clean-picked bones on the platter; he picked up the head and crunched it for the brains, salty and delicious.

Large-Son flattened his batwing ears and wrinkled his upper lip to expose long wet dagger-teeth. "You eat your share, hairball-maker-who-never-matured." Spots growled around the mouthful; he had never entirely lost the juvenile mottles in his orange pelt. Dueling scars and batwing ears at his belt showed how he usually dealt with those who reminded him of it. "And the price of a meal is nothing compared to what we owe."

Spots-Son flared his facial pelt in the equivalent of a shrug. Kzinti rarely lie; it is beneath a warrior's honor, and in any case few of them can control the characteristic scent of falsehood.

"Truth," Spots said. "My liver is chill with worry; we

are poor beyond redemption. But if we must die, at least let us do it full and soothed."

A shape brushed past the shimmer of the privacy screen. "Owe? Poor?"

They both wheeled, grinning and folding their ears into combat-position. Long claws slid out of four-digit hands like knives at the tips of black leather gloves. A human had spoken, mangling the Hero's Tongue with his monkey palate. During the kzinti occupation, a human would have had his tongue removed for so insulting the language of the Heroic Race.

"You intrude," Spots-Son said coldly in Wunderlander.

"This is a public booth," the man pointed out. "And the only one not full. Besides, we all seem to have something in common."

That *was* an insult. The fur lay flat on their muzzles, and they grinned wider, threads of saliva falling from thin carnivore lips.

"*Cease to intrude, monkey,*" Large-Son said; this time he used the Hero's Tongue, in the Menacing Tense.

"We're all warriors, for one thing," the human continued, smelling of reckless self-confidence.

Both kzin relaxed, blinking and studying the monkey. He was a tall male, with a strip of dark head-fur; the clothes he wore were uniform and also thermally adjustable padding for wear under ground-combat armor. They blinked again, noting the ribbons and unit-markings, looked at each other.

He speaks truth, Spots-Son signaled with a twitch of eyebrows. Both of them had been junior engineering officers in an underground installation before the human counterattack on the Alpha Centauri system; both had been knocked out with stungas toward the end. The human was actually more of a warrior than either of them; their defense battery might or might not have made a kill during the tag-end of atmospheric combat, but this monkey had beaten kzinti fighters at close quarters. The pips on his sleeve were so many dried kzin ears dangling from a coup belt. It was permissible to talk to him, although not agreeable.

The human smiled in his turn, although he kept his teeth covered. "Besides, we're all broke, too. My name is Jonah Matthieson, ex-Pilot, ex-Captain, United Nations Space Navy. Let me order the next round of drinks."

". . . and so we inherit the care of our dams, our Sire's other wives, now ours, and our siblings and half-siblings," Spots-Son said morosely some hours later, upending the whiskey decanter over his dish. "Honor demands it."

Harold's was half-empty now; a waiter came quickly enough when the long orange-furred arm waved the crystal in the air, setting out fresh liquor and cream. Spots-Son slopped the amber fluid into his bowl and into Jonah's glass. Large-Son was lying with his muzzle in his dish, tongue protruding slightly as he snored. Thin black lips flopped against his fangs, and his eyes were nearly shut.

"Kzinti females take much care," Spots continued, lowering his muzzle. Despite his care it went too far into the heated drink as he nearly toppled, making him sneeze and slap at his nose. "And much feeding. The properties have been confiscated by the military government — all the fine ranchlands and hunting-grounds our Sire possessed, all except the house. Where once we feasted on blood-dripping fresh beef and screaming zianyas, now our families must trade heirlooms for synthetic protein. Soon we will have no alternative but honorable suicide."

"Thas — that's a shame," Jonah said. "Yeah, after th' war the fighters get nothin' and the politicians get rich, like always." He hiccuped and drank. "Goddam UN

Space Navy doesn't need no loudmouths who think for themselves, either. Say, what did you say you did before the war?"

"I," Spots said with slow care and some pride, "was a Senior Weapons System Repairworker. And my sibling, too."

Jonah blinked owlishly. "Reminds me." He fumbled a sheet of printout from a pocket. "Lookit this. Decided it was a good deal so I'd come in here an' spend my last *krona*. Here."

He spread the crumpled paper on the damp surface of the table. The kzin craned to look; it was in the spiky fourteen-point gothic script most commonly used for public announcements on Wunderland. Printed notices were common; during the occupation the kzin overlords had restricted human use of the information net, and since then wartime damage had kept facilities scarce.

Technical personnel wanted, he read, *for heavy salvage operation.* Categories of skills were listed. *Heavy work, some danger, high pay. Suuomalisen Contracting, vid. 97-777-4321A Munchen.*

"Urrrowra," Spots said mournfully. "Such would be suitable — if we were not kzinti. Surely none will hire us. No, suicide is our fate — we must cut our throats with our own *wtsai* and immolate our households. Woe! Woe for a dishonored death in poverty, among furless omnivores! No shrine will enclose our bones and ashes; only eating-grass will cover our graves. Perhaps Kdapt-Preacher is right, and the God has a hairless face!"

Large-Son whimpered in half-conscious agreement and slapped his hands over his eyes to blank out the horrible vision of the heretic's new creed, that God had created Man in His own image.

"Naw," Jonah said. "I talked to the boss, she don't care anything but you can do the job. Or wouldn't have hired me, with a black mark next to my discharge. C'mon — bring the bottle. Talk to her tomorrow."

"You are right!" Spots bellowed, standing to his full two meters and a half of massive, orange-furred height. His naked pink tail lashed. "We will fight against debt and empty-accountness. We leap and rip the throat of circumstance. We will conquer!"

From the other side of the long room beads rustled as a tall black-skinned human stuck his head through the curtain. He was dressed in archaic white tie and tuxedo, but there was a fully functional military-grade stunner in his fist. Behind the bar several other employees reached down and came up with shockrods as guests' heads turned toward the booth.

"Shhhhh!" Jonah said, tugging recklessly at the felinoid alien's fur. "The bouncers."

"Rrrrr. True." There was no dignity in being stunned and thrown out in the gutter. "Where shall we go? Our quarters are far outside Munchen, and transport for kzin costs much." Sleeping outside would not be very wise, given the number of exterminationist fanatics ready to attack a helpless kzin.

"C'mon. I know a doss where they don't care 'bout anything but your coin, and it's cheap."

They weaved their way to the door, Spots half-carrying his brother and Jonah lifting the unconscious kzin's tail with exaggerated care.

● CHAPTER FIVE

" . . . still worth lookin', oh, yes," the old man said.

Jonah yawned and looked over at him. The two kzin were unrolling their pallets up a level in the framework; the human had a stack of blankets and a pillow instead, all natural fiber in the rather primitive way of Wunderland, and all smelling dubious and looking worse. It must be even more difficult for the felinoids, with their sensitive noses.

"Look at 'er this way," the man was saying. "You take hafnium — "

It was hard to estimate his age; he could be as young as seventy or as old as one-fifty, depending on how much medical care he had been able to afford during the occupation.

" — good useful industrial metal; or gold, likewise, and we use it as monetary backing. Usually don't pay to mine it anywhere but in the Swarm, in normal times. But there *ain't* been any normal times, not since the pussies came, no sirree. So people've been out in the Jotuns for a dog's age now, finding deposits. Don't pay to bring in heavy equipment; deposits are rich but small. You can make yourself rich that way, and that's not counting salvage on all the equipment the pussies abandoned out there, all very salable these days. I'd go myself, don't you doubt it, go again like a shot."

"Hey," Jonah called. "You sound like you've done that before; what're you doing *here*?"

The great room was noisy with the sounds of humans settling down to sleep, snores, snatches of

drunken song. There were still tens of thousands of
displaced from the war years.

"Made me a fortune, oh, yes, more than one," the
old man said. His wrinkled-apple face looked over at
Jonah, eyes twinkling. "Lost 'em all. Some the government took, and I spent the others going back and
looking for a bigger strike. Most people get into that
game don't know where to stop. Get thirty thousand
crowns worth, they want sixty. Get sixty, spend it trying
to find half a million. Stands to reason, of course; that's
why the heavy metals are so valuable. Value of 'em
includes all the time and labor and money spent by
those who *don't* find anything, you see."

"Wouldn't be like that with me," Jonah said, unrolling the blankets. *Finagle, but I'm tired of being poor,* he
thought. Odd; poverty had never come up before he
got to Alpha Centauri. Before then he'd been a Navy
pilot, or a rockjack asteroid prospector. The Navy fed
you, and rockjacks generally made enough to get by —
certainly during the war, with industry sucking in all
the materials it could find. "Just enough to set me up.
Software business." He had a first-rate Solarian education in it, and the locals were behind. "That's all I'd
want."

"Likely so, stranger, likely so," the old man said.
"Well, don't signify, does it?"

"Finagle!" Jonah swore, as the beam jerked backward towards him. He heaved at the bight of control
line. "Get it, Spots!"

"Hrrrrr," Spots growled, and caught the end of it.
His pelt laid itself flat under the harness, and the long
steel balk slowed and then touched gently on the
junction-point. A little less power in the stubby plump-
cat limbs and they would both have been crushed
against the uprights of the frame.

"Slack off!" Jonah called down.

Large-Son flapped his ears in amusement thirty meters below and turned the control rheostat of the winch. The woven-wire cable slacked, and together man and kzin guided the end of the beam into its slot. Jonah clamped the sonic melder's leads to the corners and stepped back onto the scaffolding.

"Sound on the line," he called, and keyed his belt unit.

That flashed the alarm and began the process of sintering the beam into a single homogenous unit with the rest of the frame; it worked by vibrational generation of a heat-interface, and Spots winced and crouched beside him, hands clamped firmly over furled ears. The human took the opportunity to flip up his sight goggles and take a mouthful of water from his canteen; when he noticed the kzin's dangling tongue he poured some into a saucer the felinoid had clipped to his harness. Around them the complex geometries of the retrieval rig were growing into a latticework around the hill. Humans and the odd alien — there was a kdatlyno, and a couple of unbelievably agile five-armed Jotoki, and the brothers Kzinamaratsov, as he had named them in a private joke. Beyond was a flat terrain of swamp, livid-green Terrestrial reeds and mangrove, olive-green palmlike things native to Wunderland.

He slapped at his neck; it was *hot* here, right on the equator. The bugs were native, but they would cheerfully bite humans, or kzinti if they could get through the fur and thick hide. The brothers were suffering more than he. Their species shed excess heat through tongue and nose and the palms of hands and feet, more than enough on savagely dry Kzin. Difficult in this steambath, although the kzinti's high natural body-temperature and the light gravity of Wunderland helped a little. Jonah shook his head. He had been fighting kzin for most of his adult life: in space back in

Sol System, by sabotage, and even hand-to-hand in a hunting preserve when he'd been sent in as a clandestine operative. Now he was working with a couple of them, and they turned out to be a pretty good team. Stronger than humans by far, which was valuable on this archaeological relic of a project — the contractor was too cheap to rent much of what little modern equipment could be spared for civilian projects — and quicker. Their abilities were well balanced by his superior hands and better head for heights; kzinti had evolved on a world of 1.5 gravities, climbing low hills rather than trees. They were not quite as good with their fingers as humans, and a long vertical drop made them nervous.

"More water?" he offered the other.

No, Spots signaled with a twitch of his ruff, scratching vigorously a moment later. Then, aloud: "Is that not the Contractor Human?"

"It *is*, by Finagle's ghost," Jonah muttered. "*Hey, Biggie! We're coming down!*"

Jonah did so with a graceless rush down the catwalks; he had always been athletic for a Belter, and the last two months had left him in the best condition he had ever been, but he was still a child of zero-G. The kzin followed with oil-smooth grace, and they dropped in front of the project supervisor. Fairly soon the contract would be over . . .

"Looks like it'll be finished soon," Jonah said amiably. "Should be, with the extra time we've been putting in."

"And the bonuses you'll be getting, don't forget that," she replied, wiping at her face with a stained neckerchief.

"Yeah, they sound real good on the screen — the problem is, we haven't seen anything deposited to our accounts."

Heldja made an impatient gesture, then smiled —

carefully, because the two kzin were looming behind Jonah like oil-streaked walls of orange fur. Their teeth were very white, and all were showing.

"What vould you with money be doing *here*?" she said reasonably, waving a hand. There were pressmet huts standing on the dredged island; beyond the six-meter reeds of the swamp began, stretching beyond sight. Tens of thousands of square kilometers of them, and the closest thing to humanity in there was wild pigs gone feral, fighting it out with the tigripards. "Except to gamble and lose it? I ride the float of your money — all the hands' money — this is true, because it furnishes working capital; but the bonuses more than make up for it. Transfer will be made as soon as the hovercraft gets back to Munchen."

• CHAPTER SIX

"No, Ib," Tyra Nordbo said, lowering her rifle.

"Fire!" the young man said.

"No!"

One of the prisoners looked up from his slump; tears rolled slowly down through the dirt on his cheeks and the thin wispy adolescent beard. His lips moved soundlessly.

"Squad — fire!"

The magrifles gave their whispering grunt, and the five prisoners toppled into the graves they had spent the last half-hour digging. Behind, the villagers gave a murmur, halfway between shock and approval; they were Amish, men in dark suits and women in long black skirts. The half-ruined houses of the farmtown beyond were slipping into shadow as Alpha Centauri set; the moon was up, and Beta, leaving it just too dark to tell a black thread from a white. The air smelled of death and of moist turned earth from the graves, and from the plowed fields beyond, purple-black rolling hills amid the yellow of reaped grain and the dusty green of pasture. Orchards and vineyards spotted the land, and small lakes behind dams. Woodlots were the deep green of Terran oak and the orange-green of Kzin, tall frondlike growths in Wunderland's reddish ocher. Westward the last sunlight touched the glaciers and crags of the Jotuns, floating like a mirage seen through glass. The mountains were close, the dense forest of the foothills less than a day's walk away.

It was hard to imagine war had passed this way, until

you saw the graves. Many fresh ones in the church-yard, and these five outside it, along the graveled main street. The other soldiers in the squad lowered their weapons and turned to watch the exchange between brother and sister.

Tyra Nordbo was 180 centimeters, as tall as her brother, but she lacked the ordinary low-gravity lankiness of Wunderlanders; she was robust and full-bosomed, and strikingly athletic for a girl of eighteen. Her brother was only four years older and much alike in his high-cheeked, snub-nosed looks. There was a hardness to his face that she lacked, although she matched the anger when he swung to confront her.

"Karl, Yungblut," he snapped over his shoulder, "bury them. Kekkonen, get the dogs back to the van." He raised his voice to the villagers. "You people, return to your homes. Justice has been done."

The black-clad farmers stirred and settled their hats and turned back to their houses.

"Justice, Ib?" Tyra said, her voice full of quiet fury. She slung her rifle and reached to tear off the Provisional Gendarmerie badge sewn to the arm of her bush jacket. It landed at Ib's feet with a quiet *plop* of dust. Her holoprinted ID card followed it.

"Those were bandits!" Ib said, jerking his head at the graves where earth fell shovelful by shovelful.

"Thieves, murderers, and rapists," Tyra said, nodding jerkily. The sight was not too bad; the prefrag penetrators were highly lethal but did not mangle flesh much. She had seen much worse, working in an aid station for the underground army, during the street fighting in Muchen at Liberation. "They deserved to die — after a fair trial."

The Amish here were strict in their pacifist faith, and had made little resistance when the gang moved in; the investigation had been ugly hearing. This part of the Jotun foothills had been guerrilla country during the last days of the occupation, full of folk on the run from the collaborationist police, from the forced-labor gangs, or simply from spreading poverty and chaos. Not all of them had gone back to the lowlands when peace came, to the sort of badly-paid hard work that was available. Many had turned to raiding, and were difficult to catch. The Wunderlander armed forces were stretched thin, and most of their efforts had to go to the fighting farther into the kzinti sphere, as the human fleets pressed the aliens back.

"They were guilty," she went on. "They still deserved a trial, and it wouldn't have taken any effort at all to carry them back to Arhus," she went on bitterly. Her eyes stung, and she blinked back anger and grief. *I will* not *cry.*

"General Markham —"

"You and your precious Ulf Reichstein-Markham. He's as bad as a kzin!" she snapped. Some of the other troopers scowled at that. Ulf Markham had been among the fiercest of the space-based Resistance fighters in the Serpent Swarm, and he had a considerable following in the military. "Compared to a *real* hero, like Jonah Matthieson, or — Enough. I quit. My pay's in arrears" — everyone's was — "so I'll take the horse and rifle in lieu. Goodbye."

"Stop — " Ib called to her back. "You're running away, running away like Father did!"

"*Don't you ever mention Father like that again,*" she said coldly, forcing her hand away from the weapon slung at her back. Her hands were mechanical as she unhitched the horse and vaulted into the saddle, an easy feat on Wunderland.

His voice followed her as she cantered out into the falling night.

And so the Commission leaves us only the home farm, the Teufelberg forest, and the Kraki, *of the properties*, Tyra

Nordbo read, tilting the paper towards the firelight. The letter took on the tones of her mother's voice, deliberately cheerful and utterly sad, as it had been ever since Dada left. Was taken away on that crazy astrophysical expedition by the kzin, Yiao-Captain. *But this is more than enough to keep all of us here busy. It is a relief not to have the management of so much else, and we must remember how many others are wanting even for bread.*

She started to crumple the printout in one hand, then carefully smoothed it out and folded it, tucking it back into the saddlebags and leaning back against the saddle. In the clearing on the other side of the fire her horse reached down and took another mouthful of grass, the rich *kerush* sound followed by wet munching and the slight jingle of the hobble chain. Her new dog Garm looked up and thumped his tail on the grass, the firelight ruddy on the Irish Setter — mostly Setter — hairs of his coat. Elsewhere the flicker caught at grass, trees, bushes, the overhanging rock of the cliff behind her and the gnarled trunk and branches of an oak that grew out of the sandstone ten meters above her head. Overhead the stars were many and very bright; in the far distance a tigripard squalled, and the horse threw up its head for a moment in alarm. Nowhere in the wilderness about her was there a hint of Man — save that the tree and the grass, woman and horse and dog were all of the soil and blood and bone of Sol.

"So," she whispered to herself. "It is not enough that we are stripped of our honor, they must make us paupers as well."

Not quite *paupers*, she admitted.

That had been among the first things her father taught her; not to lie, first and foremost not to lie to herself. They would be quite comfortably off; the home farm was several thousand hectares, the timber concession would be profitable enough now that the economy was recovering, and the pelagic-harvester *Hrolf Kraki* was a sturdy old craft. The household staff were all old retainers, loyal to *Mutti*, and very competent. *It's not the money*, she knew; it was a matter of pride. The Nordbos had been the first humans to settle Skognara District, back when the Nineteen Families arrived. They had been pioneers, ecological engineers adapting Terran life to a biosphere not meant for it and a planet not much like Earth; then guides, helpers, kindly landfathers to the ones who came after and settled in as tenants-in-chief, subtenants, workers.

It was not the loss of the lands and factories and mines; in practice the family had merely levied a small percentage in return for governing, a thankless privilege these past two generations. But Gerning and Skognara *belonged* to the Nordbos, they had *made* them with blood and sweat and the bones of their dead. For the Commission to take the rights away was to spit on the memories. Of Friedreich Nordbo, who had sponsored a tenth-share of the First Fleet, of Ulrike Nordbo, who discovered how to put Terran nitrogen-fixing soil bacteria in fruitful symbiosis with the native equivalents, of Sigurd Nordbo, who lost his life fighting to save a stranded schoolbus during the Great Flood. Of her aunt Siglide Nordbo, who had piloted her singleship right up to the moment it rammed a kzinti assault transport during the invasion.

And of Peter Nordbo, who had stood like a rock between the folk of Skognara and the conquerors' demands, every day that he was able. Who was ten years gone, shanghaied into space because he told a kzin who was half a friend of an astronomical curiosity, leaving a wife who had no choice but to yield more than he had, as conditions grew worse. Condemned for a traitor *in absentia*, by a court that thought it was merciful . . . and *Mutti* was all alone now in the big silent house on the headland at Korness, looking out over the waves. Few friends had been willing to visit, much less speak in her defense.

"*Dada-mann*," Tyra whispered, laying her head on her knees and weeping aloud, because there was nobody to hear. That was what she had cried out when he left. There had been no words he could say to a child of eight . . . Presently Garm came, creeping on his stomach and whining at her distress, sticking his anxious cold nose against her face; she clutched him and sobbed until there was no more.

When she was functional again she took the coffee pot off the heater coil — the fire was for comfort, and predators — and poured herself a cup. The other letter was still sealed; she had nearly discarded it, until the return address caught her eye. Claude Montferrat-Palme, a Herrenmann of ambiguous reputation. Frowning, she pressed her thumb to the seal to deactivate the privacy lock and then opened it.

"Dear Fra Nordbo," she read. "A possible juncture of interests — "

"Yes, there are workings in the mountains," the old villager said.

At least, that was what Tyra *thought* he had said. These backwoodsmen had been up in the high country for the better part of two centuries, pioneers before the kzinti came and isolated by choice and necessity since. Their dialect was so archaic it was almost *Pletterdeutz*, without the simplified grammar and many of the loan-words from the Baltic and Scandinavian languages that characterized modern Wunderlander. Back further in the Jotuns were tiny enclaves even more cut off, remnants of the ethnic separatists who had come with the third through seventh slowship fleets from Sol System.

"What sort of workings?" she said, slowly. Her own accent was Skognaran, more influenced by Swedish and Norse than the central dialect of Munchen; modified by a Herrenmann-class education, of course.

The Nordbos were formerly of the Freunchen clan, one of the Nineteen Families. *Formerly*. Luckily, these primitives were out of touch with the news; they barely comprehended that the alien conquerors were gone.

"Ja, many sorts, *Fra* Nordbo," the old man said deferentially.

The von Gelitz family had owned these lands — still did, pending the Reform Commission's findings — but that ownership had always been purely theoretical, except for a hunting lodge or two. Nobody but the Ecological Service ever paid much official attention to this area, and they had gotten careless during the occupation. There was an old manor house outside Neu Friborg's common fields, but it had been ruins for the better part of a century. He had called them the "old herr's place."

Old, she thought with a shiver, looking at the man. They were getting by on home remedies here, and what knowledge their healer could drag out of an ancient first-aid program. The wrinkles, wispy white hair, liver spots . . . this man might be no more than seventy or eighty, barely middle-aged with decent medicine. *Markham should spend less on his precious fleet — the UN Navy is fighting the war now — and more on people and places like this!*

Apart from premature aging and the odd cripple, it was not too bad as backcountry towns in the Jotuns went. Built of white-plastered fieldstone and home-made tile, around a central square with the mayor's office, the nationalpolezi station — long disused — and the Reformed Catholic church. There was a central fountain, and plenty of shade from eucalyptus and pepper and featherfrond trees. They were sitting under an awning outside the little *gasthaus*, watching the sleepy traffic of midafternoon: bullock-carts and burros bringing in firewood or vegetables, a girl switching along a milch cow, tow-haired children in shorts tumbling through the dust in some running, shouting game. A rattletrap hovertruck went by in a cloud of grit, and a waitress went about watering the flowers that hung from the arches behind them in earthenware pots.

That was all there *was* to see: the town and its four-hundred-odd inhabitants, the cluster of orchards and fields around it in the little pocket of arable land, and wilderness beyond — mostly scrubby, in the immediate vicinity, but you could find anything from native jungle to forest to desert in a few days' journey. All about the peaks of the Jotuns reared in scree and talus and glacier; half a continent of mountains, taller than Earth's Himalayas and much wider. Wunderland had intermittent plate tectonics, but when they were active they were *active*, and the light gravity reduced the power of erosive forces. These were the oldest mountains on the planet, and not the highest by any means.

The old man finished fanning himself with his straw hat and continued:

"Jade, of course. No mines, but from the high mountain rivers; that is how we paid our tribute to the kzin. We are not ignorant *knuzen* here, Fra Nordbo!"

There was a pathetic pride to that; a hovertruck had come once a month from the lowlands, until the final disruption at liberation. Tyra felt a slight stinging in her eyes. Once even the most isolated settlement had been linked to Munchen, with virtual-schools and instant emergency services . . .

"Then, sometimes hunters come through; hunting for tigripard hides, quetzbird feathers. Or prospectors. There is gold, hafnium . . . when I was a small boy, scholars also from the Scholarium in Munchen."

"Scholars?" she said, pricking up her ears.

"Yes; they said little — this was just after the War, you understand, people were suspicious then — but there were rumors of formations that could not be accounted for. But they found nothing, and had to return to Munchen when so much of the Scholarium was closed by the government." The collaborationist authorities had other priorities than education; their own profits, primarily. "And — but your supplies, they have arrived!" He rose and left, bowing and murmuring good wishes.

Another hovertruck pulled into the square; big and gleaming by contrast with the single ancient relic the village of Neu Friborg owned, although shabby enough by Munchen standards, much less Earth's. The man who stepped down from it was tall, 190 centimeters at least; his black hair was worn in a shag cut, although she knew he had kept it in a military-style crop while he was Police Chief of Munchen. Chief for the collaborationists, and notoriously corrupt even by the gang's standards. Claude Montferrat-Palme, of the Sydow clan. He wore expensive outbacker clothes, leather boots and grey usthcloth jacket and breeches, with a holstered strakkaker, and a beret. A small, neatly clipped black mustache lay on his upper lip, and his mouth quirked in a slight smile.

"Fra Nordbo," he said, bowing formally over her hand with a click of heels.

"Fro Palme," she replied, inclining her head with equal formality. A server bustled up with steins of the local beer.

"Prosit," he said.

"Skaal," she replied. "Now that the amenities are over, could you tell me exactly what you had in mind?"

Her voice held a chilly correctness; he seemed to recognize the tone, and smiled wryly.

"Fra Nordbo, I'm very strongly reminded of your father."

"You knew him?" she said, with a raised eyebrow. "Perhaps you will claim to have been his friend, next?"

He surprised her by letting the smile grow into a deep laugh. "Quite the contrary," he said, shaking his head. "He treated me with the most frigid *politesse*, as befitted an honorable Landholder forced to deal with noxious collaborationist scum."

She relaxed slightly. "He couldn't have known you were involved with the Resistance," she said.

"Ach, at the time I wasn't," he replied frankly. "I *was* a collaborationist at that point. My conversion came later; people do change. As some claim your father did, later."

"*That is a lie!*" she said. More calmly: "My father was an astrophysicist, it was his . . . hobby, since he had to govern Skognara from a sense of duty. How was he to know the enemy would think a mere energy-anomaly a thing of potential miliary importance? The kzin — Yiao-Captain — forced him to accompany them on the expedition."

"From which he has never returned, and hence cannot defend himself. And the Commission has been in no charitable mood."

Tyra's blond head drooped slightly. "I know," she said quietly. "Ib . . . my brother and I, we have discussed resigning the Nordbos from the Freunchen clan."

"Advisable, but it may make little difference. Unless I've lost my political feelers — and I haven't — the Reformers are going to strip the Nineteen Families of everything but ceremonial power. And from all but their strictly private property, as well."

Tyra nodded jerkily, feeling the hair stir on her neck as her ears laid back. That mutation was a mark of her heritage, of the old breed that had won this planet for humankind.

"It is unjust! Men like my father did everything they could to shield — " She shrugged and fell silent again, taking a mouthful of the beer.

"Granted, but most of the kzin are gone, and a great deal of repressed hatred has to have a target." He turned one hand up in a spare gesture. "Even our dear Grand Admiral Ulf Reichstein-Markham has been able to do little to halt the growth of anti-Families feeling. Which means we of the Families — as individuals — had better look to our own interests."

Tyra looked down into her mug. Montferrat laughed again.

"How tactful you are for one so young, Fra Nordbo. I have a reputation for looking after my own interests, do I not? *Old Sock* is the nickname now; because I fit on either foot, having changed sides at just the right moment. Unfortunately, most of my accumulated wealth went on securing my vindication."

He nodded dryly at her startled glance. "Yes, our great and good government of liberation is very nearly as corrupt as the collaborationists they hunt down so vigorously. Not Markham; his vice is power, not wealth. A little too nakedly apparent, however, and I doubt he will retain much of it past the elections, when the junta steps down. Which it will, given that the UN Space Navy is overseeing the process . . . but I digress."

"Ja, Herr," Tyra said. "You spoke of a matter of mutual interest?"

"Indeed." He took out a slim gold cigarette case, opening it at her nod and selecting a brown cigarillo. His gaze sought the mountains as he took a meditative puff. "After *you* mentioned rumors of something . . . strange in these mountains."

"I was a student at the Scholarium before the liberation, and afterwards a little. Before my brother . . . Well, he greatly admires Admiral Markham."

"Of whom you no longer think highly, and who is notoriously unfond of myself, thus showing his bad taste," Montferrat said suavely. "Yes. Thank you for the information on that little atrocity, by the way; it may come in useful as a stick for the Admiral's spokes." He frowned slightly, looking at the glowing tip of the cigarillo.

"I don't believe in fate, but there's a . . . syncronicity

to events, sometimes. Your father vanished, seeking an artifact of inexplicable characteristics, near this system. You come across evidence of another here in these mountains. And I —"

Tyra made an inquiring sound.

"Well, let us say that this is the third instance," Monferrat went on. "More would be unsafe for you to know; it has to do with General Markham, and his Sol-System patrons the ARM. It would *certainly* be unsafe for me to be openly involved in any such search."

"You implied that you would be commissioning a search?" Tyra said.

"No. *Searchers.* Who will be looking, but not specifically for that. It *is* necessary that someone guard these unaware guardians; and since this presents me with an opportunity to do a lovely lady a service —"

He smiled gallantly; Tyra retained her look of stony politeness. Monferrat sighed.

"As you will." A puff made the cigarillo a crimson ember for a moment. "First I must tell you a story, about a man named Jonah, and some friends he has made recently. Unusual friends —"

● CHAPTER SEVEN

The hovercraft that carried the outgoing shift back to the Munchen docks was an antique. Not only would the design be completely obsolete once gravity polarizers were available for ordinary civilian work; it had been built before the kzinti frontier world of Hssin had decided to send a probing fleet to investigate the promising electromagnetic traffic from Alpha Centauri. That was nearly sixty Terran years ago, fifty Wunderlander, and it had soldiered on ever since, carrying cargo and passengers up and down the Donau river and out into the sheltered waters of Spitzer Bay. It was simplicity itself, a flat rectangle of light-metal alloy with a control cabin at the right front corner and ducted fans on pivots at the rear. Other fans pumped air into the plenum chamber beneath, held in by skirts of tough synthmesh; power came from molecular-distortion batteries.

Jonah and the kzinti squatted on their bedrolls in the center of the cargo bay, with the hunched backs of the other workers and the waist-high bulwarks at the edge between them and the spray cast up by the river. Spots hated to get his pelt wet, spitting and snarling under his breath, while Bigs endured stolidly. The human rolled a cigarette of *teufelshag*, ignoring the felinoids' *urrows* of protest. They were well up into the settled areas now. Thinly settled, but the banks of the middle Donau had been where humans first came to Wunderland. The floodplain and benchland were mostly cleared, or in planted woodlots; farther back from the floodplain the old Herrenmann estates stood, bowered in gardens, whitewashed stone and tile roofs. Many were broken and abandoned, during the occupation, by kzin nobles who had seized a good deal of this country for their own, or by anticollaborationist mobs after the liberation. They passed robot combines gathering rice, blocks of orange grove fragrant with cream-white flowers, herds of beefalo and kzinti *zitragor* under the watch of mounted herdsmen. Villages were planted among small farms, many of them worked by hand; machinery had gotten very scarce while the kzinti were masters.

The hovercraft slowed as traffic thickened on the river, strings of barges, hydrofoils, pleasure craft with their colored sails taut in the stiff southerly breeze. The steel spire of St. Joachim's Cathedral blazed in the light of Alpha, with Beta high in the sky as well. Farther north there were parks along the waterside, with palm groves and frangipani, but the section the hovercraft edged toward was workaday and bustling, sparkling with welding torches as the old wrecked autocranes were replaced with temporary steel frames; in the meantime stevedores sweated to haul rope pulleys. Jonah flicked the butt of his cigarette into the water like a minor meteor undergoing reentry.

"Nice to be affluent," he said cheerfully.

Bigs made an indescribable sound and turned away from the irritating human, lying flat on the decking with his chin extended. Spots waggled his ears in the kzin equivalent of an ironic chuckle.

"Three thousand krona each," he said dryly. "The prospect heats my liver — I truly feel one of Heaven's Admirals. This for thirty diurnal periods of laboring like a slave in a swamp and improvising machinery out of muck and junk. There is fungus growing on my fur. I may never be able to eat fish again."

"Let's collect, then," Jonah answered.

They heaved themselves erect under the burden of their kitbags and shouldered their way to the bows as the big vehicle ran up on a concrete landing ramp and sank to the surface. It was easy enough, although the cargo well was crowded; nobody on Wunderland was going to jostle a kzin, liberation or no. Legal prosecution would be cold comfort after you fell to the ground in several pieces. The surf-noise of voices sounded tinny after the long hours of engine roar.

"Fra Eldasson," Jonah called. The contractor was slipping out of the control cabin and walking up the ramp. "Finagle dammit, wait for us!"

She turned, frowning, then smiled without showing her teeth as she saw the three of them wading through the crowd toward her.

"Problem you haf?" she said brusquely.

"I thought you were going to pay us as soon as we got back to Munchen," Jonah said.

"Certainly," she replied, glancing out of the corner of her eyes at the two towering orange figures behind him. They grinned at her. "I've told everyone" — a hand waved at the others disembarking — "credit chips or account transfers will be made at the opening of bank hours tomorrow. It *is* Sunday, you know."

Jonah blinked in bewilderment for a moment, then realized what she meant. Wunderland was a *very* conservative place; about what you would expect from a settlement founded by North European plutocrats in the late twenty-first century. Even now they still observed religious holidays.

"*May we eat it if it attempts to snatch away our gain/prey?*" Bigs snarled in the Hero's Tongue: in the Menacing Tense, at that.

"Shut up," Jonah whispered; Bigs was uncivilized, even for a kzin. "A lot of people around here understand that language — do you want to start a riot, talking about eating a human?" Far too many *had* been eaten; compulsory holocasts of kzinti hunting parties chasing down political prisoners had been a staple of the occupation.

Tanjit, I was the quarry *for a kzinti hunting party*, he reminded himself. *Me and Ingrid.* He pushed the memory out of his mind; thinking about Ingrid was too painful. Besides, the kzin hunting him had died.

From Eldasson's narrowed eyes and slight smile, he suspected that she had understood. *Tanjit. If there's a disturbance, she might* really *try to stiff us.* Kzinti were not popular with the courts, understandably enough — although Jonah's war record would help. It was not everyone who had assassinated a Planetary Governor like Chuut-Riit.

"Look, Fra Eldasson, we're broke until we get paid — we don't even have enough to buy a drink," he said reasonably.

"*Ja.* Hmmm. Here" — She took him by the arm and lead him to one side, behind a wrecked crane. The thick synthetic bars had frayed out into tangled fiber fragments; heavy beam-rifle hit, from the look of it. Composites did not weather, so it might have been from last year, or from the street-fighting fifty years ago when the kzin landed.

"Here's four hundred in cash," she said. "Don't let any of the others know, or everyone will be about me like grisflies. Meet me at Suuomalisen's Sauna later tonight, and I'll transfer the rest for you and your two ratcats."

"All right."

"*Hrraer.*"

"I thank Eldasson for the drink and the meat," Spots said, "but the delay is irksome. We will have much to set at rights in our households; our younger siblings are still immature, of shrunken liver and rattlepate."

Bigs wrinkled his upper lip in agreement and

stropped his claws on the table. Shavings of tekdar curled back, creamy yellow beneath the darker patina of the surface.

Jonah nodded. They were in one of the quieter rooms of the Sauna, which despite its name was an entertainment center of varied attractions, some shocking even to him; the tamer floor shows were interesting, but of course wasted on non-humans. The kzinti had eaten on their own — no human felt comfortable with a feeding kzin, and the felinoids detested the smell of what men ate — but had returned to wait with him.

"Yeah; I'm anxious to get the credit deposited myself," he said. *And you're not bad company for ratcats, but you're not half as pretty as what I have in mind*, he thought: it had been a long month in the swamps. "Eldasson had better show up soon."

"Eldasson?" a voice said.

Jonah looked up, slightly surprised. A man who associated with kzinti got used to being ignored, or left to his own thoughts, whichever way you preferred to look at it. The speaker was a thickset man for a Wunderlander, with a blue-jowled stubble of beard and a grubby turban; from one of the little ethnic enclaves that hung on even here in Munchen. The light from the stained-glass overhead lamps flickered across his olive skin.

"She owes you money?" the man went on.

"A fair bit," Jonah replied.

The other man giggled and lifted his drink; the steel bracelets on his wrist tinkled.

"Then you had better have a written contract," he said. "Notarized."

"Notarized?" Jonah said in alarm. "We've got the contracts, right here." He tapped his belt-unit. "With mods for bonuses and overtime."

"A personal recording?" the turbaned man said scornfully. "How long *have* you been on Wunderland, flatlander?"

Jonah bristled and ran a reflexive hand down his Sol-Belter strip of hair; his great-great-grandmother had been the last of his family to be born on Earth.

"Sorry — I knew by your accent you were Sol-system," the other said, raising a placating hand. "I just wanted to warn you; Eldasson and Suuomalisen are like *that*" — he held up two fingers, twined about each other — "and they're both crooked as a kzin's hind leg. You'd better be ready to sue for that money."

A gingery scent filled the air; the stranger backed off in alarm, as the two kzin stood and grinned, lines of slaver falling from their thin black lips. The same thought had occurred to Jonah; a kzin was not likely to receive much justice from the Wunderland junta's courts, these days.

"Let's go hunting," he said.

"*Hraareow.*"

Munchen was the biggest city Jonah had ever traveled: over a quarter of a million people. There were many times that in the Belt, but not even Gibraltar Base had as much in one habitat. Of course, much of Earth was one huge city — over eighteen billion, an impossible number — but he had been born to the Belt and the war against the Kzin. The other problem was that it wasn't a habitat at all; it was uncontained, sprawling with the disregard for distances of a thinly settled planet and a people who had been wealthy enough to give most families their own aircar. The open space above still made him a little nervous; he pretended it was the blue dome of a bubbleworld, one of the larger farming ones with a high spin. Luckily, it was unlikely that Eldasson was in the residential neighborhoods, or the slums that had grown up during the occupation. Nor was she at the address Public Info listed as her home, which had turned out to be a townhouse with several loud, extremely xenophobic — or at least anti-kzinti — dogs.

"Hrunge k'tze hvrafo *tui*," Bigs said; he stopped, opened his mouth and wet his nose with his tongue. "*Tui, tza!*"

I think I scent the prey, Jonah translated mentally. He let the length of skeelwood he was carrying up the sleeve of his overall drop until the tip rested on his fingers. *The prey is* here.

The nightspot they were staking out was a few hundred meters behind them, around a slight curve in the tree-lined road. It was a converted house, and the buildings here stood well apart; hedges lined the outer lawns, making the turf roadway a glimmer of green-black under the glowglobes. The summer night was quiet and dark, the moon and Beta both down and the stars little dimmed by city lights; the smell of dew was stronger than that of men's engines. Feet came walking, several pair. Then he saw them. Eldasson right enough, but dressed in a fancy outfit of black embroidered tunic and ballooning indigo trousers. A dark woman in a tight shipsuit to one side of her, arm in arm, talking and laughing. Another behind them, tall even for a Wunderlander but thick-built, almost a giant, shaggy ashblond hair . . .

"Fra Eldasson," Jonah said, stepping into the pool of light under one of the globes that hung from the treebranches; they were biologicals, hitched into the tree's sap system. "How pleasant to meet you."

He could sense the kzinti spreading out behind him. Not hear them — their padded feet were soundless on the grass — but a whisper of movement, a hint of sour-ginger scent. Kzin anger: it sent the hair on his own backbone to bristling as conditioned reflex said *danger*. His smile was grim. Danger in truth, but not to him.

Eldasson stopped, blinking at him. "What are you doing here?" she snapped. Her companions looked at Jonah, then recoiled slightly at the sudden looming appearance of Spots and Bigs. The tall blond rumbled a challenge; the two women crouched slightly, spreading to either side.

Finagle, Jonah thought. *These aren't flatlanders. I miscalculated*. Even after decades of war between Man and Kzin, most Earthers were still culturally conditioned against violence. That had never gone as far on Wunderland, and there had been little law here for humans while the kzinti ruled. Nobody who prospered in those years was likely to be a pacifist. Jonah tapped his belt unit, for emphasis and for a record of what followed.

"We got a little tired of waiting for you to show up with our money, Fra Eldasson," he said calmly. "We'd like it now, if you please."

"You'll get it as soon as the transfer to me clears," she said. The voice was flat and wary; her right hand was behind her back.

Calm settled on Jonah, a comforting familiarity. The feeling of being completely immersed in reality and completely detached at the same time, what the adepts who trained him for war had said was the closest he would ever approach *satori*. For the first time in a year, the wounds within his mind ceased to itch.

"Not good enough. We want it *now*."

"No! Now get out of this neighborhood; you're not welcome here."

Bigs spoke; his Wunderlander was more thickly accented than his sibling's and distorted by anger as well:

"*Why do you think you can cheat a Hero and live, monkey?*"

"Ah, a racial slur," Eldasson said, smiling tightly. "Jilla, von Sydow, remember that." To the kzin: "*Go ch'rowl your Patriarch, ratcat.*"

Bigs screamed and leaped. Everything seemed to move very slowly after that. Jonah dove forward and down, the yawara-stick snapping out into his hand, then sweeping toward Eldasson's wrist as it came out with the chunky shape of a military-grade stunner. She was throwing herself backward; the wood met the synthetic of the weapon instead of flesh, and there was a high karking buzz before the stunner flew off into darkness. Bigs's leap turned from fluid perfection into a ballistic arch, and his body met the earth with a thud that shook through Jonah's body. The human came up coiling off his hands, one long leg pistoning out into Eldasson's stomach.

That *hurt*. She was wearing impact armor, memory-plastic that stiffened under rapid stress. The heelstrike still sent her back winded and wheezing against the hedge. Spots came on in a hunching four-footed rush, like a giant orange weasel; the blond giant roared and swept out a chopping cut with a Gurkha knife. They circled, eight claws against a knife. The kzin was limping as he turned, dark-red blood running down one columnar thigh, naked pink tail held out rigidly to sweep around as a weapon in itself. The man had been wearing armor too; it showed through the rents in his tunic, glittering where the claws had scraped. Bigs was stirring and muttering, no longer a mute limp pile of orange fur. Only the edge of the beam could have clipped him.

Enough. The woman in the skinsuit came for Jonah, hands stripping two black-plastic rods out of sheaths along her thighs, each baton a meter long. Shockrods; the touch would bring utter pain, possible brain damage or even death in the wrong place. She had delicate Oriental features, lynx-calm, and the movements were unmistakable. Well, Nipponjin were common in the Alpha Centauri system too, out in the Serpent Swarm. He lunged, using the length of arm and leg, the point of his yawara punching out for her throat.

This is uncivilized. Maybe the ARM were right.

The hard wood clacked on plastic as both rods came

around, one smashing at the stick, the second driving for his elbow with bone-breaking force. He let the force of the blow help him pivot the stick to block the second rod. *Clack*. Faint brushing contact against his left arm. *Pain!* A datum, nothing more. Pain did not hurt; paying attention to it hurt. Snap-kick to the inside of her knee, damage done but she rolled forward with the fall and backflipped, coming up crouching with the rods before her in an X, guard position.

Eldasson was straightening up, whooping for breath. Her hand snapped out a flat black lozenge and clenched; a shimmering appeared in the air before it, and a tooth-gritting whine. Jonah knew what that was; ratchet knife, a wire blade stiffened and set trembling thousands of times a second by a magnetic field. It would slash through tissue and bone as if they were jelly.

Things just became more serious, he thought, feeling his testicles trying to draw themselves up into his abdomen.

He rushed toward the woman with the shockrods, bringing his yawara down in a straight overarm blow. It smacked into the X, and she slid the shockrods down toward his hand. Jonah accepted it, accepted the sudden agony that froze his lungs and sent shimmers of random light across his pupils. His other hand flashed up to her wrists and he bore forward with his full weight and strength. They went over backward; he landed with a knee in her stomach, and the rods came down across her throat. The face beneath him convulsed, the galvanic reaction tossing him aside before she slumped into unconsciousness. Wheezing with pain he shoulder-rolled erect, both arms trembling as he brought them back to guard position.

Eldasson was on her feet and shuffling toward him, the ratchet knife extended. Behind her the big human and Spots were still circling. It could only have been thirty seconds or so. She lunged at him, the blade invisible in the dimness, but he could hear it keening malevolently. Jonah twisted aside desperately, felt something like a hot thread stroke along his side. He tried for a kick and snatched the foot back when the knife moved down, backing and feeling at the cut along his side. *Not too deep*, he realized with a hot surge of relief; only enough to break the skin. Blood flowed down his flank and soaked into his coverall around the waistband. He retreated a little faster, looking around for something to use.

Then Bigs rose in the shadows by the sidewalk.

"Look behind you," Jonah suggested helpfully, flexing his arms to try and work the feeling back into them. Eldasson snorted contempt and bored in, holding the ratchet knife before her like a ribbon saber and lunging as he skipped away. She was breathing more normally now, and the twin red spots on her cheekbones might have been anger as much as the aftereffects of being gut-kicked. A grunt of triumph as he dodged to the side and went down on the pavement; the ratchet knife went up for a slash, night air peeling back from its buzzing wire edge. There was a yawp of sound; the woman's eyes rolled up in their sockets, and the knife went silent as fingers released it. She crumpled bonelessly to the ground, her head going *thock* on the asphalt.

Bigs clipped the stunner to his belt. Spots unlocked his jaws from the knife-man's right shoulder and threw him a dozen paces to crumple bonelessly on the soft turf of a lawn. Jonah swept up the ratchet knife and flipped the hilt in his hand, the molecular-distortion battery making it heavy even in the .61-G field of Wunderland. The contractor's eyes were open; Bigs had taken time to reset the stunner's field to *light*. That meant that Eldasson could feel and see, although not move the main voluntary muscles. The Sol-Belter drove his heel into her ribs with judiciously calculated force.

"Paytime, Fra Eldasson," he said. "Payback time."

Her lips worked, trying to spit at him. Bigs picked her up by the back of her tunic and shook her at arm's length, as effortlessly as he might have a rag doll. When he was finished he brought her close and smiled in her face, tongue dangling and carnivore breath hot.

"How . . . how much?" she croaked.

"Just what you owe us," Jonah said. "Not one fennig more . . . in money."

General Buford Early looked a little less out of place in Munchen than he did in his native Sol System, these days; men as black as he were rare on Wunderland, and mostly from the Krio enclaves. They were even rarer in the polyglot genetic stew of Earth. That was not true at the time of his birth. He had been born while there were still distinct human sub-races, a fact he took some care to disguise. Not least by keeping a careful ear for the changes in language, and by muting the inhuman gracefulness learned through the centuries. Other things he hid more deeply; but the power he held from his rank in the UN Space Navy, from his role in the ARM, and from his own force of personality, he did not bother to conceal. Heldja Eldasson looked a little intimidated, sitting across the wide oak desk in the upper offices of the Ritterhaus, once more headquarters of Wunderland's government.

"What else could I do?" she said sullenly. The autodoc had healed the worst of her injuries, but she had not been allowed enough time to clear up the bruises that marked her face with red and blue splotches. "The ratcat-lover had his tame kzin *grin* at me until I transferred the funds and authenticated the contract."

"You could have gone to the police," he pointed out, lighting a cigar. That was also more common here on Wunderland than on Earth, among the many archaisms he found rather pleasant.

"*Teufelheim!* They had the contracts — and would the police believe me, with my record? I wouldn't have chanced stiffing them, if you hadn't suggested it."

He stared at her for a moment, and she dropped her eyes before the steady yellowish glare of his.

"Excellency," she finished sullenly.

"It should have occurred to you that — " Early stopped. *That I have influence with the courts, and the police.* Both quite true, although not to the extent he would on Earth. There, opponents of the ARM — or the Brotherhood, if they were unlucky enough to learn of its existence — could be ignored so completely that they found nobody even acknowledged their existence any longer. Harsher measures were rarely necessary; overt fear was a crude tool. The Secret Reign had survived the centuries by manipulating men, not by trying to rule them directly. It was already far older than any mere state in the year Buford Early was born . . .

"Never mind," he continued. "You'll be compensated for your loss." *Loss of stolen money,* he thought ironically. "And keep me informed of *anything* to do with Matthieson. Understood?"

"Jawul," she replied.

• CHAPTER EIGHT

Jonah pulled his head out of the fountain and shook it; the two kzin looked up from tending their wounds and complained with yeowls as drops hit their fur. The human restrained an impulse to grin at them; from the way they were wagging their ears back at him, they felt the same way.

"Well, we're rich," he said. "Comparatively speaking. Rich in spirit, too — I never did like being cheated." *And this time I got to do something about it,* he added silently. *Finagle, but I feel good!* Better than he had in a year. Better than he had since the psychists released him and Early began his campaign of persecution.

Bigs grunt-snarled. Spots answered aloud: "We have fought side by side," he said. His whiskers drooped. "Although there will be little enough left of this money when our debts are paid and supplies laid in for our households."

"Considering that you were contemplating suicide the night I met you, that's not bad," Jonah observed dryly, turning and sitting on the cornice of the fountain. "How much *will* you have left?"

"If we pay no more than the most pressing of our debts . . . " Spots turned and consulted with his sibling in the Hero's Tongue; kzin felt uneasy with a language as verbal as English. "A thousand each."

"Hmmm. The idea is to let money make money," Jonah replied. "You ought to invest it."

Bigs folded his ears in anger, and the pelt laid itself

flat on his face, sculpting against the massive bones. Spots lifted his upper lip and let his tail twitch in derision.

"If we had the skill, we would not have the opportunity. Business — who would do business of that sort with a kzin?"

"Well, I — " Jonah snapped his fingers. "Wait a minute! Remember that dosshouse we stayed at, the night I told you about the job?"

"I would rather forget," Spots said.

"Vermin," Bigs rasped. "Human-specific vermin at that. If the Fanged God is humorous, they will die from ingesting kzin blood."

"No, the old man I talked to — he'd been on prospecting expeditions into the Jotuns."

Spots had bent his head to lap at the water in the fountain; now he raised it, hands still braced on the rim, long pink washcloth-sized tongue lapping at his jowls and whiskers.

"You are altruistic, for a monk — for a human," he said suspiciously.

"Tanj," Jonah replied. "There Ain't No Justice. You two are out of luck because your side lost the war; I'm in bad odor with . . . hmmm, an influential patriarch, let's say. And we've just pounded on some people who, if not respectable, are certainly established citizens of Munchen. Reason and health both say we should get out of town. If nothing else, living's cheaper in the countryside. The Jotuns are pretty wild; we could hunt most of our food."

That brought the kzinti heads up, both of them. The aliens stared at him with their huge round lion-colored eyes for a moment, then looked at each other.

"I've got three thousand, you've got thirty-five hundred, our two friends here have a thousand apiece. No, that's not enough. Mm-hm. Need about twice that."

The old man's name was Hans Shwartz, and he had been perfectly willing to discuss an expedition. His honesty was reassuring, if depressing.

"Why so much?" Jonah asked. "I've done rockjack work, back in the Sol-Belt, but this is planetside — the air's free."

"*Ja*, but nothing else is," Hans said. "Look. You've got animals — no sense in trying to take ground vehicles, it's too rough in there — and you've got personal supplies, you've got weapons —"

"Weapons?"

"Bandits. Worse now than during the war. Weapons, then there's detector equipment. Southern Jotuns have funny geography, difficult — that's why it's worthwhile going in there. Scattered pockets of high-yield stuff; doesn't pay for large-scale mining, even these days."

Jonah nodded, and the two kzin flared their nostrils in agreement. The Serpent Swarm had been stripped of experienced rockjacks; they made the best stingship fighter-pilots, and the Alpha Centauran space-navy had inherited plenty of shipbuilding capacity from the occupation. Thousands of small strike craft built in Tiamat and the other space fabrication plants were riding in UN carriers deeper and deeper into kzinti space. Even so, the natural superiority of asteroid mining was only somewhat diminished. There would have been little or no mining and industry on the surface of Wunderland but for the kzinti. Kzin had been in its late Iron Age when the Jotok arrived and brought with them the full panoply of fusion power and gravity polarizers. The polarizer made surface-to-orbit travel fantastically cheap, and with fusion power pollution had never been a problem either.

"Ja, lot of stuff we'd need to make it worthwhile going. I'm willing to invest my savings, but not lose them — why do you think I'm sleeping in flophouses with three thousand krona in the bank? The return would be worth it, but only if we're properly equipped."

Jonah rubbed at his jaw; the stubble was bristly, and he reminded himself to pick up some depilatory, now that he could afford it.

"What prey is in prospect?" Bigs said.

Shwartz understood the idiom; he seemed to have had some experience with kzin. Enough to know basic etiquette like not staring, at least.

"Depends, *t'kzintar*." *Warrior*, in the Hero's Tongue; a derivative of *kzintosh*, male. "Possibly, nothing at all! That's the risk. Have to go way outback; anything near a road or shipline's been surveyed to hell and back. Take in filter membranes, then build a hydraulic system if we discover anything. Pack it out. Only the heavy metals and rare earths worth enough. With luck, oh, maybe ten, twenty thousand krona each — profit, that is, after expenses. Depends on when you want to stop, of course."

"Twenty thousand sounds fine to me," Jonah said. About the price of a rockjack's singleship, in normal times. More than enough for independence, if he managed carefully; passage back to Sol System, if he wanted it. "Excuse us for a minute?"

"*Ja*," the old man said mildly, stuffing his pipe and turning away to sit quietly on his cot, blowing smoke rings at the grimy ceiling of the dosshouse.

Jonah and the kzin brothers huddled in a corner; the half-ton of sentient flesh made a barrier as good as any privacy screen.

"Sounds like the best prospect going," he murmured.

"Yes," Spots said. He took a comp from his belt and tapped at the screen; a kzin military model, rather chunky, marked in the dots-and-commas of the aliens' script. "That would repurchase enough land to sustain our households. With an independent base, we could contract work to meet our cash-flow problems."

"I am tempted," Bigs cut in; they both looked at him in surprise. "My liver steams with the juices of anticipation. With enough wealth, we need no longer associate so much with humans." His ears folded away and he ducked his muzzle. "No offense, Jonah-Matthieson. You hardly seem like a monkey."

"None taken," Jonah said dryly. *Actually, he's quite reasonable . . . for a pussy,* he thought, using the old UN Space Navy slang for the felinoids. *That was flattery.* Accepting defeat violated kzin instincts as fundamental to them as sex was to a human. Walking among aliens who did not recognize kzinti dominance without lashing out at them took enormous strength of will.

"Hrrrr." Spots closed his eyes to a slit; the pink tip of his tongue protruded slightly. "How are we to raise the additional capital?" He brightened, unfurling ears. "A raid! We will — "

Jonah groaned; Bigs was grinning with enthusiasm . . . aggressive enthusiasm. How had these two survived since the liberation? *Badly,* he knew.

"No, no — do you want to end up in *prison*?"

That made them both wince. Kzinti were more vulnerable to sensory deprivation than humans; they were a cruel race, but rarely imprisoned their victims except as a temporary holding measure. Kzin imprisoned for long periods usually suicided by beating their own brains out against a wall, or died in raving insanity if restrained.

"No, we'll have to go with what the old coot had in mind," Jonah concluded.

Huge round amber-colored eyes blinked at him. "But he said he did not have access to sufficient funds," Spots pointed out reasonably, licking his nose and sniffing. Puzzlement: *I sniff for your reasoning.*

It was amazing how much you learned about kzinti,

working with them for a month or two. Back in Sol
System, nobody had known squat about the aliens,
except that they kept attacking — even when they
shouldn't. Now he knew kzin body language; he also
knew their economic system was primitive to the point
of absurdity. Not surprising, when a bunch of feudal-
pastoral savages were hired as mercenaries by a
star-faring race, given specialized educations, and then
revolted and overthrew their employers. That had
happened a long, long, *long* time ago, long enough to
be quasi-legend among the kzin. They had never
developed much sophistication, though; nor a real
civilization.

What they had done was to freeze their own
development. The kzin became a space-faring power
long before they understood what that meant; and
with space travel came access to genetic alteration techniques. The kzin used those, both on their captives and
on themselves. The plan was to make them better; but
better to the Race of Heroes meant to be even more
primitive, even more dedicated to the Fanged God,
even more loyal to the Patriarch. Civilization breeds for
rationality; but the kzin used gene mechanics to build
in proof against that.

While they were at it, they altered their social customs,
then changed their genes so the new customs would be
stable. The result was a race of barbarians, culturally well
below the level of the Holy Roman Empire, roaming
through space in wars of conquest and slavery.

Fortunately they had also changed their genes to
make themselves more Heroic; and to a kzin, Heroes
were rarely subtle and never deceptive.

Heroes don't lie, and they don't steal. *It should be
enough*, Jonah thought. So—

"He'll have a backer in mind," Jonah said. "A
beneath-the-grass patriarch. A silent partner."
Explaining the concept took a few minutes. "Otherwise

he wouldn't have talked to us at all."

The huge kzinti heads turned toward each other.

"*We need him*," Spots said. "*Badly.*"

"*Truth*," Bigs replied morosely.

Each of them solemnly bared the skin on the inside of a wrist and scratched a red line with one claw, then stared at him expectantly.

Oh, Finagle, the human thought. "Can I use a knife?" he said aloud.

"I won't take money from Harold Yarthkin," Jonah said bluntly.

He stared narrow-eyed at the lean Herrenmann face across the table, with its arrogant asymmetric double spike of beard. The room was large, elegant, and airy in the manner of Old Munchen, on the third story of a townhouse overlooking the Donau and the gardens along its banks. Almost as elegant as Claude Montferrat-Palme in his tweeds and suede, looking for all the world like a squire just in from riding over the home farm. He lounged back in the tall carved-oak chair, framed against the bright sunlight and the wisteria and wrought iron of the balcony behind him. His smile was lazy and relaxed.

"Oh, I assure you, there's no money of his in this. We're . . . close, but not bosom companions, if you know what I mean."

Ingrid, Jonah's mind supplied. An old and tangled rivalry; resolved now, but the scratches must linger. His were about healed, but he hadn't spent forty years brooding on them.

"Although he probably *would* back you up. You did save both their lives, there at the end."

Jonah felt a cold shudder ripple his skin, but the sensation was fading. *There are no more thrint*, he told himself. None at all, except for the Sea Statue in the UN museum, and that was safely bottled in a stasis field until the primal monobloc recondensed. After an instant the sensation went away. A year ago the memory attacks had been overwhelming; now they were just very, very unpleasant. Progress, of a sort.

"Not interested," he said flatly. *For one thing, our dear friend Harold might have left me here for the pussies, if it wouldn't have made him look bad in front of Ingrid.* Harold Yarthkin was a hero of sorts; Jonah knew the breed, from the inside. As ruthless as a kzin, when he was crossed or almighty Principle was at stake.

"But as I said, it's my money."

"Why are you spending your time on this penny-ante stuff, then?" Jonah asked. His nod took in the room, the old paintings and wood shining with generations of labor and wax.

"I'm not as rich as all that," Montferrat said to Jonah's skeptical eyebrow. "Contrary to rumor, most of the money I, hmmm, disassociated from official channels during the occupation didn't stick. Much of the remainder went after the liberation — my vindication wasn't an automatic matter, you see. Too many ambiguous actions. And I'm not exactly in good odor with the new government. The ARM doesn't like any of us who were involved in . . . that business, you know. Therefore the most lucrative investments, like buying up confiscated estates, are barred to me. But yes, backing an expedition like yours isn't all that good a bet. I've funded a number, and no more than broken even."

"Why bother?"

"For some reason, the Provisional Government —our acquaintance Markham, and General Early — doesn't really want exploration in that quarter. Among the many other things they dislike. Just to put a spoke in their wheels is satisfaction enough for me, so long as it doesn't *cost* money. And besides, perhaps the horse will learn to sing."

Jonah shrugged off the reference and sat in thought for a moment.

"Accepted," he said, and leaned forward to press his palm to the recorder.

" . . . and that, my dear, was how Jonah Matthieson came to be prospecting in these hills," Montferrat finished.

Night had fallen during the tale, and the outdoor patio was lit by the dim light of the town's glowstrips. Insectoids fluttered around them, things the size of a palm with wings in swirling patterns of indigo and crimson; they smelled of burnt cinnamon and made a sound as of glass chimes. Tyra took a cigarette and leaned forward to accept the man's offer of a light; she leaned back and blew a meditative puff at the stars before answering him.

"You certainly don't believe in letting the left hand know what the right does, do you, Herr Montferrat-Palme. Claude."

His grin was raffish and his expression boyishly frank. "No," he said. "But I'll tell you everything . . . "

She raised a brow.

" . . . that I think you need to know. I'm still uncertain of Jonah — uncertain of what the psychists did to him. I need someone to watch him; to report back to me, if there's any sign he's not what he pretends to be. And unobtrusively check up on any attempt to sabotage his expedition. You're the perfect choice, young and obscure . . . and Jonah is likely to trust you, if that's necessary."

"Well and good, and I can use the employment," Tyra said, giving him a level stare. "But what are your *purposes* here, myn Herr?"

"Money." After a moment he continued: "For a reason. I've got political plans. Not so much ambitions — with my history I'll never hold office — but I have candidates in mind. Harry, for one . . . I intend, in the long run, to put a glitch in Herrenmann

Reichstein-Markham's program; he'd make a very bad *caudillo*, and I think he's got ambitions in that direction." Tyra nodded grimly. "Beyond that, I want to get the ARM out of Wunderlander politics — a long-term project — and ease the transition to democracy.

"Not," he went on with a slight grimace, "the form of government I'd have chosen, but we have little choice in the matter, do we? In any case, I need money, and I need information, which is power. This business is just one gambit in a very complicated game."

"I've never been called a pawn so graciously before," Tyra said, rising and extending her hand. The older aristocrat clicked heels and bent over it. "Consider it a deal, Claude."

• CHAPTER NINE

The convoy was crowded and slow as it ground up the switchbacks of the mountain road. Hovercraft had a greasy instability in rocky terrain like this, setting Jonah's teeth on edge. The *speed* was disconcerting, too. Insect-slow, in one sense, compared to the singleships and fighter stingcraft he had piloted in the War, but you could not see velocity in space. Uncomfortably fast in relation to the ground; he kept expecting a collision-alarm to sound. He ignored the sensation, as he ignored the now-familiar scent of kzin, and scrolled through the maps instead. The flatbed around them was crowded, with farmers and travelers and mothers nursing their squalling young, and a cage full of shoats that turned hysterical every time the wind shifted and they scented Bigs and Spots. The kzin were sleeping; they could do that eighteen hours a day when there was nothing else to occupy their time.

Hans tapped the screen. "No sense in looking anywhere near here, like I said," he went on. "Surveyors found it all, and then when it got worth taking the contractors took it all out, twenty, thirty years ago. We'll buy some animals in Gelitzberg and —"

An alarm *did* go off, up in the lead truck. Almost at once an explosion followed, and a slow tide of dirt and rock came down the hillslope to their right, with jerking trees riding atop it like surfboarders on a wave. The autogun on the truck pivoted with smooth robotic quickness and its multiple barrels fired with a noise like yapping dogs, streaks of light stabbing out at other lines of fire reaching down from the scrubby hillside. Magenta globes burst where the seeker missiles died, but more lived to smash their liquid-metal bolts into engines; then the guard truck took the avalanche broadside and went spinning down the slope to vanish in a searing actinic glare as its power core ruptured. Molecular distortion batteries could not explode, strictly speaking, but they contained a *lot* of energy.

By that time Jonah had already rolled off the flatbed and dived for the roadside bush; he had seen boarding actions during the war, and had trained hard in gravity. He landed belly-down and eeled his way into the thick reddish-brown native scrub, ignoring the thorns that ripped at his exposed hands and face. To his surprise, Hans was not far away and moving rather more quietly. The response of the two kzin was not surprising at all; they went over the heads of their human companions and up the hillside in a series of bounding leaps, then vanished into cover with an appalling suddenness.

Jonah licked at the sweat on his upper lip and took up the trigger slack on his magrifle. It was a cheap used model, and the holo sight that sprang into existence over the breech quivered slightly and never reached the promised x40 magnification. It was still much better than nothing, and he used it to scan the upper slope carefully, starting close and working back. The bandits were visible in short snatches, working their way cautiously toward the wrecked convoy. Fire still crackled overhead from passengers and guards; the bandits returned it with careful selectivity, not wanting to damage their loot more than was needful. One face showed through a gap between rocks for an instant, a heavy pug countenance with brown stubble and a gold tooth.

If they had seeker missiles, they've probably got a good jammer, Jonah thought. No help to be expected anytime soon.

"Here goes," he whispered softly, laid the sighting-bead on a blurred shape screened by bush, and stroked at the trigger.

His rifle was set for high-subsonic; the slug gave a sharp *pfut* and the weapon bumped gently at his shoulder. The bandit folded and dropped backward, screaming loud enough to be heard over a thousand meters. One of the weaknesses of impact armor; when there was *enough* kinetic energy behind the projectile, the suddenly-rigid surface could pulp square meters of your body surface. Very painful, if not fatal.

Hans was firing too, accurate and slow. Jonah snap-shot, raking the slope and clenching his teeth against the knowledge that they would be scanning for him, with better sensors than an overage rifle sight. They had heavy weapons, too.

Another scream, this time one of kzin triumph, inhumanly loud and fierce; instincts that remembered tiger and sabertooth raised hairs under the sweat-wet fabric of his jacket. A human body soared out and tumbled down the hillside, limp in death. Seconds later, a globe of flame rose from nearby, the discharge of a tripod-mounted beamer's power cell. Another heavy beamer cut loose, but this time directed back upslope at the bandits. Jonah's sights showed Bigs holding it like a hand weapon, screaming with gape-jawed joy as he hosed down the hillside. Bush flamed, and men ran through it burning. Jonah shot, shifted aimpoint, shot again, as much in mercy as anything else. When he shifted to wide-angle view for a scan, he saw a swarthy-faced bandit in the remnants of military kit rallying the gang, then leading them in a swift retreat over the hill.

And the two kzin pursuing. *"Come back!"* he screamed incredulously. Hans looked at him; the humans shrugged, and began to follow.

Horses did not like kzin. That, it seemed, was an

immutable fact of life. Hans watched the last of them go bucking off across the dusty square of Neu Friborg with a philosophical air.

"Waste of time, horses, anyway," he said. "Die on you, like as not. Draw tigripards. Mules are what we need; mules for the gear, and we can walk. Kitties'd have to walk anyhow, too heavy for horses."

"I *eat* herbivores, I do not perch upon them," Bigs said, and stalked off to curl up on a rock and sulk.

"Will these . . . mules be more sensible?" Spots asked dubiously.

The stock pens had been set up for the day, collapsible metal frames old enough to be rickety; most of the work animals being offered for sale had been stunned into docility by the heat. High summer in the southern Jotuns was no joke, with both suns up and this lowish altitude. Jonah fanned himself with his straw hat, wiped sweat from his face and looked dubiously at the collection of bony animals who turned their long ears towards him. It was probably imagination, the look of malicious anticipation . . . *and planets have lousy climate control systems*, he added to himself. His underwear was chafing, and he was raw under his gunbelt. The pens stank with a hot, dry smell and buzzed with flies, Terran and the six-winged Wunderlander equivalents.

"I haven't had much to do with animals," he said dubiously. Except to eat them sometimes, and he preferred his meat prepared so its origin wasn't too obvious. In space you ate rodent, mostly, anyway, or decently synthesized protein. It made him slightly queasy, the thought of eating something with eyes that size and a large head.

"You'll learn," Hans said, running his hands expertly down the legs of one animal. "Won't do," he added to the owner, in outbacker dialect. "Galls. Let's see t'other one.

"Yep, you'll learn," he continued to Jonah. "Unless you want to carry three hundred kilos of gear yourself."

"I see your point," Jonah replied.

The mule stretched out its neck at Spots and gave a deafening bray with aggressive overtones. The kzin's fur bottled, and he hissed back at the mule, which blinked and fell silent. From the way its eyes rolled, it was keeping a wary watch on the big carnivore . . .

"Thiss'un 'll do," Hans told the owner. "And the other five."

The grizzled farmer nodded and whistled for the town registrar, who came over with a readout pistol and scanned the barcodes laser-marked into the mules' necks.

"Set down," she said, tucking the instrument into a holster in her skirts. "New system, just back on line — haven't had a computer link like this since way back in the occupation." She gave Spots a hard glare; that was extremely bad manners by kzinti standards, but the felinoid stared over her head.

Poor bleeping pussy must have had a lot of practice at that, Jonah thought with some compassion. Stares and jostling and tobacco smoke; life was not easy for kzin under human rule. *On the other hand, we don't enslave or eat them, so matters are rather more than even.*

"Might as well get started," Hans concluded, after slapping palms with the farmer. "You fellas need to learn how to do up a pack saddle. Got to be balanced, or you'll get saddle galls and then we'll be stuck without enough transport to carry our gear. Couldn't have that. All right, first lesson."

He handed one of the wood-and-leather frames to Spots, together with a blanket. "Fold the blanket, then put the saddle firmly across."

Spots picked up the gear in his stubby-fingered four-digit hands, conscious of the village loafers and small children watching him. So conscious that he did not realize what the mule's laid-back ears meant, and the way it turned its head to fix him with one distance-estimating eye. The kick was swift even by kzinti standards, and precisely aimed. Spots made a whistling sound as he flew back, folding around his middle. The onlookers laughed; he fought back to all fours. His back arched, fur bottled out, ears folded away in combat mode, and his tail stood out like a pink column behind him. He was beyond lashing it, in his rage, and his lower jaw sank down on his breast in the killing gape as he whooped for breath. Adrenaline surge and lack of oxygen sent gray across his eyes and narrowed his vision down to a tunnel. When a human moved at the corner of it, he whirled and began the upward gutting stroke with barred claws.

The motion froze. It was the human Jonah, and he stood calmly in the position of respectful-nonaggression, with no smell of fear. His teeth were decently concealed. Slowly, slowly, willpower beat down the aching need to kill and the rage-shame of mockery. The loafers had tumbled backward at the blurring-swift kzin leap that left Spots back on his feet, though some of the children had cried out in delight as at a wonder. Spots's pelt sank back toward normal, and he forced his ears to unfold, his tail to relax. Jonah bent and picked up the saddle and its blanket pad.

"Shall we do this together?" he said in an even voice. "I wouldn't care to be kicked by that thing, myself — I don't have cartilage armor across my middle the way you Heroes do."

Stiffly, Spots's ears waggled; the equivalent of a forced smile. "Mine is not in very good condition, at the moment. How shall we approach?"

"One on either side," Jonah said. "We shouldn't give him a target."

"*Hrraaaeeeeeeeee!*" Bigs shrieked and leapt.

The gagrumpher froze for a fatal instant, its six legs

tensed and head whipping backward, then spurted forward in a desperate bound. Spots rose out of the underbrush almost at its feet and lunged for the exposed throat, fastening himself with clawed hands and feet to the big animal and sinking his fangs into its throat. Blood bubbled between his teeth, hot and salty and spicy across his tongue, but he concentrated on squeezing his jaws shut. Air wheezed through the punctured windpipe and he gave a grunt of triumph as it closed beneath the bone-cracking pressure of his grip. Suffocation killed the prey, when you got a good throat-hold. The animal collapsed by the forelegs, then went over on its side with a thump as Bigs arrived and threw his massive form against its hindquarters. A few seconds more and it kicked and died.

They crouched for a moment, panting, forepaw-hands on the warm body. The soft night echoed to the throbbing killscream of triumph, and then they settled down to the enjoyable task of butchering and eating. Spots cuffed affectionately at his sibling as they ripped open the body cavity and squabbled over hearts — gagrumphers had two, one major and one secondary, like most Wunderland higher life-forms — and liver. It was a big beast, twice the weight of an adult male kzin, half a human ton, but they made an appreciable dint in it, before feeling replete enough to pile the remainder in torn-off segments of hide; it would be fresh enough to eat for a couple of days. With the chore done they could lie at leisure, cracking bones for marrow with rocks and the hilts of their wtsai-knives, nibbling at treats of organ and tripe, grooming the blood and bits out of each other's fur.

"It is well, it is well," Bigs crooned, working over the hard-to-reach places at the back of his sibling's neck. It was amazing where the blood got to, when you stuck your head into the prey's abdominal cavity.

"It is well," Spots confirmed, yawning cavernously. "If

I never eat synthetic protein again, it will be far too soon. Nothing is lacking but ice cream, or some bourbon with milk."

"Your pride-mate provides," Bigs announced, unslinging a canteen and two flat dishes that collapsed against it. "The bourbon, at least."

A throaty purr resounded from both throats. *This is how the Fanged God meant kzinti to live*, Spots thought. The night was bright to their sight, full of interesting scents; a gratifying hush of terror was only gradually wearing off, as the native life reacted to the roar of hunting kzin.

It was how kzin *had* lived, for scores of scores of millennia, on the savannahs and in the jungles of Kzin itself. The scent of his brother was rich and comforting with their common blood. So had young warriors lived in the wandering years, cast out by their fathers and the home pride. They grouped together in the wastelands, brothers and half-brothers and cousins, growing strong in comradeship and skill, until they could raid the settled bands for females of their own — or even displace their fathers and become lords in their own right. From those bonds sprang the pride and the clan, foundations of kzinti culture. So had the Heroic Race lived through the long slow rise to sentience, through all the endless hunting time. Before iron and fire, before the first ranches. Long, long before the Jotoki came from space, with their two-edged gifts of technology and education to hire orange-furred mercenaries.

"I scent a path that might have been," Spots mused, over a second drink. "If the Jotok had never come to Kzin-home, would we ever have been more than wandering hunters, with castle-dwelling ranchers as the height of our civilization? My liver trembles with ambiguity — perhaps that would have been best?"

"And miss the Endless Hunt?" his more conventional sibling retorted. "The flesh of these excellent gagrumphers?"

"The Endless Hunt is endless time spent in spaceships and habitats, living on synthetic meat, never feeling wind in your fur," Spots replied. They had both done tours of duty offplanet during the war, and served longer in fortresses on the surface that might as well have been battlecraft. "And living among aliens."

"The Fanged God created them to serve us," Bigs said reasonably, rolling onto his back in the gesture of relaxed trust and looking at Spots upside-down. "Thus freeing the Heroes for the honorable path of war."

"So said the Conservors of the Patriarchal Past," Spots said, with a sardonic wave of his bat-wing ears. "You will note that there are few of them around. We *lost* this war."

Bigs's posture grew slightly rigid. "My nose is dry with worry," he said, in an attempt at lightness. "Our impoverished but noble line is about to be disgraced with a Kdaptist."

"Lick your nose, kshat-hunter; I do not yet imagine that God created Man in His image. Kdapt-Preacher I have seen; he is of great liver, but rattlebrain as a kit. As a kzinrett. His experiences in the war . . ."

Bigs nodded wisely. "Yet I will not challenge him claw-to-claw," he said.

Spots snorted, lips flapping against his teeth; the self-proclaimed prophet had made many converts among the remaining kzinti in the Alpha Centauri system. It was soothing to the self-esteem to blame defeat on God, Who was the ultimate Victor in every life. He had made even more with an uninterrupted series of personal victories in death-duels; his belt was like a dried-flesh kilt with the ear trophies he had garnered since proclaiming his mission. Luckily, he had also proclaimed his intention of voyaging to Kzin itself and trying to convert the Patriarch. The Riit would deal with him in due course, one assumed.

"Yet still, we lost."

"We have suffered a setback," Bigs replied stubbornly, scratching his belly. "It was unfair — the Outsiders intervened."

Spots twitched tail. The mysterious Outsiders *had* sold the hyperdrive to the human colonists of We Made It; it was still a matter of furious controversy among the Wunderland survivors whether the Fifth Fleet so painfully accumulated by the late, great Chuut-Riit would have overwhelmed the human homeworld. Neither species would have stumbled on the hyperdrive themselves, he thought, despite knowing some such thing had been made by the ancient thrint and tnuctipun. It was so . . . *unlikely*.

"Unfair," Bigs repeated.

"As the great Kztarr-Shuru said, fairness is the concept of those whose leap rams their nose into a stone wall. They open their eyes and complain. Four fleets were destroyed by the monkeys," Spots said meditatively, likewise scratching. The salt of blood made for a pleasantly itching skin; his belly was drum-tight with fresh meat he had killed with his own teeth and claws, an intensely satisfying feeling. "Even when they had no tradition of war. I have studied them."

"Too much, my brother," Bigs said, rolling over onto his stomach to talk seriously. "Even as you speak too much with the Jonah-monkey."

"The Jonah-monkey is a warrior," Spots said sharply. "He has saved our honor . . . not to mention our lives."

"For its own monkey purposes," Bigs grumbled, holding down a legbone with both hands and gnawing. The tough bone grated and chipped beneath his fangs. "Remember, in the end, there can be only Dominance toward such as it."

Spots rose and stretched, one limb at a time, his tongue curling pinkly. "When we are not paupers living on enemy territory . . ." he said, and rippled his fur in a shrug at the sharp scent of annoyance from his sibling. It faded; it was difficult for any young kzintosh to maintain anger on a full belly after a kill. "We should return to their camp. As Jonah said, the old one will have difficulty setting a decent pace — he needs his rest."

"Hrrraweo. Journeying with humans! Their cremated meats . . ."

Spots joined in the shudder. "Yet we may hunt — we have not eaten so well since the war ended."

"Truth." Bigs looked around at the minor scavengers, already congregating for the scraps. "Yet in my inmost liver, I feel we are now such as these."

With a sigh, they slid off into the friendly night, back toward the human campfire.

• CHAPTER TEN

"ID cards? We don' need no ID cards! We don' need no stinkin' ID cards!"

The bandit chief struck his fist on the table and snarled; the jugs of drink jumped, and one flask of sake fell. The porcelain was ancient and priceless, an heirloom from Earth; one of the black-clad attendants had crossed the room to catch it before it had time to travel half the distance to the floor. Scalding-hot rice wine cascaded across his wrists and forearms, but there was no tremor in them as he set it reverently back in place, bowed, and stepped smoothly to his guard position along the wall. Shigehero Hirose spared him the indignity of sending him to the autodoc; repairs could be made at any time, but an opportunity to demonstrate true loyalty — and to accumulate *giri* — was more rare.

The bandit, Gruederman, lost some of his bluster. Hirose thought that was merely from the guard's speed, not from the true depths of disciplined obedience it showed; but any lesson learned by a barbarian was an improvement. "Herr Gruederman," the Nipponjin said. "I have gone to some trouble to secure false identities for you and your group as members of the Provisional Gendarmerie. I am sure you will find them very useful."

Gruederman threw himself back in the chair, taking up his bottled beer and gulping at it. Hirose hid a cold distaste behind his bland smile. The other man was short and thickset, bouncy-muscular, which was something; many Wunderlanders who did no manual labor were obscenely flabby. Humanity had had only a few centuries to adapt to the .61 gravity, and millions to develop a physiology suited to 1.0. But for the rest he was a slobbering pig, not even bothering to depilate — Hirose suppressed a shudder at the sheer *hairiness* of *gaijin* — with great bands of sweat darkening his khaki tunic under the armpits and at the neck. Granted, the hotel room was hot, even with the ceiling fan, but . . .

He wrinkled his nose. Gruederman didn't wash very often, either, and he had the rank body odor of a red-meat eater.

"More guns is what we need, more equipment," he was saying. "Not stinkin' ID. Why can't you get us guns? You slants fence what we take, you've got to have good contacts."

"Our contacts are our concern," Hirose said quietly. "We have provided a valuable service; you may purchase weapons elsewhere with the valuata we supply." *And we are not going to make you so much of a menace that the Provisional Government looks too closely, which would happen if we provided you with the equipment you desire.* "In return, we ask only that you do an occasional favor . . ."

Gruederman frowned. "*Ja*, no problem, we boot some head. Who you want done?"

Hirose pushed the holos across the table and sipped delicately at his sake.

"Lieber Herr Gott!" Gruederman swore, taking another swig of beer. "Ratcats!"

"The humans are the crucial targets," the oyabun said quietly.

"I know these fuckers! They were on the convoy to Neu Friborg last week. Shot us up! You say they're goin' into the Jotuns?" Hirose inclined his head. "No problem, we boot their heads *good*."

"Excellent," Hirose said, nodding.

Gruederman belched hugely, pushed back his chair

and swaggered to the door. "We boot them good." The bandit hitched at his belt and went out without bowing. The *oyabun* walked quickly to the window and flung it open; without needing orders, the others began to clean the room and lit incense.

The things I do for the Secret Rule, he thought ironically. *Or for fear of the Secret Rule*. Once your family was in the Brotherhood, there was no such thing as resignation. That was how the world had been knit together, back on Earth; slowly, but oh so surely. *"Until Holy Blood fills Holy Grail . . ."* he quoted to himself. And now, it seemed, the extra-solar colonies would go the same way. He sighed; it had been pleasant, the degree of autonomy four and a half light-years interposed between Earth and Alpha Centauri. Virtual independence, the way it must have been on Earth before Nippon was opened to the West, when the Eastern Way families had received their orders from the Elders only once or twice in a generation. All things came to an end, though; the kzinti had come, the hyperdrive had followed, and now the universe had shrunk drastically once more.

It was useless to think of resistance. Even more so to think of rebellion, or exposing the Brotherhood; it had been exposed a dozen times, and *it did not matter*. In more than one century investigators had managed to publish books with most of the details of the Brotherhood, its origin, many of the membership, even some of the signs of the Craft. They hadn't mattered. The books were not believed. They were buried under a mountain of disinformation, the tale-tellers ignored if outsiders, silenced if initiates. Outright rebels like Frederick Barbarossa and Lenin were crushed. Invincible, secret beyond secret, the conspiracy at the heart of all conspiracies and secret orders, the Brotherhood went on. Just at the moment it took the form of the ARM and Buford Early, and demanded that certain individuals vanish in the dangerous, bandit-haunted wastes of the Jotuns. That, at least, was easily arranged, with willing tools who knew nothing of what purpose they served.

"Go." He turned, nodding to the attendant who had caught the spilled wine. "See to your hurts."

He kept his voice curt, but the man sensed the approval. *When the time comes to silence Gruederman, I will send that one*, Hiroshe decided. None of Gruederman's band could be allowed to live, of course. They would be no loss to anyone.

"It's a very tempting proposition, Herr Early — or should I say Herr General Early? — but I'm afraid it's not what I had in mind at the present time," Claude Montferrat-Palme said.

His current mistress set a tray between the two men and withdrew; she was a spectacular blond in red tights and slashed tunic, and Early's eyes followed her out of the lounge with appreciation. Low gravity could do some interesting things for the human figure, things only prosethics or special effects could accomplish on Earth. Belters were usually too spindly to take advantage.

They were meeting on Montferrat's home ground, the manor-house of his grudgingly restored estate. Grudgingly, since his allegiance to the Resistance had been so late and politic, but the conversion had been spectacular when it came. Also he turned out to have used much of the graft that came the way of a *collabo* chief of police for Munchen to help refugees, most of whom had showed their gratitude in electorally solid ways . . . *Rather surprising me,* Montferrat chuckled inwardly. *Sometimes I wish the world would not keep chipping away at my cynicism so.* You needed the vigor of disillusioned youth to maintain a really black, bitter cynicism. In his seventh decade and settling into middle age, Claude felt a disconcerting mellowing effect.

Early leaned back, coffee cup in one hand and

brandy snifter in the other. "Excellent," he said after sipping at one and then the other. Continuing: "I'm surprised you're not interested, *Herrenmann*. You struck me as an ambitious man."

"Pleasant to meet someone who appreciates the finer things," Montferrat said, swirling the amber liquid in his snifter and inhaling the scent. Most of the plutocrats who founded Wunderland had been German or Netherlander or Scandinavian; his Montferrat ancestors were a French exception, and they had worked long and hard to establish the true vines of Cognac on this property. Along with the coffee plantations, things were possible in Wunderland's climate that were not on earth.

"And I *am* ambitious, Herr General," he went on, setting it down and taking out his cigarette case.

Early accepted one of the cigarillos, and they both lit from the candle on the table. The big room was dimly lit, letting in moonlight and warm garden scents through the tall louvered windows on three sides. Blue smoke drifted up toward the molded plaster of the ceiling.

"Strange you should be willing to risk all this, then," he said, waving an arm at the outer wall; taking in the mansion and estate beyond, in spirit.

"If you mean the inheritance of the Nineteen Families," Montferrat said, blowing a smoke ring, "it's already more-or-less lost. And in any case, what business is it of yours?"

"I'm merely advising General Markham, as liason with the UN Space Navy," Early said mildly.

"Advising him that his dreams of returning Wunderland to the pre-War status quo can be accomplished," Montferrat said dryly. "Absurd. For a variety of reasons, good and bad, the Families were too closely involved in running the planet during the Occupation. Their rule is doomed, even if the Provisional Government's

Gendarmerie has stopped the rioting and looting against them."

"You haven't thrown in with the Democrats, either," Early pointed out.

"No, because I recognize a certain fine Terrestrial hand behind them — you've been puppeting the new Radical Democrat party too — financing it, in fact."

"You'll never prove a word of *that*," Early replied.

"Of course not; I'm not entirely sure what you and your masters are after, but you're certainly no fool. There isn't even enough evidence to convince Markham, and he's a clinical paranoid, I wonder his autodoc doesn't fix him. My best guess is that you want to use Markham to restore order, infiltrating our military in the process — then use him to discredit the aristocrats completely with his ham-handed repression. Thus leaving the field to the Radical Democrats, who want a constitution that's a carbon copy of Earth's — complete with a technological police. Which the experience of the UN shows is equivalent to handing the government *over* to the technological police, since to control technology in a modern society you have to control everything."

For a moment the mask of affability slipped on Early's face, and Montferrat felt a slight prickling along his spine. *How much of that is genuine?* he thought. *The man is* ancient, *for Gott's sake.* At least three times older than himself . . . and he ought to be sitting wheezing in a computerized wheelchair in the Strudlebug's Club back on Earth. *Secrets of the ARM.*

"You *are* ambitious," Early said softly. "I'd hoped to talk you out of this party you're promoting."

"Many people are involved with the Centrists," Montferrat corrected; Early waved his hand.

"Please, I know the signs of secret influence when I see them." For some reason he grinned at that. "Separatism is not a viable alternative."

"Independence is," Montferrat said. "And

Wunderland — the Alpha Centauri system — is going to be independent. Of the kzin, and of Earth and the UN."

"You'd better be sure you've got ample bargaining power before you sit down to bargain with me," Early warned.

"Oh, exactly, my dear General. Which is why, as you will have noticed, I'm not bargaining with you now."

Unexpectedly, Early laughed; it was a deep rich sound, thick as chocolate. "You aren't, are you?" He took another sip of the brandy. "Well, in that case — perhaps you could expand on the remark you made at dinner, about local performance techniques and classical Meddelhoffer?"

● CHAPTER ELEVEN

"He's not *human*," Jonah gasped, flopping down on a rock and watching Hans swing along up the mountainside.

Bigs rolled a baleful eye at him as he lay prone in the track, twitching expressive eyebrows; Spots carefully poured water from a plastic container over his body, from head to the base of his tail. Then he trudged down to the small stream and poured several more over his own head before returning to repeat the process with his brother. Both kzin were panting, their tongues lolling, the palms of their hands and feet and their tails oozing sweat. Those were the only ways kzinti *had* to shed excess heat; Kzin was a cooler planet than Earth or Wunderland. Besides . . .

"If — " Spots stopped, thrust his muzzle into the plastic container and lapped down a torrent "— if I remember my instructors, you monk-hrrreaow, you Men evolved into omnivores by taking to running down your prey in long chases."

"Think so," Jonah replied.

His feet hurt, and he felt dizzy from the amount he'd sweated. A swallow from his canteen to wash down salt tablets, and he poured more on a neckerchief and wiped his face and neck. The hollow where they had halted was shady at least, big gum trees and whipsticks, but the steep rock to either side concentrated the sunlight, and it was humid as well. The air hummed and buzzed with insects, drawn to sweat, landing and biting and stinging. The human ignored them; there was no

relief until they made camp and set up the sonics —
and those had to be turned low or the sensitive ears of
the kzin found them unbearable in frequencies
humans could not hear.

"Well, we Heroes evolved from stalk-and-leap
hunters!" Spot snapped. Literally: his jaws closed on
the word with a wet *clomp*. "Of *course* we don't shed heat
as well. We don't chase prey that escapes our ambush!
We never needed to! We developed brains cunning
enough to catch meat without following it for days!"

There was a teeth-gritting whine in the kzin's voice.
Bigs was in worse shape, heavier and thicker-pelted; he
simply lay with his tongue hanging out on the ground.
Jonah nodded wordlessly, stumbling down to the stream
and refilling his canteen. *He* had never had the slightest
interest in chasing prey of any sort, except kzinti Vengeful Slasher-class fighters during the War — and that
could be done in the decent comfort of a crashcouch,
right next to a good food synthesizer and autodoc. Fighting in space was war for gentlemen: either you won or
you died, usually quickly, and you did it in climate-
conditioned comfort. There had been a couple of
boarding actions when the Fourth Fleet was smashed,
but even those had been done in space armor.

He shuddered slightly, swallowing hard. There had
been *tubing* in the meat last night.

The water looked cool and inviting as he dipped his
head once more. The pebbles in the bottom were
unusual — he noticed the dull glitter of them through
the rippling water, and idly lifted a handful. *Heavy*, he
thought, and threw them skipping across the surface.
One struck a shovel lashed to the pack-saddle of a
mule, startling the animal out of its torpor and into a
brief bucking frenzy. The sound of pebble on steel was
a dull, metallic *clunk* . . .

"Wait a minute," Jonah whispered. He scrabbled at
his belt for the sample spectroscope and scooped again

for more pebbles; his hands were trembling as he shoved one into the trap of the instrument and flicked the activator. "*Platinum!*" he yelled. The kzinti unfurled their ears to maximum, like pink radar dishes. "54% platinum, by Finagle's ghost!"

Jonah Matthieson had been a rockjack, an asteroid prospector, in the brief intervals of peace in Sol System; the methods in that were a great deal more mechanized, but he knew what was valuable. He scrabbled in the streambed, then tore back to his mules for the pan. Pebbles and heavy sand washed out as he swirled the water and flicked off the lighter material. Readings glowed as he jammed more samples into the scanner: 57%, 72%, an incredible 88%. His stomach ached with the tension as he worked his way upstream; Bigs and Spot were following, howl-spitting at each other in the Hero's Tongue. At last he thought to call Hans. The Sol-Belter was still fumbling with the belt radio when the old man came up, leading his mules and looking nearly as phlegmatic.

"Ja," he said calmly. "Platinum all right. Nice heavy concentration." He took the pipe out of his mouth to spit aside. "Worthless."

Spot gave an ululating howl, jaws open at the sky. Bigs collapsed again, this time into the stream with only his eyebrows and black nostrils showing; his tail waved pink in the water, and little fish-analogues came to nibble at it. Jonah felt an overwhelming urge to break the spectroscope over the Wunderlander's head, and then a sick almost-headache at the back of his neck.

"It's a perfectly good industrial metal!" he protested, slogging to the bank of the stream and sitting down on a wet rock. A kermitoid croaked and thrashed away through the spiny underbrush. "It's used for everything from chemical synthesis to doping crystal fusion cores. Back in the Sol Belt, it was the first thing we looked for."

"Ja, so useful the kzinti hauled seven or eight asteroids from the Swarm to near-Wunderland orbit as reserves, back during the Fifth Fleet buildup," Hans nodded. "Still a lot of it left. We need something valuable but not so valuable they thought to get a supply set up," he went on. "Gold, hafnium, something like that. Well," he went on, "rest-period's over. Got to get a move on if we want to get anything done."

Spots and Bigs whined. So did Jonah.

"Give me two," Spots said, throwing two cards into the pile.

Jonah dealt, watching the kzin across the campfire narrowly. His scent was calm — he had long since learned to recognize the gingery smell of kzinti excitement — but that could simply be control enough to keep it down below the stun-your-nostrils level humans could recognize. Bigs seemed to be watching him intently, ears out and fur fluffed up around his face. Spots's tail was held rigidly and quivering just slightly at the tip . . .

"Fold," he decided. Nobody else wanted more cards.

Spots flapped his ears, and his eyebrows twitched. "See you and raise you three."

Three *krona*, to the humans; the brothers were playing each other for kzinretti, of which they both had more than they wanted, due to the surplus after most of the kzintosh — male kzin — in the system died. Evidently numbers in the harem were a status matter for kzinti.

"See you," Bigs said in Wunderlander: "*And smell you, you vatch-in-the-grass*," he muttered under his breath in the Hero's Tongue, in the Mocking Tense.

"And two," Hans added. He puffed ostentatiously on his pipe, and the two kzin closed their nostrils in an exaggerated gesture. Their huge golden eyes caught the firelight occasionally, silver disks in the darkness.

Well, it is pretty foul, Jonah conceded. On the other hand, Hans was sitting downwind.

"Call." Bigs's tail was quivering visibly.

Spots sighed and let his ears droop. "Three queens," he said, flipping his hand upright.

Bigs lunged and snapped close to his nose. "I thought you were bluffing!" he said, throwing down his pair of tens.

"You should have listened to the Conservors and learned to control the juices of your liver," Spots said sanctimoniously, purring slightly and letting the tip of his tongue show through his teeth. The pelt rose around his neck, and his whiskers worked back and forth; he licked a wrist and smoothed them back. "That is fifteen kzinretti you owe me — my selection, remember."

"Sorry, fellers," Hans laughed. "That's fifteen krona you three owe *me*." He turned up his hand; three aces.

Spots shrieked, sending the mules snorting and pulling on their curb chains out at the edge of sight. Bigs waved his ears and thumped his tail back and forth, flapping his lips against his fangs in derision.

"Now whose liver is overheated?" he said, then stretched and yawned. "You have first watch."

Spots stalked off into the night, ears folded away and tail a rigid pink length behind him.

"I think even Hans is getting tired," Jonah said over his shoulder.

Then he raised the cutting bar and slashed again at the thick, matted vegetation ahead of him. It was almost all native, with the cinnamon scent of Wunderlander growth; the local varieties seemed to run mostly to thorns and silica-rich stems, though. The cutting bar was a thin-film of diamond sandwiched between vacuum-deposited layers of single-crystal iron, and it should have gone through vegetation with scarcely more effort than air. Two of the teeth had broken off on rocks, and the matted stems pulled irritatingly at his wrist.

Spots scarcely bothered to flap his ears; Bigs was morosely silent again. Last night he had even turned down the evening poker game, a very bad sign.

"Your turn," the human wheezed.

Bigs squeezed past him and began chopping methodically. From the way his lips moved and the slight murrling sounds from his chest, he was fantasizing each bush as an enemy to be killed. Hans was to their right and a thousand meters upslope, up in the open. Hotter up there, no shade, but at least there was some wind, a little air. The olive gloom around Jonah seemed as airless as the bottom of the sea; sweat clung and curdled, drying in the creases of his body, chafing at the small sores the thorns had left on his arms and face. Even the tough synthetic of his clothing was starting to give way, and the zitrigor leather of his boots had begun to wear thin in a place or two. He was leaner by about ten kilos than he had been at the beginning of the trip, and tough as the strip of dried meat he chewed at mechanically as he marched. The kzinti had lost weight too, and their pelts were so matted with tangles and burrs that even their obsessive nightly grooming could scarcely keep pace.

So much for the mighty hunters, he thought snidely. That was a little unfair; whatever their instincts, Wunderland kzin were the descendants of space travellers. Their immediate ancestors came from Hssin, a sealed-habitat colony on a world with poisonous atmosphere. Spots and Bigs had hunted in their father's preserves, but their home environment was as artificial as any human's.

"I begin to dream of talcum powder and blowdriers," Spots said unexpectedly. Bigs grunted. "And of kzinretti. My palazzo will be in chaos."

Jonah grunted in his turn. Thinking about women was a *bad* idea out here; easier for a kzin, since their responses were so conditioned on smell. They turned upslope to avoid an outcrop of granite and emerged blinking onto the steep brushy slopes of the hill; they were in an interior depression of the Jotuns, with eroded volcanic peaks on all sides, and it focused the summer heat like a lens. Wearily they all sank to the ground, letting the mules browse for a moment. The kzin had taken to wearing conical straw hats the humans wove for them, and now they fanned their dangling tongues. Jonah shook his canteen and decided half-full was still enough to warrant a drink; he sipped at the water, letting each drop soak into his tissues. Far above a contrail streaked across the sky, some vacationer in an aircar off to the beaches of Heleigoland Island. Sitting under an umbrella, sipping at drinks with fruit in them. Watching girls diving into the surf . . .

"There's not much point in going on," he said wearily. It was only the thought of retracing his steps that had kept him from saying it until now. Going forward with some hope was bad enough; going back with none was unbearable. "We've got those tigripard hides, that'll cover most of our expenses. We could sell the gear."

Bigs was lost in his brooding. "I begin to think you are correct, Jonah-human," his sibling said sadly. "My nose is dry with worry at what will befall our households — but still, we — "

Hans jumped down from a boulder near them. "Ready to give up, are we? The valiant Heroes, the UN Navy hotshot?" He cackled laughter, his ancient leathery face crinkling. "You're so stupid you don't know a fortune when you're standing on one. You're so stupid you'd shit on a plate and call it steak!" The Wunderlander was practically dancing around his bewildered companions. "Jonah, you're sitting down, you've got your thinking apparatus jammed on money — can't you tell when you're rubbing your cheeks on wealth?"

"Something hit so hard the planet *splashed*," Hans said, leaning on his pick.

They had been working up the side of the hill, following the gullies and taking samples. The gold was patchy, but the deposits caught in folds and ripples in the ground were increasingly rich. Off to their left a waterfall stretched down the surface of a cliff, a thread-thin line of silver against the pink granite rock; where it struck down in the valley bottom an explosion of mist blossomed, amid a great circle of whipstick and jacaranda trees, with tall silver-gums towering over all. Ahead the slope was jagged and eroded, soft crumbly rock and clay streaked with bright mineral colors. The scent of the scrub under their feet was dry and intense, like a perpetual almost-sneeze, cut occasionally by a drift of cooler air and mist from the falls. Kermitoids peeped and croaked, and a red-tailed hawk dove down the slope after a rabbit and then rose with the struggling beast in its claws, *skree-skree* as it flapped off heavily toward the cliffs.

"Ja, big astrobleme — way, way back. Punched right through the crust. Wunderland's got slow continental drift, you know, ja? Starts and stops. This made a hotspot, kept burning through every time the crust moved across it. The whole line of the Jotuns, east-to-west across the Aeserheimer Continent is here because of it — this is the active part. Erosion . . . that's why you get pockets of metallics here. None very big, but by Herr Gott, they're rich."

"Where do we dig?" Spots asked. He was drooling slightly, always a sign of impatience in a kzin.

"Not down here," Hans said; the beatific smile still quirked at the edges of his mouth. "No, no use digging down here. Oh, there's gold, but we need water to set up the ripple membranes and get it out." He used the haft of his pick as a pointer. "Up there. We can cut a furrow 'cross the hillside from the creek."

"Tanj," Jonah said, measuring distances. Trivial by spatial terms, but he'd acquired a whole new perspective on "kilometer" since he started spending so much time dirtside. "That's quite a job, without any equipment."

"We've got cutter bars and thirty kilometers of monofilament," Hans said cheerfully. "My brains, and you three for strong backs and simple minds, plus four mules. That's plenty of equipment for what we'll need."

"There ain't no justice," Jonah muttered, dragging a forearm across his face. Still, it wasn't much harder than the contracting job, and promised to pay a good deal better.

"You said it, son. You said it," Hans chuckled.

"Hrreeeaaaww!" Bigs groaned, rising from all fours with a gut-straining effort; their flexible spines made a straight lift harder for a kzin than for a man. The timber across his shoulders was ten meters long, and even on Wunderland it weighed three times his body mass. The other three hauled on the cable rigged over a wood-frame block and tackle, and the long gum-tree timber rose slowly in swaying jerks until it settled into the predug hole with a rush and stood nearly upright, vibrating. The two kzin took turns bracing it upright and hammering rocks into the hole to hold it so. Three more of equal size stretched in a line across the gully; up on the lip the humans returned to slicing other trunks into square-cut troughs with the cutter bars. When the line of supports was complete, they would swing the troughs out and lash them to the poles with monofilament.

"We're doing the slave's part of this," Bigs complained to his brother, as they climbed down the boulders to where the next upright waited to be dragged up to its hole.

"Suck sthondat excrement," Spots said.

They set themselves on either side of the massive timber and braced themselves, securing a good hold on the oozing slab-cut timber with their claws. The sharp medicinal scent of eucalyptus sap was overwhelming.

"*Strike!*"

The kzin heaved in unison, lifting the end of the beam and running it half a dozen steps upslope before letting it fall.

"It's the heavy lifting," Bigs went on, as they rested for a second, panting. His tongue worked on nose and whiskers, reaching almost to his tufted eyebrows. "*They* slice planks off trees, we carry the trunks."

"We are larger and stronger," Spots pointed out reasonably. He had tied a wad of cloth over his head and soaked it in water; now he patted at it, and runnels fanned down his neck and muzzle, plastering the fur to his skin. Mud streaked his legs and the paler-colored pelt of his belly. "If the monkeys were hauling these trunks, they would go very slowly — or we would have to take more time to rig a dragway with a winch and tackle."

"Hrrrr. Then we should get more of the gold," Bigs went on. "Now — *strike*."

They moved the log another dozen meters. This time they dropped it next to a rock-pool full of water and crouched to lap up a drink; instinctively, their muzzles rose every second or two to scan the surroundings.

"We contributed less than a quarter of the capital, yet we are to have equal shares," Spots replied. "You would complain if a monkey brought you a zianya with its muzzle already taped."

Bigs yawned enormously and licked his lips. "Zianya — ah, the first mouthful, full of fear-juices! With dipping sauce and grashti on the side." He paused. "Yet I *would* complain if a monkey brought one. It is disgraceful to be dependent upon them."

"Silence, fool. You did not complain when they were our slaves — and we were even *more* dependent on them then! Ready — *strike*."

This rush carried them to the line of supports, where the next hole waited.

"You are a whisker-splitter," Bigs said, unlimbering his cutting bar. They had dropped the thigh-thick end of the log across a boulder, leaving it at comfortable chest height. With four swift strokes he trimmed the hard wood to a point.

"Besides," Spots continued, raising his voice slightly from the other end of the log, where he belayed a loop of cable to a hole punched through the wood. "There are probably no zianyas closer than Hssin."

They whined; zianyas were a homeworld beast, and they had never flourished in the ecology of Wunderland, unlike many other kzinti animals. Before the human hyperdrive armada arrived some kzin estates had specialized in rearing them, coaxing them to reproduce and investing in expensive gravity-polarizer sheds to rear them under homeworld gravity, 1.55 of Earth's. Most of those had been smashed in the fighting, or confiscated in the aftermath of liberation, and the markets were vanished now that kzinti were few and poor in a human-ruled Wunderland.

"Reason enough to shake the dust of this world from our paws," Bigs went on. "Push — slowly, slowly."

Spots heaved with a steady pressure on the smaller end of the log, as his brother guided the point to the lip of the hole. As he did, his ears waggled ostentatiously.

"Yes — I can see us prostrating ourselves before the Patriarch's Cushion. '*Admittedly we did surrender to the omnivores and obey them; nevertheless we long to have Full Names and be permitted to maintain the noble-sized households we, the penniless refugees, have brought.*' Aha! The

Patriarch's liver overflows with kin-feeling for us! His pelt stands on end with joy at our scent! With his own hands, he serves us tuna icecream. He awards us Names; he allows us possession of every one of our kzintretti; he grants us vast estates on the *extremely expensive* savannahs of Homeworld . . ."

His lips flapped derisively against his teeth in imitation of a kzinti snore; *you dreamer*, it implied. "We could not even afford passage to kzinti space without human help."

"That may change," Bigs said, grimly sliding out his claws. Long silvery needles against the black leather of his hands. "That may change . . ."

"Not without gold," Spots replied. He took the end of the cable in his mouth and climbed the wall of the canyon with a bounding four-footed rush; kzinti had evolved hands to help them climb rocks.

"Next one ready!" he called, dropping back into Wunderlander. Jonah and Hans straightened; the older man groaned, kneading his hands into the small of his back. "Reave this to the block line."

● CHAPTER TWELVE

Gracious lord God, but these are primitive! Tyra Nordbo thought.

Friendly enough, but so *backward*. The village was hidden, with dwellings of straw and bamboo tucked deep under an overhang of rock. There was a waterfall at one end of the little valley, and channels irrigated gardens of banana, citrus and vegetables. There were goats and sheep, a few horses . . . and that was all. There was plenty to eat here, but not a book, not a powered tool, not a single comp or receiver. The only metal or synthetic was what their ancestors had brought in, fleeing as refugees from the first wave of kzinti conquest. There were things here that had been only names to her before: opthamalia, cataracts, clubfoot, harelip. She shuddered at the thought, even as she made herself smile and accept an opened coconut from a smiling woman. At least the settlement was fairly clean. And the people walked with pride.

I thought we were badly off in Skognara during the occupation, she mused. Machinery wearing out, more and more hand labor, the kzin tribute abating not one whit. *It was paradise compared to this.* The thought of the labor and loneliness these people had endured was chilling. Only by cutting themselves off completely from the money economy had they been able to stay out of the kzinti sight, but that meant no machinery, no medicine, no help in the disasters of everyday life . . . They were touchingly awed at having one of the Nineteen Families here, as well. There was no mistaking what she was, of course; everything from her accent to the mobile ears that twitched forward at a sound betrayed it. *It is humbling*.

"Why did you stay here?" she asked the leathery old headman of the . . . village seemed inappropriate. Compared to this, Neu Friborg was like downtown Munchen. And the headman was probably only fifty or so, not even middle-aged by civilized standards.

His grandfather had been a orbital shuttle pilot.

"We are *free*, Fra Nordbo," the man said proudly. "Here, we pay no tribute to the enemy. None of them has ever came here — except one on a hunting trip."

He nodded proudly to a ledge above the plaited-cane doorway. The skull that grinned with yellowed fangs looked much like a cat's, or a tigripard's, until you saw the long braincase that swept back from the heavy brows. A creature that thought, and made tools, and hunted Man. Until some Men hunted it . . .

"We had the pelt," the villager went on regretfully, "but it rotted in my father's time."

"The kzinti are gone," Tyra said gently. "Gone from all this world. None remain except those who accept human rule. You have no need to hide any more."

The man's face fell slightly. "I know," he said. "A fur hunter told us the news ten months ago." More slowly: "You are of the Herrenfolk, Fra Nordbo," he said. "Since the war is over, folk have come from the Great City. They speak of taxes, of land titles — of taking our children for schools."

"You understand," he went on, leaning closer earnestly. "We do not want to be isolated any more . . . not really. We know we have forgotten much. But we are *free*. Some say the folk of Munchen wish to grind us down, that they think of us as ignorant savages."

You are, poor creatures. No fault of yours, Tyra thought sadly.

"What shall we do?" he said. "We know nothing of

these matters — only what the officials of the new government tell us. Some say we should move again, as our ancestors did — move back even further into the mountains, and live free. There are others like us in the Jotuns, they might help."

"Even the Jotuns are not large enough to shield you from Time and Fate," Tyra said gently. "You need a friend who can intervene for you in Munchen. I know a good man, a Herrenmann, who would be your protector. But even so, change will come. It must; your children deserve to have the world opened up to them once more. Wunderland is once more a planet of Man, and there is no reason to deny them the stars."

"Thank you," the headman said, wiping at his eyes one palm; the calluses scraped against the blond-gray stubble on his cheeks. "We will try it."

The headman's daughter came in, with a tray: slices of roast wild boar and gagrumpher, steamed plantain, sauces, the rough homemade wine. Tyra's mouth filled at the smell; her own camp-cooking had grown tiresome.

"It is good of one of the Freunchen clan to take time for our troubles," the headman went on.

"Duty," Tyra mumbled. *Embarrassing*. Perhaps only in a place as out-of-the-way as this, as completely isolated from the past century, could you find that sort of faith in the Nineteen Families and their tradition of stewardship.

"We must do what we can for you, who helped those who were strangers," he said.

"Murphmmhg?" she replied, then swallowed. "You've already helped me," she said. Quite sincerely; a month in the wilderness with nobody but her horse and Garm to talk to had been a chastening experience.

"There are . . . bad people in the mountains," he said. "Some of them have been here for a long time — they fought the ratcats a little, stole from us more. The real fighters, to them we gave without asking, but they went back to the towns when the liberation came. The others have become worse, and more have joined them since. They do not come this far back into the mountains often — we have little to steal, and we will fight to keep what we have. When the police chase them, then they run deep into the Jotuns. Some of the ones who were here during the war, they know their way around, a little."

"Do you help the police?"

"Yes." Flat and decisive. "The outlaws, they are *advokats*." That was a small, scruffy, unpleasant-smelling carrion eater common to this part of the continent; it travelled in packs, attacked sick or wounded animals, and would eat anything including dung. Eat until it puked up, then eat the vomit. The beast was almost all mouth and legs, with very little in the way of a brain, an evolutionary holdover. "If we had more guns, we would shoot them ourselves."

"Thank you," she said. "I'll be cautious."

"And . . . " he looked down at his feet in their crude leather sandals. "You said, you were looking also for unusual things?"

Tyra felt a sudden prickle of interest. *Unusual* could mean anything, back in here; jadeite, a meerschaum deposit, abandoned kzinti equipment from a clandestine base . . . or news of the party she had been told to look out for. Business for herself, or for Herrenmann Montferrat-Palme. It was about time *something* turned up, it was cheap to live in the outback but not free, and she would be damned if she was going to be a burden on Mutti. Doubly damned if she would go asking Ib for help.

"Yes, if you please," she answered.

"Here."

He pulled out something small but heavy, wrapped in cloth, and placed it on the table between them. The work-gnarled fingers unfolded the homespun cotton with slow care and the young aristocrat leaned over, holding her breath. A dull-shining piece of . . . not metal, she thought. About the size of her palm, with a curved surface and a ragged edge, as if it had been torn lose from a larger sheet. Not any material she recognized, but there was a cure for that.

"Excuse me," she said, and rummaged in the packsaddle braced against one bamboo wall. The sample scanner Montferrat had gotten for her was late-model, a featureless rectangle with a pistol grip and readout screen. She pressed it against the whatever-it-was and pulled the trigger.

No data, it told her.

"What do you mean, no data?" she muttered. Perhaps the contact wasn't close enough: she turned the piece over and made sure there was no airspace.

No data.

"Swine of a gadget!" she said, and tried it on the surroundings. No problem with the table, a rock on the floor, the bamboo wall, or her own hand. Tyra pressed it firmly against the artifact.

No data.

"Hmmpfh." The girl tapped at the back, running the diagnostic. Everything fine.

Her hand stopped in mid-motion. The scanner worked by firing a tiny but very intense burst of laser energy into the sample, then analyzing the result. The material involved was minuscule, too little to even feel if you used it on yourself, unless you pressed it to your eye, of course. But the laser was *very* energetic.

She tapped out *temperature*. At ambient, which was no surprise. Then she squeezed the trigger for the sample function — *no data* — and asked for hotspots. Nothing: still at ambient temperature. Whatever this was, it was absorbing the energy and not ablating; not even warming up.

Odd, she thought: *very odd*. Back home in Gerning, the manor-house had had a functioning computer system with good educational programs. Tyra Nordbo had received a sound university-entrance level scientific education, and offhand she could not think of *anything* with those characteristics. A moment's conference with her belt-comp's reference functions confirmed her ignorance. It could be a kzin product, or something military that was not in the general databases . . .

"Do you mind if I test this?" she said to the headman.

He grinned. "We tried shooting at it. Then we dropped large rocks on it. Nothing we could do would so much as scratch it. The smith's forge didn't even heat it up."

She nodded. That did not mean much, since the only thing these outbackers had in the way of weapons was old-fashioned chemical energy rifles. There were plenty of modern materials that would be untouchable to anything they could do, and which would reflect away a lot more thermal energy than charcoal could produce.

A crowd of children gathered as she came out into the sun, blinking for a moment in the brightness; all dressed alike in shorts, bare feet and varying degrees of grime. They clustered bright-eyed as she drew the magrifle from its sheath beside her saddle, on the porch of the hut, and held up the piece.

"Would one of you like to help me?" she said. A sea of hands waved at her amid eager clamor. She picked a girl of nine or so, with strawberry-blond braids and a gap in her teeth. "What's your name?"

The girl blushed and dug at the packed dirt with a toe. "Helge," she whispered.

"Well, Helge, why don't you take this all the way down there — down by that big boulder — and put it in at ground level? Jam it in tight, facing me. The rest of you," she went on, "get back — back behind me. Yes, that means *you*, too. One of you take the little one."

A few adults had come to look as well; some of them with envy at her equipment, more in curiosity. *Gracious lord* Gott *but it must be boring here,* she thought. The cassette of regular ammunition came out with a *clack* sound, and she slid in the red-flagged one from the bottom of her war-bag. The normal rounds were single-crystal iron, prefragmented for antipersonnel or hunting use. These were narrow penetrators of osmium, in a ferroplastic sabot that would peel off at the muzzle. Antiarmor darts, and at a hundred meters they would punch through two hundred millimeters of machinable steel plate. Much less of real armor, and it drained the batteries like the *teufel*, but she had a solar-charging tarpaulin spread out over a sunny patch of ground. She tapped the velocity control to maximum and set the weapon for semi-auto.

Helge ran like the wind, heels flashing, and used one to pound the piece of material into the angle between ground and rock. Tyra gave her a smile of thanks and waved her back into the crowd as she sat, pushed her hat back and brought the rifle up with her elbows on her knees. A final check to be sure that everyone was behind her — Dada-mann had taught her about firearms as soon as she could walk; even under the occupation Herren-mann families had been allowed hunting weapons — and she took up the slack on the trigger. The sighting holo sprang up before her eye on x5, and she laid the target blip on the center of the gray material. Squeeze gently —

Whack. The recoil was punishing, several times worse than normal; there was not all that much mass in the darts, but they were travelling *fast*. She let the tremor die out of her arms and shoulders and the sight settle back on the target as the muzzle came down with its own weight. *Whack. Whack. Whack. Whack.* Five rounds, as much as her shoulder could stand and more than should be necessary.

"Don't touch it!" she called sharply, as some of the children ran ahead of her.

The older ones pulled their younger siblings back, making a circle around her as she knelt. The impacts had driven the fragment back against the stonè; into the stone, in fact, cutting a trough. The surface was shiny, plated with a film of osmium, and splashes had colored the earth and rock. She reached out with a stick, and it sizzled as the end came in contact with the shiny film. The osmium layer peeled away at the touch, falling to the battered earth below.

"Scheisse," she whispered. *Nothing. Gottdamned nothing.* The dull gray surface of the material was utterly unmarked, to the naked eye at least. She shifted the rifle to her left hand and pulled out the scanner. Another *no data*, and the temperature was still at ambient . . . no, about .002 of a degree higher. That after being struck with penetrator darts that splashed across its surface in a molten film!

Well, Herr Montferrat-Palme wanted the unusual, she thought. *And this is* certainly *unusual enough.*

Another thought struck her as she lifted the material and turned it. The edges were *torn*, twisted as if something had struck a sheet of whatever-it-was and belled this piece out beyond the breaking strain of the material. Considering what the tensile strength must be, that would have to be a fairly drastic event.

"Careful about that," she said to a curious child who was poking at the film of osmium; the edges would be razor sharp even though it was thinner than tinfoil. She crumpled it with the heel of her boot and stamped it into a harmless lump. Turning to the headman:

"Where did you find this stuff?"

"The Muttiberg, Fra Nordbo. We pan a little gold in the rivers below it, to trade for things we must have. In the wash beneath —"

• CHAPTER THIRTEEN

"Let her rip!" Hans called into his beltphone. "Don't get your underwear in a knot," he went on to Jonah. "And that's enough dirt."

"My back agrees with you but my greed dissents," Jonah said, straightening up.

The water-furrow that fed their wash was nearly half a kilometer long, dug along the hillside or carried in troughs of log slab. Nothing in it had come with them, except the monofilament line that held it together. The wash itself was a series of stepped wooden boxes, ingeniously rigged with baffles so that the flow of water would shake them.

Their bottoms were different; memory-film, made in Tiamat, the central manufacturing asteroid of the Serpent Swarm asteroid. Leads hooked them to a wooden stand where their computer and main distortion-battery lay. A single keystroke would activate the memory-film; each box's floor was set to form an intricate pattern of moving ripples. Rushing water would dissolve the mixture of water-deposited volcanic soil and gold granules Jonah shoveled in to the first box; a thin layer of water would then run over the rippling film. Gravity would leave the heavier metal particles in the troughs of the ripples, and they would move slowly down each box to deposit the gold in a deep fold, ready to be scooped out. The surface had a differential stickiness, too, nearly frictionless to the useless garague, catching at any molecule the computer directed.

From higher up the water-furrow a rumbling

sounded. Spots had lifted the sluicegate, and the flood was rumbling along. Raw timber vibrated and thuttered, and the beams reinforcing corners groaned as the first weight threw itself against them. A meter across and deep, the wave bore dirt and twigs before it, and a hapless kermitoid that peeped and thrashed. It curled and rose as it struck the pile of gold-rich dirt, then washed it away and into the settling tanks like a child's sand-castle. The tanks themselves began vibrating back and forth, their squealing groans almost deafening.

"Shovel, boy, shovel!" Hans called. "That's a pocketful of krona with every shovelful of dirt."

Jonah cursed and wiped at his face, covered in an oil of sweat and dirt; more moisture ran from the sodden rag around his forehead, trickling down to cut runnels over his face and drip onto his bare chest. He had always been muscular for a Belter, but the weeks of labor had thickened his arms and shoulders, besides burning his face and body nearly the color of teak. The loads of dirt still felt heavy as he swung the long handle. Hans was spindly and wrinkled beside him, but his movements were as regular as a metronome.

"You're putting too much heave into it," the old man said after a moment. "Remember what I told you. Don't jerk at it. Just enough to get the shovel moving, then turn your wrists and let the dirt slide off into the water. No need to waste sweat *sticking* it in."

Jonah grunted resentfully, but he followed Hans' advice. He was right; it *was* easier that way. Zazen helped too. His training was coming back to him, more and more these days. Use the movements to end thought; become the eye that does not seek to see itself, the sword that does not seek to cut itself, the unself-contemplating mind. Feel sensation without stopping its flow with introspection, pull of muscle, deep smooth breath, aware without being aware of being aware. The two humans fell into lockstep, working at the high pile of precious dirt. Presently the pile grew smaller, and Spots came up with more. He was dragging it on a sled made from more of the film, set to be nearly frictionless on the packed earth of the trail. There was a rope yoke around his neck and shoulders, and he pulled leaning far forward, hands helping him along. When he was level with the men he collapsed to earth, panting.

Jonah stuck his shovel in the pile and helped him out of the rope harness, then handed him a bucket made from a section of log. The kzin lapped down a gallon or so and then poured the rest over his head, scooping out another from the trough and repeating the process. Then he licked his whiskers back into shape and shook himself, showering Jonah and Hans with welcome drops from his fur. The air was full of the smell of a quarter ton of hot wet carnivore.

"Bigs needs someone to help with the shoring," he rasped, drinking again. "He digs more quickly than we thought."

"Guess I'd better," Hans said, rubbing a fist into the small of his back. "See you later, youngster." He walked off up the trail to the shaft they had sunk into the hillside, whistling.

Spots paused as he gathered up the drag harness and the film. "Ah — adventure!" he said. "Travelling to far-off lands; ripping out the gizzards of hardship and danger; winning fortune and Name. Is it not glorious? Does your liver not steam with —"

"Go scratch fleas," Jonah muttered, spitting on his hands and reaching for the shovel.

"Better that than hauling freight like a zitragor," the kzin replied, flapping his ears ironically as he turned to go for the next load. "Far better."

"I cannot believe it! I do not believe the testimony of

my own nose!" Bigs said, pawing through a pile of datachips.

"Believe what?" Spots replied.

Across the campfire Jonah looked up at the sound; the hiss-and-spit of the Hero's Tongue *always* sounded like a quarrel, but this was probably the real thing.

"That I was stupid enough to let you pack the virtual-reality kit!" Bigs said.

That was a late-model type, with nose implants for scents as well as ear and eye coverings for visual and aural data.

"It's in perfect working order."

"The chips, fool, the chips — you forgot the *Siege of Zeeroau*, the *Hero Chruung Upon the Ramparts*, no *Warlord Chmee at the Pillars* — all our good stuff. None of the classics at all!"

Spots flapped his ears and fluttered his lips against his teeth. "You run too many of that graypelt sthondat excrement," he said. "You will curdle your liver and stultify your brain living in the past that way; you should pay more attention to the modern world, sibling. Renovate your tastes! Entertainment should be instructive!"

"Modern — heeraaeeow — *The Kzinrette's Rump*?" Bigs said sarcastically, throwing one chip aside and digging for more. His voice rose an octave as he listed titles, and his tail quivered and then began to lash.

"*Blood and Ch'rowl*? *The Lost Patriarch of the Hareem Planet*? *Energy Swords at the Black Sun*?" He screamed, a raw sound of rage. "Is there *nothing* here but smut and cheap, trashy science fiction adventures?"

He abandoned the carton of chips. The two kzinti faced each other, crouching low and claws extended: their ears were folded away and their tails held rigid. The air smelled of ginger as they growled through their grins, and their fur bottled out. Jonah started to rise in genuine alarm; most of the siblings' spats were half in fun, but this looked like the real thing — and when kzinti got angry enough to stop exchanging insults in the Mocking Tense, they were milliseconds away from screaming and leaping. It must be the sheer frustration of the hard labor . . .

Hans broke in first: "You two tabbies interested in our results, or are you too set on killing each other and leaving it all for us monkeys?" he said dryly.

The kzin relaxed, breaking the lock of their unwinking eye-to-eye stare. The huge golden orbs turned on the old man instead, and they both licked their lips with washcloth-sized pink tongues. After a moment their fur sank back and their tails relaxed, but they both drooled slightly with tongues lolling. Hans brought out the portable scale and a set of bags of tough thermoplastic, setting a heatrod at one hand.

"That's the last of it," Hans said.

He took the container off the scales and dropping the dust into a bag; then wrote the weight on the outside and sealed it shut with the rod. Jonah watched the digital readout blink back to zero. They were sitting in front of the humans' tent — the shelters of the felinoids were longer but much lower — and the sunken firelight was flickering on their faces, shining in the eyes of the kzin. Tonight it was scarcely brighter than the moon, full and larger than Luna from earth, leaving a circle of blackness in the sky where the stars were outshone. The dust had not looked like gold, save for a few granules larger than pinheads. Mostly it was blackish.

"Not much to look at," he said, hefting one of the bags. It was a little larger than his fist, but heavy enough to bring a grunt of surprise.

"No nuggets," Hans nodded. "It's rich, but not that rich. We've cleared about three thousand krona. Not bad for the first day's work."

"First month's work," Bigs grunted, lying flat on his belly with his hands on either side of his chin. "Not counting walking *in* to this verminous spot."

"There is that, yes," Hans went on cheerfully, and spat into the fire before lighting his pipe with a twig. "Thing is, we'll get as much tomorrow. For a while, too. Sort of time for it all to pay off. Remember what I said back in Munchen; getting the benefit of all the labor that everyone *else* who went looking put into it. Now we reap the results. Should be tasty, very tasty."

Spot's tongue moistened his nose. "How much?" he said. At their looks: "How much shall we take out before we stop?"

Hans pursed his mouth. "Twenty thousand over our expenses would do me fine. Twenty thousand's enough to get the shop I've had my eye on."

"Not enough for me," Bigs said; the humans looked at him in slight surprise. Usually the larger kzin spoke as little to them as he could. "For what I want . . . I need more."

"More is good," Jonah nodded, remembering to turn away his eyes. *Never stare at a kzin.* Seven times, *never stare at a* hostile *kzin.* "I'd like forty thousand myself. Starting a business is risky. Plenty of people have gone bust just because they didn't have enough cash to tide them over until the returns started."

"Forty thousand would satisfy me," Spots mused, using a branch he had whittled to scratch himself on one cheek, then under his chin. He slitted his eyes and purred, tongue showing slightly. "Plenty of land coming on the market; we might even be able to buy back some of our Sire's lost estate. Enough over to start a consulting firm; there are kzinti in the Serpent Swarm, on Tiamat, who would be glad to have Wunderland agents."

"Forty thousand it is, then," Hans said. He hooked the coffeepot off the fire and poured himself a cup.

"Nothing like a cup of hot coffee to settle you for sleep."

Bigs spoke up. "When shall we divide it?"

The old man's hands stopped and he looked up, face carefully calm. "Well, that's a question. We could split it up when we leave, or when we get back to civilization, or each day. Something to be said for all three."

"Each day, where I can see it," Bigs snarled. Literally; talking with kzinti made you realize that humans never really snarled. "I labor in the earth like a slave. The prey I toil for shall rest in no monkey's larder."

Spots hissed at him; he turned and hissed back through open jaws, and the smaller kzin shrugged with an elaborate ripple of spotted orange fur.

"I will be content either way," he said. "By all means, divide it. It makes no difference."

Jonah locked eyes with Bigs for a moment, then shrugged himself. It *didn't* make any difference. Except . . . why was the kzin so insistent? A surly brute, to be sure — if Jonah had been in the habit of naming kzinti, he would have christened him Goon — but it was also a little strange he had never so much as mentioned what he intended to do with the money. In modern kzin society few ever satisfied the longing for physical territory with game on it, and their harem and retainers about them; that was reserved for the patriarchs. It must have been doubly cruel for a noble's sons to have the prospect snatched away; Spots daydreamed about it constantly, and Jonah could see him imagining the wilderness about them to be his own. Whereas Bigs seemed more and more withdrawn, as if Wunderland were not really real to him any more.

Again, he shrugged. Kzinti psychology was still a mystery to those humans expert in it. Jonah Matthieson had killed quite a few kzin, and worked a few months with two. That was no basis for easy judgement — in fact, just enough to lull your sense of difference and put you most at risk of anthromorphizing them.

That could be dangerous; besides the weird culture the orange-furred aliens had produced, dragged straight from the Iron Age into an interstellar civilization, their basic mental reflexes were *not* like a human being's. And never had been, even before they used the new technology to alter their own genes.

They wanted to be more like their folk heroes. So they did genetic engineering to make it so. That was what the ARM intelligence people decided was the only plausible explanation for Kzinti behavior and customs. Usually civilization changes things. Defects don't result in death. Evolution stops, then works backwards. Bad genes are preserved. *Not with the kzinn. They really are like the Heroes they admire.*

Hans wordlessly set out the scales, checking that each bag was identical. Then he divided them into four piles, and silently invited his partners to take their pick. Bigs scooped his up and disappeared into the dark; they heard him stop and make a long leap onto bare rock further up the slope, hiding his trail. Spots sighed and trotted out into the night in the opposite direction.

"Of course, now we've each got to wonder about our goods," Hans added; the smaller kzin hesitated for a second, then continued. "Wonder if any of the others has found them, you see. Couldn't tell *who*, not if some of it just disappeared."

Jonah halted with an armful of small, heavy bags. "Finagle's hairy arse, *now* you mention that?"

"Well, son, if it was all in one place it'd also be a teufel of a temptation, now, wouldn't it?" There was a twinkle in the little blue eyes beside the button nose, but they were as hard as any Jonah had ever seen. "Been at this business quite a few years now. Not the first time I've had partners, no indeed. Something to be said for all the methods."

Jonah yawned cavernously over his morning coffee,

then hauled the crisp air deep into his lungs as he stretched work-stiffened muscles. It was a cool morning, a relief before the long blazing heat of the day. Alpha Centauri was rising red over the mountains to the east, and the eye-hurting bright speck of Beta hung on a peak like a jewel on a wizard's staff. No mountain on Earth could have been so slender and so steep, but Wunderland pulled its heights less fiercely. Birds and orthinoids were waking down in the ribbon of forest that filled the valley, purling and cheeping. None of the kzin were present, which was not surprising in itself. The aliens had fallen into a gorge-and-fast cycle which seemed to be natural to them, and the bacon and eggs frying in the pan would be repulsive to them.

They used to be that way to me, he admitted: far too natural. After this much pick-and-shovel work, he just felt hungry all the time.

"Want some hash-browns?" Hans asked.

"You're bleeping right I do," Jonah said, yawning again.

"See you didn't get any more sleep than the rest of us," Hans said.

"The rest of us?" Jonah paused with his fork raised over his loaded plate.

"Oh, I may be getting on, but that don't make me sleep any sounder. Just the opposite. First the big ratcat goes out to check nobody's found his goods — then the little one. Then you. Then the big one again . . . "

Jonah flushed. "I just had to piss," he said.

"Funny you went in that direction, then," Hans said, and cackled with laughter. "This'll get worse the longer we're out here. That's why I wanted to stop at twenty thousand, mostly. Now we'll all have to check nightly. And each of us worry about the others ganging up on him."

Jonah forced himself to eat. His body remembered his hunger, even if his mind was telling him his stomach was full of lead.

"You don't seem too worried," he said.

"Well, it's a matter of possibilities," Hans said. "The two ratcats could take us out — but they don't get on too well, you may have noticed. Still, blood counts for something. Or you and Spots could take the rest of us — Spots will be seeing Bigs as a real challenge down in his balls, while we're just monkeys. Or —"

"Or you could know where it all is and just take it and clear out," Jonah said harshly, feeling the hair on his back creep. As a programmer, he knew what an infinite regression setup could do to your logic; also how the Prisoner's Dilemma generally worked out in real life.

Hans lit his first pipe of the day with a stick from the fire. "No, don't think so. You three are a lot tougher than you were when we started. You'd catch me and kill me. Still, it's something to think about, isn't it?" He blew a cloud of smoke. "Enough lollygagging — nobody told us to stop working."

"Sure," Jonah muttered to himself. "Send *me* back to Neu Friborg for supplies. Why *me?*"

Another charge of water went down the sluice, to his left past the beaten trail up to the shaft. The wood groaned less now after a week of operation; water had swollen it until the pegged joints were tight, and there was less leakage too. He ignored it, concentrating on strapping the pack-saddle tight; the mule just seemed quietly relieved to be free from hauling loads out of the mine. The pack was mostly empty, except for some hides and dried meat to lend credence to their cover-story of hunting for pelts. The *last* thing they needed was contact with the authorities. The Provisional Government was hard-up and had even more than the usual official determination to see that the citizenry and their money were soon parted. All four of them agreed on that, if nothing else, although it had been a bleeping struggle to get the kzinti to skin their kills before they ate them.

Is Hans out of his mind? Or is he in it with them? Jonah thought. It would be a four-day trip. Four days he'd be unable to check on his goods, and that was nearly fifteen thousand krona by now. Without that gold he'd be back cadging handouts in Munchen soon enough. *I put up more money than the others*, he thought bitterly. *As it is, I'm getting less than my share. Tanjit, but it's hot.* He reached for the canteen and poured more water on the cloth draped over his head. He could hear Spots coming down the trail, dragging another load of dirt for the boxes. With a scowl, he led the mule behind a boulder; it was downwind from the trail this time of day, so he wouldn't have to talk to the kzin.

Spots stopped for a moment, moaning softly and pulling the rope yoke over his head. His effort at grooming the matted, worn spots on his sloping shoulders seemed half-hearted, and after a few swipes he simply lay down in the roadway, groaning more loudly. Something he would never do if he were aware of being watched, of course . . . Jonah felt a moment's guilt. *I should cough or something*, he thought. Then: *No.* If he did, he would have to explain why he was hiding behind the rock — and that would make Spots more suspicious than he was already. At least they were still talking when business made it necessary, while Bigs was barely speaking even to his sibling and not at all to the humans.

The kzin lay still, panting in the sparse shade a pile of rocks threw over the path. Then his head came up, the big pink bat-ears swivelling downslope. Jonah held his breath, eyes narrowing in suspicion. Spots drew his wtsai and headed down the steeper slope, leaping over the water furrow and dodging along agile and swift as the hillside grew steeper. When the kzin stopped to cut a pole from a broombush and began prying up a large flat rock suspicion grew to rage. Jonah drew his magrifle out of its slings along the pack saddle and stepped out from behind the rock.

I should let him have it right now, he thought, taking up the slack. *No*, he decided, as the back of the kzin's head sprang into the holosight. *No, I want him to see it coming*.

"Freeze, ratcat!" he shouted, and sent a round *whack* through the air over him.

Spots whirled and leaped backward instead, the stone thumping back down on the others that supported it. His ears flared wide with surprise, as did the wet black nostrils, then folded away in anger. He crouched, opening his mouth wide and extending his hands to either side; one gripped the wtsai, and the claws slid out on the other, needles against the black leather of the hand.

"What — put that rifle down, monkey!"

"Right," Jonah sneered; the ratcat had gotten good enough at Wunderlander to put indignation into its tones. "So you can cut me up — and then take my goods."

Spots's pupils flared wider still, in surprise. "Oh, so *that* was where you put them," he said. "Clever, clever, the spray from the furrow would obscure your scent."

The human had been moving downslope; he climbed across the furrow carefully, not that there was any danger with sixty-nine rounds still in the cassette, and halted beyond leaping distance.

"Drop the knife," he said, his voice flat and ugly.

"I saw a fuzzball crawling under there," Spots went on, staring at him in deliberate rudeness. "I was going to pry up the rock and kill it."

"Murphy, can't you invent something more plausible than that?" Jonah jeered. There was a bounty on fuzzballs . . . although they were commoner here in the Jotuns than in more settled regions.

Another footfall sounded on the trail. Jonah risked a quick glance upslope; it was Hans, trotting up with his rifle at high port. He stopped at the sight of the tableau below and then climbed down, standing midway between Spots and Jonah but out of the line of fire, with the muzzle of his weapon carefully down.

"You fellers mind telling me what's going on?" he said mildly.

They both began to speak at once. Jonah gestured Spots into silence with the rifle.

"The bleeping ratcat found my goods, and I caught him trying to lift the rock" — he nodded at the lever still jutting into the air, and then at the boulder upslope where the mule still stood — "and clean me out."

He tensed slightly; Hans *might* be in it with the alien. Not likely, since Hans had voted to send Jonah off for the supplies. If it was Hans, they would have waited until he was gone and they could do it safely. Or wait — Spots could be double-crossing *Hans* by promising to wait until Jonah was gone, and then looting the cache first himself!

"Of course," Jonah went on sardonically, "he *claims* it was all because he saw a fuzzball crawl under there."

Spots had risen from his crouch. Ostentatiously, he sheathed the wtsai and stood up to his full two-meters plus of height, staring down his muzzle at Jonah with ears half-unfurled. That was an insult as well; it was the Posture of Assured Dominance, rather than the fighting crouch used to confront an adversary.

"There is an easy way to find out, monkey," he said. "Put your arm in through the gap you used to hide the bags of gold. If there is no fuzzball, it is perfectly safe."

He backed up along the slope, still in clear sight but more than leaping distance away from the tumbled rocks. Jonah licked his lips, tasting the salt of sweat, and moved closer to his once-secret cache.

"Of course, you know that fuzzballs never let go once they bite, don't you?" Spots said, as Jonah bent toward the hole. "The jaws have to be broken and pried loose. Not that that matters a great deal. The neurotoxin venom is quite deadly. Convulsions, bleeding from all the orifices, hallucinations and agonizing death."

Jonah snorted and bent further. Then he stopped, looking at Spots. *Kzin don't lie well,* he thought. The slick film of sweat that covered his body suddenly seemed to cool. *They don't get enough practice — they can smell each other lying.* Spots could be relying on human inability to smell, nearly total by kzinti standards . . . but Jonah knew enough of their body language to know that he really *was* relaxed. Even amused. And if there *was* a Beam's Beast hiding down there — With a convulsive movement he turned and hauled one-handed on the lever. The big volcanic slab toppled backwards slowly in Wunderland's .61 G, and the fuzzball cowered for a second as the light stabbed its dark-adapted eyes.

"Pappy-*eek*!" it shrilled, the characteristic warning cry.

Jonah gave a shout of loathing and pumped two rounds into the vermin. The little biped flew backward, half its torso torn away, but still snapping at the air. Beam's Beast — the origin of the name was lost in the early settlement of the planet — was about half a meter long, covered in titan-blond fur. They had huge eyes, filling nearly half their faces, and clever monkey-like hands to match their demonic cunning. They could even be considered cute, if you didn't notice the over-lapping fangs. In a frenzy of disgust the human leaped forward and stamped the heavy heel of his boot into the big-eyed face. Then he had to spend a minute using the muzzle of his magrifle to pry the jaws out of the tough synthetic.

That was a welcome distraction. When he looked up Hans had slung his rifle and was looking at him with a speculative stare; Spots was grinning in contempt-threat. Jonah clicked his rifle onto safety.

"Guess I'd better get back to the mules—" he began.

Then the earth shook, and a cloud of dust rose from over the ridge where the mineshaft lay.

None of them wasted words as they ran.

Spots was the first to reach the entrance, but he hesitated. The exterior shoring on the hillside was still intact, but choking dust and grit billowed out. Most kzin are natural claustrophobes unless they are lactating females, and it had raised his opinion of his brother's courage, if not his intelligence, when he volunteered for the job at the pit-face. It also kept Bigs more out of contact with the humans . . .

Without a word, Jonah plunged past him into the interior.

The outer stretch was intact, but the air broiled with metallic-tasting debris; hacking and coughing, he stopped for an instant to tie the wet headcloth over his mouth and nose and snatch a glowrod from the wall. Murk surrounded him, glowing with reflected light, thickening as he advanced wiping his streaming eyes. Ten meters in the roof had collapsed, and a tangle of dirt, rock, broken timbers and planking lay across his way. He dropped to the floor and raised the glowrod. A triangle of empty space in the lower right-hand corner of the pile gaped at him like a toothless mouth. He crawled close and shouted:

"Bigs! Can you hear me?"

Nothing; nothing but the trickling sound of dirt falling, and the groan of raw timber stressed to its limits. The rest might come down at any moment. He repeated the call in the Hero's Tongue, shouting as loud as he could, grit raw in his throat and lungs.

A sound; faint, and it could be wood collapsing as readily as a kzin moaning in pain. Spots and Hans came up behind him, and he turned urgently.

"This looks like it might go through. Get me a cutter-bar and a rope."

Spots stared at him oddly as Hans handed him the tools. Jonah tied the rope around his waist and went down on his belly.

"I'm — " he hesitated for a moment and took a deep breath. "I'm going to go in head-first. I'll tie a loop under Bigs's forelimbs, if I can, and you pull him out."

That might work with a kzin; they were so flexibly jointed that they could get through any space big enough to pass their head with a centimeter to spare on either side of the skull. That was a conscious kzin, of course.

"You are going in that hole?" Spots asked, in a low voice. His pelt was bristling in a ripple pattern, as if he tried to order it flat and his nerves rebelled. He looked over his shoulder; the entrance was a spot of light. More dirt trickled down from above. "Bigs might be dead."

"I *said* I'm going, didn't I?" Jonah asked, his voice rough with more than the bad air. A wave of gooseflesh ran over his own skin; he looked at the hole, and remembered the piping cry of the fuzzball. *Don't try to talk me out of it. You might succeed.*

"Pain does not hurt," he muttered to himself. "Death does not cause fear; fear of death causes fear."

The mantra was little protection as he squirmed into the hole. He could feel it shifting above him, and the jagged edges of broken wood clawed at his back and flanks. He could feel the blood trickling down, feel the salt sweat stinging in the wounds. One meter, then ten, infinitely cautious. Controlling his breathing helped control the overwhelming impulse to squirm backward. The glowrod was little help, in air so thick with floating dust, and his passage stirred up more.

At least it's fairly straight. After a time that could have been a minute or twenty, his outstretched hand touched something softer. Kzinti fur, that twitched under his hand. Timber creaked.

"Brother?" Bigs whispered, in the Hero's Tongue.

"Jonah," the man said, and felt the kzin start again. "Careful, it's still unstable! Can you understand me?"

"Yes," the alien rasped. The heavy scent of its fear was detectable even through the dirt; he could smell urine, too.

"Are you badly injured?"

A moment's silence, full of heavy panting. "No. I think not. There is a timber resting on my thighs, but they are only bruised, not broken. My shoulder is dislocated." That hurt a kzin less than a human, but it meant the arm was useless until the joint was set back. "I am bleeding a little, but I cannot move."

Jonah had been feeling around, raising the glowrod. Bigs was in a bubble of space, spindle-shaped with the narrow end at his feet. There was a main vertical support across his legs just down from the crotch; one jagged end of a fastening peg had driven into the flesh for a centimeter or so.

"I'm — " Jonah paused to cough. "I'm going to have to get in there with you," he said. *Tanjit. There Ain't No Justice. I don't even* like *the bleeping pussy — never did.* It was mutual, too. "I'll tie this rope under your forelimbs and then sever the timber with my cutter-bar. Then we'll slide you out on your back, I'll follow and get you past the obstacles. Understand?"

"Brother," the kzin whispered again, and something in his own language too fast and faint for Jonah to follow.

The human shook him, and barely dodged the instinctive snap that followed.

"Finagle shave you bald, *do you understand me?*"

"Yesss . . ." followed by a mumble.

Oh, joy. Concussed. Jonah shone the light into the big golden eyes. One pupil was slightly larger than the other, and that was a cross-species indicator. No blood from the nose or ears, though.

"Here I come," Jonah said, keeping up a flow of

words to maintain Bigs's attention. *And to boost* my
morale too. "I'm going to have to do a forewards somer-
sault." That took an eternity, but when it was
completed he was lying along the kzin's side. "Here
comes the rope. Can you lift your forequarters?"

Another eternity before the dazed kzin understood,
and the slipknot loop went under his armpits. He
made a short convulsive sound between clenched fangs
as the rope touched his dislocated shoulder, and the
claws of his other hand stabbed into the dirt close to
Jonah's stomach.

"Be a Hero," Jonah said sharply, in that language.
Bigs twitched his whiskers affirmatively. It was not that
the kzin was unable to control his fear, but the blow to
the head was leaving him wavering in and out of full
consciousness. A quarter-ton of kzin acting from
instinct and reflex was not something you wanted to
have with you in a confined space.

"Here we go," the human muttered, and reached
down with the cutter bar.

This was the one with no broken teeth, and it sliced
smoothly through the tough gumtree wood. Pale curls
of shavings came free as he drew and pushed, with a
faint *shirrr-shirrr* sound. His own pelvis was under the
timber. If it was bearing weight, it would shift when he
cut through and smash his hipbones to splinters. Not
that that would be of much interest to either of them
when the dirt closed 'round . . . Halfway through, and
the log had not pinched shut on the cutter bar, that was
a good sign. Three quarters of the way, and something
went *crack* over his head. Man and kzin froze, peering
upwards. Another *crack* and the sound of rock grinding
on wood. Jonah's arm resumed movement, more
quickly this time. He closed his eyes for the last cut.
There was a deep *tung* sound as the wood was cut —
and the severed end rode *up*, not down towards him.

He let out a shaky breath, suddenly conscious of how

thirsty he was. No time for that. He dropped the cutter-bar, carefully, and wedged his knee under the end of the timber that now lay across Bigs's thighs.

"This is going to hurt," Jonah said, and repeated it until he was sure Bigs was fully conscious. "Here goes."

"*Eeeeraaeeeewwooww!*"

The kzin scream was deafening in the strait space, like being in a closet with a berserk speaker system. After the jagged wood was free of his flesh Bigs was silent save for rapid shallow panting.

"*All right,*" Jonah shouted, mouth to the hole. "Get ready to pull!" The slack on the rope came taut. "Carefully. If the rope gets caught on a timber, it could bring the whole thing down on us."

The ten meters of passage might as well have been a kilometer. Jonah had to follow behind Bigs' nearly inert form, pushing on his feet and easing the cable-thick tail over obstacles; when the rope caught, he had to crawl millimeter by millimeter along the hairy body until his hands could reach and free the obstruction. More skin scraped off his back and shoulders as he did so, a lubrication of sweat and human and kzinti blood that made the wiggling, gasping effort a little easier. After the first few minutes he lost track of progress; there was only effort in the dark, an endless labor. Until light that was dazzling to his dark-adapted eyes made him blink, and a draft of air cool and pure by comparison brought on another coughing fit. Hands human and inhuman pulled him and the comatose kzin out of the last bodylength of the wormhole.

Jonah had only an instant to lie and wheeze. The groaning and creaking from above became a series of gunshot cracks, and streams of loose dirt poured down. A board followed, ripped free as the scantlings twisted under the force of the earth above and weakened with the forward sections brought down in the first fall. He told his body to rise and run, but nothing happened but a boneless flopping sensation; there was nothing left, no reserve against extremity. Death was coming, smothering in the dark, coming at the instant of victory.

Spots had been squatting while Hans manoeuvred the larger, heavier body of his sibling across his shoulders. One hand was up, steadying that; the other reached out and gathered Jonah to his orange-furred chest.

"*Run,*" he grunted.

Hans ran beside him — a staggering trot was a better description — steadying the load on his back and taking some of the dragging weight. Jonah was clutched beneath him, turning his progress into a three-limbed hobble that turned into a scrambling rush as the innermost section of the shoring gave way behind them. Wood screamed as each successive section took the full weight for a moment and yielded; the collapse nipped at their heels, its billow of choking dust enclosing them like the hot breath of a carnivore in pursuit. They shot out of the mouth of the diggings like a melon-seed squeezed between fingers and collapsed half a dozen meters from it; Spots was barely conscious enough to turn sideways and avoid crushing Jonah beneath the half-ton weight of two grown kzintosh.

Jonah was still sitting with his head in his hands when Hans returned with the medical kit and water.

"Better look at Bigs first," he coughed, drinking a full dipper in one long ecstatic draught and blinking up at the sun. It had hardly moved; less than two hours since the cave in, difficult to believe.

"Hmmm-*hmm,*" Hans agreed.

He and Spots went to work. "No broken bones," Spots pronounced. "There is a lump on the skull but the bone is sound beneath it. Reflexes are within parameters. Concussion, but I doubt any major damage."

"Speak for yourself," Bigs whispered. "More water."

He drank rather than lapping, to wash down the handful of antibios and hormonal healing stimulants his brother handed him.

Hans had been examining the thigh wound. "Splinters in here," he said, slipping his hand into the debrilidator glove. "Want a pain-killer?"

"I am a Hero — " Bigs began. Then the miniature hooks in the computer-controlled glove began extracting foreign matter from the wound. " — *so of course I do*," he went on, in a thready whisper.

The work was quickly done, and Hans stepped over to Jonah; then he whistled, watching as the younger man doused himself with water. Fresh blood slicked great patches of skin and raw flesh.

"You done a good job on yourself, youngster," he said, rummaging for the synthskin sprayer. "Hold on."

Jonah did his best to ignore the itching sting of the tiny hooks cleaning dirt and dead skin out of the scrapes. The synthskin was cooling relief in comparison, sprayed on as each area was cleansed.

"What the tanjit were you doing digging that deep?" he asked Bigs. "You were way beyond the shored-up section. You know the routine; timber and shore *every* meter you go in."

Bigs' eyes were glazed. "Hull," he mumbled. "I found the hull."

"You found the *what*?" Jonah asked, looking up sharply; then he gasped. Hans had done likewise, and braced himself against a flayed area. Spots halted with his muzzle halfway into a bucket.

"Hull," Bigs said more distinctly. "Like nothing I've seen before. Spaceship hull. Small."

● CHAPTER FOURTEEN

The little trading post had a dusty, abandoned feel. There was the adobe store, two houses and a paddock, all planted where three faint mule-tracks crossed a creek. The houses had roofs of tile with tiles missing, carrying solar-power panels with some of the panels missing; the pump that filled the watering troughs before the veranda of the store was still functioning, and the metered charger available to anyone who wanted to top up their batteries. The satellite dish on the rooftree looked to be out of order for some time, though. A straggly pepper tree shaded the notional street, and a big kitchen garden lay behind a dun-colored earth wall.

Tyra Nordbo tethered her horses where they could drink; Garm stood on his hind paws to lap beside them. Two meters further down two pack-mules looked up at her animals, then returned to their indifferent doze. She blinked at them thoughtfully as she loosened girths and patted her horse's neck, put a hand to the stock of her rifle where it rested before the right stirrup in its saddle scabbard, then shook her head.

"Hello the house," she called, from outside the front door; outback courtesy.

The inside was just as shabby as the exterior, if a little cooler from the thick walls, and the fan-and-wet-canvas arrangement over the interior door. A counter split the room in half, with a sleepy-looking outbacker standing behind it; boxes and bales were heaped up against the walls. And another man was at the customer's side, reading from a list:

" . . . two four-kilo boxes of the talcum powder. Two kilos of vac-packed vanilla ice cream. One kilo radiated pseudotuna. A thousand meters of number-six Munchenwerk Monofilament, with a cutter and tacker. Ten hundred-nail cassettes for a standard nailgun . . . "

Both men looked up, then looked again, squinting against the sunlight behind her. A third look, when she stepped fully inside and became more than an outline; the storekeeper straightened and unconsciously slicked back his thinning brown hair. Tyra sighed inwardly. There were times when being twenty and a pattern of Herrenmann good looks was something of an inconvenience. Here in the back of beyond it made you stand out, even in smelly leathers with a centimeter of caked dust on your face and a bowie tucked into the right boot-top. Then her eyes narrowed slightly; after the first involuntary reaction, the customer was looking at her with suspicion, not appreciation.

He's changed, she realized. Harder and stronger-looking than the holo Montferrat had shown her. Burned dark-brown from outdoor work, dressed in shabby leather pants and boots with a holstered strakkaker at his waist and a sleeveless jerkin. The Belter crest still stood alone on his head, legacy of a long-term depilation job, but it had grown longer and tangled.

"Guetag, herr," she said politely, nodding.

What the tanj is she *doing out here?* Jonah thought suspiciously. His gaze travelled from head to toe. Young, very pretty, with the indefinable something — perhaps her accent — that indicated Herrenmann birth. Definitely not an outbacker. Not the sort to be bashing the bundu. Although there were plenty of Herrenmann families down on their luck these days, of course. He started to estimate what she would look like without the bush jacket and leather pants . . .

Get back to business, mind, he admonished himself,

with a mental slap on the wrist. *Think of ice and sulphur.*
Besides that, his experience with Wunderlander
women had not exactly been overly positive.

"Been out here long?" she asked.

"Not long," he said shortly.

"Prospecting? Odd to find a Sol-Belter prospecting
dirtside."

Jonah stopped, a finger of cold fear trailing across
his neck. His crest marked him, and his accent. For that
matter the standard Sol System caucasoid-asian mix of
his own genetic background was uncommon here,
where unmixed European stock was in the majority.

"Hunting," he grunted, jerking his head at the pile
of pelts on the counter.

Suddenly they looked completely unconvincing.
The beautiful wavy lines of tigripard, the fawn and red
of gagrumphers, all might as well have been cheap
extrudate. She met his eyes and smiled, face unlined
but crinkles forming in the reddish-grey dust on her
skin. It was a charming smile.

"Hunting good?" she asked. "Enough to keep all of
you in business?"

"Good enough," Jonah replied, lifting a sack of
beans to his shoulder. Then he turned back. "All of us?"
he said.

"Not really smart to be out in the bundu alone," she
pointed out. "Let me give you a hand."

Before he could prevent her she scooped up a
double armful of sacks — a very respectable armful, for
a Wunderlander born and raised in this gravity — and
carried them out the door. Jonah followed, torn
between fear and embarrassment. Outside, she was
tying them down to a mule's packsaddle with brisk
efficiency.

"What's wrong with hunting alone?" he asked, when
the silence began to be suspicious in itself. She turned
and looked at him with open-eyed surprise; blue eyes,

he noticed, with a faint darker rim.

"Break a leg and die," she said. "Or a dozen other things. Not to mention the bandits."

Jonah moved to the other side of the mule and began strapping the sack of beans to the frame of the saddle, moving it a little to be sure the load was balanced. She had neat hands, slender for a tall woman but strong-looking; her nails were clipped short and clean enough to make him feel self-conscious about the rim of black grime under his. It was difficult to object to the lecture; coming out here alone *would* be insanely risky. Too risky even for a flatlander.

"Heard the Provisional Police have the bandits under control," he said.

"Oh, they're getting there. Not much on trials and procedures, but they track well enough. Big job, though. It'll be a while before these hills are safe for a man alone — or a woman, of course. Tempting fate to go out there with a mule-train of supplies, too."

Jonah worked on in silence, turning on his heel for another load and ignoring the presence at his heel.

"Tyra Nordbo, clan Freunchen," she said after a moment. "Besides which, a man alone usually doesn't require that much tuna and ice cream. You don't look like you drink that much bourbon by yourself, either."

"Manse Chung," he replied shortly. "I've got unusual tastes."

"Not Jonah Matthieson?" she enquired sweetly. "The man with the unusual, large, hairy *friends*?"

Jonah stepped back half a pace, snarling and reaching for his strakkaker; he paused with the vicious machine-pistol half out of the holster, half from prudence and half from the genuine shock on her face.

"Please, be calm, Mr. Matthieson," she said soothingly, hands held palm-down before her. "We have a mutual friend in Munchen who asked me to look you up. And," she added with a gamine grin, "you're a girlhood hero of mine, anyway — some people *did* hear a *little* of what went on out in the Serpent Swarm, you know."

"I don't have any friends in Munchen, and I don't have any here either," Jonah barked. *Montferrat. He's checking up on us, the scheming bastard.* "I've got a *backer* in Munchen, and he'll get the return on his capital he was promised, *if* he leaves me alone to do my work. Now if you'll pardon me, Fra Nordbo or whatever your name is, I'm a busy man."

"What took you so long?" Hans said.

"Making sure I wasn't followed," Jonah said. "Got it out?"

"Out to the mouth of the diggings," the old man said. "Didn't think it would be all that smart to leave it out in plain view."

"Show me."

Film sheeting had been rigged over the mouth of the shaft and covered with dirt and vegetation. Jonah ducked through into the interior chamber, lit by glowrods stapled to the timbers of the shoring, and whistled silently.

The . . . craft, he supposed . . . was a wasp-waisted spindle four meters long and three wide. One end flared with enigmatic pods; a hole had been torn in it there, the only sign of damage. Through the hole showed the unmistakable sheen of a stasis field. A Slaver stasis field, except that no thrint could be held in a ship this size; the thrintun were Man-tall and much more thickly built. Jonah shuddered at the memory of icy tendrils of certainty ramming into his mind . . . but he knew thrint naval architecture as few men living did, and *they* had been programmed to forget it. Thrintun ships were always large; the thrint were plains-dwelling carnivores by inheritance, and not intelligent enough to suppress their instincts.

"Tnuctipun," he breathed.

The Slavers' engineers, the ones whose revolt had brought down the Slaver Empire three billion years before. The revolt had wiped out both races and every other sentient in the galaxy save for the bandersnatch; humans and kzinti alike had evolved from Slaver-era tailored foodyeasts, along with the entire ecosystems of their respective planets. As a master race, the thrint had not been too impressive, apart from their power of telepathic hypnosis — with the Power, they did not *need* intelligence. An IQ equivalent to human 80 was normal for thrintun. Little was known of the tnuctipun, but it was clear that they had been very clever indeed.

"Or something else from then," Hans said. "That hull's like nothing in Known Space, that's for sure. Tensile strength and radiation resistance is right off the scale; none of the gear we brought can even test it." He scratched in the perpetual white three day's beard that covered his chin. "Wish we hadn't found it. Gold I understand. This I don't. Don't like it."

"This could make us one bleeping lot richer than all the gold on Wunderland," Jonah said.

"We do not know if there is *anything* valuable in the artifact," Spots said. "Not yet."

"There is a stasis field!" Bigs replied. "Neither the Patriarchy nor the monkeys have that as yet. There is the hull material. Think of the naval implications of such ships! We know the ancients had superluminal drives — undoubtedly the secret of that is inside as well. Matter conversion . . ."

He licked his chops and forced his voice to quietness; they were near the disused gold-washing boxes, but the humans could be anywhere and both of them had some command of the Hero's Tongue.

"You said we could not return to the Patriarchy — we, defeated cowards with nothing to offer. Now we can return. Now we can return as *Heroes*, assured of Full Names — assured of harems stocked from the Patriarch's daughters, and a position second only to his!"

Spots nodded thoughtfully. "There is some truth in that," he said judiciously; his voice was calm, but his eyes gleamed and the wet fangs beneath showed white and strong in the morning light. "*If* we could get the secrets, and *if* we can get them offplanet — you do not hope to ride aloft in the alien craft, I hope," he added dryly.

Bigs snorted; neither of the humans could fit in any likely passenger compartment, much less a kzin.

"We must get the pilot, or download the data from the craft's computers," he said decisively.

"Easy to say," Spots said, flapping his ears. Bigs grinned at the reminder that his sibling had always been better with information systems. "The hardware and programs both will be totally incompatible — fewer similarities in design architecture than kzinti-human system interfaces have. At least we and the monkeys have comparable capacities, and integrating *those* systems was a reborn-as-kzinrett nightmare. I did some of that during the war. What kind of computer would the monkey slaves of the thrintun build?"

"And yet. To be a true Hero, to have a name, it never was easy. Until not it was not possible. Now it is."

Spots paused thoughtfully, scratching himself under the jaw. "And the monkey authorities — if they sniff one trace scent of this, they will bury us so deep that we will stay submerged as long as that spacecraft did."

Bigs's fur rippled, and he gave an involuntary dry retch. Ever since the cave-in he had been unable to force himself closer than the outer entrance of the shaft. The darkness, the stifling *closeness* . . . he retched again. As nearly as they could estimate the tnuctipun spaceship had spent the last three thousand million years in the planetary magma, bobbing around beneath the Aeserheimer Continent's crustal plate. The hot spot must be connected with it, somehow — the how of it was beyond them; none of them was a specialist in planetary mechanics — and only chance had ever brought it to the surface again. Vanishingly unlikely that it should be then, although erosion would have revealed it in another few centuries. On the other paw, it had to be discovered *sometime*. It looked to be eternal.

To be buried *that long*, though. His mind knew that it had been less than an instant; inside a stasis field, the entropy gradient was disconnected from that of the universe as a whole. Less than a single second would pass inside during the entire duration of the universe, from the explosion of the primal monobloc to the final inward collapse into singularity. His mind knew that, but his gut knew otherwise.

Spots chirred. "For that matter, what of the humans here? They seem no more anxious than we to attract the *government's*" — he fell into Wunderlander for that; the Hero's Tongue had no precise equivalent — "attention. Yet they may be reluctant to allow us to depart with the data — they are monkeys, after all."

"We can bury their bones. They are outcasts, not dear to the livers of the monkeys in authority. Who will miss their scent?"

The smell of anger warned him; he looked up just in time to jerk his head backward, and Spots's claws fanned the air over his nose rather than raking through the sensitive flesh.

"Honorless sthondat!" the smaller kzin hissed. "Did you forget the oath we swore with Jonah-human? You are alive because of the Jonah-human! Oath-breaker! Are you without regard for the bones of your ancestors? The Fanged God will regurgitate your soul."

Bigs bristled, swelling up to a third again his size; his ears folded back.

"They are *monkeys*," he growled back; the sound was a steady *urrreeuueeerree* beneath the modulations of his words. The Menacing Tense in Imperative Mode.

"That *monkey* crawled into the darkness to rescue you as you lay helpless," Spots said; he stood higher, unwilling to let Bigs' height give him dominance. All eight claws on his hands were out. "Blood for blood."

They began to circle, tails rigid. "What of our duty to the Patriarch?" Bigs spat.

"Our first duty to the Patriarch is to be Heroes," Spots replied. "Heroes do not break their solemn oath!"

They both sank on their haunches for the final leap. Then Bigs let his fur fall and looked aside.

"There is a true trail among the prints of your words," he admitted with sullen reluctance. *Earth rumbling and the walls closing around* — "If the monke . . . if Jonah-human refuses to let us leave with the data, I will challenge him to honorable single combat."

Spots straightened suspiciously; he sniffed with his jaw open and licked his nose for a second try.

"I smell reservations. They smell stronger than a dead kshat," he warned. "Be sure, I will not permit less. No under-the-grass killing. And if you duel Jonah-human, you must preserve his head for the Ancestral Museum of our line."

"Agreed. We shall all act as Heroes. Even the Jonah-human."

Spots's pelt rippled in a shrug. "We quarrel over the intestines of a prey that grazes yet," he said. "So far, all we have is an impenetrable mystery."

• CHAPTER FIFTEEN

"What did you *do*?" Spots demanded, springing back and bruising his tail against a timber upright. He rubbed at it absently, eyes locked on the tnuctipun spacecraft with the same intent longing that they might have fixed on a zianya bound in the blood trough of a feasting table.

"I did *nothing*," Bigs said.

Jonah grunted, and Hans whistled softly. For the better part of a week, nothing. And now the stasis field had vanished, seemingly of its own accord.

The hull had turned . . . translucent, as well. Much of the interior seemed to be packed solid with equipment of various sorts; none of it familiar, although he thought he recognized something like the wave-guides of a gravity polarizer. *If it's that small, and can lift this ship, it's better than anything we or the kzin can make*, he thought. Nothing this size could make space on its own — the power-plant alone would be too large — and nothing this size could possibly mount a superluminal drive, from what little was publicly known about them. On the other hand, nothing humans or kzinti knew would stand three billion years of immersion in liquid metal, either.

"Tnuctipun," he whispered, awed. In the center of the forward bulge was a capsule, and inside that he could dimly see the outline of a body inside a cocoon of tubes and wires.

Small, was his first thought. He knew from his time on the thrintun ship *Ruling Mind* that tnuctipun were

small; they had built that thrintun vessel, and many of
the crawlspaces were too cramped for a human to
enter. Long limbs in proportion to the body, and twelve
digits, longer and more jointed than human fingers.
Another indication; there was a rough correlation
between manual dexterity and the length of time a
species had been sentient. Dolphins and bandersnatch
were exceptions, of course. Overall he thought it
would come to about his waist standing erect, but the
arms were as long as his. A single nostril in the long
snout, ahead of an even longer swelling of braincase; a
pattern of holes on either side of the head that might
correspond to ears, or might not; two large eyes and a
smaller one set where the forehead would be if there
was one. The eyelids closed side-to-side rather than up
and down.

I'm the first human ever to see a tnuctipun, Jonah
thought, slightly dazed. He stepped forward, acutely
conscious of the smell of his own sweat, of the ginger
scent of the kzin. They were staying well back; not that
they were more fearful than he, just less driven by
curiosity.

"It's hurt," he said, peering closely with his hands on
the absolute smoothness of the hull; it was an odd sensation, the palms always trying to slip away.

Whatever the tnuctipun was floating in was liquid,
and reddish blood was hazing the egg-shaped chamber; it thinned and flowed away as he watched. *An
autodoc*, he realized. Doubling as a pilot's crash couch.
Some small scoutcraft and atmosphere flyers used that
arrangement, with a high-oxygen liquid for breathing.
A body with open air spaces inside it was much more
vulnerable to acceleration than one whose lungs were
solidly filled with incompressible liquid. *Why bother, if
they had gravity polarizers?* he wondered. Then: *ah.*
Gravity waves were detectible, and the ones from a
polarizer much more so than the natural variety. A

clandestine operations craft, no doubt. The tnuctipun had probably been a spy, and the ship designed to slip onto thrintun-held planets during the war of the Revolt. Jonah was willing to bet a great deal that the hull material was superlatively stealthed, as well as near-as-no-matter invulnerable.

"You realize what this means?" he said, looking at the others. "It means we four are potentially the richest beings in known space."

"Means we could all lose our heads, hearts and testicles when the gov'mint gets its claws on us," Hans said dourly. The kzin both snapped their jaws shut: *We are meat*.

"We certainly are if Markham or the ARM get hold of us," Jonah mused.

And the bleeping ARM wouldn't even use *this stuff, particularly now we're beating the pussies.* At that thought his head came up, raking his eyes across the kzin. Both returned his glance blandly, looking aside in carnivore courtesy. *The Patriarchy would use it*, he knew. Kzinti had never been able to afford antitech prejudice; they had less natural inventiveness than humans to begin with. *Tanj. And we were ready to kill each other over* gold, *much less this.*

A voice spoke in his ear, in the Hero's Tongue: *"What did you* do?"

Jonah jumped backwards; then he noticed everyone else around the spacecraft had done likewise; the kzinamaratsov brothers were whirling in place, trying to find whatever was speaking beside their ears.

"*It's hurt,*" the voice said, in Wunderlander with a trace of Sol Belt accent. The wet sound of kzin jaws closing on air followed.

The kzin were bristling. "Haunted weapons," Spots said, snapping twice.

"Translator program," Jonah said. "The systems are active, if not the pilot. It's trying to talk to us." It was vibrating the air beside their ears somehow, not too startling compared to the rest of the technology.

* * *

"That is beyond my parameters," the computer said. "I must consult my operator before I can make further judgements."

Jonah opened his mouth to reply, and found himself croaking. A startled glance outside showed darkness.

"We'd better knock it off for a while," he said. *Nerve wracking work.*

Especially when the translator program had spent an hour trying to find out which side they were on in the tnuctipun-thrintun war; it seemed to have a bee in its bonnet about that, understandably enough. He strongly suspected that it also had a self-destruct subroutine, and would engage it if it 'thought' that they were part of a thrint slave-species. The type of suicide bomb available to a culture whose basic energy source was matter conversion did not bear thinking of. You could tell a good deal about the people who designed an infosystem by talking to one of their programs, and there was a pristine ruthlessness to this one that even the kzin found chilling.

No wonder the Revolt wiped out intelligent life, he thought. They had had to take a datalink out and show the ship's system the stars before it really seemed to believe them about the length of time that had passed. At that, it was probably fortunate that the pilot was still comatose. The computer had limited autonomy; it was very powerful, right up with the great machines that ran the UN Space Navy from Gibraltar Base in the Sol Belt, but not a true personality, as far as he could tell. Neither human nor kzinti designers had ever been able to make a really sentient system that did not go catatonic within months. Evidently the ancient world of the Slaver Empire had been no more successful. At least the AI was completely logical; Finagle alone knew what a conscious but traumatized tnuctipun would do on realizing it was the only member of its species left in a universe changed beyond recognition.

Jonah shivered again. That did not bear thinking about either. When the *Yamamoto* dropped him and Ingrid Raines off into the kzin-occupied Alpha Centauri system two years ago they had decelerated by using a stasis field — one of the few the UN had been able to make — and skidding through the photosphere of the star. A little, little mistake and they would have spent the next several billion years in stasis themselves — until Alpha Centauri went nova, perhaps. Then the invulnerable bubble of not-time might have been flung out, eventually to land on a planet. To wait while intelligent life arose or arrived, then be opened. He swallowed, mind exploring the concept the way a tongue might probe at a sore tooth. *At that, there would have been two of us*, he thought. *And I'd still have gone off the deep end.*

Jonah was preoccupied enough not to notice the extra figure at the campfire, as he walked downslope to the tents. Spots and Bigs had better senses; he looked up sharply at their angry hisses of territorial violation.

"You all seemed to be busy," Tyra Nordbo said, crouched by the fire. "So I thought I'd help myself to some of this coffee."

With her free hand, she pitched something small and heavy out into the firelight. All of them recognized the material. After a moment, they recognized the shape; the hole in the rear section of the tnuctipun ship's hull matched it exactly.

"No, of *course* I haven't reported back to Herrenmann Montferrat," Tyra said. "How could I? The government — which means the ARM, remember — is monitoring all frequencies and all the cable and satellite links. There *is* still a state of military emergency on, you know."

Jonah relaxed slightly; out of the corner of his eye, he could see Spots and Bigs doing likewise, the ruffs of fur around their throats and shoulders sinking back to the level of the rest of their pelts. Their eyes stayed locked on the young woman, ominously steady, glints of silver and red in the gathering dark against the ruddy orange of their fur. Hans was imperturbable as he sucked his pipe to a glowing ember.

"You really don't have much choice but to go through with your agreement, as far as I can see," she went on.

"Oh?" Jonah said, softly. "We didn't bargain to hand over the Secret of the Ages for a pat on the head and a few thousand krona."

Bigs snorted agreement, followed by a low growl. Spots was silent, but the tip of his tongue showed as he panted slightly.

"It's *too* big," Tyra said. "The ARM would give anything to suppress this — they'll take the tnuctipun back to Earth, put it in the museum next to the Sea Statue, that thrint they bottled up again, and that'll be that. You know them. They have a *lot* of influence here on Wunderland these days. To make any use of the secret, you'd have to have a powerful patron of your own — or," she added with a gamine chuckle that made her look twelve for a second, "you could take it and sell it to the Outsiders or the Patriarch of Kzin. No offense," she added in the brothers' direction.

Bigs snarled, a sound like ripping canvass. Spots snorted, a *flupp* sound. "None taken," he said.

"Besides which," she went on, "*I* know about it, and it's my duty to see that the most responsible authority takes charge of it for the benefit of Wunderland — of everyone, eventually. That means Montferrat. Of course, you could kill me and bury my body." She leaned back against her saddle. "Up to you, mein herren."

Blast, she had to go and say *it*, Jonah thought. His palms were damp. *I'm a — moderately — law abiding type*, he mused. *And normally, I'd be against offing anyone that good-looking on general principle. But* Finagle *there's a lot at stake here!*

Odd, how ambition struck. He had never been

conscious of wealth as something he lacked, before.
Enough to be comfortable, yes; the loss of that had
been shocking when Early had him railroaded out of
the UN Space Navy and then blacklisted. A little more
of the gold, yes; independence had looked awfully
desirable. The tnuctipun's secrets were more than
wealth, they were *power*. The problem was, they were
proportionately risky.

"Ja, Fra Nordbo," Hans said mildly. "Those look to
be the alternatives, don't they?" Tyra stiffened; she had
not meant to be taken literally. "If you'd let us talk it
over in private, for a minute?" He waggled his pipe
towards the kzinti; it would be futile to try and run in
the dark, with them ready to scent-track as accurately
as hounds and with intelligence to boot.

As soon as she had withdrawn, Bigs spoke: "Kill him. I
mean her." Kzinti females were mute and subsentient,
probably another consequence of genetic engineering,
and kzintosh — male kzin — had trouble remembering
that sexual dimorphism was not so extreme among the
race of Man. The matter was academic to them, of
course. "We owe the monke — hrreaheerr, Montferrat-
human only money. We can pay him off with gold. The
secrets in that craft will make us Patriarchs!"

"Or make us dead," Hans said. "Killing the girl —
the Provisional Gendarmerie, they don't worry about
trifles like proof. They just shoot you. Can't spend if
you're dead. I wish we hadn't found it, I truly do."

"I also," Spots said surprisingly. "But it is done." His
breed wasted little time on regrets. "My sibling is right
— in potential. Hans-human is also right — as to the
risk. I scratch dirt upon the dung of risk . . . but there is
no glory in defeat. It is a difficult matter."

"We can't kill Tyra — the girl," Jonah said
reasonably.

The two kzin looked at each other. Bigs rolled his
eyes toward Jonah and made a complex gesture,

involving fingers wiggling at the muzzle, flapping ears, a ripple of the fur and an arch of the back. It meant *mating frenzy*; also *stupidity* and *madness*.

"Hrrrr." Spots lay his chin on his hands and turned his eyes on Jonah. "We must agree, whatever we do. Or else fight each other." He added kindly: "If all agree to kill the female, we will do it; you need not watch. We will even forgo eating it."

"Bleeping hell you — " Jonah forced calm. *Breath in. Breath out. Ommmm* — "Look, I know it's tempting for you, but I've decided; we really can't do anything but sell to Montferrat. Wunderland's our only market. They won't let us get off planet! Montferrat is the only market on Wunderland that won't slap us in a psychist's chair. And kill you two, by the way."

"I think Fra Nordbo should go," Hans said. He gestured with his pipe as Jonah stared round. "Nothing against her personal. No, seems a nice enough sort. Still, I'm a Wunderlander — commoner, like my parents before me. Don't like the thought that we hand this to the new government; too cozy by half with the Earthers. Don't like the idea of the Herrenmenn getting it, either — tired of them running things, and throwing us scraps." He smiled across at the kzin without showing his teeth. "Since you fellers' friends back home *can't* get it, that don't come into the picture."

Tanjit! Jonah thought. Aloud: "Look, we've had a long day. What say we turn in? She isn't going anywhere. We can consider it in the morning."

"Logic will be the same in the morning," Spots said reasonably. "Also, you will not find the decision easier once you have mated."

"I don't *intend* to mate!" Jonah snapped. *Although Finagle knows I'd like to.* Aliens had trouble with the details of human social interaction. "And I say let's think it over in the morning."

CHAPTER SIXTEEN

Spots-Son of Chotrz-Shaa whimpered softly in his sleep. He was hiding from his father. Chotrz-Shaa had seen the vids from the Fourth Fleet sent against Man-Home. Three elder sons and a brother had sailed with the Fourth Fleet; $sis-Captain, Second Gunner and Squadron Analyst. Chotrz-Shaa raged through the home complex; the scent of his anger was terrible. In the palazzos of the harem, mothers tucked their kittens into cupboards or piles of pillows and yowled their fear and defiance, prepared to fight to the death to keep the enraged male from eating the young. *That* was an instinct older than the Patriarchy, older than speech and tools.

Spots-Son followed in his father's wake; the smell of killing rage repelled and led. Occasionally a faint *euuuw-euuuw* trickled past the young kzin's lips; his brother the Big One gave him a contemptuous look, that was the infant's distress call. They followed down corridors of black basalt with trophies of ceremonial weapons, into the communications room. Sometimes their father brought them there for lessons with the teaching machines, but now it was in turmoil; smashed crockery, modules thrown here and there. A human servant huddled bleeding in one corner, then scuttled out as the youngsters entered.

Pictures were up on the wall holo. For a long time the two youngsters stared at them without comprehension, until Spots recognized the face in one.

"Uncle Ssis-Captain!" he cried. "Sire's Brother!"

Bigs reared back beside him with a *reeearrwowow* of protest, hair bottling out and tail stiff. Uncle Ssis-Captain was *dead*. He was floating in zero-G, with the bottom half of him *gone*. The brothers were old enough for preliminary education; they both knew about spacecraft, and kzinti anatomy.

"But . . . but Uncle Ssis-Captain went to conquer the monkeys!" Spots wailed.

Uncle Ssis-Captain had picked him up and swung him around, and promised him an elephant-hunt when he came to visit on the estate on Earth . . .

"The monkeys killed Uncle Ssis-Captain," Bigs said shakily. "That . . . that is Brother and Brother." The other two forms in the holo were calcinated to ash and bone, but one had a chased-tungsten arm ring. Their father had given that when the Fleet left on its mission of conquest.

Two shrill cries of grief and rage rose, higher and higher until an adult roar cut them off.

"*What are you doing here?*" it bellowed.

Spots threw himself down flat, paws over eyes and fur laid flat. Bigs was more reckless; he stood upright, met his father's eyes.

"I shall kill all the monkeys — they killed Uncle and — "

"*Silence, cub!*" Chotrz-Shaa bellowed, backhanding the youngling into the wall and whimpering silence. The huge face bent low, filling Spots's vision, all glaring eyes and teeth and rage-smell.

"*No, Father!*" he cried, and woke.

I detest that dream, he thought, shaking his head and rolling up to all fours.

It was the hour before dawn, with the moon down and the air chilly; it felt good to be comfortable in his fur, and scents were marvelously clear. Eyesight was flatter and less color-sensitive than in daylight, but otherwise not much less as the pupils of his eyes expanded until the iris was only a yellow thread around the black pits of sight. Something moved, a human — he sniffed deeply — yes, the blander, earthier odor of the female.

Good, he thought. That dream usually came when something serious disturbed him in his sleep. If the human-female was trying to escape, he could kill it without angering Jonah-human; that would be best. *Jonah is a fine monkey*, he thought. If the thought were not slightly blasphemous, one could wish that he had been born a Hero. *I will make him my Chief Slave when we reconquer Wunderland.* As they would, if Bigs was right. If only. *My liver says yes, but my brain disagrees. Enough. The longest leap begins with setting your hindclaws. First the Tyra-human.*

He crept forward, belly to the earth, tail straight back to balance his weight and hands touching down occasionally to guide it. Ready for the sudden overwhelming rush, the final leap; he needed no weapon for this. Excitement folded his ears back into knots and drew lips back from teeth, brought the claws sliding out on all eight digits. Almost, he was reluctant to end it; Tyra-human moved very quietly, for a monkey, and he might have had trouble following her if the breeze had not been with him. Eagerness brought him forward faster, but with only a little more noise; a pebble displaced, a thorn snagging his fur and snapping. Then he went rigid with shock.

"*Quiet*," she said, turning and calling softly. "They're moving up the valley."

She looked directly at him, with the bulbous shape of nightsight glasses hiding her eyes. She spoke in the Hero's Tongue, as closely as a monkey could come to pronouncing it; in the Warning Tense. He nearly screamed and leapt then; only caution at the sight of her magrifle gave him pause. Then the sense of the words sank home.

They? he thought. Quickly he came level with her and followed her pointing hand. Motion, over a kilometer away; he took the glasses from his belt and looked. Humans on horseback, leading other horses. Octal to the second of them, all heavily armed, and he recognized the shapes of knock-down beamers on the lead horses.

"Who?" he breathed. *I lay my fur flat in shame. Claw your own nose and roll in sthondat excrement, Spotted Fool! We should have kept lookouts.*

"Don't know," she replied. Even now a thought flickered, how easy it would be to reach out — only arm's reach — and slash her throat open.

No. Not with an unknown factor . . . unless she led them to us? His lips went further back in rage, but it was unlikely.

"Could be the Provisional Gendarmerie," she said softly. "Or it could be bandits. Either way, bad news for us. They'll be here by dawn at that rate. Can't miss the trail and the water-furrow."

Us, Spots thought mournfully. *Us expands to too many monkeys.* The Fanged God would have his jokes on those so lost to honor that they surrendered.

I will rip your throat yet, he thought, staring resentfully up into the sky for a second. The God appreciated a good fight.

"I will wake the others," he went on aloud.

"Well, they've got Provisional Gendarmerie *armbands*," Jonah said, lowering the magnifier.

"Cloth's cheap," Hans replied.

Jonah nodded, mind busy. "All right. Spots, you take your beamer and dig in behind those rocks over there. Hans, get the mules back into the diggings and then set up on the hill over the entrance."

Hans was the best shot of all of them; it was difficult to be a *bad* shot with a military magrifle, but he was superb.

"I'll take the center, here."

"What about me?" Tyra Nordbo said.

I wish to Finagle you were far, far away, Jonah thought. Aloud: "Ever used that rifle?"

"Yes."

The reply was bitten off, and from the expression she hadn't enjoyed it. All to the good; he'd known people in the UN Navy who enjoyed combat, and none of them were types he'd like to have backing him up. They tended to fly off the handle like . . . like kzinti, come to think of it.

"You get about ten meters to the east of me and take that little knoll." He turned to eye the two kzin. "And *nobody* fires unless they open up, or I give the order. Understood?"

Bigs looked skeptical. "What if they flank us?" Spots asked. "There are enough of them."

"Then we'll retreat," Jonah said. "And someone else will have the headache of what to do with *that*." He jerked a thumb towards the entrance to the diggings.

The mounted column wove over the ridge opposite and down into the morning shadow of the valley, disappearing into the dense vegetation along the streambed. Jonah burrowed deeper into cover, showing nothing but the lenses of his field glasses, their systems keyed to passive receptors only. IR would show their locations, of course; a good deal depended on how much the whatever-they-were had in the way of detection systems. Quite a bit if they really were Provisionals, anything from the Eyeball Mark I to military issue if they were bandits. The dawn was coming up in the east, to his right; the snowpeaks and clouds around the summits of the Jotuns turned red as blood, while Beta was a point of white fire overhead. The waterfall toned and thundered to his right, mist rising out of darkness into light.

He pulled the audio jack on his field glasses out and

put it in his ear. The instrument clicked, sorting out sound not in the human-voice frequencies. Then:

" . . . *boot some head* . . . "

"Shut up, scheisskopf! Turn it on!"

A crackling hiss filled his ear. *Wonders of modern technology*, he reflected sourly; it was always easier to make things not happen than to make them happen, so countermeasures generally ran ahead of detection. The rustle of boots and the clink of equipment came more clearly, and the *tock . . . tock* . . . of synthetic horseshoes on firm ground or rock. The strangers were in no hurry. They stopped to water their horses and picket them, to set up a firing line along the edge of the brush, before two walked out from under the trees and began climbing the hill.

"Everybody stay calm," Jonah warned again, as the pair halted and looked upslope.

They looked tough, shabby and a little hungry; or at least the rat-faced thin one did. The leader had a beer belly that hung over his gunbelt, and even in the cool morning sweat stains marked his armpits. He carried a strakkaker at his belt and a magrifle in his hands; his companion had the chunky shape of a jazzer slung from an assault sling. That fired miniature molecular-distortion batteries set to discharge into any living tissue they met. An unpleasant weapon.

The big-bellied leader smiled, a false grin creasing his stubbled face. His Wunderlander had a thick accent, maybe regional, or he might have come from one of the many ethnic enclaves that dotted the planet:

"Hey, you up there? Why you hiding?"

"Why are you here?" Jonah replied. "Ride on. We'll mind our business, you mind yours."

"Hey, we can't do that, man!" the other man said. "We're the Provisional Gendarmerie — you know, the mounted police? We're inspecting the area for illegal weapons. New order, to confiscate all illegal weapons, peace and order, you know?"

"What's illegal?" Jonah asked.

"Just military stuff, man. You know, magrifles, jazzers, beamers — hunting rifles, they are fine."

"Let's see some ID, then."

"ID? We got *plenty* of ID. Here, I show you."

The fat man pulled something out of a leg-pocket on his stained pants and handed it to the smaller figure beside him. He murmured an order, which the other seemed to resent; then he took off his hat and began thrashing the little man over the head and shoulders.

"Ja, boss, Ja, I'll *take* it," the small man with the big nose said.

"Here!" he called out, climbing towards Jonah's position.

"Toss it over that rock and get back down," Jonah shouted.

Ratface scuttled to obey, and Jonah signed to Tyra. She leopard-crawled with her rifle across her elbows, over to the plastic card and examined it with a frown of puzzlement; then she ran it past the scanner of her beltcomp. That brought another frown, and she kept crawling to within arm's length of him to pass the ID. He glanced down at it; a holo of the fat man's face, looking indecent without its stubble. Serial number, and *Leutnant Edward Gruedermann, Provizional Staatspolezi.*

"My comp recognizes the codes, and I updated about a month ago, but . . . "

"But?" Jonah bit out. If he had stood off a real Gendarmerie Lieutenant, they were all in serious trouble. Wunderland was under martial law, and out here a mounted police officer could be judge, jury and executioner all in one. Staging a shoot-out with the police would be absolute suicide, even if he won. Jonah Matthieson's ambiguous status would harden into "desperate criminal" quite quickly, then.

"But if that lot are Provisionals, I'm a kzinrette." She bit her lip; even then it was interesting . . . "Look, herr

Matthieson — up until two months ago, I was *in* the Provisional Gendarmerie. My brother Ib's a captain. I spent six months riding with them. That lot down there smell wrong, completely."

Jonah met her eyes, a changeable sea-blue; tinted with gray this morning, desperately sincere. *Tanj, why couldn't she be a middle-aged battleaxe of eighty?*

"All right," he said. "I'll play it safe." *Because if we do give up our guns, there's our options gone right there.* "You get over there east of the Brothers Kzinamaratsov; they might come up the gully."

To his surprise, he heard her chuckle — he had only taken up ancient literature in the last year himself; data was free, if nothing else — and she touched a finger to her brow before heading off east with an expert's use of cover.

"If this ID is genuine," Jonah called down to the man halfway up the slope, "then you won't mind me calling in to Munchen for confirmation. Leutnant Gruederman."

Gruederman began a snarl, and forced it back into a smile. *Docking contact*, Jonah told himself. *Tyra was right.*

"Hey, man, we don't want to *steal* your guns — it's the law, you know. Here — " he shoved the other man " — we'll give you compensation."

"See," the little man said, rummaging in his knapsack. "This is worth three, maybe four hundred krona!" He held up a briefcase sized box, an obsolete model of musicomp and library. "Good stuff, pre-war!"

Stolen from some farmer you bushwacked, Jonah thought grimly. He took up the slack on his trigger and put the aiming point on the musicomp. *Whack.* The casing exploded and the little bandit went howling and whirling away, face slashed by the fragments. The sharp sound of the high-velocity round went echoing off down the valley in a *whack*-whackkkkk of fading repetitions.

"Get moving," Jonah called flatly.

The bandit chief's face convulsed, going from a broad grin to an expression that was worthy of a kzin. Spittle flecked out as he screamed:

"*You can't do this to Ed Gruederman! I will* boot your head!"

The smaller bandit had recovered enough to unlimber his jazzer. A round cracked over Jonah's head; by reflex he shifted aim and sent a short burst into the man's torso. It blossomed out in a mist of sliced bone and flesh as the prefrag bullets punched in and disintegrated, a thousand crystalline buzzsaws of adamantine strength. By the time he shifted back it was too late. Gruederman threw himself backward in a desperate flip, somersaulting and rolling down the short distance to cover. Bullets pecked at his shadow, and then the whole treeline opened up. Magrifle bullets chewed at the stone, and a boulder exploded as a tripod-mounted beamer punched megajoules of energy into its brittle structure. Thunder rolled back from the cliffs.

"Let 'em have it!" Jonah yelled.

Unnecessary, but satisfying. He rolled a half-dozen paces to his right, rose, fired a burst, ducked and rolled again. Hans was shooting from his position over the diggings, single shots. A man screamed and fell from a tree in the valley below, and the beamer fell silent. Over to the left the kzin were popping up for fractional seconds and sending bursts from their captured beamers, using heavy weapons like rifles, inhumanly quick and accurate. Trees below exploded into steam and supersonic splinters. Their screams sounded louder than the noise of battle, daunting in a way that the mechanized death they wielded was not. Hair rose on human spines, a fear that went back to the caves and beyond.

Wonder what Tyra's doing, Jonah thought in a second of calm. *Hope she hasn't got buck fever.*

***

Spots flicked himself up with a heave of his body. It was just enough to clear head and hands above the scree ahead of him; the aimpoint of the beamer settled on the target he had picked on his last shot, and it exploded with steam. From vegetation, and as he dropped and rolled he could smell flash-cooked monkey as well. He shrieked exultantly:

"*Eeeeeerreeieiaiïaaiawiowiue!*" The kzinti are upon you! He had a wide arc before him, with a deep narrow ravine full of brush that stretched right down to the river. Already an arc of riverbank forest before him was burning. He looked down at the power readout of the beamer; almost half discharged. A pity, since he liked this weapon. The two strakkakers strapped to his thighs seemed like feeble toys in comparison, although the grips had been modified for kzin hands.

The next shot almost brought disaster. A fragment caught his forehead, and stinging blood covered his eyes as he dropped back into the protection of the rock. With a yowl of impatience he felt at the injury, even as rounds chewed at the tumbled volcanic basalt ahead of him. It was painful enough to wake him to full fury, the area above his brow-ridges cut to the bone and a flap of skin hanging free; his ears rang, and his mouth filled. He swallowed and forced pain and dizziness back. That had almost killed him; many monkeys would die for their presumption, and he would chew their livers. In the meantime he had to get the blood out of his eyes; it was blinding him, and the rank scent of kzin blood dulled his nostrils.

A yowl from Bigs meant that he had caught that smell too. "All's well!" he snarled back. "Look to your front."

There was a length of gauze in his beltpouch. He pushed the flap of skin back into position — he would get a worthy battlescar out of this, but in the meantime it *stung* — and began binding the wound with an

X-shaped bandage, anchored by a loop under the base of his jaw and around the rear bulge of his skull. Hurriedly he poured water from his canteen over his brows and eyelashes, snuffling and scrubbing and licking his nose to clear his senses. A sharp scent of eucalyptus almost made him sneeze; some tree damaged in the fight, he supposed.

"*Behind you!*" a human voice screamed.

It was utterly unexpected, but Spots' reflexes wasted no time on surprise. He dropped sideways.

A bandit lunged through the space he had occupied a moment before, with a vibroblade outstretched before him. It whined into uselessness as the humming wire edge sliced into rock. The knifeman's face had just enough time to begin to show surprise when the kzin's full-armed swing ripped out his throat almost to the neckbone and threw him ten meters through the air. The instinctive full-force effort swung Spots around in a three-quarter turn, his body betraying him in a G field barely a third of the one for which it had evolved. That exposed him to fire from below for a moment — rock spalls stung his shoulders — and left him helpless as the second bandit six meters away raised a strakkaker left-handed. The forty-round clip of liquid-teflon filled bullets would rip the kzin's body open like an internal explosion.

The bandit's head vanished from the shoulders up in a spray of red, gray and pink. The body stood for two seconds with blood fountaining up to where the face would have been, took two stumbling steps forward, and collapsed across Spots' tail. He blinked surprise and looked.

Tyra-human lay prone beside another boulder, slapping another cassette into her rifle. She gave him a brief nod before moving off to a fresh firing position; her face was gray, and she smelled of fatigue poisons and nausea, an acrid scent.

Spots went flat again and readied his beamer, but the savor had gone out of the fight. *Bigs owes a life to Jonah-human. Now I owe a life to Tyra-human. Two lives the honor of the House of Chotrz-Shaa owes to Man. It is too much. How will I know the balance of debt and obligation, unless the Fanged God tells me?* Like most modern kzinn, Spots had worked at rejecting religion as unfashionable. The effort wasn't entirely successful. Intellect was one thing; but belief in the Fanged God was built deep into the kzinn culture, and a desire to *believe* had been built into their very genes. The Conservators of the Patriarchal Past had a fertile field to sow. Now Spots wished he had listened more closely to the Conservators. It would take a God to figure out this tangle.

Oh, well — there are monkeys down there I can kill, he thought gloomily.

"*Sssisssi!*" Bigs snarled, and forced his clawed hand down again. "We should have pursued," he went on.

"Shut up," Tyra said, working the sprayskin around the depilated patch of singed flesh that ran down the barrel ribs of the big kzin's body. "We're not in any shape to pursue three times our number. Defending gave us an advantage."

Jonah sighed and sipped again at his canteen, looking around the campsite; they had moved into the outer edge of the shaft, in case the bandits tried to sneak a sniper back, and left sensors scattered about outside with Spots to oversee. The kzin seemed depressed; not so Bigs, who was a little manic by his own surly standards. He lifted his beltphone.

"Spots, anything?"

"No. They ran, and continued to run to the limit of the audio sensor's ability to detect the footfalls of their riding beasts." A sigh. "Must we really leave all those bodies?"

"Yes!" Jonah snapped, swallowing at certain memories of his own. *Every once in a while, you remember that they're not humans in fur suits.* "Last thing we want is a posse-mob of outbackers on our trail, understood?" Wunderlanders would *not* react well to the thought of kzin eating even dead bandits.

"Understood." A long, sad sigh.

"Come on in."

Silence crackled between them as they waited; Jonah met Hans's eye, and got a slight nod in return. Tyra finished with Bigs and stepped quickly away, aware that an injured kzin was unlikely to tolerate much contact with a human. *Got brains, that girl,* Jonah thought admiringly. Spots ducked in between the screens and stopped, turning his head inquiringly towards his brother, ears cocking forward and nostrils flaring. Then he rippled his fur in a shrug and squatted against the restraining timbers of the far wall, hands resting on the ground before him.

"We can't stay here," Jonah said abruptly. "There's something you should know: I don't think that those bandits were acting on their own."

It took a few minutes to sketch in Jonah's relations with Buford Early, and Early's campaign of persecution. Silence followed, and he went on:

"We can't lug *that*" — he jerked a thumb over his shoulder at the tnuctipun spyship — "either. Either the bandits will come back with more men, or the real Gendarmerie will show up. The bandits will kill us, the Gendarmerie might — and the government will *certainly* stamp everything Excruciatingly Secret and silence us, one way or another. I'm a pariah, you two are kzin, Fra Nordbo here comes from a suspect family subject to pressure — "

"And I'm a worthless old bushcoot," Hans said cheerfully.

"If we were lucky, they might buy us off," Jonah continued. "If we want to make anything of what we've got, we'd better get out quick and make a sale to the only one who has the resources to make something of this — to Montferrat-Palme. At least we'll have *some* bargaining position with him."

"*That . . . is . . . not . . . all,*" a voice said behind him.

Jonah shot erect, turning before he came down again. Within its sac of fluid, the tnuctipun's eyes had opened. It stayed in its fetal position, hands wrapped about knees. The three eyes blinked vertically, and the mouth moved; the lips seemed almost prehensile, and they were not in synch with the words that he heard. The translator program, then.

"*I . . . will . . . not . . . be . . . buried . . . again.*"

• CHAPTER SEVENTEEN

Durvash whimpered to himself, eyes squeezed tightly shut. Agony, agony to speak. Agony to *think*. Last. He was the last. *I failed*. Suicide night had succeeded. The thrint had won. *Egg mother. Womb mother. Father. Siblings. All dead.* The tnuctipun race was dead, and he was the last. The last by three *billion* years. One-celled organisms had evolved to intelligence while he lay within this planet's crust. He was not even sure it was the planet he had lost consciousness on; there was more than enough time for his damaged craft to have drifted through several systems. Time for all the bodies of thrint and tnuctipun and shotovi and zen-gaborni to rot away, and the fabric of their cities to erode to dust and the dust to be ground down under moving continents, and for stars to age and—

Rest, the faithful machines said; they had no souls, no souls that longed for the deep red velvet sleep of death. *Your functions are at less than 45% of optimum and you must rest for the healing to be complete.*

He jerked. *No. I must think.* He was *not* the last tnuctipun! His race had won, not the mouth-beshitting Slavers. Joy brought Durvash tears as painful as despair. He existed; his autodoc and computer existed. They contained the knowledge to clone his cells, to modify the genetic structures to replicate individuals of all three sexes. Genetic records of *thousands* of tnuctipun; that was part of the general autodoc system. His rubbery lips peeled off his serrated teeth in aggression-pleasure. Tnuctipun were pack-hunters of great sociability; group survival was sweet ecstasy.

I will need facilities. Laboratories, tools, time. The current sentients here would be complete fools to allow a rebirth of the tnuctipun species, of tnuctipun culture — and all of *that* was encoded in the memory of his computer as well.

They were not complete fools. Not very bright by tnuctipun standards, but then few races were. They were certainly more acute than thrint — by about a fifth to a third, he judged, from the hour or so of conversation, and to judge from their technology. It was fairly advanced, in a quaint sort of way — the beginnings of an industrial system, interstellar travel and fusion drives.

They were divided, too. Species from species, as was natural: the tnuctipun word for "alien" translated roughly as "food that talks". Also individual from individual, a common characteristic of inferior races — he quickly suppressed memory of his own rivals at home. Durvash knew what to make of that. He had been trained as a clandestine agent, and his proudest accomplishment had been an entire thrint world wiped clean of life by engineering a civil war between thrintun clan elders.

The large carnivore, he decided. Carnivores were easiest to work with, in his opinion — as he was one himself. *He is in a minority of one.* It should be easy to persuade him to use the neural-connector earplug. That would make communication easy, and certain other things, if the biochemistries were similar enough.

Durvash squeezed his eyes shut. No warrior of tnuctipun had ever been so alone as he. He had lost a universe; there was a universe to win.

If I do not go mad, he thought; although his autodoc would probably not let him do so. He did not know if that was fortunate, or the most terrifying thing of all.

Sleep . . .

* * *

The little caravan prepared to depart in the blueish half-light of Beta dawn, with Alpha still a hint on the horizon, blocked by the peaks whose passes they would have to traverse. The mules had become inured to kzin scent — somewhat — and were loaded first, to proceed Tyra's skittish horses who were doubly disturbed by the smell of carnivore and the dead horses from yesterday's battle. Fading woodsmoke and coffee smells mixed with the crisp earthy scent of dew on the bushes, and the cries of birds and gliders cut a sharper undercurrent through the sound of the waterfall. That came into focus again, now that they were leaving it after so many months of labor.

"Done right well by us, this mountain," Hans said reflectively, strapping the packsaddle of his mule. "Wonder if it has a name? Not likely," he decided. "Too small." The little eroded volcanic peak was a midget among the Jotuns, even in the comparatively low hollow.

"Muttiberg," Tyra said, passing by with her saddle over her shoulder. The dog Garm pressed against her leg, casting another apprehensive look back at the two kzin. He had been trying to keep himself between her and them since she rode into camp, despite the flattened ears and tucked tail of intimidation. Kzinti were nightmares to canines, of course. "The locals call it the Mother Mountain — for obvious reasons."

Probably a man named them. This and the hill opposite did look like a woman's breasts, if you squinted and had the right attitude. Muttiberg.

"Let me give you a hand with that," Jonah said; then he was a little surprised at the weight of the saddle. *Strong for a Wunderlander,* he thought; but then, you could tell that from her build, almost like an Earther's.

Bigs lifted the life-capsule possessively. It was lighter than it should be, some application of gravity polarizer technology beyond current capacities, and opaque now as well. The whole assemblage had seemed to *ooze* through the wall of the spaceship, leaving no mark of its passage. For the first time in his life Bigs felt lust as a purely mental state, not just the automatic physical reaction to kzinrette pheromones. It was an oddly cerebral sensation, yet it had the same obsessive quality of excluding all other considerations. The tnuctip un-voice murmured in his ear, and he commanded them not to twitch. Only the slightest subvocalization was necessary to reply, too faint even for Spots's ears to catch.

He fitted the life capsule into one side of the pack saddle; the other was balanced with sacks of gold dust, worthless as dirt now. '*We have a means of converting matter into energy along a beam*,' the voice said. Bigs's mind blossomed with visions of monkey warships flashing into fireballs, galaxies of fire to light the triumphant passage of kzinti dreadnoughts. Planetary surfaces gouted upward, gnawing down to fortresses embedded in the crusts. '*Matter-energy conversion is also available as a power source.*' Fleets crossed between suns in days, weeks. Once or twice, no more, in the history of the Patriarchy a warrior — a Hero — had been adopted into the Riit clan, promoted to the inmost lairs. What reward would be great enough for Chotra-Riit, savior of the kzinti? What glory great enough for the one who brought the Heroic Race domination not merely over the monkeys, but over a galaxy as well? Man was not the only enemy of the Patriarchy. *None* of them could stand against the secrets of the tnuctipun. The Eternal Pride would sweep the whole spiral arm in a conquering rush.

Slaver dripped down from his thin black lips to the fur of his chest. He ignored it, taking the mule's bridle as tenderly as he might have borne up his firstborn son.

* * *

" . . . and so after Father was forced to leave on that crazy astrological expedition with Riao-Captain, Mutti had more and more trouble with the kzin," Tyra went on.

Jonah leaned his head closer, interest and concern on his face. They were strung out over rocky plateau country, following a faint trail upwards toward the nearest pass through the central Jotuns. The mountains curved away northeastward, this slightly-lower hilly trough between the main ranges heading likewise; directly east and south were the headwaters of the Donau, and the long road down to the fertile lowlands where Munchen lay. Tyra hesitated and went on; Jonah seemed to be that rare thing, a man who knew how to *listen*. Not to mention looking at you without salivating all the time, something that was more subtly flattering than open interest.

"She had not his strength of body. Or," she went on more slowly, "his strength of will — they were very close. So she must yield more to the kzinti, and the replacement for Riao-Captain was less . . . willing to listen, in any case. Things were growing worse all over Wunderland then; the war was going against the rat-cats, and they squeezed harder on the human population." She scowled. "Yet Mutti did her best; more than can be said for some others, who were punished less."

"I agree with you," Jonah said. "Your family seems to have gotten a raw deal. Mind you," he went on, "I wasn't here, dealing with the kzin occupation. That twists people's minds, and there's little justice in an angry man — or a frightened one."

She nodded, liking him better for the honesty than she would have for more fulsome support.

"In the meantime," he went on, lowering his voice, "I'm worried about our kzin here and now." He dropped into English, which was a language they shared and the sons of Chotrz-Shaa did not. "They're not acting normal."

Tyra blinked puzzlement. They had been sullen, true. "Kzinti are not supposed to be talkative or gregarious, are they?" she said.

"Tanj, no," Jonah said, taking a moment to fan himself with his hat. This high up the heat was dry rather than humid, but the pale volcanic dirt and scattered rocks threw it back like a molecular-film reflector.

"Bigs is surly even by kzin standards, but now he's downright *euphoric*. Not talking, but look at the way his fur ripples, and the way he holds his tail. Spots *is* talkative — for a kzin. Now he's miserable."

Tyra looked more closely. The smaller kzin was plodding along with back arched, the tip of his tail carelessly dragging in the dirt, even though it must be sore. His nose was dry-looking and there was a grayish tinge to its black, and his fur was matted and tangled, with burrs and twigs he had not bothered to comb out. Bigs's pelt shone, and his head was up, alert, eyes bright.

"It is a bad sign when a kzin neglects his grooming, isn't it?" she murmured.

"Very bad."

She glanced aside at him. "You know them very well. From having fought them so long?"

He shrugged. "I know these two," he said. "You have to be careful you don't anthropomorphize, but offhand I'd say Spots is thoroughly depressed and worried. I don't know if that worries me more than Bigs being so happy, or not."

Spots folded his ears. "Must you torture that thing?" he said to Hans, as the old man blew tentatively into his harmonica. "It screams well, but the pain to my ears is greater."

Off curled asleep around the canvass-wrapped

tnuctipun module, Bigs's ears twitched in harmony. His hands and feet were twitching as well, hunting in his sleep, and an occasional happy *mreeowrr* trilled from his lips.

Hans shrugged and put it away, picking up his cards. "Don't signify," he said mildly. "You want to bet?"

"Sniff this group of public-transit tokens," Spots snarled, throwing down his hand. "I fold. Count me out of the game." He stalked off into the night, tail lashing.

"Ratcats don't have the patience for poker," Hans observed. "Bids?"

"I fold too," Jonah said. Tyra had dropped out a round before.

"Neither do youngsters," Hans observed, showing his hand; three sevens. He raked in the pot happily. "Could be we'll all be very rich, but I never turn down a krona."

Jonah made a wordless sound of agreement and looked over at the girl. She was sleeping, curled up against her saddle with one hand tucked beneath her cheek. He smiled and drew the blanket up around her shoulders . . .

"*Awake!*" Spots shouted, rushing back into the circle of firelight on all fours.

Jonah leaped. Tyra awoke and stretched out a hand for her rifle in its saddle-scabbard; Garm growled and raised his muzzle.

The kzin kicked his brother in the ribs and danced back from the reflexive snap. "*Awake.* Are you injecting sthondat blood? Get ready!"

He turned to the humans. "A dozen riding beasts approached; their riders dismounted and are coming this way, a half-kilometer. They will be within leaping distance in a few minutes."

Bigs awoke sluggishly, shaking his head and licking at his nose and whiskers. Spots efficiently stripped the beamer from a pack-saddle and tossed it to his brother before freeing his own weapon. Jonah checked his rifle; Tyra and Hans were ready.

"Careful," he said. "These might be the bandits —
but they might not. We can't fight our way back to Nev
Friborg through a hostile countryside."

Spots snorted. "Who would be pursuing us but the
ones we fought, thirsty for blood and revenge?" he
said. Bigs was growling, a hand resting on the module.
Still, the smaller kzin licked his nose for greater
sensitivity and stood stretched upright, sniffing open-
mouthed.

"The wind favors us," he said after a moment. "And I
do not recognize any individual scents. That does not
mean these are not the ones we defeated — I had little
time to pay close attention then." He sounded disappointed, thwarted in his longing to lose himself in combat
and forget the decisions that had been oppressing him.

"Spread out and we'll see," Jonah said; it made no
sense to outline themselves against their campfire.
"No, leave the fire. If you put it out, they'd know we'd
spotted them."

Not bandits, was his first thought, as he watched
through his field glasses. The bandits had been in a
mismatch of bits of military gear and outbacker clothes.
These were in coarse cotton cloth and badly tanned
leather, with wide-brimmed straw hats and blanket-like
cloaks. Their weapons were a few ancient, beautifully-
tended chemical hunting rifles, and each man carried a
long curved knife, heavy enough to be useful chopping brushwood. *Tough looking bunch*, he thought, but
not particularly menacing. They stopped a hundred or
so yards out from the fire and called, a warning or hail.
He could not follow their thick backcountry dialect, but
Hans and Tyra evidently could. They stood and called
back, and Jonah relaxed.

"Act casual," Hans said as they all returned to the
fire. "These people are deep outback. They've got
peculiar ways." He frowned a little. "Don't think they'll
like we've got kzin with us."

The men did stiffen and bristle when they saw the silent red-orange forms on the other side of the fire, but they removed their hats and squatted none the less, their hands away from their weapons. One peered across the embers of the fire at Tyra and smiled, nudging the others. That brought a chorus of delighted, crook-toothed grins; the kzinti controlled themselves with a visible effort.

"I passed through their village," Tyra explained.

"What do they want?" Jonah asked.

Now that fear was gone it was a nagging ache to be delayed. They *must* get to Nev Friborg before Early and his cohorts could think up something else. Jonah never doubted for a moment that the bandits had had Early's backing, doubtless through his Nipponjin friends. The ID cards proved that, the forgery was far too good for hill-thieves to have managed.

"Got to handle the formalities first," Hans said. "Go on, light up."

The outbackers were passing around their pouch of tobacco; Jonah clumsily rolled a cigarette and passed it to Tyra, who managed the business far more neatly, even one-handed. She poured cups of coffee and handed them around as Hans filled his pipe, lit it with a burning stick from the fire and passed that likewise; the kzinti were pointedly ignored, crouching back with their eyes shining as red as the coals. Time passed in ritual thanks, in inquires about their health and that of their horses and mules, talk of the dry weather . . .

Tyra leaned forward intently as the real story came out. "They had a brush with our bandits," she said. "And — oh, Gott, no!"

Hans took up the story, listening intently; Jonah could catch no more than one word in three. "Sent some of their kids up-hill for safety. Ran into an ambush. Couple of men killed; they got the kids back, but they'd been hit with some sort of weapon they don't understand. The kids are alive and breathing, but they won't wake up."

Jonah's skin crawled. He relayed a few questions through the two Wunderlanders. "Neural disrupter," he said, when the villagers had answered. "Didn't know they had one — nasty thing, short-range but effective."

"They want — they want us to do something for them, heal the children," Tyra burst in. "What can we do?"

"Hmmm." Hans broke off to rummage through their medical kit. "Yep. That *might* work." He spoke to the headman of the strangers; they stood. "Wants us to come right away. That'd be better. Take a day or two to get to their settlement, two three days there."

Jonah opened his mouth to object — couldn't they call in to one of the lowland villages and get a doctor in by aircar? — and then shut his mouth again when Tyra looked at him. *Damn. Shame works where guilt wouldn't.*

Bigs felt no such objection; he shot to his feet, sputtering in the Imperative Mode of the Hero's Tongue, with his brother only half an expostulation behind. A dozen outbacker heads turned to the aliens like gun-turrets tracking, hands moving towards rifles and machetes. A sudden chill hit Jonah's stomach as he heard Bigs:

"We *will not* delay."

Even then, Jonah frowned in puzzlement. His command of the Hero's Tongue was excellent if colloquial, and he could have sworn that that had been in *Ultimate* Imperative Mode — which only the Riit, the family of the Patriarch, were entitled to use. Not that there was anything on Wunderland to stop Bigs using any grammatical constructions he pleased, but it was an unnatural thing for the big kzin to do. He was a traditionalist to a fault, that much had been clear for months. Spots stopped in mid-yowl to glance aside at him, confirming Jonah's hunch.

No matter. Both kzin were on the verge of fighting frenzy, and a very nasty little battle could break out at any second with a scream and leap. Garm backed up, bristling and barking hysterically; the kzinti ears twitched, and that was just the extra edge of hysteria that might set them off.

"*Shut* that damned dog up!" he barked. Tyra grabbed its collar and soothed it. "You two, you won't get extra speed by starting a battle now."

"What are the kittens of these feral omnivores to us?" Spots said, all his teeth showing. "You pledged to cooperate in this hunt with us, Jonah-human. And you were the one who said we risk failure with every minute of delay. Is the word of Man good, or is it not?"

A weight of meaning seemed to drop on that last phrase; Spots was watching him intently, not staring at the outbackers the way Bigs did. Jonah had a sudden leaden conviction that more rested on his decision than he could estimate.

"Look . . . " he began. Then an idea struck. "Tyra, these people, they're trustworthy?" An emphatic nod. "You and Hans are the ones with the medical training. You two go to the village; Spots and Bigs and I will take our . . . load on ahead. You can catch up — the outbackers will lend you a horse, surely, Hans."

Bigs' head jerked around to look at him, and his muzzle moved in the half-arcs of emphatic agreement. Spots brushed back his whiskers, as if confirming something to himself.

"That would be according to your oath," he said softly. "I apologize." Jonah was a little surprised; 'sorry' was something kzinti were reluctant to say, especially to other species.

The outbackers followed the exchange with wary eyes. Hans turned to them and spoke, then smiled at Jonah:

"As it turns out, young feller, they don't want our kzin anywhere near their place anyway. Just me and Fra Nordbo here are fine. We'll start right away, if that's all right with you. Sooner begun, sooner done."

Tyra rose. "Will you be all right?" she asked softly.
"We'll manage," Jonah replied.

"I do not have to account to you," Bigs said loftily.
"*Stop using that tense!*" Spots snapped in a hissing
whisper, glancing ahead to where Jonah walked beside
the lead mule. "Who contacted the Fanged God and
promoted you to royalty, Big-son of Chotrz-Shaa?"

"I am self-promoted," Bigs replied softly, but with no
particular effort to keep his voice down. "And the
Fanged God fights by my side. How else would the two
monkeys remove themselves? We will take the north-
eastern path, abandoning all but the beast necessary to
carry the capsule. Alone, we will make better time.
There is a kzin settlement at Arhus-on-Donau. We will
seek shelter there. We will *build* a means to get offplanet, or buy it — these monkeys will do anything for
money."

"You are self-befuddled!" Spots said. "*Fool.* What will
Jonah-human say to this?"

"It is what Durvash says that is important," Bigs said,
resting his hand on the module. "He becomes clearer
all the time."

Spots recoiled. "Now you, oh *patriarchal* warrior, take
orders like a slave from that little horror?"

Bigs bristled, suddenly swelling up and hulking over
his smaller sibling in dominance-display. Spots forced
himself to match it, letting his claws slide free.

"At least it is a carnivore, you . . . you *submitter-to-
omnivores*," Bigs grated. "Your breath stinks of grass!"

Spots's mouth gaped at the horrendous insult. All
their lives they had sparred and tussled for dominance,
insulting each other in the friendly fashion of non-
serious rivals. That was a blood libel.

"Is your oath nothing to you?" he grated.

"Oh, I will allow the monkey to fight me . . . barehanded," Bigs said, with a sly, horrible amusement in

the twitch of his ears and brows. "That fulfills the oath." He paused for effect. "What of *your* blood-obligation to the Patriarchy and the Heroic Race, Spots-Son of Chotrz-Shaa?"

Abruptly, Spots collapsed into a fur-flattened, droop-eared, limp-tailed puddle of misery. "I know," he muttered. "I am ripped in half! If you have forgotten your honor in madness, I have not. We are the last of the line of Chotrz-Shaa. Two lives and the life of our House we owe these monkeys. Your life to Jonah-human. Mine to a female! Yet we owe blood and honor to the Patriarch."

Bigs smirked, and Spots flared into a gape-jawed scream of rage: "*Stop whacking at my tail, fatherless sthondat-sucker!*"

He could see Jonah turning, alarmed at the sound, and he forced calm on himself with an effort greater than he had thought was in him.

"No killing by stealth," he finished, dropping into the Menacing Tense. "Or you die."

Bigs smirked again, and continued in the infuriating inflections of a Patriarch: "You will conspire with a monkey against your own sibling?"

"No. But I will not allow you to kill him."

A sneer, just showing the ends of the dagger incisor-fangs. "He is helpless as a kit at night."

"I will be watching."

"How long can you go without sleep, *brother*? I will feast on his liver yet." Bigs stalked off after the train of mules. As he came level with the last his hand rested on its pannier, and Spots could hear the edge of a whisper.

My tail is cold, he thought in panic. *What can I do? What can I do?*

Three nights later Spots watched desperately as Jonah prepared for sleep, tilting his broad-brimmed hat forward over his eyes; it was a bright night, alive with the shooting stars so common on Wunderland and with Beta Centauri overhead near the moon. The human gave him a puzzled look as he settled in, and then his breathing grew slow and steady, his heartbeat sounded like an ancient Conundrum Priest drum to Spots's straining ears. A heavy drum, regular, soothing. Heavy as his eyelids, so soothing as they dropped across dry and aching eyes, so pleasant. Making the ground soft like piled cushions, like piled cushions in the palazzo when he was young, and his father was crooning:

"Brave little orange kzin
Brave little spotted kzin,
Turn to the din
And if it makes you smile,
Leap
But if it is nothing at all
Really nothing at all
You may turn-in;
And droop your eyes while
You sleep."

Spots sighed and turned, drifting, content. Then shot half-erect, trembling, his fur laid tension-flat on the bones of face and body, tail out and rigid.

Bigs was halfway from his lair of blankets to Jonah, moving with ghost-lightness. Moonlight and Betalight glinted on the heavy blade of the wtsai in his hand. He caught his brother's eye and shrugged with fur and tail, grinned insolence, flared his nostrils.

I scent that which you do not. Slowly, insultingly, he sauntered back to his blankets, laid himself down. Then he yawned, a pink-and-white, curl-your-tongue yawn of drowsy contentment, stretching every limb separately and grooming a little. He circled, finding exactly the right position, and curled up with tail over nose. One eye remained open for a second, glinting at Spots from beneath the tufted eyebrow.

You were lucky. But I only have to be lucky once.

Spots whimpered, tongue dangling as he panted with envy and despair.

"Are you all right?"

Spots blinked. *What am I doing lying on the ground?* he thought.

The mule had stopped, pulling at the brushes nearby with a dry tearing sound as leathery leaves parted. One limb at a time, the kzin pulled himself up. Heavy, heavy, more heavy than the battle-practice in the old days, when their Sire worked them to exhaustion under kzin-normal gravity in the exercise room of the palace. Something seemed to hold his hands to the dry packed soil, and pains shot up his back as he stood and squinted into the bright daylight. He ran his fingers through the tangled mass of his mane, and hanks and knots of hair came loose, the furnace wind snatched it from him and scattered the long orange hairs on the air, on the dirt, on the scrubby bushes and sparse grass. He stood, dully staring after them.

"Are you all *right*?" Jonah asked again. Then he recoiled hastily from the vicious snap that nearly ripped open his arm. "If that's the way you want it," he said, tight-lipped, and went back to the lead mule.

Bigs's ears smirked as he came by, his hand on the capsule. He never left it, now. "Soon we will camp for the night," he jeered. "Won't it be good to sleep?" More seriously: "It will be for the best, brother."

"I have no brother," Spots rasped, and stumbled forward to take the reins of his mule.

Even the scream hardly woke Spots. His eyes were crusted and blurred even when he opened them. The savage discord of metal on metal jarred him to some semblance of consciousness, and the scent of hot fresh-shed blood. He stumbled erect, mumbling, and stepped forward. The raw-scraped tip of his tail fell across the white ash crust that covered the embers of the fire, and he shot half a dozen meters into the air, screeching.

When he came down, he could see. Bigs's first leap had failed, and Jonah had gotten out of his blankets and erect. Now the two were circling; Jonah had a four-furrowed row of deep scratches across his chest, and the very tip of Bigs's tail was missing. The wtsai gleamed in the kzin's hand, and Jonah had his arm-long cutter-bar whistling in a figure-eight between them. Totally focused, Bigs lunged forward. Density-enhanced steel shrieked against the serrated edges of the bar and Bigs danced back, smooth and fast. There was a ragged notch in the blade of his honor knife, and his snarl grew more shrill. For a moment Spots thought desperately that his brother would walk the narrow path of honor, weapon against weapon.

"Get back," Bigs flung over his shoulder, reaching for the strakkaker at his waist.

The world stood still for Spots. *I owe my life to Jonah-human. I owe my life to the Patriarch. This is my brother. That is my—* There was no more time for thought.

Spots screamed and leaped. "*No!*" he howled. His leap carried him onto the larger kzin's back.

There was nothing wrong with Bigs's reflexes. Even as Spots fastened on to him with all sixteen claws he ducked his head between his shoulders to avoid the killing bite to the back of the neck and threw himself backward, stabbing with reversed wtsai. The blade scored along Spots's massive ribcage, but there was no soft unarmored midsection to a kzin body. He twisted to lock the arm as they rolled, accepting the savage battering and the pain as they rolled across the campfire, fangs probing deeper and deeper through fur ruff and into the huge muscles of Bigs's neck. Groping for the vulnerable spine, to drive a spike into the nerve.

Jonah stepped forward, cutter bar raised to strike in a chop that would have cut through Bigs's torso to the hearts. To the hormone-speeded reflexes of the battling kzinti, the movement might as well have been in slow motion. A full-armed swipe of Bigs's free hand caught him across face and neck and shoulder, sending him spinning limp to the ground in a shower of flesh. In a tuck-and-roll that was a continuation of the same movement Bigs levered his brother off his back and sent him a dozen meters away. They screamed together and met in a flowing curve of both their leaps, mouths open in the killing gape, hands and feet ripping and tearing and stabbing. Rolling over and over in a blurred mass of orange fur, blood, distended eyes, flashing steel and gleaming inch-long fangs.

Spots's grip on his brother's knife-wrist weakened, the claw-grip on his throat choking him until his eyes bulged almost out of their deep-set sockets. Stronger and fresher, the muscles of the short thick arm straining against his were as irresistible as a machine. Pain shot through his hand as his thumb popped out of its socket, and then something cold and very hot at the same time lanced into his body. Gray swam before his eyes as vision narrowed down to the killgrin of his brother's face, then winked out.

Sleep, he told himself. *You fought to the death.*

Victory was cold and pain and nausea, after the first liver-jolting flash of adrenaline. Bigs staggered away, away from the body that lay at his feet with blood bubbling on its chest-fur, blood in mouth and nose and eyes where his teeth had savaged it. He threw away the broken hilt of his wtsai and gave a sobbing shriek of grief and triumph at the risen moon.

"I have killed my brother. *Howl for God!*" His brother, guardian of his back in the tussles of childhood. Last son of Chotrz-Shaa beside himself.

"Not now," the voice whispered in his ears. "You have work to do. Gather the equipment. Bury the bodies. We must move."

Bigs shook his head as if shaking off water, clawing at his own ear. The little implant seemed impossible to dislodge; sometimes these days in evil dreams he felt that it was growing tendrils into his brain from his ear. Pain shot through his head at the thought.

"Nonsense. Now, get to work."

Howling again, Bigs beat fists on the capsule until the mule reared and kicked and nearly escaped. Then he seized the halter and dragged it after him into the night. He must run, like Warlord Chmee, run from his guilt. Had not Chmee broken an oath for ultimate power? He must *run*.

"Stop, you brainless savage! Obey!" The pain again, but Bigs ignored it.

"I did it for the Heroic Race!" he screamed into the night. "None shall command us. No more monkey arrogance. *I did it for you, my brother!*" His grief rose shrill, a huge sound that daunted even the *advokats* pack that had come to prowl at the edge of sight, attracted by the blood. Dragging the mule behind him, Large-Son of Chotrz-Shaa ran into the darkness.

The pain in his head was continuous now. Sometimes he felt as if his brain were being dragged out, and he found himself walking in a circle to the left, head bent to his shoulder. When it lessened, he was conscious of the voice again. It was daylight, but he was uncertain of the day. They were over the pass, and the ground on either side was covered in long grass, with patches of trees on the higher slopes. The cool damp scent from the lowlands spread out below him was like a benediction in his nostrils; there was no sight of Man, not even of his herdbeasts.

"Very well," Durvash said. "We will proceed straight.

That pack of scavengers probably finished them off in any case. No time may be spared to go back, in any case."

Bigs mumbled something. He felt he should resent the tone; did the ancient revenant not know he was speaking to a Conquest Hero? Soon to be the greatest of all Conquest Heroes? Yet the emotion was far away, as if muffled behind a thick layer of sherrek fur. Why was his mind wandering so? Great chunks of time seemed to be missing, and sometimes his vision would blur like a badly adjusted holoscreen. It kept the grief at bay, though. With that he began to weep, an *eeeuuureuee* sound.

"My brother fought for me when the older kits pulled my nose," he mumbled to himself. "I grew bigger, but he never quarreled with me." Not enough to really draw blood. "We shared our first kzinrett." An under-the-grass transaction with a warrior needing quick cash to cover a gambling debt. "We —"

"Silence."

"Urr-urrr— " Bigs's throat would not work any more, and he found he had lost interest in speaking.

Well, now I know how the implant will work on these kzin, Durvash thought sourly. *Badly.* It had been designed to use on thrint and thrintun slave species, of course, with multiband capacity. Kzinti seemed very resistant to pain-center stimulus, and on a strange species the control of volitional routines was impossibly coarse.

Report, he thought/ordered the autodoc system. Impatiently, he ran through the diagnostic and came to the conclusion. *Prepare to decant me,* he told it. Warnings flashed, but he overrode. The autodoc would be priceless as part of his breeding program, since it was capable of acting as an artificial womb, but he must not run down the base supplies of organic molecules for recombinant synthesis before he was sure of obtaining more. The local biochemistry was unlikely to have all a tnuctipun metabolism required.

Besides, I am hungry and mad to see the sky, to smell fresh air again. If he was to be reborn into this new world, let his fangs and tongue take seizin of it.

"I will emerge," he said to the kzin. It stood apathetic, eyes dull; he ordered the machine to jolt its pleasure centers and relax forebrain restriction, and awareness returned to the big golden eyes. "Where are we?"

"Near . . . hrreeawho, how did we come here so fast? Where is . . . we are near Neu Friborg, I think. We are there, I think."

It lifted the module to the dirt and sank exhausted to the ground. Fluid began to cycle out of Durvash's lungs, and he wrapped his lips against the pain.

CHAPTER EIGHTEEN

Something was biting his tail.

Spots groaned and tried to open his eyes, but they were gummed together. The biting stopped, and water fell across his face. He heard shouting. Feebly, he scrubbed at his eyes with a wrist, and blinked back to wakefulness. An *advokat* slinked in the middle distance, huge jaws working, matted pelt stinking of carrion.

Jonah-human was looking down at him, from a safe distance, canteen in hand. Matted blood covered one side of his face, and fresh blood glistened on clumsy bandages around his neck and one arm. They glanced aside from each other's eyes, and the human stepped forward and sank down by the kzin's side.

"Got to stop the bleeding," he rasped. "Here, drink."

Spots lapped water from his cupped palm, and then seized the canteen to guzzle with his thin lips wrapped awkwardly around the spout. He coughed and felt tearing pain in his chest; water spurted out of his mouth. Looking down, he could see the bright gleam of steel among the tangled red mass of his flank.

"It is not as bad as it looks," he wheezed, after taking a careful deep breath. "See, the steel must have turned aside and snapped on the ribs — thanks to your cutter bar, which weakened it. My lungs are not pierced, nor my intestines." He licked at his nostrils and sniffed again. "I would smell that."

"Could be stuff inside hanging on by a thread," Jonah said worriedly.

"I will survive while you pursue the oath-breaker,"

Spots said grimly. Then the voice broke into a howl of woe.

"Not until we get you to help. This *would* happen while Hans and Tyra are away with the medkit . . . that'll be the closest place. You can lean on one of the mules, I can catch them. I think."

My sibling attacked him dishonorably, yet he will forego revenge to save my life, Spots thought. *I am ashamed.*

"First," he said aloud, "you'll have to get this out of me."

Jonah blanched as he looked down at the knifeblade. The stub of it moved with every breath.

"We really *should* get under way," Tyra urged, with a sigh.

"Yep. Figure we should."

Hans smiled beatifically, and leaned back in the hammock. His was strung between two orange trees, and a few blossoms had fallen across his grizzled face. He brushed them aside and took another sip of the drink in his hollowed-out pineapple. There was rum in it, and cherries and cream and a few other things — passionfruit, for example — and it helped to make the warmth quite tolerable. So did the tinkling stream which flowed down the narrow valley under the over-hanging cliff, and the shade of the palm trees. Hans Shwartz had been a grown man when the kzinti came; he was into his second century now, and even with good medical care your bones appreciated the warmth after so much hard work. The air buzzed with bees, scented with flowers.

"Thank you, sweetling," he said, as a girl handed him a platter of fried chicken; it had fresh bread on the side, and a little woven bowl of hot sauce for dipping. The girl smiled at him, teeth and green eyes and blond hair all bright against her tanned skin. Someone who looked like her twin sister was cutting open a watermelon for them. Not far away in a paddock grazed six horses, three for him and three for Tyra, and they had been turning down gifts of pigs and sheep and household tools for a solid day now.

"These are sweet people," Tyra said, as the girl handed her a plate as well.

"No argument," Hans said, gesturing with a drumstick. The batter on it was cornmeal, delicately spiced; he bit into the hot fragrant meat with appreciation. "They need some help, though. Someone to guide them through the next few years, getting back into contact with things. Otherwise they'll be taken advantage of."

"True enough," Tyra said, more somberly. "I was surprised at you, the way you diagnosed those children and managed the treatment." Her young eyes were guileless, but shrewd. "What *did* you do before the conquest, Freeman Shwartz?"

"This and that, this and that," Hans said, repelling her curiosity with mild firmness. The youngsters were all up and about, although they would need further therapy. Unfortunately, that would cost; it would be some time before Wunderland could afford planetary health insurance again.

"And we *should* get going; I'm worried about Jona — about Freeman Matthieson, alone with those kzin."

Hans suppressed a smile. His tolerant amusement turned to concern as the headman of the village dashed up, sweating, his eyes wide.

"Your friend," he gasped out. "Your young friend — and one of the accursed ratcats — they are here. They are hurt!"

Hans tossed his plate and drink aside, yelling for his medkit as he landed running down the pathway. Tyra was ahead of him, her long slim legs flashing through the borrowed sarong.

* * *

"Finagle, there is a heaven after all," Jonah murmured.

The cool cloth sponged at his face and neck as he looked up through matted lashes at Tyra's face. Sheer relief made him limp for long moments, his head lolling in her lap. *A man could get used to this*, he thought.

Then: "Spots!"

"He's all right," Tyra said. "In better shape than you, actually. The locals were a bit leery of having him in the village, but they put up a shelter for him and Hans has been working on him."

"Speak of *der teufel*," Hans said, ducking throught the doorway of bamboo sections on string. "Aren't you sitting pretty, young feller," he added. Tyra blushed slightly and set Jonah's head back on the pillow.

"Your furry friend is fine, as far as I can tell," the old man went on. "Growling and muttering about that brother of his."

"Who nearly killed both of us," Jonah said grimly.

He felt at the side of his face; the swellings were gone, and his fingers slid over the slickness of spray-skin. From the slightly distant feel from within, he was on painblockers, but not too heavily.

"He *would* have killed me, if Spots hadn't jumped him." Jonah shook his head. "I'm surprised. Usually, if a kzin swears a formal oath, they'll follow it come core-collapse or memory dump; look at the way Spots stood up for me. I can see Bigs challenging me, but to try and kill me in my sleep — "

"Temptation can do funny things to a mind, human or non," Hans said shrewdly. "Seem to remember one feller who wouldn't believe there was a fuzzball under a rock, on account of temptation."

Jonah flushed, conscious of Tyra's curiosity. "When will I be ready to ride?" he said.

"Not for a week at least," Tyra said firmly.

Hans tugged at his whiskers. "Funny you should

ask; Spots said the same thing, more or less." His button blue eyes appraised the younger man. "Neither of you was infected." Wunderland bacteria were not much of a threat to humans; the native biochemistry lacked some elements essential to Terrestrial life, and vice versa. "He's healing real fast, seems to be natural for him. You're dehydrated, and those cuts shouldn't be put under much strain, sprayskin or no. Say three days, minimum."

"One," Jonah said grimly. He held up a hand at Tyra, stopping her before the words left her lips. "It's not just what we — Montferrat — could do with the knowledge. It's what that tnuctipun could do, once it's out of its bottle. I think we badly underestimated it. I believe it's controlling Bigs, somehow. Control, hypnosis. Maybe what the Thrintun do for all I know. That thing is a deadly danger every instant it's free, never *mind* what the government or the ARM would do with it. I think it would be better if the ARM *does* get it. Maybe they can dispose of it."

Hans nodded. "Can't say as I like it, but you're talking sense," he said.

Slowly, reluctantly, Tyra nodded too. "I might have expected boldness like that from you," she murmured.

"Tanj. It's common sense."

"Which is not common."

Bigs shook his head again, trying to clear the stuffed-wool feeling. It refused to go away, even though he was thinking more clearly again. More calmly, at least. The mule-beast brayed in his ear, then shied violently when he threatened its nose with outstretched claws.

Stupid beast, he thought with a snarl, then exerted all his strength to haul it down again and hold it back; they were both very thirsty, but he could not let it run to the little watercourse ahead. *It is does not even have enough brains to obey through fear.* The ruined manor-house was half a kilometer ahead, and Neu Friborg beyond that. He would rest for the day in the ruins, and help Durvash when he emerged from the autodoc. Then he would pass the town in the dark and walk down the trail to Munchen until he could buy a ride on a vehicle.

"And abandon this stinking, stupid mule-beast," he muttered to himself.

With grim patience he led it down the steep clay bank to the slow-moving creek and moved upstream, throwing himself down to lap. It was the ground-scent that alerted him, since the wind was in his face. That and the clatter of pebbles as feet walked the bank behind him. He was up and turning in a flash, but his feet and hands were further away than they should have been, and he shook his head fretfully again. *Spots. I smell Spots. Stand by me, brother. Bare is a back without brother to guard it.* Spots was dead, he remembered, and forced his fur to bottle out.

Four humans, all armed but scruffy and hungry-looking, their ribs standing out. The leader-beast a taller one with heavy facial pelt and the remains of a swollen belly. Bigs grinned and waited.

"Hey, what's a ratcat doing here outback?" the leader asked. The voice had a haunting familiarity, except that the stuffing in his head got in the way.

"Nice mule," one of the others said, examining the beast. It snapped at him, and he slapped its nose down with an experienced hand. "Hey, good saddle too."

Bigs snarled. "Away from my possessions, monkeys," he said, backing toward the animal and retreating slightly to keep all the humans in his field of vision. They were ambling forward, not seeming to spread out deliberately but edging around behind him all the same. His head swivelled.

"Hey, that's not polite!" the big manbeast said, grinning insolently. "You shouldn't call us monkeys no more, on account of we kick your hairy asses."

Bigs felt fury build within him and his tail stiffen,

then inexplicably drain away. *I must dominate them*, he told himself.

"We just poor bush-country men. You got any money? That's a fine strakkaker you got, and a nice beamer. Maybe I recognize the beamer — maybe we had one like it a while ago, before my luck got bad?" The leader's face convulsed. *"Maybe Ed Gruedermann should boot some head, hey?"*

"Get back!" Bigs said. The monkeys continued their slinking, sidling advance.

His hand blurred to the strakkaker, and he pivoted to spray the monkey nearest Durvash, he would turn and cut them all down. The weapon clicked and crackled — there was sand in the muzzle! He crouched to leap, but something very cold flashed across the small of his back. Something huge, like his father's hand, slapped him across the left side of his head, and he was falling. Falling for a very long time. Then he was lying, and he hurt very much, but his head seemed clear.

"Forgive me, brother," he whispered. Soft hands reached down out of time to lift and hold him, and a tongue washed his ears. A voice crooned wordlessly. He closed his eyes, and welcomed the long fall into night.

"Hey, Ed — look at that!"

Ed Gruederman glanced over to where a rifle muzzle prodded the huge wound on the dead kzin's head, right where his left ear would have been. Silvery threads were lifting out of the blood and grey matter, almost invisibly thin, twisting and questing in the light. He slid his cleaned machete back into the sheath behind his right hip and walked over to the mule.

"Get back from that, you scheissekopf," he called to the man by their victim. *Stupid ratcat, not to think we had a sniper ready.* "That's some kzin shit, it may be catching, you know, like a fungus."

The bandit jumped back and leveled his rifle, firing an entire cassette into the dead carnivore. When it clicked empty the torso had been cut in half, but the tendrils still waved slowly.

"Watch it, fool, we're close to town — you want them to hear us and call the mounted police?" Then: "Yazus Kristus!"

They all crowded around, until he beat them back with his hat. "Gold," he said reverentially, lifting one of the plastic sacks from that side of the packsaddle.

They all recognized it, of course. Nobody could be in their line of work in the Jotuns and not recognize gold dust; for one thing, nothing else was that heavy for its size. They counted the bags, running their hands over them until their leader lashed the tarpaulin back.

"Ten, fifteen thousand krona," one muttered. "Oh, the verguuz and bitches I can buy with this."

"Buy with your share, if Ed Gruedermann can keep your shitty head on your sisterfucking shoulders that long," their leader replied. "Back! There's an assessor's office in Neu Friborg. We'll stop there and get krona and sell the mule, and then head for Munchen or Arhus-on-Donau, the Jotuns is no place for an honest man these days — too many police. Look at them, letting ratcats wander around attacking humans."

That brought grins and laughter. "What's this, boss?" one asked, lifting the smooth featureless egg that balanced the mule's load."

It shifted in his arms, and he dropped it with a cry of surprise. That turned to horror as it split open, and a spindly-limbed creature rose shakily from the twin halves; it was spider thin, blue-black and rubbery with three crimson eyes and a mouthful of teeth edged like a saw.

"Scheisse!" the bandit screamed. The mobile lips moved, perhaps in the beginning of *wait*.

The motion never had time to complete itself. A dozen rounds tore the little creature to shreds, until

Gruedermann shouted the bandits into sense — they were in more danger from each other's weapons than from whatever-it-was. Even then three of them hacked it into unrecognizable bits with their machetes. Their fear turned to terror as the twin halves of the egg began to glow and collapse on themselves.

"We get out of here," Gruedermann said. "The *advokats* will take care of the bodies." There were always a pack of them around a human settlement, waiting for garbage to scavenge, impossible to exterminate. "Come on. Money is waiting."

"Not more than an hour or so," Jonah said, with an odd sense of anticlimax. *And yes*, he thought. *Sadness.* The mangled remains of the tnuctipun were pathetically fragile in the bright light of Alpha Centauri. *To come so far, so long, for this. There Ain't No Justice.*

Tyra shied a stone at a lurking *advokat* that lingered, torn between greed and cowardice. It yelped and ran back a few paces; tears streaked her face.

"Come look at this!" Hans said sharply. He reached down with a stick and turned the dead kzin's head to one side. Not much of the soft tissue was left after the *advokat* pack, but for some reason they had avoided the shattered bone.

Spots began a snarl of anger, then stopped as he saw what was revealed. The others stood beside him, watching the silver tendrils move in their slow weaving. Hands probed with the stick; several of the threads lashed towards it and clung for a moment. A button-sized piece of the same material was embedded in the shattered remains of Bigs' inner ear.

"Stand back," Spots said, unslinging his beamer.

None of the others quarreled with that; they crowded back with the gaping outbackers as the kzin stood on the edge of the creekbank and fanned a low-set beam across the bodies until nothing was left but calcinated ash. The tendrils of the device in his brother's brain shriveled in the heat, and the central button exploded with a small *fumf* of released pressure. Spots kept up the fire until the wet clay was baked to stoneware, then threw the exhausted weapon aside.

"That . . . *thing* explains a good deal," Jonah said; Tyra nodded, reached out an hand and then withdrew it.

"I am owed a debt of vengeance by a race three billion years dead," Spots said, in a voice that might have been of equal age. "How shall I requite it?"

"There's a debt of vengeance only about three hours hold," Hans said sharply. "Those tracks are heading for Neu Friborg."

"Let's do it then," Jonah said grimly. "Let's *go*."

"Hey, it's a good mule," Ed Gruedermann said. "But we don't need it any more — we had good luck up in the mountains."

His men were on their best behavior; grinning like idiots with their hats clasped to their chests, and keeping their mouths silent the way he had told them. Gruedermann felt a swelling of pride at their discipline; he'd had to boot plenty of head to get them so well-behaved. A big crowd had gathered around the mule with the unbalanced load as the four of them led it into town. Well, nothing ever happened in little arse-pimple outback towns like this, even if it did have a weekly run down to the lowlands. Fine well-set men like themselves were an event. He caught the eye of a young woman, scowling when she looked away.

"This the assessor's office?" he said. It should be, the best building in the town and the only one of prewar rockmelt construction.

"Ja."

A young girl of ten or so had slid under the mule, examining the girth and then running a hand down the neck. She seemed interested in the bar-code brand;

not many of those out in the hills, he guessed. Then she ran up the stairs into the building.

"How long did you say you'd been up in the Jotuns?" a man said, his tone friendly.

The crowd was denser now; Gruederman felt a little nervous, after so long in the bundu, but he kept his smile broad, even when he felt a plucking at his belt. Nothing there for a pickpocket to get, but in a few hours he'd be *rich*. With luck, he might be able to shed the others before he got to Munchen and cashed the assessor's draft. Pickings were slim in the Jotuns these days. From what he heard, Munchen was a wide-open town with plenty of opportunities for a man with a little ready capital and not too many foolish scruples.

A woman in a good suit came down the steps with the little girl and touched a reader to the mule's neck.

"That's the one," she said quietly.

Danger prickled at Gruedermann's spine. He shouted and leaped back, reaching for his machete. It was gone, hands gripped him, the honed point of his own weapon pricked behind his ear. He rolled his eyes wildly. All his men were taken, only one had unslung his weapon and it was wrestled away before he could do more than fire a round into the air. The crowd pushed in with a guttural animal snarl.

"Kill the bandits!" someone shouted.

The snarl rose, then died as the woman on the steps shouted and held up her hands:

"This is a civilized town, under law," she said firmly. "Put them in the pen — tie them, and two of you watch each of them. We'll call the police patrol back, they can't have gone far."

"Take your hands off me!" Gruedermann screamed, as rawhide thongs lashed his wrists behind his back and a hundred hands pushed him through the welded steel bars of the livestock pen. "You can't do this to me!" He spat through the bars, snapping his teeth at an unwary hand and hanging on until a stick broke his nose. "Motherfuckers! Kzinshit eaters!"

He screamed and spat through the strong steel until the square emptied.

"What do we do now, boss?" one of the men asked, from his slumped position on the floor of the cage.

"We fuckin' *die*," Gruedermann shouted, kicking him in the head. His skull bounced back against the metal; it rang, and the bandit fell senseless.

Neu Friborg seemed deserted in the early evening gloaming, as Jonah and his party rode down the rutted main street. He stood in the saddle — painfully, since riding was not something a singleship pilot really had to study much — and craned his neck about. He could hear music, a slow mournful march, coming from the sidestreet ahead, down by the church.

A little ahead of the riders, Spots lifted his head and sniffed. "They are there," he said flatly. "Also a large crowd of monke — of humans. Many armed. They do not smell of fear, most of them; only the ones we hunt."

"Odd," Jonah said.

He swung down from the saddle. *Finagle, but that beast was trying to saw me in half from the crotch up,* he thought. It had been downright embarrassing in front of Tyra, who seemed to have been born in the saddle from the way she managed it. She'd said something, about how a spacer must know more *real* skills than riding, though . . . *quite a woman.*

"Cautious but polite," Jonah said, leading the way. "Remember that." For Spots' benefit; the kzin seemed to be in a fey mood, bloodthirsty as usual but *relieved*. Perhaps that his brother hadn't broken an oath entirely under his own power, although Jonah suspected the tall kzin had been a willing victim at the start. The temptation was simply too great. *There are times when I think Early is right,* he mused. *But they never last.*

The little laneway opened out into a churchyard, and a field beyond that; the crowd stood in an arc about the outer wall of the graveyard. There, outside the circle of consecrated ground, four men were digging graves. A double file of armed men and women faced them, with Provisional Gendarmerie brassards. Seeing the genuine article, Jonah wondered how he could have been taken in by the bandits, even for a moment. He also decided that the mounted police were decidedly more frightening than the freelance killers had ever been. Beside him, Tyra checked for a moment at the sight of the tall crop-haired blond officer who led the firing party.

Jonah scanned the slab-sided *Herrenmann* face, and reluctantly conceded the family resemblance. *If you subtract all the humor and half the brains*, he decided. Aloud, in a whisper:

"Your brother?"

"Ib," she confirmed.

One of the digging men swung his shovel too enthusiastically, and a load of dirt ended up in the middle grave. The man there climbed out and leaned over to swat the culprit with his hat, cursing with imaginative obscenity. Hans shaped a soundless whistle.

"Seems the Provisionals got in before us," he said. "Can't say as I'm sorry."

"Neither am I," Jonah said.

"*I* am," Spots grinned.

The bandits stood in front of the graves they had dug. The rifles of the squad came up and Ib Nordbo's hand swung down with a blunt finality.

Whack. The bodies fell backward, and dust spurted up from the adobe wall of the churchyard behind. A sighing murmur went over the watching townsfolk, and they began to disperse. The Gendarmerie officer cleaved through them like a walking ramrod, marching up to the little party of pursuers.

"So," he said, with a little inclination of his head. "Sister."

"Brother," she replied, standing a little closer to Jonah. Ib's pale brows rose.

"This is most irregular," he said, and turned to Jonah, ignoring the kzin and Hans as an obvious commoner. "You are the owner of the stolen mule and gold?"

"We are," Jonah said with a nod.

"You understand, everything must be impounded pending final adjudication," he said crisply. "Proper reports must be filed with the relevant — why are you laughing?"

"You wouldn't understand," Jonah wheezed. Beside him, Tyra fought hiccups, and Hans' face vanished into a nest of wrinkles. Even Spots flapped his ears, although his teeth still showed a little as he watched the work-crew shovel the dirt in on the dead bandits.

"Ah, life," Jonah said at last; twin red spots of anger stood out on the young policeman's cheeks. "Tanj. And now, we'd like a line to Herrenmann Claude Montferrat-Palme, and transport to Munchen — *if* you please, Herrenmannn Leutnant Nordbo."

"Except for me," Hans said, turning his horse's head. He leaned down to shake hands. "Goin' back. These people, they need me. You know where to reach me — always more fried chicken and rum for visitors!"

Jonah began to laugh again as the old man touched a heel to his horse and the outbackers fell in behind him.

"One happy ending at least," he said.

"Oh, perhaps more," Tyra said.

"Perhaps," Spots murmured.

• CHAPTER NINETEEN

Buford Early's laughter rolled across the broad veranda of the Montferrat-Palme manor. Evening had fallen, purple and dusky across the formal gardens, still with a trace of crimson on the terraced vineyards and coffee fields in the hills beyond. The ARM general leaned back in his chair, puffing at his cigar until it was a red comet in the darkness. The others looked at him silently; Montferrat calm and sardonic as always, Jonah stony-faced, Tyra Nordbo openly hostile. Only Harold Yarthkin and his wife seemed to be amused as well, and they were not so closely involved in this matter. With the human-style food out of the way Spots had joined them, curled in one of the big wicker chairs with saucers of Jersey cream and cognac, still licking his whiskers at the memory of the live zianya that had somehow, miraculously, been found for him.

"Glad you're happy," Harold said sardonically, pouring himself a glass of verguuz and clipping the end off a cigar.

"Why shouldn't I be?" Early said. "An excellent dinner — it always is, here, Herrenmann Montferrat-Palme — "

"Please, Claude."

" — Claude. And fascinating table talk, also as usual. Politics aside, I enjoy the company here more than I have on Earth for a long, long time. But you said you had something to negotiate! It seems to me you've wound this affair up very neatly, and just as I would have wanted. All the evidence buried or gone, the bandits conveniently dead, and nothing of the tnuctipun but rumors. You might," he added to Jonah, "consider writing this up as a holo script. It'd make a good one."

"Not my field," the ex-pilot said with a tight smile.

"You're forgetting something, my dear fellow," Montferrat said with wholehearted enjoyment. "You know the *approximate* location of the tnuctipun spaceship. We know the *exact* location, and as you love to point out, you don't believe in swift direct action. We can get to it before you can — in fact, we just *might* have secured and moved it already. In which case you could look forever, it's a big planet. Treasure-trove law is clearly on our side too, for what that's worth. We could decipher some of those secrets you're so afraid of, and send them off — to We Made It and Jinx, for example. Think of the joy you'd have trying to suppress it *there*."

"No joy at all," Early sighed, taking the cigar out of his mouth and concentrating on the tip. "I don't suppose an appeal to your sense of responsibility for interstellar stability . . . no. You *might* try not to be so gleeful," he went on. "What terms did you have in mind?"

"Well, my young friends here — " Montferrat nodded at Jonah, Tyra and the kzin "— and their rather older friend back in the outback, have all gone to a great deal of trouble and expense. I think they should be compensated. To about the extent of a hundred thousand krona each, after tax."

"Agreed," Early said, sounding slightly surprised. "What's the *real* price?"

"Well, in addition, you might get the blacklisting on Jonah removed — and have him and Fra Nordbo given security clearance for interstellar travel."

Tyra's face lit up with an inner glow at the ARM general's nod.

"And?" he said with heavy patience, sipping at his cognac.

"And you go home. Or to another star system, but you get out of Alpha Centauri."

Early laughed again, more softly, and set the snifter down. "I hope you don't think I'm the only agent the . . . ARM has?" he said.

Jonah cut in: "No. But you're the smartest — or if you're not, we're hopeless anyway. It's a start."

"It will win me time, which I will use," Montferrat added.

Early sat in silence, puffing occasionally, while the sun set finally; the stars came out, and a quarter moon, undimmed by Beta Centauri. A flash of shooting stars lit up the night, ghostly soft lightning across the hills and the faces of humans and the kzin.

"More time than you might expect," he said. "Bureaucracies tend to get slower as they age, and mine . . . " More silence. "Agreed," he said. "It's time for me to move on, anyway. I'm getting too well known here. Lack of discretion was always my besetting sin. There's still the war — we have to organize the ex-kzin slave worlds we're taking as reparations — and doubt-less other work will be found for me. *Ich deinst*, as they say." He looked over at Montferrat. "Checkmate — for now," he said, rising and extending his hand.

"For now," Montferrat agreed. "Harold here to hold the stakes?"

"Agreed; we can settle the details at our leisure." He bowed to the ladies, an archaic gesture he might have picked up on Wunderland. Or not, if he was what they suspected. "And now, I won't put a damper on your vic-tory celebrations."

He strolled like a conqueror out to the waiting aircar, the stub of his cigar a comet against the night as he threw it away and climbed through the gullwing door. The craft lifted and turned north and west, heading for Munchen, an outline covering a moving patch of stars.

"I doubt he's going to accept defeat gracefully," Jonah said, sipping moodily at his coffee. Montferrat had winced a bit when the younger man dumped his cognac into it. "Especially when he discovers the interior of the spaceship melted down into slag when the tnuctipun bastard died."

"The hull alone is a formidable secret; he'll have the satisfaction of putting that in the archives," Montferrat said judiciously. "You know, I could almost pity him."

That brought the heads around, even Spots's. "Why?" Harold demanded, pulling himself out of reverie.

"Because he's so able, and so determined — and his cause is doomed to *inevitable* defeat," Montferrat said. At their blank looks, he waved his cigarillo at the stars.

"*Look* at them, my friends. We can count them, but we cannot really know how many. The number is too huge for our minds to grasp! With the outsider's gift of the hyperdrive, we have access to them all — and the kzinti will too, in their turn, you cannot keep a law of nature secret forever, despite what the ARM thinks."

His voice deepened. "The universe is too *big* to understand; vastly too big to control even by the most subtle and powerful means, even this little corner of it we call Known Space. There is an age of exploration coming — as it was in the Renaissance, or the twenty-first century. Nothing can stop it. Nothing can stop what we — all the sentient species — will do, and venture, and become. *That* is why I pity Buford Early — and why I never despair of *our* cause, no matter how bleak the situation looks. Tactically we may lose, but strategically, we *cannot*."

Jonah looked thoughtful, and Harold grinned across his basset-hound face. Tyra Nordbo laughed, and leaned forward to put a hand on his arm. The jewels in her tiara glistened amid the artfully-arranged piles of blond hair, and the shimmering silk of her gown clung.

"Thank you for everything," she said.

"Nonsense," he said, watching Jonah's gaze on her, warm and fond. *Bless you, my children*, he thought sardonically. *And if I wasn't a middle-aged eighty and didn't have commitments elsewhere, you wouldn't have a chance, Jonah the Hero.*

"The *stars*," she said. "For both of us."

"Perhaps," Montferrat said. "Someday."

"Someday."

Jonah laughed. "Myself, after the past couple of years, I'm not so sure I'll ever want to leave the confines of Greater Munchen again."

Tyra laughed, but Montferrat had a suspicion the Sol Belter might mean what he said; he sounded very tired, at a level below the physical.

"May," Jonah added, standing and extending his crooked arm, "I show you the gardens, Fra Nordbo?"

"I would be delighted, sir," she said.

Montferrat watched them go. "A satisfactory conclusion, all things considered," he said. "Very satisfactory indeed."

● EPILOGUE:

Harold's Terran Bar was far too noisy and crowded and smelled of tobacco smoke. Spots-Son of Chotrz-Shaa still felt it was appropriate, in memory of his brother. He had taken the same booth for the evening, and the remains of a grouper lay clean-picked on his plate. Glen Rorksbergen and jersey mingled in yellow and amber delight in a saucer, beside his belt computer.

It will take many years to decode that download, he thought. There had been far more in the tnuctipun spaceship's system than the mere fifty terrabytes his belt model could hold, as well. Piecing together the operating code with nothing but fragmentary hints and sheer logic would be a torment.

Still, he had time.

To you, my brother, he thought silently, dipping his muzzle towards the drink. *I dedicate the hunt.*

THE END

Hey Diddle Diddle

by Thomas T. Thomas

"A kzinti warship!" Daff Gambiel called from the watch-keeping station at the mass pointer in the ship's waist. "No — a whole fleet of them!" he corrected. "Dead ahead!"

Up near the control yoke Hugh Jook, *Callisto*'s navigator, spun on his own axis and dove toward the detector. He braked by grabbing a nearby stanchion and going into partial parabola around it. Once he stabilized, Jook studied the thin blue line that peeked out of the milky globe.

"Relax, Daff." He sketched the line with his finger. "Is that what you're excited about? Look at the mass actually showing there. Way too much for hull metal, even in a tight formation. That's an asteroid."

"So far out?" Gambiel said doubtfully.

"It's a rogue. A rock that got perturbed from its orbit."

"Perturbed enough to reach stellar escape velocity?" Gambiel still sounded unconvinced, but the Hellflare tattoo on the Jinxian's blunt forehead glowed violently with the flush that was creeping up from his cheekbones. "I'd rather believe the Navy's conclusions. *They* say it should be a fleet."

"Coming through on gravity polarizers? Oh sure!" The navigator's native Wunderlander superiority leaked out around the edges of his debating style. "And if they were accelerating, pointing away from us, then they would mask the gravity wave so thoroughly our detector wouldn't budge. Pointed toward us, in braking mode, they'd show the shadow of a couple of solar masses.

"This line's just right for a small iron or carbonate body." The Wunderlander pulled his chin. "How it got here, and moving so fast — probably pulled out by the gravity well of a passing star or black hole. . . . No kzinti need apply for that picture, however much you want to believe. Anyway, the Navy is dead wrong. We blasted the Patriarchy back to a collection of cinder worlds and a basketful of kittens in the Third War. They're harmless."

Jared Cuiller, commander of the *Callisto*, listened casually to this conversation. By now, it was going through its seventh or eighth cycle among his tiny four-person crew. They were thirty-six days out of Margrave and twelve light-years beyond the Chord of Contact between Known Space and the Patriarchy. Although his ship's mission had come up fast, the debate behind it had been years in the making.

Over the decades since the Third Man-Kzin War, various industrial conglomerates had gone in to rebuild the shattered Kzinti homeworld and reconstruct the Patriarchy's fractured system of colony and tribute planets along more market-oriented lines. The organized religions had sent in missions to introduce concepts of peace and love, equality and reciprocity — as far as they would go. The universities had sent archaeological and sociological study teams. All of these observers insisted that the Kzinti were pacified, if not exactly civilized. And the U.N. Peacekeeping Commission still controlled strictly the production facilities of Kzin and its colonies, as well as the goods they could buy and sell. So conventional wisdom said the Kzinti had neither the war spirit nor warmaking capability left in them.

But in the last six months, the Admiralty had

convinced the U.N. politicians, the ARMs, and the Peacekeeping Commission that an anomaly existed in the economic and cultural profiles that these on-the-spot observers had sent back from the Patriarchy. The tactical-analysis computers at Naval HQ had found indications that this sudden docility among the kzinti was just a clever screen.

Or that's what the dockyard scuttlebutt was saying. No one at Jared Cuiller's lowly rank — lieutenant commander, with two years to go on the list for his next promotion — had ever been invited to read the Admiralty's secret reports.

On the basis of HQ's analysis, the Navy had received appropriations to restock its fleet, at least in part, and establish a cordon of patrol vessels around the Patriarchy to monitor and screen future kzinti activities. They had a huge volume of space to cover, and resources were still spread thinly. So *Callisto* was a General Products No. 2 hull bought at auction, stripped down to its keyway holes, and rebuilt up from the slippery monomolecular surface, inside and out. Cuiller knew that this was the hull's fifth incarnation, but what their vessel had been before — scout ship, miner, or pleasure yacht — not a scrap of material remained to show. Now it was simply a slender, 200-meter-long spindle hastily fitted out with inertial thrusters, regenerative weapons, sensors and controls, sleeping cocoons and energy pods, and a massive hyperdrive engine, assigned a small scratch crew, and pressed into blockade-and-reconnaissance service — although the Navy preferred to say "deep-space survey."

As to who was right in the debate, Jook or Gambiel, and whether the Patriarchy was indeed ready for another fight, Jared Cuiller wasn't even trying to decide anymore. About the mass of the approaching body, the navigator probably knew more than Daff Gambiel. But about the warmaking capabilities of the

Patriarchy, Cuiller would trust the weapons officer's instincts over Hugh Jook's. After all, the Jinxian had trained to take on the kzinti hand-to-hand.

But, then, maybe in this debate the more relaxed Jook was right. Gambiel's Hellflare tattoo might be making him too eager for a fight. Cuiller tried to place himself in the mental state of a human male who had prepared most of his adult life for just one battle. To pit his entire strength in one synaptic burst against 200 kilograms of angry catflesh tipped with ten-centimeter claws. That would put unique stresses on anyone's body and mind. After all, could a man be truly at ease knowing exactly *how*, if not when, he will die?

But, then, the tactical computers at HQ did back up Gambiel's version. Jook was being too simplistic in thinking that the last war had cured the kzinti of their natural instincts. The universe was a perpetual challenge to the kzin psyche, pure and simple. It was *there* to be stalked and seized. And perhaps this time they would practice a more subtle form of stalking and less outright seizing.

No, Cuiller sighed, neither of his crewmen had the final answer. Nor, probably, did the technical experts at Naval HQ. And Cuiller himself didn't, either. He was just going to follow fleet orders and see.

Nyawk-Captain dreamed of monkeys and his fingers twitched. He hung in the control cradle at his leading station aboard *Cat's Paw*. The interior spaces of the former Scream of Vengeance-class interceptor were eaten up with extra ship's stores and a station cradle for a third kzin. So the crew members had no private space to themselves at all and only a cruelly limited area where they could loosen their limbs — one at a time, in rotation. Otherwise they ate and slept while plugged into their panels. And dreamed there, too.

For most kzinti, if their dreams ever crossed the

sweat-scent of human flesh or their minds played on the shallow softness of a human face, the experience was pleasurable. Then breath quickened, the tail twitched, ears fanned out, fingers and toes splayed slightly, and the tips of razor claws peeked involuntarily from behind black pads.

But when the monkeys danced in Nyawk-Captain's dreams, his breath stopped, his tail went stiff, and his fingers curled nervously, anchoring his bulk into the crash couch. Nyawk-Captain — reputed to be the best fighter pilot of his generation — in his secret dreams was terrified.

Years ago, during Most Recent War, he had been Tactician aboard a much larger vessel. His duties there had once required him to be present when Telepath peeled the brain of a human prisoner. This specimen also served as Tactician aboard his own human ship, although he had his own name, too. Chatterjee. While Telepath gnawed at the edges of Chatterjee's awareness, seeking the plan of an expected attack, the human had thrown up unrelated memories and concepts as a screen. And Telepath had reported them faithfully. One of these memories — or perhaps it was simply an evasion — concerned a person called Hanuman.

This Hanuman was either a clan chief or a god, depending. Chatterjee did not make the distinction clear. Hanuman spoke and moved as a full-grown person, and yet he had a sense of morality more suited to a kzitten. He told lies and untrue stories for amusement. He played tricks on his enemies in battle, dodged their arrows, and routinely ambushed them instead of engaging them openly and honorably. Then he danced and laughed when they were discomfited.

From Chatterjee's telling, filtered through Telepath's own awareness, it was uncertain that Hanuman was even, in fact, a human Being. One part of him was otherness: pre-human or perhaps proto-human. Chatterjee sometimes called him a "monkey." Monkeys, it seemed, had no true adulthood but lived and danced as lively, happy, cruel children all their lives. They screamed and threw things. They told lies, stole from each other, taunted their peers and inferiors, and made a joke of anything they could not desecrate or steal. They ate fruit out of the trees or the flesh of their dead, and copulated with great frenzy at any time.

These monkeys depicted an aspect of personal behavior that stayed in Tactician's, later Nyawk-Captain's, mind long after this Chatterjee was dead. Any creatures that could waste such a huge fraction of their lifetimes in frivolous, carefree, and even disgusting activities — and not die of them — must be very powerful indeed and have brain capacity to spare. They must be devastating.

This Hanuman, whom Chatterjee had revered as either leader or god, a man or a monkey, embodied for Nyawk-Captain all that was creative, lively, resourceful, and *awful* about the humans. This god had no fighting skills worth mentioning but instead defeated all his enemies by trickery. Low, unworthy — and devastating.

The interrogation incident had driven another nail of fear home into Nyawk-Captain's brain. While this Chatterjee was a full human, he considered himself different from those around him, even from his shipmates. He thought of himself as "Hindu-human," and seemed to be more Hindu than human in the shape of his life and thoughts.

Nyawk-Captain tried to imagine sapient beings who could endure diverging breeds and varieties — Hindu, Chinese, Belter, Lunatic, Russky, American, Wunderlander, Englishman, Jinxian — and *not* fight each other down to a single pride governed by a single patriarchic family! The fact that so many could live and work together, without continual killings, spoke to Nyawk-Captain of great inner resources, huge mental agility, varying strengths. Perhaps the humans had grown so cunning through learning to deal with the differences among themselves. Frightening thought! A race that did not need enemies to fight and test itself against, because it provided its own.

In Nyawk-Captain's dreams, the monkeys danced and chattered, and he trembled.

The fifty-eighth day, and twenty light-years beyond Known Space . . .

". . . *not* put your butts in the 'cycler!"

Sarah Krater's soprano voice rang out, echoing off hard surfaces of the ship's interior and rising toward an unpleasant screech. From the context of her complaint, Jared Cuiller could identify without effort both her location and the object of her wrath. *Callisto's* communications officer, linguist, and fourth crew member had cornered Hugh Jook in the cocoon that was fitted out for the combination ship's head and recycler unit.

"Now, Sally," the Wunderlander's voice began in his usual, joking defense. "I've told you a dozen times that cocasoli is a perfectly harmless alkaloid derivative, which the 'cycler absorbs completely. The carrier is a totally organic fiber which is likewise converted. You *can't* be tasting it."

"Wrong!" she barked. "It makes lime gel taste like wet leaves."

"Then the machinery must be a tad out of adjustment."

"I checked. It isn't. If you would just *not* put your butts down the can—"

Which was where that conversation had started, Cuiller thought. It looked like time for him to intervene officially. The captain unhooked from the forward control yoke and exchanged glances with Gambiel, who was strapped in beside him.

"Better you than me," the Jinxian said quietly.

Cuiller did not reply. But he took a leisurely pace, choosing his handholds carefully, as he worked his way downship.

Four people should not be asked to seal themselves in a glass bottle and venture beyond the magnetosphere of a G-type sun, he told himself. They should not have to hurl themselves through a dimension of the universe that had no dimension. And even though they dropped out of hyperdrive regularly to examine new systems, prepare charts, and leave probes, four people should not have to go for months with no other distractions than they could devise for themselves inside a crammed hull.

But four people was optimal minimum crew size, or so the Bureau of Personnel had ruled. Four was the minimax of personality variations, sleep cycles, pairs of hands, and skill levels required for an extended patrol. A crew of four has the available brain capacity and viewpoints to interact as a population. And when disagreements arose, as now, four allowed for a referee, a judge and jury, or even an innocent bystander.

Four was the optimal minimum — if, Cuiller reminded himself, you had the right four.

It took a lot, Cuiller knew, to break through Jook's easygoing persona. But even as a failed aristocrat, the Wunderlander had developed habits and tastes certain to bring out the worst side of people who had not enjoyed parallel advantages. Like Sarah Krater, who had been brought up under the strict air disciplines of a Belter mining cooperative. She would react instinctively against anyone who wanted to burn fibers and chemicals in the open, and draw the residue into his lungs, just for the psychological effects, no matter how harmless the substances under discussion.

Rather than change his behavior to suit her, Jook had simply adopted a light and laughing tone. His personal defense mechanism was to let others go their own way, and he only asked the same of them in return. Nothing seemed to bother him too much. And the navigator did have his good points. Jook was level-headed and philosophical, with a bent for mathematics and ship propulsion technologies.

Krater, by contrast, was touchy and aggressive. A perfectionist in her work, she was always finicky about her personal surroundings and was quick to note the shortcomings of others. That sort of tightass was out of character for a trained xenobiologist. Perhaps greater perspective did *not*, as Cuiller had once thought, provide for greater tolerance. But then, Belters could be strange. She was also ambitious and, from her first day aboard had made clear that she did not intend to stay with "this bucket of a patrol ship" for very long. Krater wanted a command of her own, and to get that she would have to transfer aboard a bigger vessel and begin working her way up into the command structure. As *Callisto* had no formal wardroom and was not going in any direction that would win ship and crew much distinction — at least, not on a peacetime patrol — Krater's frustrated ambitions spilled over into her personal contacts.

Double that frustration once she had learned that both Cuiller and Jook had served on those bigger ships and then been rotated down to *Callisto*. She was beginning to realize that accidents can happen in a Navy career, even hers.

And, much to the frustration of the three males in the crew, the willowy Belter had also announced her intention of keeping all her shipboard contacts purely professional. She was married to her career, she pointedly told them, and didn't fool around on the side. But that was hard if you were a healthy young man sharing less than 12,000 cubic meters of mostly machinery-filled space with a healthy young woman whose eyes were a lovely shade of violet, whose cheek-bones stood out above a full and pouting mouth, and whose long, blonde roostertail haircut begged to be stroked.

When Cuiller reached the cocoon's dilated sphincter, he found Krater and Jook floating practically nose to nose. They were about three seconds from an exchange of blows.

"Do you two want to go back to the gym-bag and strap on the pads?" he asked.

Jook half-turned away at the sound, but Krater remembered her basic training and never took her eyes from the vacant point off her opponent's left shoulder.

If it came to hard-edged hands, Cuiller would bet on the woman. Growing up in a near-weightless environment, she had the reach on Jook and was strong from an early life of wrestling rock drills and mandibles. The navigator once boasted that he had never lifted anything heavier than a booktape, a fork, or a squinch racquet.

"I guess not, Cap'n." Jook shook his head.

"Any time, boy," Krater said into his ear.

"Cut some slack, Lieutenant," Cuiller told her. "... And that's not a suggestion."

"Yes, sir." And *still* she did not relax the position of her limbs.

"Now, Lieutenant! Make space!"

Her hands flexed out of their semi-rigid, thumbs-in shape and her arms came down. Krater pirouetted a half-meter away from the navigator.

"That's better. . . . Sarah, I think you ought to take that 'cycler apart and find out why it's making you sick. Adjust it to your own taste specs, if you like."

"If that means I've got to clean out *his* shit, Captain —"

"It means you'll tend to the equipment, Lieutenant. Your turn on the roster."

She glared at him, then lifted her chin. "Aye, sir."

"Jook, take station forward and get me a report on our mission profile to date."

"That I can tell you at once. We're only — "

"*With* a detailed threat analysis, based on all reported contacts logged throughout the Chord. Don't rush yourself. Do it right. Work on saving our asses."

"But, sir! We *know* the kzinti aren't coming through here. That cyber projection is just — "

"Just the reason we're out here. But I don't want you taking an expert system's analysis on faith. Do your own homework. Down in the library. Move it."

"Aye, Cap'n."

With Jook and Krater moving in different directions, on assignments that would occupy each of them for an hour or more, Cuiller could relax for a bit — unless Gambiel wanted to pick a fight, too. The commander drifted back up to the control yoke.

"Get it all settled?" Gambiel asked.

"Not that it's your business," Cuiller said shortly.

"Sorree!"

Nyawk-Captain awakened slowly. He spat the rusty taste of fear out of his mouth as soon as his brain had caught up with local reality and he could herd the monkeys back to their secret hiding places.

He checked the navigational repeaters at his station, verifying that Weaponsmaster had not let them drift off course during his watch at helm. No, *Cat's Paw* was still headed far out into neutral space, away from the network of manned patrols and passive trip-monitors that the humans maintained along their nearer borders with a much-reduced Patriarchy.

The course his ship was following had evolved among the Patriarch's closest strategists. These were kzinti so highly placed that each one had a full name, and it was death ever to speak of them as mere "strategists," even in the aggregate. Except that they and their counsels were secret, and thus Nyawk-Captain and his crewmates could not *know* their names, and so could never speak of them. Clever.

Their plan, like its origins, was a similarly constructed puzzle, a series of boxes within boxes for the humans to discover and open. This was not perhaps as satisfying for Nyawk-Captain and the other kzinti as a scream and a leap, nor as honorable as one massive attack. But it was more likely to win results under the current circumstances.

A plan almost worthy of Hanuman.

Cat's Paw and three other, similarly enhanced interceptors were moving secretly out into space that the humans had not yet explored. There, unobserved, each would soon turn and find its own path back into human space. Each would pass through a different sector, and the timing of their entries would be staggered, too, just enough to appear to human strategists as individual attacks. The humans would dismiss these transits as the movement of renegade kzinti, secret traders and raiders, and so not responsible to the Patriarchy and the humiliating papers that had been signed after Most Recent War.

Each interceptor would make an isolated attack against a single human world. The *Paw* at Margrave, the others simultaneously at Gummidgy, Canyon, and Silvereyes. With the new weapons they now carried, they could do a massive amount of planetary damage. Of course, the *Paw* would have to move very quickly through the Lambda Serpentis system — and find the Margravians very much asleep — if they were to be successful and still escape with their lives into deep space on the far side of the system.

But escape was not important. Survival was not important. Timing was everything.

The suddenness and brutality of the attacks would awaken the humans' highest strategists to a possible military action. But an action falling *where?* To meet it, the humans would spread their fleet. "Trying to cover all the bases" was the human phrase his orders had referenced. It had the smell of a *sports* term, and true kzinti did not practice sports.

While the humans dispatched their ships and spent their resources investigating and healing the four damaged worlds, the kzinti Last Fleet would be riding behind only one of the interceptors. Just how far depended on the humans' calculated reaction time and the reports of brave kzinti agents among the survivors on those shattered worlds. When human strength was at maximum dispersal, the Last Fleet would overwhelm the patrol screen, engulf the target planet, consolidate, and move on. The fleet would take two, three, perhaps even four key colony worlds before the humans could regroup and mount a defense. But by that time momentum and purpose would be riding with the kzinti. Confusion and alarm would be hindering the humans.

As a plan it was flawless.

As an actual attack, it just might work.

But timing would be everything.

On the seventy-first day, and twenty-four light-years into the unknown . . .

Uncharted but not unknown, Cuiller reminded himself. A thousand, a million times over the millennia, humankind had looked outward toward this sector and seen its stars — stars now hidden in the *Callisto*'s Blind Spot. Some of these stars, judging by their lines in the mass pointer, were even bright enough to be visible from Earth. But no one had taken a survey mission through here. Not after bumping into the kzinti coming the other way.

"Captain . . ." from Jook at the comm down by the pointer. "We're going to graze the singularity limits of a star — "

"Initiating evasive."

"No, wait. The mass says it's a sol-type, G1. We might drop in for a look."

"Again?"

"I've got some scatter that might be planets," Jook said hopefully.

"Or another fully developed Oort cloud?"

"Well, we can't know till we look. . . ."

"We've got a mission to perform, Hugh," Cuiller told him.

"Survey data is valuable, sir."

The commander sighed. Jook was right. And it was time for them to drop in and see some stars in visible light for a change, if only for an hour or so.

"Very well. Sing out when it's time to decouple the hyperdrive."

"*Now!* . . . sir."

Cuiller hit the switches on reflex. It wouldn't do any good to wander into a singularity. Stars bloomed in the nothingness beyond the wide window stripes in the ship's surface covering.

"Which direction?" he asked.

"Off our port bow and now rolling up at, uh, 230 degrees."

The commander looked and saw a bright yellow bead, big enough to begin showing a disk.

"Start plotting the planets, or whatever they are. I'll wake Lieutenant Krater and get her on the console."

"I'm awake," she said, rolling out of her sleeping cocoon. "I felt the ship acquire momentum."

"Jook's got another possible planet. Give it the once over, will you, Sally? Full spectrum."

"Gotcha."

The crew settled into their workstations, except for Gambiel. Cuiller let the weapons officer go on sleeping, held in reserve against a probable long watch when they were underway again.

After ten minutes, both Jook and Krater spoke at once. "Hello!"

"I've got —"

"One at a time," Cuiller ordered.

"I've found a planet," the navigator said. "One body, no moons. It has an equatorial radius of about 3,400 kilometers, about the same as Mars. But it's got a lot higher mass, pulls about point-seven-nine gee. We can move around easily enough, but if there's an atmosphere it's going to be dense and hot. The planet is far enough out from the primary for water to go liquid but not start icing down."

"Spectral analysis says there's atmosphere," Krater confirmed. "Sixty-eight percent nitrogen. Twenty-two percent oxygen. Nine percent water vapor — so the air is pretty steamy, too. The rest is traces. We can breathe, unless we find pockets of poison gas or spores or something. . . . But that's not the big news. I've got a hard return!"

"On deep radar?" Jook asked eagerly.

"Of course. I thunked your planet once just for luck. And the return shows either a chunk of neutronium, or —"

"You weren't scanning at the core?" Cuiller asked quickly.

"Naw, it shows up right near the surface."

"Well, well."

"You're not going to make us go down there, are you, Captain?" Jook asked, inserting a mock whine in his voice. "You know we've got a mission to complete, with lots of phantom kzinti to chase."

"Stow it, Hugh." Cuiller grinned. "Give me a vector to the planet. Sally, when we get close enough, localize that hard return for the navigational console and send it to Hugh. . . . We make one pass over it in low orbit, Hugh, to get a fix on landing sites, and then we head in. Right? Look sharp, everybody. We could be going home rich."

"Aye, sir!" from both of them.

From more than ten million kilometers out, they could see with the naked eye that the planet's disk was unbroken. It showed a pale green atmosphere, banded with broad strips of white.

"Looks like a gas giant," Cuiller said uneasily.

"No way, Cap'n," Jook answered. "We definitely have rock."

The green was the color of dilute free chlorine — lots of it. On a hunch, Cuiller asked Krater to recheck the spectralysis, which was taken by comparing incident light from the G-type primary with sunlight reflected off the planet.

"I do get some dropout lines for chlorine," she said. "But not enough to color the atmosphere like that. The machine still says what it's got is breathable."

From a million kilometers away, they could see little more.

"The green is probably chlorophyll," Krater observed. "We're looking at grass fields, swamps, taiga, or all three."

"Should be greener then," said Gambiel, who was awake by now and at his forward station.

"Remember all the H_2O in the air," she told him. "We're looking through a mile or two of light haze. A lot of reflectance there."

"Oh."

The haze appeared to deepen and grow whiter as they locked into an orbit. "More scatter effect," Krater called it.

"Do you have any features around our deep return?" Cuiller asked.

"Captain, you're looking at a billiard ball," Jook announced. "I'm doing a navigational scan in the point-one-meter range, and the spherical deviation is nil. A trifling amount of oblateness. Otherwise smooth. I mean, a rise of fifty meters would be a mountain range down there."

"Then we can set down anywhere," Cuiller summarized.

"Well . . ." Jook hesitated.

"Give me a fix on that deep radar pattern, Hugh," Cuiller told him, "and I'll kill the orbit."

"You've got it, Cap'n. Deceleration point coming up in two minutes."

"Sally, do you see any change in that pattern?"

"No, what you're looking at is just what we've had from the first, allowing for scale change. I read the return image as just about a meter in any dimension."

"Better all the time. . . . You'll have to reel in the whip now," he told her.

Because a General Products hull blocked all radiation outside the visible spectrum, *Callisto* communed with her environment through a trailing string of antennas and sensors that wound on a reel in her tail section. The sensor string would not survive the buffeting of an atmospheric entry. "Aye, Captain." Krater keyed the proper contacts.

"All right, people," Cuiller called out, "strap in."

He counted the *whir*s and *click*s as the crew pulled out the gravity webbing and made themselves fast at station. Cuiller fastened himself down last.

"One minute to mark," from Jook. "You going to take this one in manually?"

"I need the practice," Cuiller said.

"Easier to let the computers do it. . . ."

Cuiller thought about that, looking down at the nearly white curve of the horizon. "We've got room to play around, surely."

"All right . . . Mark!"

The commander closed a series of switches, engaging the external ion engine. The ship vibrated, and Cuiller felt his body sway forward against the retaining strands.

Callisto glided down in a long curve. Her forward

quadrant glowed where the external ceramic coating
— which deflected laser attacks tuned in visible light —
covered the impervious General Products surface. The
hull itself remained serenely clear, except for a buffeting layer of ionized air.

At 2,000 meters above the surface, Cuiller ter-
minated the ion drive and brought her gliding around
on inertial thrusters, maneuvering under his own eye-
hand coordination. He glanced at the repeater from
Krater's station.

"I'm going to set down about two kilometers from
that reflection," he announced. "Not too far to walk,
but not close enough to disturb it."

No comment from the crew, which he took for
agreement. As *Callisto* cut through the mist, the
planet's surface was revealed as a deep and startling
green. Cuiller was reminded of pictures he'd seen of
Ireland but then amended that. This was bright
enough to be an enhanced color graphic of Ireland,
with overdrive on the yellow and cyan pigments. Jook
had not overstated the flatness. Even from a hundred
meters up, Cuiller could not see any hill or wrinkle
higher than two or three meters. No valleys either. And
no boulders, trees, rivers, lakes, nor any other feature.
Just a deep and rustling green vegetation.

"Settling in," he said, killing forward motion and
dropping the lift smoothly toward a steady seven-
point-seven-three meters per second, just enough to
counter local gravity. When the greenery — it looked
like large and feathery leaves — reached up to touch
the clear window in the hull's underside, he backed the
thrusters down to zero and switched them off.

"Captain!" Jook called out. "Check your navigational radar!"

"What? Oh shit!" He saw the 120-meter discrepancy
immediately.

The leaves flared back around the window below

and revealed lighter green strings of moss and the wet black bark of tree branches. Between them, Cuiller could see more layers of green and black strands, receding indefinitely, with nothing solid under them.

He got his hands back on the switches for the inertial thrusters and initiated a restart. But before he could key in the full sequence, *Callisto*'s tail, weighted down with the unbalanced mass of the hyperdrive engine, broke through the surface.

It happened too fast. Cuiller was still thrusting on the ship's long axis, but *Callisto* was now falling nearly vertically. He tried to correct — and only pushed her backward into a tangle of branches and vines. Their springiness absorbed the horizontally vectored thrust for ten meters of travel, then rebounded, shoving *Callisto* down her own hole.

They all felt the shock when the stern contacted firm ground at last. No one cried out, but someone among the crew gave an involuntary gasp. Cuiller, glancing down the spindle into the maze of machinery, could see a subtle misalignment. Internal structures had shifted. He could also hear things falling, *plink* and *clunk*, along the hull. Not all of them were personal effects shaken out of the sleeping cocoons.

The bow and the forward band of windows, around the control yoke, were still angled above the leaf layer, exposed in misty sunlight. Cuiller's fingers were dancing over the switches, trying to get thrust under them and lift clear. But the ship was sliding, changing orientation too fast. He and Gambiel watched the world rotate and sag as the hull's weight found paths of least resistance among the branches and vines. *Callisto* swung and turned, walked and slid. A green gloom rose up around their window. Cuiller quit trying with the controls and lifted his hands clear.

"Hang on, people!"

Finally, only the forward tip of the spindle was caught in the branches, and they were slipping away to the left and right, passing *Callisto* side to side, as they got out of the way of her mass. In two more seconds, the ship was free and fell a hundred meters at the bow along her own length.

Wham!

More clatter came up from the hull behind Cuiller, but then his ear caught a louder groan. At first he thought it came from one of his crew, until Cuiller realized that one of the weapons pods, located forward of the control yoke, was moving. Right before the commander's and tactical officer's widening eyes, it turned on its own axis and fell through the open space ten centimeters in front of their toes. Severed conductors in a cable tray snapped and fizzled before the automatic extinguishers kicked in with a chill cloud of carbon dioxide.

The ship rolled almost 180 degrees in settling, and the weapons pod swung back, now poised above them. It caught up on the lateral strut that braced Cuiller's and Gambiel's watch-keeping station, and it stopped moving.

"Everybody sit tight till the ship quiets down," the commander ordered. They were all hanging by their ears now.

"I got nowhere to go," Gambiel breathed beside him.

The infrastructure creaked and groaned, but nothing more came loose.

"Let's try to get damage reports before we shut down."

"Aye, Captain," the crew called back raggedly.

In the space of two minutes, they had logged the ship's status — weapons, propulsion, sensors, life support — at their various duty stations. *Callisto* had lost that forward weapons pod for certain, and the sensor whip was not reporting, even from its reeled-in position. Two portside thrusters were impaired, if not inoperable. The recycling system had lost function.

Auxiliary power was down by three charge cells. And the ship was oriented horizontally in a 170-degree roll — standing on their heads, as it were.

"I should try to get off a position report," Krater said. "If that's possible, with the antenna cable damaged — "

"Do what you can," Cuiller told her. He swiveled around in the stirrups, hanging head down in the webbing, to observe the crew at their stations. "Anybody take injuries in that last fall?"

"Well . . . it's my knee, you see," Jook said. His webbing was loose enough that he had bashed his leg against the mass pointer. No damage to that piece of equipment, of course, but Jook's knee was swelling rapidly. Otherwise the crew was shaken but unhurt. Cuiller directed Krater, who doubled as medical assistant, to help the navigator into the autodoc.

"Daff, take air samples," he ordered. "And if it's clean, pop the hatches. Let's get outside and see where we are."

The main entry hatch, normally oriented toward the underside of the hull, was now positioned near the top. Cuiller, Krater, and Gambiel climbed up handholds and over equipment bracing to reach it. Jook stayed inside, nursing his knee in a bubble cast foam-molded by the 'doc. While they went outside, he would use the time to catalog and schedule their estimated repairs.

After levering themselves through the opening, the three crewmembers stood on the roughened ceramic surface and surveyed the landing site. *Callisto* lay on clear ground, angled slightly upward at the bow, where the hull was wedged between the smooth trunks of two trees. Those trees, and every other tree in view, supported a high forest canopy whose underlayer was more than ninety meters overhead.

Cuiller searched for the hole they must have made in passing through it but found nothing. No clearings punctuated the vaults of leaves and trailing moss that soared above them. The surrounding world was a uniform green gloom, without a splash of sunlight.

"Beanstalk," Krater said suddenly. "That's what we'll call this planet."

"What?" from Gambiel. "This patch, maybe. But who can say what's going on in the next county over."

"*I* can say," she answered. "There is no 'next county.' We've been around this world once and taken a radar image of it. This is one huge, unbroken rainforest, girdling the planet, covering probably sixty percent of its surface."

"Well, at the poles, then . . ." the weapons officer said, trailing off.

"There ought to be what?" Krater asked. "This planet's rotational axis is perpendicular to its ecliptic. So you won't get seasonal temperature variations, as you do on Earth. You can expect the temperature to drop uniformly at the higher latitudes, because of the sun's lower angle in the sky. But that only means that the rainforest is going to peter out in low scrub, then mosses and lichens, and eventually frozen deserts. This planet clearly has no plate tectonics, which means not much in the way of topography ever formed here. So no mountain ranges, no valleys, no river floodplains, no oceanic heat sinks. That means there can't be any weather."

"What about Coriolis effects?" Cuiller asked. "You'd still have moving air masses, trade winds, horse latitudes — any planet that's turning has them."

"All right, I'll agree to trade winds. But on a smooth ball like this, they sorted themselves out long ago. Even flows without much intermixing. That's the cloud banding we saw from far out."

"Hugh said he detected a smooth surface, and it was — even a hundred meters up in the treetops," Cuiller said. "That's what fooled me, I guess," he added sheepishly. It was a close as a commanding officer could come to officially apologizing to his crew for that fiasco of a landing. "Daff, if you would rig a rope ladder or something like it, we can go down and check out the ground."

"Aye, sir." Gambiel climbed back down through the hatchway.

The commander looked off into the distance, a perspective of spaced tree trunks vanishing into a brownish-green mist. Something about the trees . . . He turned his head one way, then the other. He moved his head sideways, left then right, along the baseline of his shoulders. He widened that line by taking two steps to the side. As the angle changed, the trunks seemed to line up in a geometric pattern. And then the pattern faded out as he moved farther to one side or the other.

"Sally? Does it look to you like the trees are — "

"Lined up? Yeah, I was thinking that, too. They're spaced in a matrix, actually."

"Like an orchard," he agreed.

"As if they had been planted on purpose. But it's not a simple design of rows and columns. More like pentagrams or hexagons."

Cuiller itched to get down and begin taking measurements.

Gambiel returned with a length of spare optic-fiber cable in which he'd tied small, tight knots at half-meter intervals. He anchored it inside the open hatchway and dangled the rest across the smooth curve of the hull. They all heard its trailing end thump on the ground.

"We might be needing that cable to make repairs," Cuiller observed quietly.

The Jinxian stared at him. "We won't. I checked with Jook."

"Well," he went on, "you might have brought up a spider rig from the EVA equipment."

Gambiel turned to show his left shoulder, where

three of the rigs hung like loops of uniform braid. "We have one each. And we'll all need them."

"What for?" Krater asked.

"Climbing."

"Climbing where?"

Gambiel pointed over his head. "Deep radar was your station, Sally. You saw the return image. Whatever made it, it's still up there."

"In the treetops? But —"

The Jinxian turned toward his commander. "That was why you tried to land in the canopy. You were watching the deep display instead of the navigationals. . . . Keeping your eye on the prize."

"Well, yes . . ." Cuiller hesitated. Was *that* the cause of his error?

"Honest mistake," Gambiel offered with a shrug.

Climbing down was not as easy as Cuiller had thought it would be. They had to go one at a time, walking backwards and paying out the knots hand over hand, until their bodies were laid out almost parallel to the ground. Then they rappelled from the ship's side, slipping cautiously down the knotted cable until they were under the overhang. Finally they dragged their feet on the hard-packed ground to kill the final swing. Climbing back up was going to be harder and take longer.

With his heavyworld muscles, of course, Gambiel went up and down like a monkey.

Krater, who had the advantage of height and not much mass to go with it, seemed to step from the ship to the ground.

Cuiller, despite Beanstalk's lighter gravity, still found it a workout.

"What's wrong with this picture?" Krater asked, looking around when they had assembled under the bow. Gambiel scuffed the soil with the side of his cabin moccasin. The ground was smooth and crusted, like a section of sun-baked clay in exposed terrain. He turned over no ground cover, no dead leaves, no animal droppings or pieces of bark, nothing. They found no undergrowth, either, not even around the tree trunks. None of the vines that wove through the canopy reached down to the forest floor.

Cuiller walked over to the nearest trunk. It was at least two meters in diameter with a hard, scaly bark. He pried at the bark with his fingers but could not break off a piece. No room for invading insects, small birds, or snakes.

He looked up. The overhead leaves were as still as the underside of a green cloud. Of course, if any wind were stirring in the treetops, the sound and movement were cushioned by 30 meters of netted foliage.

Cuiller squatted down to examine the trunk's base. The bark was scraped and scarred raw there, at least on the side facing him. The wounds went a third of the way around the bole and extended more than a meter up from the ground. They wept a thick, ruddy sap. He duck-walked along the trunk's circumference and discovered that the cuts faded out into white, scraped wood, which looked almost dead. Beyond that, by another third of the circumference, was a patch of new, green bark — but even there he could see a pattern of parallel scrapes and gouges. Areas of sap, clean wood, and new growth alternated around the trunk.

Something had been abusing this tree on a regular basis, coming at it from all sides.

Cuiller stood up and walked toward the next tree, counting his paces as he went. He knew his stride was just less than a meter. Factoring the correction into his count gave him a distance of twenty-five meters between the two trees. He examined that base and found the same pattern of abuse.

He walked on to a third tree — again, covering just twenty-five meters — and saw the same thing. And he confirmed that the three trees were growing in a line.

On a hunch, he walked back to the second tree and sighted to the third. A patch of white wood there matched a similar patch here. In the same way, running sap faced sap on a tree sighted 120 degrees around the trunk's circumference. Green bark matched green bark on yet another facing tree.

Cuiller went from tree to tree, always twenty-five meters, and found the same pattern of parallel scars.

Logic said that something 25 meters wide was being dragged through the forest here like a rake. And whatever it was, it swept up leaves, scored the tree trunks, clipped any undergrowth, and scoured the soil bare, compacting it to the consistency of a mud brick.

"Did you bring radios?" he asked Gambiel.

The weapons officer handed him a palm-sized unit. Cuiller tuned and spoke into it.

"Hugh?"

"Right here, Jared. I can even see you through the window, sometimes."

"How's the knee?"

"Painkillers are kicking in."

"Can you get up to the deep radar?"

"Not without a climb, but I can work the repeater at the comm."

"Right. Give us a bearing to the return image, would you?"

"Just a sec. . . . Ten degrees off the port bow, still at a range of two and a half kilometers. And, Captain — it's *above* us now."

"I know. In the treetops, right?"

"Well, the angle is right for it, anyway. But how would — ?"

"I think we're going to find that everything interesting on this planet — which Sally has named 'Beanstalk,' by the way — is up in the forest canopy."

"All right. You're leaving me with the ship?"

"Can you lift if you have to?"

"So long as you all are clear of the area, I can punch up the main ion engine, have her hot in ninety seconds, and *scoot*."

"Do that, if you see anything."

"What am I going to see, down here?"

"Somebody's keeping the grounds swept nice and clean. Watch out for whoever it is."

"Sure thing. Do you explorer types have weapons?"

Gambiel overheard that. He turned his right hip toward Cuiller, exposing three hand-fitted variable lasers clipped to his belt. Over that same shoulder he carried a brace of laser rifles, which had a wider aperture and a longer beam pulse.

"We've got them."

"What about food, water, thermal—"

"I've got my field test kit," Krater spoke up. "And we're all carrying a foodbar or two for snacking. Quit nagging, Mother-Hugh. We've only got two klicks of ground to cover."

"Okay. Be back soon."

"In two shakes," Cuiller agreed and clicked off.

They headed out, walking easily between the trees on the bearing Jook had given them. After half a kilometer of parklike open space, they came upon their first patch of undergrowth. Green shoots, bushes, and saplings grew up in an uncleared area that was shaped like a pentagon. Cuiller noticed immediately that its points were anchored by five of the mature trees.

"Wait here," he ordered, and began to wade into the greenery.

"Captain?" Gambiel called. When Cuiller turned, the Jinxian checked the charge on a hand weapon and tossed it to him.

Cuiller accepted it with a nod.

He pushed his way into the secondary growth, bending stalks and branches aside and wishing they had brought along a few simpler weapons, like machetes. Twenty-five paces in from the nearest tree, he found what he'd been expecting: a broken stump two meters wide and a fallen section of trunk. He looked straight up, hoping to find a patch of sky. The green vault was thinner here, perhaps lighter in color, but still unbroken. Most of the saplings around him, he noticed, had tough, straight boles with flat, branching crowns.

He thumbed the radio and spoke into it. "Hugh, watch out for the groundskeepers. They're definitely intelligent."

"How do you figure *that*?" Krater cut in, having caught him on the same channel.

Cuiller described what he saw. "Whoever it is that's dragging the forest floor also knows enough to let a downed tree replace itself," he concluded. "Otherwise the canopy would thin out and fall within a generation or two. This forest is being *managed*, and that smacks of intelligence to me."

"You're leaping ahead of yourself," she said, putting on her professional xenobiologist's hat. "A lot of natural phenomena could explain what you've got there."

"Well — " Cuiller was unsure of his ground.

"I like Jared's interpretation," Gambiel said. "Anyway, let's be prepared. Err on the side of intelligence."

"Sounds good to me," Jook put in, from the ship. "I'll watch for them."

"All right," from Krater. "Have it your way. But don't be disappointed if it's a pack of grazing animals with picky appetites, some kind of stream flow, a toxic groundwort, or something."

"We can deal with those," Gambiel said.

"I'm coming out," Cuiller told them, turning around in the patch of groundcover.

"Let's start considering options," the commander

said when he was back on the swept floor with the others. He pointed at the spider rigs on the Jinxian's shoulder. "How do these things work?"

Gambiel unslung them, laid two on the ground, and spread one in his flat hands.

"This is an adjustable five-point harness. Over the shoulders, around the waist, between the legs. The takeup reel with motor winder clips on here." He thunked himself in the chest, just below the sternum. "The hand unit — " He picked up a gun-shaped object. " — launches the grapple with a gas charge that vents backward to stabilize your reaction. That's because this rig was designed for freefall, remember."

Cuiller picked up the grapple. It had a point and three spring-loaded tines — all sharpened. "We'd use a thing like this around vacuum gear?"

"The original head has a suction pad and magnets. This is a terrestrial modification."

"Right."

"What about drag from the trailing line?" Krater asked.

"For one thing, it's all monofilament. Weighs about three grams to the kilometer. But you got to watch out: put it under tension and it'll take your fingers off. Handle the line only with the winder, or with steel-mesh gloves.

"The other thing is, the line goes *with* the grapple, paying out from a cassette." Gambiel showed them, taking one from his pocket. He fitted and locked the spindle-shaped cassette into the base of the grapple, drew out a meter or so of the nearly invisible line from its end, and clicked the grapple into the gas gun. "Attach the free end to a spare reel on your winder." He took that from another pocket. "Fire the gun — " He pantomimed shooting up into the trees. " — and when the hooks are anchored, jerk it once to set a friction brake on the cassette. Then reel in and up you go."

"What happens when all your line is wound in on the takeup reel?" Cuiller asked.

"You retrieve the grapple, discard both the old reel and cassette, fit new ones, take aim and fire again." Gambiel shrugged.

"How much line in one setup?"

"Ten kilometers."

"Okay. Simple enough. Let's get into those harnesses now."

"Why?" Krater asked, her eyebrows coming together.

"Evasive action," Cuiller answered. "If we meet anything down on the ground here, we may not be able to outrun it. Or outfight it. Our best course might be to disappear. Up into the treetops."

The Jinxian nodded. "When you shoot, try to put the grapple as close to a main trunk as you can. Thicker branches there — more likely to hold your weight."

"But the canopy held our whole ship pretty well," Krater observed. "For a while."

"True," Gambiel said. "So, suit yourself."

Cuiller stepped into the harness, found the adjustment points, and pulled them snug. He fitted the winder motor to his chest, figured out the simple lever controls for its reversible gearing, and clipped the first empty reel onto it. He put a cassette in the grapple, fed out a meter of the silk-like line, and found a loop at the harness belt's left side to hold the grapple. The gun fitted into a flat holster on the right. The three of them divided up their supply of gas cartridges, cassettes, and reels.

"What happens when these run out?" Krater demanded, counting her share with her fingers.

"We won't be here that long," the commander said. He looked to Gambiel. "We still walking that way?" Cuiller pointed the direction, angling his hand around one side of the pentangle of underbrush.

The Jinxian paused, considered some inner sense, and nodded.

They walked along, deviating from a straight line only to pass around any trunks in their way.

"Whoop!" Krater shouted.

She suddenly floated away from Gambiel's other side.

Cuiller caught a glance of her white jumper flashing past and in front of them as she soared into the trees. She covered the ninety vertical meters in about twenty seconds, moving so quickly that at the end of her arc Krater barely had time to cock her feet up to reach for a toehold. The lieutenant disappeared into the canopy with the barest rustle of leaves.

"Serve her right if she cracks her head on a branch," Gambiel said. "Should we follow her up?"

The commander pointed ahead. "Our goal is over that way. We'll reach it faster walking on the ground."

"We might lose her."

"We've got visibility of what — ?" He looked around. "A hundred meters down here? And less than ten meters up there in the leaves. If she gets lost, she can always drop down and we'll spot her."

"If we're looking in the right direction."

"She'll probably scream or something," Cuiller said.

"Yeah, she probably will."

The two men walked on through the trees.

The sound came from Navigator's panel. It was a strange burring — full of enough sonics to make a kzin's neck ruff stand out from his chin. Nyawk-Captain searched his memory for a sound like it and finally decided it was not part of normal ship's operation. Perhaps a malfunction? A small, fast motor vibrating out of its bearings? But coming from inside the solid-state circuitry of the panel . . . ? Then a wrinkle of memory surfaced, a significant detail from his early simulator drills with the Vengeance-class interceptor.

"You have a return from the hardsight," he snarled over his shoulder.

"Wh-what — sir?"

"Wake up, root breath! Your station is active — and signaling you."

"Ah, yes, Nyawk-Captain. I see that now. Sorry, sir."

"Vigilance, Navigator. Now, describe the sighting."

"It is still several light-hours distant. . . ."

"Wake *up*, damn you! Give me facts in the order I need to know them. Is the anomaly along our prescribed course? Or somewhere off in the starfields?"

"The sighting's deviation is . . . fourteen degrees from our projected — "

"So we would not otherwise have walked across it. Describe the contact."

"Contact?"

Navigator's surprise was genuine, because kzinti battle referents were precise. Passive objects might be "sighted." Enemy vessels were a "contact."

"What does your training say?" Nyawk-Captain replied. "This ship was designed to cruise with its hardsight range detector automatically probing along our forward path. Why else — if not to detect the Leaf-Eaters' improbable hulls?"

"To seek out Thrintun boxes?" Navigator replied brightly.

"Fool!" Nyawk-Captain spat.

"A witticism, sir! I abase myself."

"For a Navigator who sleeps at station, you should have no comedy available to your mouth."

"I *humbly* abase myself."

"Describe the contact."

"The hardsight return is in close proximity to a star, but not within its photosphere. So the contact is either in orbit itself or lodged on a planet — although the surrounding return is too weak to show such a body. There is one object. . . . No, correction. At extreme gain I observe *two* contacts. One is sharp. The other is fainter and . . . fuzzy. It may be merely a reflection of the first. It certainly is close enough for that."

"What are the dimensions?"

"At this range, Nyawk-Captain . . ."

"Is either one big enough to be a hull?"

"One of the reflections *may* be, but the distance . . ."

"Very well. Bend your fullest attention to refining your observations."

"Shall we alter course? If we could draw nearer . . ."

"I will decide, when you give me further useful information."

"As we move to pass that system, it's possible that the two signals might show some degree of separation. From that we may learn — "

"Provide me with facts, Navigator."

"Such is my only objective, Nyawk-Captain."

"Very good. Be vigilant — and wakeful."

Sally Krater hitched her feet up, pivoting about the liftpoint at her solar plexus, where the takeup reel whined and throbbed. After the soles of her moccasins broke through the leaf veils of the lower canopy, she slipped the clutch on the winding mechanism. The pull against her chest halted abruptly, but her mass continued to rise in a flattened arc. With Beanstalk's reduced gravity, she slowly topped out, pitched forward to the length of her remaining line, and fell gently back through the leaves, swinging on the grapple anchored above her.

Krater suddenly realized that her back could be shattered against any heavy tree limb coming up behind her. She immediately dragged with her heels through the leaves, trying to kill her momentum. At this level, the greenery was dense but not cloying. The leaves were flat and veined, each about the size of her open hand. They clustered in billows around her, supported on springy whips that were either tiny branches or vines — she couldn't yet say which. As Krater swung, her head, arms,

and legs batted through masses of these leaves, stinging
where her skin was exposed but not otherwise hurting
her. When she looked down between her feet she could
see random patches of brown ground. At the end of her
last rising swing, she glimpsed in one of these patches two
pale dots that might be Cuiller and Gambiel, far below
and looking up.

Once her momentum was stopped and she hung
straight down, she began to reel in slowly, rising meter
by meter through the canopy. Within five meters she
had reached the grapple, which had fallen across the
first stout branch she had seen — up in what she
wanted to call the canopy's mid-level. She twisted
slowly on her monofilament, conscious that the
invisible strand ran just centimeters from her face. Any
sudden motion, she realized, might clip her nose or an
ear. She wondered how close she had come to cutting
her own head off when she topped out and pitched
after that first upward rush.

Krater's thighpockets held a rescue kit, and from it
she took a packet of fluorescent dye, suitable for mark-
ing a water landing. She broke it open and ran the
exposed sponge lightly up and down the line, until it
became a bright purple steak before her, like an etch-
ing laser flashing through smoke. With the remaining
dye she reached up and soaked the line spindled in the
grapple's socket, then the slack taken up on the reel at
her chest. She made a mental note to suggest this to
Gambiel, when they got together again.

As she hung there, her mass started to spin lazily,
and she put a hand against the branch above her to
stop it. The sudden pressure dislodged something up
there, and a stream of liquid cascaded down. It
splashed off her shoulder and struck a bunch of leaves
below and off to her left. She carefully tasted the drops
clinging to her uniform: water, sweet and cool.

From her other pocket, she took out her field kit. It

popped open and she keyed up the gas chromatograph and amino acid analyzer. The only samples within reach were that water and the leaves around her. Although she had no immediate plans to eat the leaves themselves, they would provide a clue to the nature of indigenous life on Beanstalk. The flora would reflect any general tendency toward toxins, heavy metals, or wrong-handed molecules. Balancing the kit on her raised knee, she tore a nearby leaf into bits and pressed them against the first sensor mesh. She dabbed a few of the drops that remained on her shoulder into the second mesh.

Something moved. Out of the tail of her eye, off to the right, she detected a pattern shift. From her undergraduate biology, Krater knew that human peripheral vision worked best at perceiving motion — a relic of primate development, both as hunter and prey. So, if she could sense something moving, it *was* moving.

"Just the wind," she whispered to herself. And yet she knew that the motion had been localized. If it had been wind, the whole canopy would be surging around her now.

She turned her head slowly, swinging her nose centimeter by centimeter to the right. She did not dart with her eyes, but shifted them only in slow blinks. But before she could begin facing the whatever-it-was, the radio strapped at her wrist crackled.

"Sally, are you all right?" in Cuiller's voice. The leaves off her right shoulder swirled with movement, as the something there darted quickly, but whether lunging or withdrawing, she couldn't tell.

Krater had no time to fool with the hand-laser attached at her belt but instead slapped the release on her cable reel. She dropped three meters in near-freefall. On the way, she bobbled and almost lost the field kit. Finally she caught it, snapped it closed, and slipped it back in her pocket. The kit would digest the vegetable sample and report later.

"I'm fine," she called into the radio, although her voice was shaky.

"You shouldn't just head off like that, Sally," Cuiller said. His tone was masked by the tinny quality of the transmission.

"I wanted some samples."

"Well, next time, ask first. Please?"

"Yes, sir. I'd like to come down now — with your permission."

"Do so."

She toggled the reel to unwind. In a few seconds her feet broke through the lowest layer of leaves into clear air.

The canopy above her did tremble then, like a breeze fluttering its lower edges. But Krater could swear that no wind had stirred since she climbed up there. She stared into the overgrowth, looking for anything that might be poking through and . . . reaching for her.

Nothing.

To rest her eyes, she looked away to the middle distance. From where she hung, about three meters below the canopy proper, the spaced tree trunks were just beginning to branch out into the flying buttresses and arching vaults that supported the greenery. The view was almost what a medieval mason might have seen, working in a sling up near a cathedral's ceiling and looking out between the stone pillars. Except these pillars were green and alive — and all were suddenly swaying.

Expecting to see the ripples of an earthquake, she looked down at the forest floor, scanning the barren ground there. That was when she saw the iceberg, moving off to one side.

"Captain . . ." She kept her eyes on the shape.

"Right here, Sally."

"Can you see me?"

"I do. You're just below where you went up, aren't you?"

"Yeah, still on the same grapple point. Now, do you see my arm?" She pointed it at the white object. "Follow that line and tell me what you see."

"Trees and deepening gloom. What do *you* see?"

"A white shape. And it's moving."

"Jared!" It was Gambiel, on another radio channel. "I can see it, too, from here." Had the weapons officer also wandered away from the commander? Krater wondered.

"Then you're closer, Daff," from Cuiller.

"Sally? How big would you say it is?" from Gambiel.

"I don't know. It's about . . . oh, six or seven trees off. Say a hundred and fifty meters over the ground. But it seems to be . . . *squeezing* between the trunks. That would make the thing more than twenty-five meters wide, wouldn't it? And I'd guess it's at least five or six times that long — but I can't see all of the creature."

"Can you see its head?" Daff asked.

"No. And I won't swear that it *has* one."

"Not important," Gambiel said. "I know what it is anyway."

"Bandersnatch?" from Cuiller.

"Yes, Captain. You've seen them before?"

"Once, on Jinx. They're intelligent — and harmless."

"Right. Sally? Which way is it moving? I can't tell from down here."

"Back the way we came, looks like," she said. "Roughly parallel to our path."

"I'll call Jook," Cuiller said. "Alert him, so he doesn't do anything rash if it shows up at the ship. And Sally, why don't you come down and join us now?"

"Aye, Captain." She paid out line and dropped toward the forest floor.

Her feet touched the ground near where Cuiller was

standing, finishing his call back to the ship. Gambiel walked up a moment later. She showed him the dye on the line and explained her reasoning. He nodded thoughtfully.

"But how do I recover the grapple?" she asked, looking up into the trees. "We can't afford to lose one each time one of us goes up and comes down."

The weapons tech reached over to her harness, locked the takeup reel, and thumbed the cover off a protected red stud on the control panel. He pushed it — unconsciously shoving her backward with his latent strength. "Step back and bend your knees," he said.

She did so, and a moment later something fell out of the canopy. When it hit the ground, she recognized her grapple, with the barbs folded in.

"Radio-controlled unlocking device," Gambiel said. "Don't use it while you're hanging around. . . . Well, reel it in."

Krater started the winder motor.

"Slowly!" Gambiel ordered. "Or you'll catch that thing right in the tits."

She slowed the winding and watched the folded grapple tumble and walk across the scoured dirt toward her. When it was a meter out, she braked the reel, picked up the grapple, and tucked it into her belt loop.

"Now what?" she asked.

"Now, we go on," Cuiller replied, pointing the way toward their objective, the calculated position of the deep radar's return image.

Hugh Jook was wedged under — or now *over*, rather — the forward control yoke. He was bent around the station-keeping stirrups, stretching as far as he could go with one leg immobilized by the bubble cast. In one hand Jook held a collection of electronics chips, all banded and tagged with alphanumerics to show what each circuit was supposed to do. In the other hand was a socket-puller. He was poking into the guts of the overturned weapons pod, hoping to get enough response from it for the ship's computer to run a diagnostic. Then it would be thumbs up or thumbs down: reconnect and rebrace the unit, or bleed away its residual charge, cut it apart with a hand-laser, and dump it out on the ground.

With his head inside the access panels, he never saw the Bandersnatch approach *Callisto*, even though the main window stripe was right behind his ear and oriented up toward the trees. His first sign of trouble was the lurch the ship took as the white beast nuzzled it.

"Yo!" he sang out and straightened up.

The exposed hull scritched and squeaked under the impact of the Bandersnatch's sensory bristles. Jook looked out into a squash of thick white tubules, like a pot's view of a scrub brush at work. Although nothing there *looked* like an eye, he had the uncanny feeling the giant was peering in at him.

"Leave it alone, and it will leave you alone," Cuiller had told him, when the ground party had called in their sighting of a Bandersnatch. "Nothing on its body is small enough, or delicate enough, to be harmed by our short-range weapons. And there's nothing much it can do to the ship, even if it sits on the hull."

"Right," Jook had agreed over the radio and dismissed the threat. Besides, Bandersnatchi were known to be harmless — and quite intelligent.

But now, with the mass of pallid flesh pushing against the side of *Callisto*, he wasn't so sure.

Jook unbent himself, steadied with his hands against the jostling that the hull was taking, and tried to reach the panels of the control yoke. He had no intention of opening hostilities, but he hoped the beast would survive the scatter from *Callisto*'s ion drive when he departed the scene.

A couple of times he got his fingers up on the buttons for the engine initiation sequence. But each time he tried to key it, the ship lurched and his hand slipped. Then it didn't matter, because the natural light coming through the window faded entirely. The Bandersnatch was riding up over the ship. It was too late to break away, even at full thrust.

Jook's ears popped.

That had to be a pressure variation, but he hadn't keyed any changes in the atmospheric specs. He looked around. The main hatch, above him and now thirty-five degrees off local vertical with the hull's current orientation, had worked open — falling inward. The hatch panel was fabricated of aligned-crystal vanadium steel. It was set in a vanadium-steel rim and keyed into the standardized opening in their General Products hull by lipping it both inside and out. Short of a patch of GP monomolecule itself, the hatch was the strongest possible seal that human technology could devise. And yet the Bandersnatch had punched it out like a baby poking his thumb through a piecrust.

Ripples of the Bandersnatch's white underside ballooned into the opening. At first Jook thought it was just normal pressure expansion, the weight of the animal forcing its underside into a new cavity as the Bandersnatch settled its mass over the ship. But as he watched, the volume of white flesh inside the hatch grew. It began lapping around the cross bracing for the portside inertial thrusters and weapons pods. As the flesh made contact there, the Bandersnatch's belly vibrated and the metal began to scream.

It also began to dissolve. Big, fuming drops of fluid wept from the point of contact and fell into the bilges. Wherever they touched, except on the hull material itself, that spot also started smoking and dissolving.

Jook moved. He climbed along struts and down handholds, swinging his stiffened leg over obstacles and bashing it twice. The pain didn't slow him down. He made it past the waist, where his nominal duty station was, and kept on going, around the hyperdrive engine. In the rear, about as far forward from the tail as the main hatch was back from the bow, the hull had another opening. This one was smaller and fitted with an airlock. He thought briefly about hiding inside the lock, but he remembered it was constructed of the same vanadium steel that had failed in the main hatch. No, his only option was to climb through while that end of the ship was still uncovered by the creature's bulk, get to the ground before the Bandersnatch noticed him, and run like hell, or as fast as his bad leg permitted.

To lower himself from the lock entrance, Hugh Jook pulled on a climbing harness and gathered up the grapple, launcher, line cassettes, and gas cartridges. Almost as an afterthought, he broke out a laser rifle and a personal radio.

While dry-locking through, he punched up the radio and whispered into it.

"Captain . . . !"

Nothing, not even static.

"Jared!"

Still nothing.

Of course — inside the lock even the strongest signal would be blocked. He'd have to wait until he was outside and clear before calling the ground party.

The outer hatch opened, and Jook was looking up into a billowing wall of rough, white flesh. There was no time to set the grapple or pay out line. He levered himself up on the hatch coaming, scrambled over the ceramic hull surface trailing down toward the tail, got his good leg lowermost to take up his impact with the ground, and dropped.

He fell over on his bad leg and cried out — then looked up to see if the Bandersnatch was interested in falling on top of him.

It wasn't. Instead, it rolled back and forth over the hull, driving the bow down and bending out of plumb the trees that had wedged it right and left. The Bandersnatch worked its rasp deeper and deeper into the main hatch, and Jook could faintly hear the screech of breaking metal inside.

Still, he didn't trust the white beast's absorption in its task. As soon as his breath was back, Jook picked himself up and hobbled into the next pentagonal clearing. There he set the line cassette in his grapple, loaded the gun, and fired up into the trees. After the few seconds it took to anchor and set the grapple, he was soaring up into the green vault.

"I can now give you more detailed information, sir, on the hardsight contacts."

"Good, uff, Navigator. Uff. Continue."

Nyawk-Captain ran full out, stretching his long muscles. At full extension, his forward-reaching claws just grazed the rack that held the brainbox of their long-range starfixer; his hind claws ticked against the panels of the weapons locker. He was exercising in a variable gravity field that could be rippled to simulate ground passing under his pads. At present, the field was going under him at twice his own body length every second. He had to stretch to keep up — or be shoved back into the locker.

"We are definitely seeing two contacts, not one with a reflection," Navigator said. "The brighter return is the smaller — an absolute return of all radiation. That would indicate an infinite density, which I cringe to propose to you."

"How big is this infinitely dense source?"

"Small, Nyawk-Captain. No bigger than a kzin's torso."

"And it orbits a star — is it dead star matter itself?"

"No, sir. It does orbit a star, but on a planet. I now have a layered return shadowing this planet's lithosphere and iron core. The object is on the surface, or near to it. The second contact — "

Nyawk-Captain growled him to silence. He then reached out in his stride and killed the gravity field, ending his run on a single, four-footed pounce into the middle of the exercise area. The cabin steamed with the heat of his exertions — but neither of his crew members would dare complain.

Navigator held the thought and obeyed silence while his captain stretched in place and considered the implications of that hard return.

Infinite density. Small volume. But not enough mass to push the object deep into the planet's gravity well. Those observations could lead to only one conclusion: a Thrintun storage container, protected by its own time-warping field.

Honor and glory, a full name and heirs, the personal friendship of the Rrit, all would go to the discoverer of such a box. The artifacts concealed in those few that the kzinti had found in the past often yielded good weapons — or the clues to improving their own armaments.

Navigator and Weaponsmaster would be having similar thoughts, Nyawk-Captain realized. It was time to distract them.

"Continue," he grunted.

"The second contact is bigger, but not as dense. It presents a volume suitable for a ship's hull — a small one, but still capable of supporting a crew, drive systems, and weapons. I hypothesize it is a Leaf-Eaters' hull, such as they make as gifts to the humans."

"Is it near the other object?"

"Almost on top of it."

Nyawk-Captain casually ran a foreclaw into his mouth, probing the gaps between his teeth. It was a habit his father would not approve of, but it relieved stress while he thought.

"Shall we alter course, sir?" Navigator prompted.

Nyawk-Captain growled him into silence.

The Last Fleet followed *Cat's Paw* with a lag of ten days and a leeway of two days. Those two days were calculated to allow *Cat's Paw* to make minor course corrections, take evasive action, and conduct a brief survey of Margrave's defensive positions before Nyawk-Captain began his attack run against the system. The ten days would allow the human forces time to reach their maximum dispersal, following the near-simultaneous attacks by *Paw* and the other outriders, before the fleet struck behind him.

Timing was everything — but Nyawk-Captain knew he operated within a window of opportunity, not under split-second coordination. . . . And what an opportunity was now presenting itself!

He could, of course, contact the Last Fleet and request a delay in the planned attack. He would ask for enough time to allow him to alter course, stop, and retrieve the Thrintun box. A few days at most. But then, Nyawk-Captain would be honor-bound to explain his reasons to Lehruff, who was the commanding admiral. And Lehruff would want to share in the discovery.

Of course, if he could move in and get out quickly enough, Nyawk-Captain might retrieve the box and still make his rendezvous with Margrave well ahead of the fleet. All honor and glory would then come to him alone, when he eventually produced the Thrintun artifacts. His two crew members, being subordinates and inferiors in rank, would defer to him on the discovery. He might even share with them for form's sake — a sixteenth of the value for each would be a graceful gesture.

Of course, if Nyawk-Captain contacted Lehruff, he would also have to report the General Products hull that lay in close proximity. It was one hull only and not a large one; such a vessel had low probability of preceding and leading a massive attack by the Leaf-Eaters and their human puppets. Yet that was how Lehruff might read it. He would then want confirmations. Analyses. Councils of war. He might even send other ships to investigate the contact. Reason for delay. And an excuse to take the prize from *Cat's Paw*.

More likely that hull belonged to a lone prospector. Some renegade Leaf-Eater or human looking for wealth, mineral or otherwise, far beyond human Space. And finding it. Nyawk-Captain had to allow for the possibility of a fight. But it would be a short one. It would be over and *Cat's Paw* would be away in less than two days— their established margin for error and reconnaissance.

He would chance it.

"Alter course, Navigator. . . . Let us investigate this Leaf-Eater's hull which stands between us and victory."

"Jared!"

Cuiller raised the radio to his mouth without even breaking stride. "Right here, Hugh."

"It's eating the ship." The voice was so faint and breathy that Cuiller thought he must have missed part of the transmission.

"Say again, please."

"The Bandersnatch is eating our ship." Jook's words were louder and more distinct that time. Still crazy, though.

"Wait one, Hugh," the commander said. He turned to his weapons officer. "You hear that?"

Gambiel shook his head. "Heard it, but I don't believe it."

"How would a Bandersnatch *eat* the hull?" Krater asked.

"It's got a rudimentary mouth scoop," the Jinxian answered, "with a pretty solid rasp inside, like a snail's tongue. It can secrete digestive juices, too. But I don't know why it would want to."

"*Eat* a General Products hull?" Krater repeated.

"Not possible," Gambiel ruled.

"All right, stand to," Cuiller ordered. "Ah, Hugh," into the radio. "We're coming back now. Take care of yourself and . . . don't disturb the Bandersnatch, whatever it does."

"Not on your life, Captain."

"Let's go," Cuiller told his party. "And at the first sight of one of them — get up into the trees."

They nodded and turned back on their trail. Without a word passing, they all broke into a jog.

As they went by the patch of young undergrowth with the fallen trunk in the middle, Cuiller began to understand it better. The "groundskeepers" were Bandersnatchi, which fed by cruising between the trees and scooping in whatever vegetable and animal matter fell from the canopy. They were intelligent enough to understand the ecology that supported their existence. They would be wary of a dead tree and leave space for a new to grow and continue the life of the forest. From that perspective, a Bandersnatch might attack the ship as a threat to the ecology — or even, marginally, in retaliation for any damage *Callisto* had done when it tried to land in the branches and fell through.

But Bandersnatchi were not known for immediate aggression. Rather, they had often exhibited heroic patience, dying in large numbers at the hands of less perceptive sentients before they would make their hurts known. On some planets they had even agreed to be hunted for human sport, accepting a calculated loss for the stimulation of the chase.

On the other hand, Bandersnatchi were a living relic of Slaver times, with germ plasm too massive to mutate and needs too simple to allow their race to die out totally. As possibly the galaxy's oldest living intelligent species, they could well have purposes and prejudices wholly unknown to humans. Defense of territory might be one of their hidden prerogatives.

But still, an aggressive and vengeful Bandersnatch just did not fit the profile.

Yet the evidence which confronted them when they arrived at the landing site could not be talked away. *Callisto* lay fully against the ground, with two broken trees squashed under her bow. The ceramic outer coating was scuffed and abraded in long swathes and ragged patches. The paired metal horns at her tail, which had been fitted for external weapons and the ion drive, were now broken off and scattered in pieces over the forest floor. Every hatch cover and through-hull fitting had been knocked out.

Cuiller walked up to the main hatchway and stuck his head through. The smell was overpowering: a mixture of acids and ketones, spoiled plastics, burned metals, and what he could only describe as elephant vomit. Holding his breath against it, his eyes watering, he looked down the length of the interior, seeing with the light that came though the masked windows and the newly worn places. He looked for as long as he could, before the fumes drove him back. The hull was nearly cleaned out. A network of optical-quality glass fibers, apparently indigestible, had been discarded in one corner like a salt-encrusted fishnet. A few curling panels of fiberglass cloth, with the resins leached out, were all that remained from the sleeping cocoons. The hyperdrive engine, thruster pods, weapons pods, struts and bracing had completely disappeared — unless the sludge of reeking green bile that ran the length of the bottom curve were their only remains.

The General Products hull, of course, was not even scratched.

Cuiller beat his fist against it, just once, for no good reason.

"Where's Hugh?" Krater asked.

They looked around. Cuiller actually hoped they wouldn't—

"Up here!" the navigator called from a distance and dropped slowly out of the canopy, suspended in his climbing rig. His toes touched the ground and, favoring his stiff leg, he retrieved the grapple.

"Where did the Bandersnatch go?" Cuiller asked.

"South." Jook pushed a thumb over his shoulder. "Right after lunch."

"What did you manage to save from — all this?" The commander waved his hand around at the hull.

"Myself. A rifle. This harness."

"Any food? Water?" Gambiel asked.

"No time."

"Why didn't you lift?" Cuiller asked. "As we agreed you would."

"Again, no time. The thing was up on the hull before I even saw it. It had punched out the hatch and was chowing down on the infrastructure before I could get to the controls. Too late then."

"You should have been watching for it. We called to warn you."

"I was trying to repair the weapons module. And anyway, we *both* agreed Bandersnatchi wouldn't harm the ship. What did you expect me to do?"

"All right. Conceded, we were both wrong."

"Can we salvage anything?" Gambiel asked.

"See for yourself," Cuiller gestured at the ship. "Take shallow breaths."

"We're marooned, aren't we?" Krater asked as the Jinxian moved toward the hull.

"Yes. It's almost as if the Bandersnatch wanted to make sure we couldn't leave," Cuiller said. "And we never did get off a position report. So no one will be coming for us, either."

"I don't . . ." Krater looked suddenly pale. "I mean, I

didn't — " She turned away and stood looking up into the trees.

"Not your fault, Sally," the commander offered, but it sounded weak even in his own ears.

Cuiller went over to the abandoned cowling of the ion drive and started to sit down. He stopped and checked the surface for corrosive liquids. Finding none, he slumped on the bent metal.

"You've been up there, Sally," he said quietly, waving at the treetops. "What do you deduce from your observations?"

"Oh! I took some samples." She turned around and slipped the field kit out of her pocket. She opened it and keyed in a series of queries. The device beeped at her.

Jook drifted closer to listen. Soon he was sitting on the other side of the cowl, but with his back to Cuiller, looking away into the forest. His posture suggested depression and a sense of rejection by his companions. He'd snap out of it, Cuiller decided.

"There's water up there," Krater reported, "and the kit says nothing in it will harm us. The leaves — all that I got to test, so far — aren't poisonous, but they're no more nutritious than any other wad of cellulose and chlorophyll. There may be game up in the branches. At least, something played peekaboo with me up there. Whether it's edible, or would find us so, I can't tell. But the native ecology seems to be generally non-poisonous. Bandersnatchi like it."

"So we won't die of thirst," Cuiller summed up for her. "And we can hunt for long as the charges on our rifles hold out."

"That's about it," she agreed.

Gambiel had come back from the ship. Cuiller noticed that when he joined their group he stood, not beside Krater, but across from her. The Jinxian glanced at her only occasionally while she reported, and he spent most of his time looking over her shoulder, scanning the forest on the far side of the hull. When Cuiller thought of it, Jook's chosen position — sitting behind and facing away from his commanding officer — was not a sign of psychological separation after all. He was watching Cuiller's back.

Before, when the three of them had gone off into the trees, Cuiller and his crew had walked separately. They had raced off to look at sights that interested them, leapt freely up into the canopy, and generally acted like a cadet class on leave. Now they were more wary. That was good. It might save their lives — for as long as they might have on Beanstalk. It was time, right now, to give them some purpose.

"Daff, see what you can make from all the metal lying around out here. Cups or basins would be nice. A jar or canteen would be even better. But think twice before you do any cutting or pounding. Don't attract visitors."

"Aye, Captain."

"Sally, take a rifle and get up into the trees again. See if you can bring down one of your 'peekaboo' critters. They might be intelligent and in communication with the Bandersnatchi down here — "

"I don't really think — "

"But if one of them holds still long enough, shoot it."

"Captain, we don't need to worry about hunting for food just yet."

"Noted. But I want you to test the indigenous fauna before we eat up all our pocket rations. Anything you see like fruit or green shoots, collect them, too."

"Yes, sir."

She turned away and readied her grapnel launcher.

"You have any assignments for me?" Jook asked.

"If your leg is solid enough — "

"I might mention that our situation is hopeless, Captain."

"So?"

"Our long-term prospects are terrible. We are all alone

on a planet that's never been charted, let alone visited by other humans. No one knows where we are — or probably much cares, because our mission had such a low priority to begin with. We are on the marches of kzinti territory — technically unclaimed but not likely to be unknown to them. We've got Bandersnatchi prowling around here, and suddenly *they* don't like us, either. The best we can hope for is mere survival, but not much more. And, unless I miss my guess, even that's a long shot unless we find some kind of vitamin supplements. We won't last more than a couple of months hunting the local game in the treetops. So why should we do anything but give up, lie down, and die?"

"Because I said so," Cuiller said grimly. "And I'm still in command."

Jook straightened up. "Oh, well then, that's different. What do you want me to do?"

"Follow Sally when she goes up. Take station behind her, and anything that tries to kill her — you kill it first."

"Easy enough." The Wunderlander stood up, kneaded the bubble cast for a moment, and readied his rig. "What are you going to do, Jared?"

"Get some exercise by kicking myself for landing us in this mess."

"Fair enough."

An hour later, Gambiel called the commander over to sort out a collection of gear he had recovered from the ground around the ship and from a few protected corners inside the hull. The weapons officer had already arranged his catch by classification.

In addition to various pieces of bent metal, he had found three battery packs for the lasers; a bucketful of damaged circuit chips that might be reworked into some kind of transmitter, given time and enough optic fiber; and half of the autodoc. What remained of the latter provided them with some unlabeled vials that might be painkillers, antibacterials, growth hormone, or vitamin supplements. The tags were all electronic, for use by the expert system that ran the 'doc. It didn't need to know English equivalents.

"So, that's our inventory," Gambiel said at last, corralling the glass vials.

Cuiller told him to hang on to them. Maybe Krater, with her background in biology, could tell the vials apart by smell or taste or something. He supposed she also knew enough basic anatomy to deal with sprains — like continued attention to Jook's knee — and other manual medical techniques. If not, Cuiller had a little knowledge of first aid and could make do with bandage and splits in a pinch.

Gambiel had found nothing of the 'cycler. So they had only the food in their pockets, unless Krater's hunt was successful, or they figured out a way to bring down an adult Bandersnatch, or found a clutch of fresh buds.

"You want to try making a fire with that laser?" Cuiller asked.

"Burning what?"

"How much of a wedge do you think you could cut out of one of these trunks without knocking it down?"

"That's green, sappy wood . . . give off a lot of smoke."

"We can stand it. None of us is going to smell too good in a day or two."

"I was thinking of our white friends. They might be sensitive to fire under the canopy."

"You're right. I — "

The sound was on them before they could hear it: the rippling crackle of tortured atmosphere parting before a heavy body traveling faster than air molecules knew how to move. What they consciously heard was the clap of a sonic boom — the air moving back in the wake of whatever had snapped it apart — *followed* by echoes of that first, searing push against the atmosphere.

Cuiller looked up, expecting to see a contrail in the sky and finding only the green gloom of the canopy above them.

"That was a ship," Gambiel said. "In a hurry, too."

"Of course. Have any idea what kind?"

"I didn't hear any reaction thrusters. They could be on gravity polarizers."

"And this close to the Patriarchy's back door . . . Can kzinti detect a General Products hull at long range?"

"The same way we go about finding a stasis-box," Gambiel said. "Keep probing with deep radar and study the return images. Our hull comes up cloudier than a Slaver box, but still defined."

"Ouch! Let's get up into the trees."

"What about these?" Gambiel pointed to the hoarded supplies.

"You take the batteries and medicines. I'll take the circuit chips. Leave the scraps — no one's going to eat them."

The Jinxian began filling his pockets.

"Captain, what was that?" Jook called on the radio.

"Company. Daff and I are coming up to join you. Stay put and — until we know more — stay off the radio."

In reply, Jook keyed the transmit twice. Two low bursts of static that could be read as "Aye-aye."

Cuiller nodded silently at Jook's quick and tactful thinking.

"The kzinti won't be out of their ionization envelope yet," Gambiel observed. "They can't hear our radio transmissions yet."

"Still . . ." Cuiller took out his grapple and launcher, hooked up a line cassette, and took aim overhead. "When we get up there, Daff, go as high as you can. You're our best at identifying kzinti ships by their silhouette. See if you can spot and evaluate the newcomers."

"Do my best."

They fired their grapples and swung up through the leaves. As soon as Gambiel was stabilized on a limb near his grapple, he released it, aimed higher, shot, and slithered away after it. Cuiller surveyed the local jungle. Radio would carry to the kzinti, but not voice.

"Hugh! . . . Sally!" he shouted.

Cuiller looked around, parting clusters of flat leaves to stare into the next meter-wide pocket of air. He called again, stepped over to another branch, recovered and reshot his grapple, and swung on a short arc toward where he thought his navigator and communications officer had gone up.

"Sally! . . ."

"Captain, you're scaring the game." It was Krater's voice, but she was invisible, screened by the foliage.

"Belay the hunting, we've got visitors."

"I know. If you keep shouting like that, you'll scare them, too."

"Well, just hang on, because — "

"Heads up, everybody! Coming through!" Small and distant, Gambiel's voice drifted down to them. It was followed immediately by the groan of branches being forced aside — much like the first passage *Callisto* had made through the treetops — accompanied by the sizzle of wet leaves burning. Cuiller could smell hot iron and dying vegetation.

The question was, where would the mass of the ship come down? If it was right over their heads, they'd never have time to get out of its way before the kzinti ship knocked them loose and crushed them among the collapsing vines and branches. But if it was coming off to one side or another, then any step might move them to safety — or take them into the line of trouble. No way to know . . .

"Hang on!" Cuiller called out, and braced himself.

The wall of leaves that defined the edge of his vision

bulged inward and then dissolved in a golden tracery of sparks and incandescent veins. Beneath the fire was the scorching flank of a kzinti warship. Cuiller thought at first it was red-hot metal — or some ceramic, equally heated. Then, from the uniform coloring, he guessed the hemispheric section was simply painted red. It disappeared below before he had a chance to make up his mind. His one glance left the impression of a globular hull. From its chord, it seemed small. He guessed it was only fifteen or twenty meters in diameter. Then the gap in the trees closed on a blackened twist of branch and a fume of smoke.

Cuiller reset his grapple and lowered himself into the feathery bottom layer of the canopy to watch the kzinti ship land. From the *whirr* of winding motors that came to him through the leaves, he knew the rest of his crew had the same idea.

At this close range, the Leaf-Eaters' special hull showed clearly on a radar scanner working at normal intensities. The spindle gleamed and sparkled under the weakly graded return of the foliage layer covering the planet that Navigator said was chart reference KZ-5-1010. Nyawk-Captain made an estimate of the hull's size — more than 200 cubits in length — and, from this, confirmed the vessel type with Weaponsmaster.

Nyawk-Captain piloted an entry through the green layer, sliding among the interlaced branches and through the nets of vine. He counted on the residual heat in *Paw*'s hull to burn through, where the gravity polarizer could not break through, the entangling vegetation.

He wanted to place his ship at visual inspection distance from the strange hull. Among these closely spaced tree trunks, that meant landing practically on top of it — too near for evasive maneuvers. *Cat's Paw* went down with every weapon fully charged, ready, and aimed. Yet his greatest weapon against the

Leaf-Eater hulls, Nyawk-Captain knew, would be the gravity polarizer itself. At the first sign of hostility, he would use an acceleration forty times the pull of the kzinti homeworld to stomp anything inside that ship into paste.

When the last branches between him and the enemy ship had burned away, Nyawk-Captain focused his optics. The first thing his eyes registered were holes in the hull material. Then scrapings on its surface and the litter of metal pieces all around it. Finally, the trees that bent under its weight and the odd angle at which it lay among them. All of this, plus the total lack of reaction to his coming, gave Nyawk-Captain pause.

It was a dead ship, certainly. But how recently dead? And had its crew died in the accident that made it dead?

Given the Patriarchy's reports on the indestructibility of the Leaf-Eater hulls, this vessel might have been killed many years and light-years from this spot, could have drifted over the distance of time and space and entered the planet's atmosphere as unguided as a meteor, crashing among these trees. But then, Nyawk-Captain would expect some kind of cratering around the ship and more damage to the surrounding forest.

It might also have landed here long ago, and then the crew had suffered some accident. The ship would have deteriorated — all but the indestructible hull — under the force of time. But how would this version account for the trees crushed under the bows?

No, to tell the full story, he needed a personal reconnaissance of the derelict.

"Navigator, break out full body armor for both of us," he ordered. "Weaponsmaster, you stay at post. Destroy any danger that may approach. We will neutralize this threat — if any threat remains here — before going on to take our prize." The two crew members growled assent and went about their tasks.

Body armor came in a single articulated piece, like a hinged kzinti skin. It fitted solidly across the back, double-folded at the sides, and clasped with a tight seam up the belly. It was not designed as an environment suit, however, and covered only the backs and outer periphery of the arms, the fronts and sides of the legs. The attack surfaces. By rolling into a fetal crouch, a kzin wearing this armor could make himself practically invulnerable. The substructure was hardened steel, the surface an ablative material that would shed a ballistic slug or energy beam with equal facility. Of course, in that curled position, it could still be blown apart by explosives or melted with sufficient heat. But what kzin would crouch and wait that long, when he could fight?

Powered joints and solenoid-driven claws — connected to the kzin's own muscles with feedback pads — increased the wearer's strength and speed fivefold. The helmet's visor was fitted with devices that increased the senses of sight, hearing, and smell; offered an air mask to protect against poison gases, dusts and pollens; and connected the wearer with his companions through laser and electromagnetic telemetry and communications.

The body armor offered wonderful enhancements for a warrior — at the cost of two disadvantages. Donning it, inside the cramped spaces of a Scream of Vengeance-class interceptor, required the skills of an acrobat. Maneuvering it into and through the ship's tiny airlock required those same acrobatics combined with insufferable patience.

But, once he got his head into the open air, Nyawk-Captain hardly needed the helmet's filter enhancements to answer his earlier questions. His head swam with the scent of a dozen different long-chain polymers, dissolved into organic soup. He knocked the filters' sensitivity back three notches and took shallow breaths.

While Navigator finished his contortions and cycled

the lock, Nyawk-Captain approached the abandoned hulk. His eyes quickly adjusted to the forest gloom and began noting details: the position of various metal pieces, the indentations they left in the ground, other impressions. As he moved toward the hull, another complex scent came up, fainter than the scream of broken plastics. Dirt, sweat, pheromones. . . .

Humans! The ship had come here under a human crew. But Nyawk-Captain could smell no blood. So whatever had become of them, the crew had clearly survived the crash. He bent toward one of the marks in the ground and sniffed it. The odors clung to it, a human footprint.

Employing the suit's visual enhancers, Nyawk-Captain traced others of these marks. All of them had a certain formal similarity, just as all kzinti paws were made to the same design. But there were variations in the size and depth of the impressions. He counted four separate sets of these prints, matching them with their right and left curves.

"What do you — ?" Navigator began as he came up.

"Stay back!" Nyawk-Captain waved him away.

Placing his own pads carefully, he walked in circles, tracking each pair of prints. They moved back and forth over the crash site, now pausing and sinking fractionally into the hardened forest floor, now skimming and scuffing lightly over the dirt. Eventually, however, each track ended abruptly — a digging in with the toes, and then gone. Nyawk-Captain looked up, up, into the treetops. He knew little enough about human physiology, but he could guess that not even the sons of Hanuman could make such a leap. But where else, then, would they be?

"This is an empty hole, My Captain," Navigator observed.

"But not too long empty. I can still smell them."

"Yes, but what of it? This ship — the only hard

contact in this system — cannot interfere with us. We have nothing to fear from naked humans, wherever they may have gone. We should immediately retrieve the Thrintun artifact and then leave here."

"Well reasoned, Navigator, if not properly expressed for your superior officer's ears. We still have the question of what could have caused such damage to this hull."

"An academic inquiry, at best."

"Perhaps. Still, we shall — "

The sound came softly at first, through the aural enhancers. Nyawk-Captain thought it might be the creep of the forest floor under thermal stresses. Standing among the lattice pattern of upright trunks, he could not at first place it. He swiveled his helmet to scan the background.

"Weapons — !" he tongued the comm switch, then let the call die in his throat. A gliding white shape, easily three or four times the bulk of his ship, had loomed behind and settled over *Cat's Paw*. Its flesh would be blocking Nyawk-Captain's radio pulse. And besides, Weaponsmaster should already be aware of his predicament.

"Best we find cover," he told Navigator.

"Where?"

"In here," Nyawk-Captain replied, and sprang toward the nearest kzin-sized hole in the Leaf-Eater hull.

They crouched against the inside curve of the spindle, gasping in the waves of resinous vapor that assailed their noses until they could fasten their masks. At the same time, the carborundum claws extruding from their armored feet tried for purchase on the slick surface in an effort to keep them from slipping into the fuming liquid that sloshed in the bilges. Through a scar in the alien hull's outer coating, Nyawk-Captain watched the white mass writhing over his ship. He briefly caught the flash of a hard, crystalline edge under the Whitefood's bulk. Something *dripped* off that edge.

Whatever Weaponsmaster decided to do, it were best he acted quickly. Nyawk-Captain was beginning to understand what processes had eaten away everything but the hull of this human ship.

Suddenly, the huge pale body trembled, bulged upward — then *blossomed* outward in a mist of blood. Bright, red drops of it coalesced on the transparent surface through which Nyawk-Captain was looking. These were followed by strings and streamers of red flesh that slid and fell out of the blood cloud.

When the dripping and pattering of raw flesh stopped, Nyawk-Captain and Navigator climbed out of their hiding place. The stench of organic chemicals had disappeared in the aroma of fresh, warm meat. Navigator swung up his visor and mask, pulled a gooey strand off the outside of the Leaf-Eater hull, and sucked it off his fingers.

"Delicious!"

Nyawk-Captain, who had been studying the flank of *Cat's Paw* which emerged from the garland of meat and bones, stopped to try his own taste. After weeks of eating reconstituted meat and artificial proteins, the flavor was wonderful. Delicate, like *grik-grik* caught in mid-spring, so that the first flush of adrenaline barely touched it. Satisfying, like a haunch of *oolerg* that had been fed on grain and then run until the acids of fatigue had fully flavored the meat. Sweet as . . . It was, Nyawk-Captain decided, whatever flavor he wanted it to be. That was how the Whitefoods had been engineered to taste.

"Enough. We waste time," he told Navigator, then switched to the comm link. "Weaponsmaster? That was quick — "

"I *abase* myself, Nyawk-Captain!"

"Explain."

"In dislodging the Whitefood, I used too much force

for proximity to such an inert mass. I have damaged our ship."

"Catalog the damages."

"Primary and secondary lifting plates, short-range weapons, long-range communications, navigational and sensory antennas."

"Can you effect repairs?"

"Eventually, if we carry the right spares."

"Can you defend against another attack by the Whitefoods?"

"With warning — and I shall guard against their approach — the long-range weapons should be more than effective."

"Begin working on the ship, then. Navigator will assist you. Out."

"And what will you be doing while we repair the ship?" Navigator asked in a tone that bordered on insolence. "Sir."

"I will go after the Thrintun box."

"Yes, the box. That most important box. For which you have jeopardized our mission and put at risk an *entire kzinti fleet!*"

Nyawk-Captain felt his armor turning, almost of its own volition, to face this errant crew member. It was bending to assume a defensive crouch, conforming to his will almost without conscious command. "Do you have more to say?" he asked stiffly, fully expecting a shrill scream of challenge.

"No, Nyawk-Captain."

"Then understand this. If we are late for the rendezvous, all three of us will be whistling vacuum — unless we have a suitable peace offering for Admiral Lehruff. That box is now our life. Do you understand?"

"Yes, Nyawk-Captain."

"Good. You should start on your work. The ship must be ready to lift by the time I return."

The chastened kzin began the process of climbing in through the airlock.

Nyawk-Captain tongued his comm switch. "Weaponsmaster. Give me bearing and range to the second hardsight contact."

"Those systems are currently inoperative, sir."

"Curse it," Nyawk-Captain said mildly. "Can you rig a hand-held unit?"

"I can modify a ranging sight."

"Do so at once, and pass it through the airlock."

"Yes, sir, but I cannot guarantee its accuracy within a thousand cubits."

"It need only give the container's general direction and a sense of its proximity."

"You will have that, at least, sir."

While he waited for the new tool, Nyawk-Captain used the suit's claw to cut fillets from the ring of blasted meat girdling *Cat's Paw*.

Watching from his hanging point in the forest canopy, Cuiller almost cheered when the Bandersnatch slid over the dome of the kzinti ship. And he blinked back tears of rage mixed with envy when the kzinti weapons blew the creature apart. There, but for the few milliseconds that had padded Jook's reaction time, might stand *Callisto*, ready to fly.

Cuiller noted that one kzin remained on guard outside the ship, clad in efficient-looking armor, while the other returned inside on some business. Then the first retrieved something through the hatch and headed off through the trees.

Although Cuiller's sense of direction had suffered somewhat from remaining suspended in his spider harness, twisting among the branches, for almost an hour, he had no doubt what heading the kzin was taking. The Patriarchy possessed its own form of deep radar.

Time to begin thinking like a soldier, he told himself, instead of a tourist.

The first problem was to coordinate his team without

radio transmissions or — given that the walking kzin's armor was probably enhanced — too much shouting. He dropped cautiously down through the leaf screen into the clear space below the canopy. The *whirr* of his winder motor must have signaled the others, for first Krater, then Gambiel and Jook, also dropped into view.

"Now what, Boss?" Jook asked conversationally.

"We're going to keep out of the Big Guy's way, aren't we?" from Krater.

"Not if we want to get that stasis-box," Cuiller answered, trying not to whisper.

"Get it — and take it where?" Krater asked. "And how?"

"First things first."

"What I can't figure," from Gambiel, "is why the Bandersnatchi on this planet are so hostile. It's not their pattern. And they *can't* evolve."

"You're assuming we've seen more than one specimen," Cuiller said. "The one the kzinti blasted down there may be the same that ate *Callisto*, coming back for dessert. Anyway, that's something to think about later. Right now, we've got a fully armed and alerted kzin on the loose. . . . Did anyone see climbing gear on that body armor?"

"He doesn't need it," Gambiel replied. "With his power-driven claws, he can go up one of these tree trunks at a dead run."

"How much does that suit weigh?" Cuiller asked.

"Seventy-five kilos."

"That means kzin and suit together mass almost three hundred kilos." Cuiller experimentally flexed his knees and pumped his back sharply — and bobbed like a toy on his almost invisible thread. "He won't have much mobility among these springy branches and vines, will he?"

"Then he'd better pick *exactly* the right tree to climb," Gambiel agreed.

"I have a decision to make," the commander announced. "Do we all follow Kzin One and try to find the stasis-box ahead of him? Or does some part of our force stay here, to keep an eye on Kzin Two and the ship? Opinions?"

"Kzinti Two and Three," Gambiel corrected.

"I thought this interceptor class was a two-man affair."

Gambiel shrugged, and started his own bobbing dance. "Someone had to fight off the Bandersnatch from inside. It wasn't done by automatics."

"All right, then it's three kzinti and a ship to divide among four pairs of eyes," Cuiller noted. "I think we should stay together," Krater said. "And go for the box."

"Reasons?"

"The other two kzinti wouldn't be going anywhere except to follow the first," she answered. "And the ship is staying put, too."

"How do you know that?" Jook asked. "The kzinti might know a lot more about this world than we do. Those two could have a dozen interesting places to visit and things to do. After all, Beanstalk might be their private hunting preserve, or something."

"Then the kzinti would have found the stasis-box long before this," Krater countered. "And they wouldn't have let the Bandersnatch surprise them. Anyway, that explosion damaged their ship."

"How do you figure?" Cuiller asked.

"Wouldn't that big a bang have knocked some widgets loose from our hull? And that kzinti sphere isn't even from General Products."

"Circumstantial evidence," Jook scoffed.

"Besides which, from where I was sitting, I saw some pieces hanging loose."

"I hate to interrupt this," from Gambiel, softly, "but while we chatter, Kzin One is getting away."

"Right," Cuiller said. He made his decision. "We'll all

go. Fan out in line abreast, keeping a space of just one tree between each person. Stay hidden in the lower branches, if you can. And stay ahead of the kzin.

"We'll follow our original vector. At half a klick out, everyone start sorting through the branches around your assigned tree grid. The first to find the stasis-box, takes it. If Kzin One interrupts while you're doing that, kill him — if you can. Any questions?"

"Why don't we just shoot Kzin One from up here?" Jook asked.

"That's ablative armor," from Gambiel.

"Oh, right."

At Cuiller's nod, they all wound up on their lines to get a foothold in the canopy. Alone among the greenery, the commander readied his grapple in the launcher and fired forward along their path — which was also the kzin's. Around him he could hear the muffled *chuff*, *flutter* and *thunk* of similar activity.

Could Kzin One hear it too?

Swinging through the trees like a goddamn *monkey!* Trying to find the Slaver box by beating the *bushes!*

Angry thoughts swirled in Sally Krater's head as she balanced her feet on a leaf-cloaked branch and got ready to fire her launcher. She held it tightly, aiming along the course that she and the others had been following.

She could hear them around her, moving quietly through the overbrush, each making no more sound than the wind or any other animal up here. Now and again, she did hear the prolonged *whirr* of a winder as one of them dropped into the lower layers and peeked out to make sure Kzin One was still on track.

Everyone was trying to move quietly — except Jook. With his bad leg and his natural clumsiness, he bumbled through the leaves, missed his footing on branches, snagged his line and cursed softly while freeing it. Not softly enough to remain unheard by his fellow crewmembers, but maybe softly enough to go unnoticed by the pair of augmented kzinti ears moving ninety meters below them.

After a kilometer of travel, Krater knew Cuiller had angled his track to intersect Gambiel's and assigned the Jinxian to watch Jook's movements and help him be quiet. Krater herself, veteran of too many biologists' observation blinds, not to mention an early life in partial gravity, knew she was more graceful than any of them in this floating greenery.

But that did not keep the angry questions from buzzing about in her mind.

For instance, just how was any of them to know when they'd traveled the full two and a half kilometers to the Slaver box? Really! Cuiller was asking them to track accurately through the jungle while swinging around tree trunks and through shallow arcs, covering anywhere between twenty and fifty meters with each set of the grapple. In all that confusion, he expected them to stop within one or two trunks — a deviation of no more than fifty or seventy-five meters — from a predefined point. It couldn't be done! And that was just one sign of how badly this expedition had gone to hell. Ever since Jook had lost the ship . . . !

Krater angled her launcher at forty-five degrees above the horizon — or where she thought the horizon might be, much as she was bouncing around inside a blob of green leaves. She fired.

Chuff-CLANG!

The grapple had flown five maybe six meters, stopped dead, and recoiled. Now she could hear it slithering, falling through the branches, its monofilament cutting a vertical slice through the jungle before her. She jigged frantically with her upper body — as much as she could without falling off her branch — trying to jerk on the grapple's friction brake. If it failed to set, the grapple would fall all the way to the forest floor, signaling her presence to their clawed and armored shadow below. The monofilament caught and twanged on a stout branch. Krater could feel by the tension on the line that the brake had activated. She began winding in, breathing again.

What had the grapple hit up there? she wondered. Vine, branch, trunk, or "peekaboo" body part . . . anything in the projectile's flight path should have absorbed the point and snagged its tines. Only a rock or —

Krater wound the grapple up into her hand and reloaded the launcher. This time she aimed higher and shot.

Chuff! Flutter. THUNK!

She jerked the brake and began reeling in, walking off her branch, skimming the vines around the slash her line had made, touching the next branch with her tiptoes. Soon she was rising almost vertically, walking with hands and the points of her knees, up the side of the nearest main trunk. When the angle that the monofilament line made with the bark wall of the trunk began to shorten, she slowed the winder.

A woman's face, her own face, stared back at her in a pool of distorted greenery. As her head moved or a breeze rippled the leaves around her, she saw a flash of bright silver. This reflection of the floating world and her own face peered out from a collar of encroaching bark in the side of the tree. Like a knot of polished metal buried in the wood.

She touched the mirror and quickly drew her fingers back. It was cold — colder than any metal would normally be, in this mild climate. Its inherent temperature was not low enough to freeze sap in the wood embedding the knot. Still, it was a chill so deep that the shock felt, to her probing fingertips, like unexpected heat. She thunked the surface with her knuckles and listened for any echo of a cavity beneath the silver skin. No sound came back. So either the object was solid — more than solid, because she could sense no resonance at all — or its insides were lodged in another dimension. A dimension turned by several degrees away from her local reality.

She had found the stasis-box.

Now, how to alert the others? Krater wished they'd worked out, in advance, a series of whistles or bird-calls to address this situation. As communications officer she suddenly realized that should have been her responsibility. Hmm. . . . Well, how could she fix it up at this late date?

Sally Krater fingered the radio at her wrist. If not for the kzinti, she might try using that. But if their enemies were monitoring the electromagnetic spectrum, a radio call would be as damning as a shout. More directional, too. But perhaps . . . Krater clicked the unit off standby and tapped her finger lightly against the microphone in a rapid and ancient dance: *dit, dah, dah, dah,* pause, *dit, dah,* pause, *dit, dah, dit* . . .

"What is it?" from the speaker, before she could go on. She recognized Cuiller's voice, low and guarded.

She brought the microphone to her lips. "Krater. I've found it."

A pause, then: "Converge on Sally." And that was all.

Krater held her breath, waiting for an energy bolt to tear through the foliage below her. None came, but the *chuff* of launchers and *whirr* of winder motors was closing in from either side.

Gambiel was the first to appear, from her right, with his weapon at the ready. He saw the mirror in the tree and slowly strapped the rifle back over his shoulder. He touched the surface and did not draw back at the chill. "That's it, all right," he said.

Jook and Cuiller appeared from the left. They, too, examined the alien artifact.

"If that thing's a billion years old," Jook asked, "how

did it get up in a tree? It should have been buried under layers of geological strata, then turned over two or three times by plate tectonics."

"We've already figured out that this world doesn't have 'em, Hugh," Gambiel said. "Plate tectonics, that is."

"This rainforest ecology must be very old," Krater observed. "As old as the Bandersnatchi and the other Slaver biota. The Bandersnatchi will have been tending this planet for a long time.

"It's just possible," she went on, "that the stasis-box was picked up by a young, growing tree. Those saplings back there looked strong enough to do it — if whatever's inside the box isn't too heavy. Then the box was absorbed into the tree trunk as the branches sprouted and spread out. Eventually, when the tree died, the box fell to the forest floor. And the next tree to rise in that place took it up again. Maybe the stasis-box did spend a million years or so underground, pulled down by the root structure. But sooner or later it always comes up."

"Why?" from Cuiller.

"Because roots and other burrowing life turn the soil over. And in any scatter of small, loose stuff, the larger and heavier objects tend to rise. . . . Have we seen any sign of streams yet, let alone rivers or lakes? Those are the forces that make sedimentary rocks — what you call 'geological strata.' But we haven't seen them."

"Well, not around here," Jook said.

"And around here is where the box is, right?"

"I give up," the navigator said. "You found it in a tree, so it must be possible."

"We'd better get it out of the tree if we want to keep it," Cuiller said. "Daff, can you cut it out with your rifle?"

"Not if you mind the top of this tree coming down."

"Alternatives?"

"None I can see."

"Start cutting."

The Jinxian unslung his rifle and took aim two centimeters from the side of the mirror. The others, dancing on their monofilament tethers, swung back from the tree trunk.

Nyawk-Captain pulled the three claws of his left foot free from the firm wood as he touched the ground again. He shook them instinctively before remembering that it was sap, not blood, on his toes. Then he arched his foot in the special way that retracted the steel hooks into their sleeves. No sense in clogging them with dirt as he walked around.

He angled the navigational tool up into the trees again and pressed the improvised trigger. The tiny readout screen blossomed with a solid return. Somewhere above him was the Thrintun artifact, but his locator — modified from a missile's ranging warhead — was too powerful for this close work. Nyawk-Captain sighed and turned toward his third and final tree trunk for climbing.

Both times before, he had gone up as far as the first heavy branchings. Then he had released his hold on the trunk and stepped out into the green world of the elevated rainforest. The foliage beneath him had been uniformly limber, sagging fearfully under the weight of his body and armor. He had made his way a few cautious steps in this treacherous environment — so unlike the rolling veldt of his ancestors. Every step had required careful placement of all four paws on a firm bough, to avoid falling through. When he was fully clear of the trunk, he had raised his torso, balanced, and aimed his locator in the four cardinal directions.

By gauging the strength of the various returns, he had determined the general direction of the artifact. And by keeping his path down the last tree all along one side, without deviating around the intervening branches, he had maintained his sense of that direction. He was reasonably sure that the way to the artifact was up the tree he now addressed.

And if it was not, then he would start over again — right up until the time his crew had the *Cat's Paw* repaired and he must continue with his mission to Margrave.

Nyawk-Captain extended the powered claws and began climbing. In his previous forays up into the canopy layer, he had perfected the technique, digging in with his hind claws for lift and using his front claws for balance. It was easier going up than coming down.

A stutter of blue-light pulses, of short and penetrating wavelength, flashed from the muzzle of Gambiel's weapon. In a second, their original impact point in the tree trunk was obscured by smoke and steam.

"Don't worry about touching the box's perimeter," Cuiller advised.

"I'm riding on it," Gambiel replied. "The reflection helps." He swung the rifle in a slow circle, keeping ahead of the billow of steam.

After about thirty seconds, he had made two circuits of the mirror's face, going deeper each time. After the third pass, he shut off the weapon.

"We can pull it now."

Gambiel gripped the outer circumference of the box, which was shaped like a keg with its flat end facing them. At first, Krater expected Gambiel to draw back his hands from the residual heat, but of course the stasis-box absorbed the laser energy into another dimension. The Jinxian did, however, try to keep his knuckles away from the charred and smoldering wood surrounding it. He worked the box left, then right. He drew a slender knife and began digging around it. Krater saw the blade make a long drag against the side when his knife slipped, but it left no scratches and made no sound. Like cutting against glass with a feather. He worked on swinging the end with his hands again. It came free suddenly, like a stopper from a bottle.

"Light," he said, surprised. "Must weigh about ten kilograms."

"Empty?" Jook asked.

Gambiel started to shake it, then stopped in mid-motion with a frown.

Jook stifled a laugh. Whatever the box held, it held in stasis. The contents would not be rattling around in this time-frame.

"Not much mass, anyway," the Jinxian said. He had been staring at the box in his hands, but in a flash his attention shifted to the tree trunk at the point his knee rested against it. He stuffed the keg under one arm and placed his free palm against the bark.

Krater tried to read his face and couldn't. She swung closer to the tree and felt it, too.

A dull, rhythmic pounding was transmitted through the wood. She looked up, expecting to see the weakened top section bending over, dragging against branches as it started to topple on their heads. But, despite the deep wound in its side, the trunk wasn't falling.

Still the pounding came.

"Kzin One has found our tree," Gambiel whispered hoarsely.

"That's him climbing?" asked Cuiller, who had also put a hand on the wood.

"Yeah. But slowly. Methodical."

"Right. Daff, you keep the box. Sally, stay with him. The two of you go east." Cuiller pointed to establish direction. "Hugh, you and I go west to provide a diversion for them. Everybody try to keep out of the kzin's way for at least a full day. Reassemble at noon tomorrow by *Callisto*'s hull — or, if the kzinti are still around, one kilometer south by the sun. Questions?"

They shook their heads.

"Go!" he hissed, pushing Krater's shoulder.

The reel motors whined as they each rose away from the burn mark, toward the scattered anchor points of their own grapples.

Once he was inside the lowest levels of the green layer, Nyawk-Captain boosted the gain on his aural enhancers. He was listening for anything that might attack. On the ground, he could trust his senses of sight and smell to detect an enemy at great range. And his armor could deal with anything short of another rampaging Whitefood. Up in the foliage, however, screened by leaves and baffled by random breezes, those senses were next to useless. Only his steel ears would save him now.

Listening hard, he could hear *twang*ing and *huff*ing noises, with the clatter of leaves closing around solid bodies. Nyawk-Captain froze. But the noises were fading, he decided, moving off into the forest. Whatever lived up here perhaps had more to fear from a kzin than he from it.

Instead of stepping off on the lower branches, as he had before, this time Nyawk-Captain kept close to the main trunk of his tree. He intended to climb as high as he could, until the width of the bole was insufficient to support his weight.

He was still climbing on firm wood when he saw a burn mark in the tree. His head came up level with a hole big enough for a newborn kzitten to curl up inside. He touched the edges of the scar, crumbling the charcoal that coated them. It was still warm. He tasted his fingerpads. Fresh soot, with the scent of smoke still in it. As he watched, a tear of yellow sap rolled down and across the curve of the hole, confirming his suspicion.

He drew his locator from its belt clip and aimed down along his leg.

No return image.

He aimed up, past his helmet.

No image, either.

He aimed to the four cardinal points, in one case reaching around the tree trunk to aim for it.

East by the sun, he got a hard return, but nowhere as close to him as the bloom had been a few minutes ago.

The artifact was on the move — and going fast.

Nyawk-Captain did not think a Whitefood would have come to take it. He did not think a sudden burst of lightning had burned this hole. And he could think of no animal living in this world of green vines which might have control of such fire. Unless it was a form of superior monkey . . . the sons of Hanuman.

Certainly they had come here in the Leaf-Eater hull. They had not died with it. And, considering its present condition, they could not leave in it.

He began the long climb down to the forest floor. As he went, he sent a call to *Cat's Paw*. It was time to get Weaponsmaster started on a wide-area sweep with those sensors they still possessed.

Daff Gambiel rested in the fork of a large branch, balancing the Slaver stasis-box on his knee. He and Krater had traveled eastward five kilometers by his own dead reckoning.

Now they were in disagreement about which way they had actually gone. So Krater had climbed higher into the overgrowth, to take bearings by the setting sun. Fine in theory — if she could keep her sense of direction while moving around in this leaf maze.

Gambiel was willing to bet she would get lost just coming down.

While he waited, he studied the stasis-box. One side had a flattened place with a dull-gray disk etched onto the mirrored surface. It was the only feature in an otherwise featureless object. It had to be the field actuator switch.

Gambiel considered it carefully. He knew he should wait on opening the box until the other team members could be present. They would all want to inventory the contents together. That way they could examine anything inside that might be fragile or valuable, offer witness of anything that might fall apart or evaporate, or try to protect each other against anything that might suddenly leap out and attack them.

But Cuiller and Jook might also have been captured by now. Or he and Krater might be captured anytime soon. Better to open the box now and know what it contained. Besides, even though it massed only ten kilos, the thing was too awkward to keep carrying around. Gambiel was tired of working his launcher one-handed, and no sling or belt he could rig would hold on to the box's slick, mirrored surface. More to the point, if the kzinti were using deep radar — or any radar at this distance — the box was a sure signal of his and Krater's location. So it made most sense to abandon it, unload and abandon it, now.

Without more thinking, he pressed down on the disk.

The box changed, its surface slowly becoming a cloudy gray. It was like watching a time-lapse video of silver tarnishing. When the transformation was complete, a crack appeared along the keg's length and down each end-face.

Gambiel forced the crack open with his hands and found himself blinking into a pair of wide-set, liquid eyes. They belonged to a face that was part of a rounded body covered in soft, white hair that was trimmed in intersecting globes of fluff. He was reminded of pictures he once had seen of Earth dogs — useless, yapping, brainless pets. This animal, however, studied him with a wary expression and made no move to climb out of the stasis-box.

Gently, in case the animal should suddenly display

teeth and snap at him, Gambiel felt around inside the box. He quickly found the remaining contents: a long, tubular device that had a fretwork of keys and finger-holes, like a flute, but no mouth-hole for blowing; and three patties of wrinkled, brownish material that looked like freeze-dried meat, each wrapped in a tight plastic sheath. Gambiel assumed the meat was some kind of food ration for the "dog."

He set the stasis-box, with the animal still sitting patiently inside it, down among the interwoven vines of the canopy. It was the "flute" that drew his attention.

He held it up with the end pointing at his mouth, like a clarinet or recorder, and tried to fit his fingers to the keys and holes. It didn't work for eight fingers and two thumbs. He frowned and looked down along the flute's length, counting. Yes, it did have more than ten positions — thirteen, in fact — but the spacing was wrong for human hands. Not surprising, considering that a billion years ago humans had not evolved on Earth, nor much else, other than bacteria and blue-green algae.

He raised the flute again, and —

Yip!

The dog had barked at him. Gambiel looked down. The animal's eyes had grown big and it was trying to shy away from him.

Daff shrugged and began pressing keys at random, still looking for a hole to blow through. He heard a faint and almost familiar strain of music. He stopped fingering. Instead of breaking off in the middle, the tune wandered away from the notes and faded in a burble of sound. If this was a flute, Gambiel decided, it was a defective one.

He set it aside and looked at the dog, which seemed to be going to sleep on him.

"Come here, Fellah."

The dog immediately straightened up and jumped out of the case. It came directly to Gambiel, sure-footing its way across the vines, and rested its chin on his knee. It looked up at him with an attitude of rapt attention.

"Yeah, you're a good Fellah, aren't you? Bright little guy, too. You know I won't hurt you. . . . It's a good thing we found you first, instead of those kzinti. . . . They probably hate dogs — would if they had any in their Patriarchy, that is. . . . And they're big enough to do something about it, too. . . . I figure they'd take you for a snack. You're just about one bite to them."

As he talked, the animal's eyes slowly closed . . . falling asleep.

The darkness was beginning to grow around them, seeping in between the leaves, and Gambiel expected Krater to come down soon.

"Are you hungry, Fellah?" He picked up one of the meat patties and looked it over. No kind of heat tab or peel point in the wrapper. He drew his knife and slit around the edge.

The dog never lifted its head from his knee.

He pulled the plastic back and sniffed the patty. It smelled vaguely unpleasant, like dried meat saturated with chemical preservatives.

"You eat this stuff?" He offered it to the dog.

Fellah slid his chin off Gambiel's leg and backed away. His eyes were still half closed and his head down between his shoulders. Gambiel knew very little about dogs, because they didn't fare well in Jinx's high gravity. But he decided the animal's reaction was purely negative, a cross between "guilt" and "disgust."

Gambiel shrugged and broke off a piece of the meat for himself. He put it in his mouth, let his saliva soak it for a moment, and began chewing. It had no flavor, like chewing on wood pulp. He rewrapped the patty, putting it and the others in his pocket.

"What the hell are you doing?" Krater asked as she brushed aside a branch and climbed the last few meters down to his level.

"Trying one of these meat pies." He took them out and showed her.

"You opened the box!"

"Well, we can't keep carrying it. The stasis-field makes us sitting ducks for the kzinti."

"But you should have — "

"Asked your permission? Well, would you have agreed?"

"Of course not."

"So why would I ask?" He shrugged.

"You should have thought it through, Daff. That's a artifact from a ancient xeno-civilization, older than life on Earth. You have no way of understanding what's inside there."

"Sure I do. A little dog, a flute-thing that doesn't work, and some rations that don't have much taste. I tried them on the dog, but it doesn't — "

"*You tried them on the dog!*"

"And ate some myself. But why does that upset you so?"

Krater ignored his question. She turned to Fellah and was peering at the little animal, which had crawled backwards in among the leaves. Only its eyes and nose, three shiny black marbles among the fluffy white fur, peered out at her.

"It does *look* like a dog," she said. "How big is it?"

"About five kilos."

"Does it have four legs, a tail, all that?"

"Yeah. I've seen holos of dogs before."

"And friendly?"

"Real friendly. I call him Fellah."

Krater reached out a hand to it. "Come here, Fellah!"

The animal's eyes grew wider and it backed farther into the foliage.

"Not that friendly," Krater said.

"Well, he came to me."

"Then *you* take care of him, because we have get moving. Our course is more — " She looked around their bubble of clearing, swung her arm off to the right. " — that way."

Gambiel stood and stuck the flute into his belt, taking care not to bend the keys. "Hey, Fellah!"

The dog came out of its leaf hole and jumped into his arms.

"He does seem to like you," Krater admitted.

Gambiel reached down for the dull-gray box, forced it shut—but with the field off—and juggled it under his left arm. "Going to be awkward," he said, hitching the dog around into the crook of his right arm. "Would you ... ?"

Krater shook her head. "I'm having enough trouble moving myself through these vines. Put the dog and the other stuff back in the box, why don't you?"

"He'll suffocate."

"Then turn the field back on."

"And let the kzinti use it to track us?"

"Then we have to leave the box," she said.

"The Navy will pay a high ransom for an operating stasis mechanism. Could be worth your pension and mine together."

"Then leave the dog!"

"No, he'll die up here. Starve to death, fall through to the forest floor, or get eaten by the kzinti. Besides, he could be valuable."

"Well, you're the one who opened the box in the first place."

"We can leave the box," Gambiel decided, setting it down on the vine mat. "Do you think you could find this place again?"

"No."

"If I left it with the stasis-field turned on, we could locate it again, easily."

"So could the kzinti."

"Yeah. And that might distract them."

"Then leave it," she agreed.

"Is that the right decision, hey, Fellah?" he asked, hugging the little dog tighter under his arm.

It looked up at him with those big eyes, seeming to understand the question. It made a sound halfway between a chirp and a whine.

"Err-yupp!"

"Oh, brother!" Krater sighed.

He bent down and activated the flat disk. The cloudy surface of the box cleared to a hard, silvery shine in the fading light.

"Let's get out of here," Krater said.

It was too dark, really, to go swinging thought the trees. But with the box set like a beacon behind them, Gambiel could see no alternative. He readied the grapple in its launcher and aimed left-handed.

Chuff!

"I need better field accuracy than this," Nyawk-Captain said, handing his jury-built locator to Weaponsmaster.

The kzin took it and inspected the pirated missile circuitry. "Perhaps I can tune — "

"Is the ship's radar back in commission yet?"

"Navigator and I were just making the final adjustments."

"Give me a sweep of the area."

"Yes, sir."

While they fired up the repaired systems, Nyawk-Captain stretched, scratched, and got himself something to eat. He had learned it was easier to shed the armor outside the ship and work the airlock unencumbered. Bad policy if a ground force attacked while all of them were inside, but he didn't think anything would come against the ship, except more Whitefoods. And Nyawk-Captain had made reconstruction of the short-range armaments a priority.

Munching a haunch of Mystery Meat — a Fleet ration consisting of amalgamated proteins and vitamins, pressed around a synthetic bone and inadequately rehydrated — he looked out through the open hatch. The armor stood sentinel there, and in more than just a symbolic sense. Before stepping out of it, he had keyed the enhancers for sound and scent, slaving them by radio circuit back into the ship's sensors.

"Ready now, sir," Navigator called.

"Locate the Thrintun box."

"Two kilometers distant but at a new bearing — uhn, different from the one you took."

"Which way?"

"North and east of here."

"Weaponsmaster, get armor. We will go together to find it this time."

"Aye, sir."

"Ouch!" came a low sound in the utter blackness.

"What was that?"

"I hit my head on a branch."

"Again?"

"Can't we slow down?"

"Still three kzinti out there. Behind us."

"One, you mean."

"One that we saw."

"The others are working on their ship."

"Yes — last time we looked."

"We'll kill ourselves, swinging through these trees in the dark."

"You want to walk? And put both feet through a hole?"

"We could stop for the night."

"The kzinti would find us."

"In this jungle, *I* couldn't find us."

"You don't have their sense of smell."

"*Ow!*"

"What now?"

"I barked my shin."

"Well, do it quietly. They have ears, too."

Nyawk-Captain aimed the locator up into the trees. The refinements Weaponsmaster had made in its circuits were amazing: they reduced the light bloom of any hardened return to a pinpoint, while stepping up the return image from woody branches and trunks into a ghost map of the tree world.

"I detuned everything else and made it selective for carbon," Weaponsmaster had explained, the first time his captain had used it. "Carbon is a component in cellulose," the kzin added.

"Very creative," Nyawk-Captain had said.

Now, two kilometers from the ship, he aimed into the treetops again and took a reading. The artifact was right above them, almost aligned with the tree by which they were standing.

Nyawk-Captain turned his helmet light up the side of the tree. "The artifact is approximately ten cubits out from this trunk in — " He oriented himself against it and pointed. " — *that* direction."

"Shall I climb for it?"

"Do so."

In five minutes, the kzin returned with the storage box under his arm.

"It feels light, sir."

"We'll open it at the ship."

"When they find it's empty, what do you think they'll do?"

"Come after us."

"They're already doing that."

"So? Did you expect them to stop?"

"No, I guess not."

Excitement overcame Nyawk-Captain. Rather than shed his armor and climb into the ship, he called on Navigator to come out with a strong worklight.

"Should not someone stay inside, sir? To guard against — "

"Come out here!"

Before Navigator could negotiate the airlock, Nyawk-Captain had the box on the ground and, in the light of their helmet lamps, had found the actuator stud.

The box turned from flashing mirror-brightness to a simple, luminous gray. A crack appeared along its top. Nyawk-Captain forced it apart with his hands. Navigator brought up the light and angled it down inside.

Nothing.

In all the records collected by the Patriarchy concerning Thrintun boxes, none had mentioned an empty box. Preserving fresh air was not a priority with any species.

Nyawk-Captain put the beak of his helmet into the space and inhaled deeply, with suit enhancers at full power. His own nose told him that some animal had once — briefly and forever — inhabited this space. The suit's flicker display began cataloging a long list of organic chemicals: oils, hormones, enzymes, pheromones.

He inspected the interior with optical enhancers, and found three hairs — finer than those on any kzin's pelt — and all without pigment. In daylight, they would be white.

"Is this a billion-year-old joke?" Navigator asked.

"No. The box was inhabited by a live animal," Nyawk-Captain replied. "Too small to be a Thrint. Unlikely to be a Tnuctip."

"But now we have nothing to show for our effort . . . and for the delay."

"Do you have a problem with that?" Nyawk-Captain asked pointedly.

"No, sir. But now we should give full attention to repairing *Cat's Paw* and resuming our flight to attack Margrave. The mission has not yet become problematical."

"We still have time to find the contents of the box — and the humans who stole it."

"Not with the sensory equipment we have at hand."

"Then use your skills as *Navigator*. Plot me a course. Use the Leaf-Eaters' stripped hull as a starting point. One vector is defined by our first sighting of this box, now a burned-out hole in a tree. The second sighting point, where we actually found the box, yields another vector. Assume, to begin with, that the humans have no means of transport nor any logical destination other than the hull. Then give me their probable locus within those limits."

"Right away, sir."

"Narrow the field for me, Navigator, and we'll find the thieves by using our native hunting instincts." He turned to Weaponsmaster. "Can you readjust the circuits of that homing radar for a slightly different concentration of carbon?"

"It's almost dawn."

"How can you tell?"

"I think I can see my feet."

"The brush does *seem* lighter."

"Ouch! Damn it! I give up."

"It's probably safe to rest here."

Without answering, Sally Krater released enough of the monofilament to allow her to sit on the branch that had tripped her. She let the rest of it float around her face — and didn't care if it snagged on anything and cut off her nose.

"We may not be as far ahead of the kzinti as Jared and Hugh now are," Gambiel said.

"How do you figure?"

"When we stopped to take bearings — "

"And open the box, remember."

" — and open the box," he agreed, "we lost valuable time. And we haven't been making it up in the dark."

"What can we do about that?"

"Listen!"

"How's that going to — ?"

"Hush!"

Krater cocked her head and listened. Faintly, through the brush, she could hear a crashing and snapping of the greenery. It was behind them, coming along their back trail.

Gambiel thrust the flute-thing and the white dog into her arms. Before she could stop it, the dog jumped free. It started to run off in the opposite direction, then turned and looked back at her. A long, hard stare that seemed to be full of meaning.

"Go along, now," the Jinxian told her.

"But you — ?"

"I'll delay them. Go."

Krater stood up and took in the slack monofilament. "Come here, Fellah!" she called in a low voice.

The dog came up to her and stood on its hind legs, putting a paw on her knee. She scooped up the animal and hit her winder's clutch. In less than a minute, she had gone twenty meters higher and thirty meters farther into the jungle canopy.

Gambiel turned about-face, called upon all his inner strength, his *chi*, and began his patient preparations. After a lifetime of training and development, he was finally going to fight a kzin in the flesh. It was likely to be wearing armor, he knew, but Gambiel had his laser rifle and the advantage of surprise.

He retrieved his grapple, loaded the launcher, and fired straight up. The grapple *thunk*ed into solid wood ten meters overhead. Slowly, so as to make as little noise as possible, Gambiel raised himself off the stable branch layer where he and Krater had paused to rest and where a full-grown kzin in armor would undoubtedly choose to walk. He stopped when he found a tunnel through the leaves that gave him an angle back to that stouter layer. His view crossed their earlier track through the area. Then he hung quietly, staring down and holding the rifle, at full charge, across his thighs. Gambiel made himself as still as a bow hunter waiting in the dawn above a game trail.

The kzin came into view, placing its feet with great care, advancing cautiously from limb to supporting limb. For all its mechanical encumbrance and the excess weight, the warrior was still moving incredibly smoothly. The body markings on this suit of armor were different from those on the kzin that Gambiel and the others had watched leaving the enemy ship the day before. (Had it been no longer than that?) This one was clearly a different member of the crew.

Gambiel raised the rifle with hypnotic slowness and sighted on the gap which showed orange fur between the jaw extender and the articulated breastplate — the place where a suit of human armor would have fastened a steel gorget.

His first pulse of coherent blue light, even masked by the gloom of the forest canopy, sent the kzin hurtling sideways. However, a flash of white smoke and a startled *"Rowrrl!"* told Gambiel that something tender had been burned.

Stumbling off balance, the kzin almost crashed through the unstable floor. Then it might have fallen ninety meters or more, to be painfully damaged if not killed. But the armored figure managed to right itself.

Gambiel lined up on the edge of his aiming hole and fired another pulse, seeking another tender spot. Instead, he touched the ablative surface of an armored gauntlet. It dissipated the energy in a spark of ceramic fragments, leaving only a small, white crater in the material. Then the kzin was up and moving forward, climbing over intervening

branches, walking into the point source of the laser pulses.
It was hunched over — not in pain, Daff knew, but only so
that it offered the thicker material of the shoulder and neck
plates to the oncoming fire.

Gambiel reeled in on his winder, moving higher as
quickly as he could, and kicked backward to put himself beyond the kzin's reach. His retreat was limited,
however, by the set of his grapple.

The kzin was upon him too quickly and knocked the
rifle aside. The weapon fell and disappeared through
the green canopy floor.

Before the warrior could strike again, Gambiel hit
the release latch on his climbing harness and dropped,
on all fours, ten meters to the canopy's base layer. He
grasped with his hands and snagged with his feet
among the vines. Once he knew he was not going to fall
through, he raised his body in a wrestler's crouch and
looked up and around, ready to meet the kzin.

The kzin — too heavy to drop like that — climbed
quickly down to his level and stopped, considering
Gambiel. Daff could read its reactions. Even though
the human was now unarmed, its stance was not that of
prey. He was actually *challenging* the kzin. And the
tattoo on Gambiel's forehead might be familiar from
kzinti training tapes. Somewhere they must have
described a breed of humans so marked, who would
actually fight barehanded.

The kzin appeared to reach a decision. Slowly and
deliberately, gesturing to make itself understood, it
keyed a release button. The armor sprang apart like a
cracked crabshell. The kzin kicked the suit aside — and
it, too, fell through the loose floor. Daff's opponent
raked its own flanks in a brief scratch. Gambiel visibly
bent his knees into a deeper crouch, preparing to
absorb the shock of the first attack across the springy
floor layer. He dug in his toes and raised his hands in a
defensive position.

Human and kzin confronted each other with a long stare. The kzin seemed to be focusing on the Hellflare tattoo. Maybe the warcat did understand its meaning.

The kzin screamed and leaped directly at Gambiel.

Gambiel lifted his left foot from the entangling vines, straightened his right leg and — hoping he wouldn't screw himself right down into the criss-crossed foliage — performed a perfect veronica around the swinging left paw. Its claws extended five centimeters outside the flashing orange blur. As the furred flank passed, Gambiel struck backhanded at the third skeletal nexus. He heard as much as felt the joint crack.

The kzin's scream rose an octave in pitch.

The warrior came back on attack with a feint. Gambiel ignored the stroke but still countered with a twisting punch. It found only air and a whisk of fur.

In two more exchanges, the kzin absorbed one painful blow, and Gambiel took a raking that opened his right arm and shoulder to the bone. As he was trying to press back the flap of flayed skin, he felt a jet of arterial blood. The fourth claw had struck higher on his neck than he thought.

The kzin, sensing imminent victory, prepared its last charge.

Gambiel then made the decision that had loomed over his entire life for so long. He would not step aside again. He met the charge full on — with a stop-kick whose perfect focus on the center of the kzin's skull was one-half centimeter longer than the warcat's reach. His blow cracked that skull a half-second before the eight claws swung across his torso in converging slices.

Disemboweled, the Jinxian's body flew sideways and caught against a tree limb. He saw it arrest his flight but could feel nothing down there. Then his eyes darkened, a red mist creeping across his field of vision. But before the mist could raise the night, he saw the orange body stagger, curl up, and disappear through a gap in the shrubbery.

The kzin did not even scream as it fell.

Hanging in her harness with just a toe-perch among the slender branches, Sally Krater listened carefully to the thrashing below her in the canopy. The fight that Gambiel was waging proceeded without cries or curses, just that one scream of challenge. If it was followed by heavy breathing and grunts of pain, she could not hear them.

The dog Fellah huddled in her arms, shivering against her chest. But occasionally it lifted its head and looked down. Then, by the tilting of its ears, she sensed the animal was following the action and weighing their chances of survival.

When the thrashing ceased, Krater released her winder and unclenched her toes, dropping down into the open vaults beneath the canopy layer and above the forest floor far below. Off to her right, about forty meters away, she saw an orange body drop through the leaves and tumble three times head over heels before it hit the hard ground. It lay there in a bundle of matted fur. Krater thought it was dead, until it twitched and moved a paw, raised itself and began to crawl.

Sally lifted herself into the cover of the leafy layer and watched. The kzin rose on its hind legs with painful, ungraceful jags of motion and started to walk away. Krater withdrew fully into the canopy. She consulted her sense of direction and moved back toward the place of the fight.

At first, all she could see were torn branches and a ruck of leaves, turned over to show their lighter undersides among splashes of blood. At the side of the clearing, however, she quickly spotted the Jinxian's uniform. She set the dog down on a firm branch and moved quickly over the vines toward Gambiel.

His coverall was curiously flat, deflated. She touched his shoulder, to rouse him and turn him over, and the torn remains slumped apart, ripping the uniform fabric across the back.

Krater found his head, his eyes open and staring. She closed them with the edge of her hand.

Then there was nothing more she could do, no words to say, and no way to bury him. She gathered up the dog and continued moving toward the noon rendezvous.

"Fellah" they had called him, these beings that lived and moved separately, apart from the Discipline. "Fellah" was the word shape that came up in their blue-green minds and arrowed at him like yellow fire. "Fellah." And they did not mean it unkindly.

As he lurched through the rushing trees, under the arm of the "Sally," the Pruntaquilun Balladeer closed his eyes to the flying wind and the green leaves, and tightened his stomach against the surgings of sensation. He called up his latent powers of intellect and considered all that he had experienced since being packed into Guerdoth's traveling case.

When the Master had prepared for a month's stay at the hunting estates of his uncle, the Magistrate Alcuin, he had taken along his favorite Balladeer. And his baton, of course. Fellah knew what the device did and how it worked. As a Pruntaquilun, with his limited insight into other minds and his facility with courtly language, he was instrumental in the Master's charades.

None other than Guerdoth's favorite Balladeer could be trusted to help the Master conceal the shame of his Powerloss and so to survive. Thus, Fellah would observe and make stealthy inquiries with the edges of his mind, accumulating bits and shadings of thought from other Thrintun and from Slaves. Then he would sing of them to Guerdoth in an ancient tongue that only the Master understood. With Fellah's espionage, and with the Baton, they cemented the impression among all who cared that Guerdoth still retained the Power and wielded it as a true Thrint.

But when the time-standing case had been opened, Fellah was arrived not at Alcuin's estates but in a green world of wild, waving plants and among wild, unDisciplined beings. Except that the "Daff" had wielded Guerdoth's Baton. Although he had used it inexpertly, still he made the commands to love and respect, to attend and obey. And he made them on Fellah himself!

Yet even as he made the commands, the Daff had not thought of himself as a Master. The word-image he used was "human." Strange it was, however, that the shape of this thought in the Daff's mind was not much different from the shape of "Thrint" in Guerdoth's. It contained the same overtones of capability, of mastery, of the expectation to control and order the world and time as one saw fit.

Similar thought-shapes had also been in the Sally's mind — although not so strongly, not since that Other had come and destroyed the Daff. Fellah himself had known the Daff was dead in the instant his mind sparked and went black.

Fellah wished the Sally would use more and simpler words in her thinking about the death, so that he might absorb them and add to his picture of these new masters, the humans. He was putting together a sense of the pattern of their minds and their language with every thought he intercepted. But it was harder this way, starting without a grammar or even a coherent picture of the world into which he had emerged from the traveling case.

The Other who had killed the Daff had used still another word-image, "kzin." It was brighter, more jaggedly lit with reddish-orange colors and blood scents, than the "human" in Daff's and Sally's minds. Yet "kzin" meant controller and shaper of destinies, too.

And nowhere, not along any of the dimensions among which Fellah cast his mind, did he find any echo now of "Thrint." The glinting hard edges of their Power was gone from the universe, creating a black and peaceful vacuum, as if it had never been.

Fellah contemplated a universe without Discipline, without the ever-present puppet strings. He tried to decide if this emptiness was a good thing in itself.

He began to suspect it might be.

Nyawk-Captain found Weaponsmaster's discarded armor through the emergency distress tone it was generating. From its position on the forest floor, with the helmet bent back and the visor digging a furrow in the dirt, he concluded that it had fallen out of the trees.

He studied the pattern of burn marks on the ablative surface. No blood or carbonized flesh on either, although the one at the throat smelled of burned hair. Clearly, Weaponsmaster had not been injured significantly while wearing the armor. Nor had he been wearing it when it fell.

Nyawk-Captain tilted his head back to study the underside of the roof layer. Nothing in its leaf pattern told him anything.

"My Captain!"

The voice was faint and coming from his left. Nyawk-Captain rose in a crouch and his armor prepared itself for violence.

Weaponsmaster limped forward from one of the rare patches of jungle growth on the forest floor. His gait reflected broken bones. He tended to circle to the right as he moved.

Weaponsmaster fell. Nyawk-Captain, moving toward him, caught his crewmate and lowered his body gently to the ground. Nyawk-Captain pawed at his belt for the field medical kit and began breaking ampules of pain-reliever.

"Do not bother," Weaponsmaster grunted. "My head is cracked and my life is at an end."

"Did you fall? I found your armor. How did — ?"

"One of the humans confronted me. He actually *challenged* me. It would have been dishonorable — to meet a naked combatant in armor. So I shed mine. . . . He fought well."

Nyawk-Captain heard this explanation but hardly believed it. The sons of Hanuman were known to fight by deceit and trickery, not by challenge in an honorable contest. And they did not kill adult kzinti in naked combat. This was most odd!

"Did you kill him?" Nyawk-Captain asked, feeling sure of the answer.

"I do not know. . . . Not for certain. But too much blood covers my paws, I think, for him to live."

"Was he alone?"

"I saw one only."

"That is never proof that there aren't others."

"I know. I failed you . . . should have . . ."

"Which way was it — were they — going?"

". . . East?"

The word ended with a huge, jaw-cracking yawn. A gout of blood came up in Weaponsmaster's throat, flowed over his tongue, and dripped between his teeth. The body went limp and, by reflex, the pink ears opened wide.

Nyawk-Captain smoothed them closed and lowered the great head to the ground.

Then the kzin considered his options. He had time, barely, to locate the humans, recover the contents of the Thrintun box, and still make his rendezvous at Margrave. But he would accomplish all this, he decided, even if it violated his margin for error on the mission. This was no longer just a matter of the box and its treasures. It was now an affair of honor.

"How far are we from the ship, do you figure?" Jook asked.

Cuiller looked up at his companion in surprise. "You're the navigator."

"Astrogation only. I'm a wreck in two dimensions."

"But I thought you were keeping track . . ."

The Wunderlander shook his head and looked down at his hands, massaging the bubble cast around his knee.

"Well, we were turning left all the time," Cuiller reasoned, "so we have to be somewhere south of *Callisto*."

"But how far?"

"Can't be more than two or three kilometers. We haven't traveled more than five or six altogether. And that wasn't in any kind of straight line."

"Are we lost?"

"Umm." Cuiller sucked his lips. "Which direction do you think the sun is?"

"Straight up."

"Then we're lost," the commander admitted. "But later on, when the sun moves west, we could work our way east and attempt to locate Sally and Daff."

"In this jungle, we could pass within forty meters of them and never know it."

"I guess it's time to try the radio." Cuiller raised the wrist unit, powered it up, and clicked the send key a couple of times.

"Captain?" from the speaker.

"Is that you, Sally?"

"Yeah. Where are you?"

"Somewhere south of the ship," he said. "I think."

"Me too. How are we going to link up?"

Cuiller thought for a moment. "One from each party should climb a tall tree, get above the forest canopy."

"It's just me now. Daff is dead. . . . What happens after I climb up there?"

"Burn some leaves or something with a rifle pulse. I'll do the same."

"All right. I'll be watching for you. Out."

Cuiller climbed while Jook stayed below. Daff was dead? As commanding officer, Cuiller would have pressed Krater for the details — except their messages had to be brief, to keep the kzinti from taking a radio fix. Anyway, Cuiller could well guess what had happened. One of the kzinti had caught up with them, and the Jinxian would not have run from that fight. Instead, with his lifetime of training, Daff had probably welcomed and invited it. And he had sent Krater on ahead, with the Slaver stasis-box, to safety.

Daff Gambiel had been a good man. Sober, quiet, strong, patient — and loyal. He never seemed to have much to say, but Cuiller knew the Jinxian was always working out problems in his head, so he would have the answers ready when needed. *Callisto*'s crew was diminished by his loss, more than they knew. . . . Cuiller could only hope Gambiel was finally at peace with his fate.

When he at last broke through the top layer, Cuiller felt like a swimmer in a great, green ocean. The treetops swelled like rolling waves above the lower branches and netted vines. The lazy winds pushed them back and forth, like the conflicting chop around a point of land. He clung to his bole with one hand and held down the fine sprouts of greenery with the other. To look east and west, he had to climb around the tree.

He gave Krater ten minutes to settle into her treetop, then faced east, unslung his weapon, and took aim at the nearest clump of leaves. Cuiller fired a long burst, circling it around to get a good fire going. Soon a puff of white smoke rose out of the canopy and blew raggedly away on the breeze.

He divided his time between watching that and

looking out for any fires Krater might have set.

Nothing. "Captain," from the radio again, softly. "I think I see smoke — or haze — about half a klick away. Try again."

He burned a fresh patch upwind of the first.

"Got you. Be there in a bit." Then the radio went dead.

Cuiller climbed back down to Jook's level.

In half an hour, they heard her winder motor, coming through the trees. At the end of a long swing, Krater burst through a fan of leaves and settled on the branch next to Jook. She was strangely encumbered.

"Daff didn't make it?" the commander asked gently.

She shook her head. "We were followed by a kzin, who climbed up into the canopy. Daff fought a delaying action — and bought me time to get away."

"Dead?" Jook asked.

"If he were alive, I wouldn't have left," she said defiantly.

"Sorry. I meant the kzin."

"Daff hurt him badly, knocked him out of the trees. But he was still moving."

After a pause, Cuiller asked, "Where is the stasis-box?"

"This is it." Krater lifted the dog out of its curled-up position, snuggled in the crook of her arm, and held it out with her fingers under its chest and around its forelegs. "Daff opened the box and found this — we call him Fellah — plus a flute-thing and some dried rations."

"I asked where the box was."

"Back along our path. It was empty, and we couldn't carry everything."

"Why did you open it in the first place?"

"Daff opened it. The kzinti were tracking on the stasis field."

"Oh . . . right." Cuiller put a hand to his chin.

Hugh Jook had taken the animal from Krater and was examining it while Cuiller absorbed her report. The commander watched his navigator move the animal's legs, feel around its eyes, look into its ears.

"Remarkably mammalian structure," Jook murmured.

"I noticed that," Krater said.

The Wunderlander felt the animal's hindquarters and lifted its tail.

"Do not . . . *touch*," the creature said in a halting approximation of Interworld. The sounds were thick as they wrapped around its long, pink tongue.

Jook dropped the dog. It landed on its feet amid the vines and glared over its shoulder at the startled navigator.

The three humans looked down at the animal, dumbstruck.

"You . . . you can talk?" Krater asked.

"Yes. You-you can talk," it replied — and waited expectantly.

Cuiller tried to decide if he was hearing a ventriloquist's trick or just some kind of mimicry, a parrot's mindless repetition. But then, he thought back, the dog's first fragmented sentence hadn't just repeated their own words. It had been wholly unprompted, arising out of nothing the humans were saying. And the words had fit the physical circumstances. So Cuiller had to accept that the "dog" was reacting to its environment, verbally, in Interworld.

"Of course, we can talk," Sally Krater went on patiently. "I was asking about *you*." And she pointed at the creature.

"*You?*" it asked. "Ah . . . 'You' means this — ?" The animal swiveled its broad head around, including its own body in the gesture. "Fellah?"

"That's right. You're Fellah, and I'm Sally."

"Sal-lee. Daff. *Yowryargawsh*. Fellah."

"*Yowr* — ?" Krater began, then shook her head.

"Other . . . that deaded the Daff. *Yowryargawsh* named itself."

"Oh, the kzin warrior."

"Yes, *kzin*. Dead itself now. But other still to come.

Find *you*-Sallee." Fellah seemed to grow agitated. "Find *you*-human. Make dead too."

"Excuse me," Jook interrupted. "But what the hell are you?"

The creature paused. "You-Fellah means, is one, of-class *Pruntaquilun*. Named itself Coquaturia."

"But *what* are you?" Jook insisted.

"You-Fellah is . . . sing-maker?" it answered, unsatisfied with the result. "*Song*-maker. You-Fellah is owned-thing of Thrint named itself Guerdoth. You-Sallee, you-human, are not owned-thing? Yes. You have no . . . no Discipline?"

"Of course we have discipline," Cuiller responded quickly. "We're a Navy survey team, after all. Without discipline we couldn't perform—"

"Captain," Sally Krater said quietly, putting a hand on his arm. "You're going too fast. And I don't think that it's — that Fellah is questioning your authority."

"Of course not," Cuiller said stiffly.

The dog was staring hard at him. "You-Captain are Thrint?"

"Thrint? Are you calling me a Slaver?"

"You-Captain . . . you impose Discipline." The creature exhibited a rippling motion that might have been a shrug. "Thrint."

"There are no Thrintun anymore," Krater said. "They died out — oh, a long, long time ago, while you were in the stasis-box that Daff opened."

Fellah turned its head patiently and watched her speak, studied the way her mouth moved, as if trying hard to understand.

"Many Thrintun," Fellah said gravely. "Too many to be deaded, to die soon. . . . What means 'long, long time'?"

"That's an approximation of age," Jook interposed. "Consider it to be a large part of the age of the universe itself. About one-fifteenth of that age." Jook had to explain this using his hands. He waved his free hand all around, to indicate the universe at large. Then he flashed his spread fingers three times, curling them off each time with his other hand.

The animal seemed to absorb this, to think about it, and then looked stunned. "No Thrintun anymore. No Pruntaquila anymore. No universe anymore." Fellah made a noise back in the throat that might have been a whimper or a moan.

"The universe is still here," Sally said easily.

The creature just stared at her.

"Hey, are you hungry?" Krater suddenly asked. She pulled out of her pocket some plastic-wrapped patties, which looked to Cuiller like some kind of dried meat. "We found these in the stasis-box," she explained to the commander. "Daff tried them but he thought the taste was pretty bland." She offered part of one patty to Fellah.

The animal backed away.

"Tnuctipun," it growled. "Head-stuff. Made dead, made cold, dry."

"What?" Krater dropped the fragment, and it slid between the leaves. "Why were the Tnuctipun killed?"

"Secret." Fellah turned away. "Big secret."

"Kill them and freeze-dry their brains?" Cuiller wondered. "Why would a Slaver want to do that? It's barbaric!"

"Maybe the Thrint wanted to preserve them," Jook speculated. "Any sufficiently advanced technology would be able to reconstruct the brains later, rebuilding their RNA linkages through some kind of computer setup — and remember, the Tnuctipun were genetic engineers. Rendering the brain inert is like insurance. That way you could keep your pet scientist quiet, but you also keep him around in case you need him to make adjustments in whatever he built."

From the position of Fellah's head, Cuiller could see

that the dog was listening closely. How much was he understanding?

"So what did these Tnuctipun build?" Cuiller asked. "Fellah himself?"

"Not likely," Sally Krater offered. "Fellah said he was 'of-class,' part of a race, called the Pru . . . Prunta-quilun. But here!" She drew a long, sticklike device out of her belt. "This was in the stasis-box, too."

"What is it?" Cuiller asked, taking it from her.

"I don't know. It looks like some kind of musical instrument."

Fellah at first regarded it with keen-eyed interest, then turned his head away.

"Fellah?" the commander asked suddenly. "Do you know what this does?"

The animal looked back at him, reluctantly. "Stick-thing."

"But what did the Thrint do with it?"

"Point at head. Work fingers. Reach deep inside. Set mind in —"

"Is it something the Thrint used to fiddle about with your brains?" Jook asked, trying to overcome the word-hurdles for Fellah.

"Yes, fiddle. Itself name, *Fiddle*."

"It's the source of the Slavers' power, then," Jook went on eagerly, to his crewmates. "It has to be! And all this time we thought they were mentalists. But instead they had these shock-rod things. 'Fiddle,' he calls it."

"My-Thrint," Fellah said slowly, "my — *master*, used it, it was secret. . . ."

"Of course it would be a secret," Jook explained. "They would keep the existence of the Fiddle from their subject races, hiding it as a musical instrument or pretending it was something else benign. In that way they could maintain the myth of their innate power. And they would be willing to kill in order to preserve their secret — as those freeze-dried brains prove."

Cuiller, who still held the Fiddle, brought it up near his face and fitted his fingers awkwardly to the keys. He pressed them in no particular order. And nothing happened.

"I can hear music," Krater said. "Or, sort of. Anyway, it's . . . silvery, like bells and woodwinds, far off."

Cuiller tried a different pattern of fingering.

"Yeah, me too," Jook said. "Kind of . . ."

Nyawk-Captain had been trailing the remaining human for hours, walking in his powered armor across the ground while the human swung invisibly through the high branches. His reworked radar easily tracked the quarry's particular carbon pattern as it moved east then south, pausing occasionally to rest in the trees.

Twice he had to detour around the glimmer of large white shapes, which passed in the distance under the forest roof. They did not see or sense him, and each time Nyawk-Captain was able to regain the trail of the human's passage.

After most of the morning, when the sun was high, the prey paused once more. This time, however, it joined two more pattern signatures that had been showing to the west of it. The monkey troupe was forming up.

Nyawk-Captain shed his bulky armor, left the locator beside it, and began climbing a nearby bole. By his calculations, he was almost under the humans as they paused in the forest canopy. He moved as quietly as he could, gripping with his forepaws around the trunk's side and pushing with his feet and claws against the bark.

Arriving approximately at the humans' level, and shielded by green fans from their sight, he extended his natural ears and listened to their ongoing conversation. He understood only the vaguest fragments of spoken Interworld but soon realized the humans were talking about the Thrintun and their long-ago time. He picked up the word for "master."

Nyawk-Captain was preparing himself for the forward rush that would put an end to these human thieves and intruders on his mission — when he suddenly froze. Through a gap in the greenery he saw one of them pointing a wandlike object at him. And he could not move!

The human diddled its fingers, and Nyawk-Captain felt his paws twitch, his leg kick, his tail go stiff. Either the humans had recently developed a psychokinetic power unknown to the Patriarchy, or this was a display of power from the Thrintun artifacts they had discovered in the box. Experience and common sense suggested the latter.

As the device worked his body over, Nyawk-Captain could also feel his attitude toward the human holding it begin to change, becoming mellow and accepting. Nyawk-Captain hated that! After a few seconds, the human stopped diddling the keys of the device and turned away.

Nyawk-Captain was himself again.

Without the traditional challenging scream, he leaped through the wall of leaves and slashed left and right. One of the humans went down under his blows, flagging bloody strings of tissue. Nyawk-Captain paused only to shake fragments of meat and fabric off his paws.

The human holding the Thrintun device dropped it and rolled to one side. The artifact skittered through the leaves, up-ended, and dropped. The human reached for it.

Realizing its immediate value, Nyawk-Captain dove after it, pushing that human away with a forehand swipe that snagged cloth and skin. He fought his way down through twigs and vines, into the lower levels of the canopy.

Too late!

He could see the wand falling, spinning, finally striking the brittle soil of the forest floor.

Whatever the device might be, Nyawk-Captain's instincts told him that by retrieving it he would preserve his honor and buy his way back into Admiral Lehruff's good graces. He leapt for a nearby trunk and raced down it headfirst, moving just slower than terminal velocity. Nyawk-Captain did a diving roll across the ground and gathered up the fallen prize.

He paused only to stash it with his powered armor and then headed back up the tree to finish off the remaining humans.

Hugh Jook was messily dead, scattered in four pieces across the center of their clearing. Several meters away, Sally Krater crouched in fetal position with her hands locked around a tree limb. Fellah had disappeared.

The attack had broken Cuiller's left arm, that much he could tell from its angle, although the onset of shock had spared him much pain yet. He also felt blood oozing from four puncture wounds in his upper chest. Possibly some cracked ribs, too.

Cuiller lifted himself and approached Krater slowly, not wanting to frighten her more. He spoke gently and touched her head, massaging her temples with his good hand.

"Lieutenant? Sally? Are you hurt?"

No response.

He began moving his palm in wide circles across the nape of her neck and shoulders.

"Sally. It's all right. Time to wake up."

"N-no-oh," she moaned.

"Time to move, Sal."

"It'll come back!"

"No, no. The cat's all gone. Come on now, wake up."

Cuiller reached for her hands, still clenched around the limb, and pulled on them gently. Reason began to return to her eyes. She straightened. Her fingers slipped loose. The hands fell inertly into her lap.

He lifted them with his good hand, and worked his stiff arm gently around her shoulders. He pressed it against her as much as he could without grating the ends of broken bone.

Sally slid close to him and nestled her face against his uniform collar. Her hands crept up, around his shoulders, locking behind his neck. Cuiller rubbed her back in slow, smooth circles, pulling her closer.

Sally's mouth lifted. Her lips first touched the corner of his jaw, then moved south to find his own.

He kissed her for the first time, for a long time.

Then the world began to catch up with them, and Cuiller pulled back just enough to look into her face.

"Hello," he said, smiling.

"What happened?" She seemed newly awakened, disoriented, lost.

"We had a visitor. Kzinti kind. Are you hurt at all?"

"I — I don't think so. You?"

"Some. Not a lot of pain yet."

"Where's Hugh?"

Cuiller glanced over his shoulder. "The kzin got him. . . . He seems to be dead."

Krater roused. "Seems to be . . . ? Maybe I can — "

He pulled her back down and locked eyes with her. "You can't, Sally."

She sagged, leaning against his good arm. He caressed her once more.

"Come on," he said. "We can't stay here. That kzin may come again."

"Where can we go?"

"Anywhere away from here. Back toward the ship. I don't know."

"Can you use the harness?"

"Not with this arm."

Careful not to look directly at Jook's remains, she began to feel for his pack and gather their scattered possessions and laser weapons.

"Then we'll have to make slow time," she said.

The two of them moved off quietly. Cuiller remembered

to keep a hand over his chest wounds so as not to leave blood spoor.

The Elders of Pruntaquila, those inventors of language and studied readers of emotion, believed that *being* is the process of *becoming*.

"And if I do not stay out of that orange monster's reach," Fellah muttered to himself, "then I will become *lunch*."

He crept under and through the varied leaf-layers, hiding after the kzin's brutal attack. He spent a few solemn moments studying the remaining humans as they crouched in place, wasting time. Then he moved on, toward a place of greater distance and safety. And as he moved, Fellah considered all that the humans had been saying.

Clearly they *did* believe themselves the inheritors of the Thrintun Masters. In their own inverted language, this Interworld, they were both givers and receivers of Discipline. Their talk hinted at complex relationships and exchanges of Power in patterns that even a Balladeer had never contemplated. And yet they were not alone in their desire for control. That kzin had thought of himself as "free," too.

Much had occurred in the "long, long time" since Guerdoth had packed Fellah away in the time-bending case. And that implied other things. . . . If the Thrintun were all dead and these new creatures risen unpredictably in their place during these three-times-five unimaginable spans of time, then so were the Pruntaquila gone from this universe.

"I will have no mate," Fellah said aloud, mournfully, in his native tongue. "I will leave none of my line. Nor any student. And I will make no mark on the future." It was a dismal thought. For a brief span, Fellah considered offering himself up to the kzin's claws.

Then something else occurred to him.

All his life he had known the straitjacket bindings of

Thrintun Power and had endured the frivolous whims to which the Masters were prone. But in the few hours he had spent among these humans, even when they were threatened by the terrible kzin, he had felt uncertainty and . . . excitement! Fellah saw now that the iron course of Discipline, even when it was shaped as commands to love and respect, had been like a heavy weight on his mind. And that weight had been totally missing from his thoughts ever since the time-box was opened. Except for a brief moment when the Daff had used the Baton — or "Fiddle," as it was called in Interworld — on him.

The only trace of Power now left in this universe was the Baton itself. And it was under control of the kzin. From what Fellah had seen, they were almost as clever as the humans. They certainly had the use of fire, metals, and other sophisticated technologies. And the awareness Fellah had tasted from mirrored a whole race, millions more like this one savage kzin, waiting beyond the distances between the stars.

They were intelligent enough to use the Baton, perhaps even to copy it, creating mind-weapons of unimaginable power. Although his experience of these creatures was limited, Fellah supposed it would not displease the kzinti to have worlds full of creatures such as the Sally and Cuiller commanded to jump on cue into their wide, waiting mouths.

Suddenly, Fellah's mind firmed. There was indeed one thing he could do, one last gesture he could make, to leave his mark on the future.

Nyawk-Captain climbed quickly up into the canopy. He oriented himself on the remains of the one dead human.

No live ones presented themselves. He was sure, however, that at least one of the remaining two was wounded. How far could they have gone? He tried to smell them out, but the scent of the kill in the immediate area was too strong and distracting, the odors of the humans too similar and confusing. Nyawk-Captain had made a shallow box search of the area, and found nothing, before he remembered his carbon-pattern detector.

He returned to the ground, retrieved it, and sighted the locator back up into the leaf layer.

No return signal from any direction.

And that should not be surprising. By this time the humans, even slowed and wounded as they were, might have gone beyond the sensitivity of his locator. Though honor demanded an accounting, there was certain danger in carrying any plan of vengeance too far.

Nyawk-Captain decided to take his prize, the Thrintun artifact, and return to *Cat's Paw* in order to continue his mission. Success, victory, and lasting honor were all still possible!

After a stumbling kilometer, Cuiller finally collapsed into the leafy layer, half-afraid — but only half — that his body would find its way through to the long fall. His arm throbbed now with the pain and swelling of the break. He could feel a raw heat creep up to his neck from the wounds in his chest. Was he developing a fever?

"Sally . . ."

"Wait here, Jared." Krater settled him across a solid branch and dug the remains of their autodoc out of her pack. She held up a vial of painkiller. "I'm guessing about the dosage," she said, breaking open a needle and injecting twenty cc's of clear fluid.

A few minutes after the shot, Cuiller roused himself. Already he was feeling warm and gauzy and . . . better.

"I should see to your arm," Krater said.

"What're you . . . gonna to do?"

"Set it, splint it, wrap it."

"D'you ever — ?"

"No."

She examined his left arm, which angled slightly outward about halfway above the elbow. Before he could offer further advice, she gently extended the arm, placed her left palm against the front of his shoulder, curled her right thumb under his elbow, wrapped her fingers over his forearm, and — pulled.

White fire boiled up in his arm and he could actually feel the ends of bone clicking together. Then Cuiller passed out.

When he came to, Krater had already cut up one of the pack-frames with a laser and made L-shaped splints with it. She had used the pack straps to bind it to his arm and tied the pack-cloth into a sling. Now she was cutting his uniform away from the puncture marks in his chest and dabbing them with an astringent.

"Sorry I've got nothing for bandages," she said. "But these holes don't look that deep."

"S'all right."

"What do you think the kzin was trying to do?"

"Kill us," he said with authority.

"Then why did it leave so suddenly? With us not dead."

"I don't . . . Just before it pushed me, I seem to remember dropping the Fiddle."

"It went through the leaves," Krater agreed, "and fell."

"And the kzin went after it — as if he *knew* it was valuable."

"Do you think he found it?"

The foliage around them rustled, and both humans tensed for a renewed attack. As Cuiller tried to lever himself more erect he stirred sharp pains in his arm and shoulder. Krater stilled him with her hand.

"It's Fellah," she said, pointing toward the small animal as it crept out of the leaf-cover near their feet. "The big cat must have scared him badly, too," she concluded.

"Other kzin . . . it's gone," Fellah said.

"Did you *see* it go?" Sally asked. "I mean, how do you know?"

The Pruntaquilun raised its head, closed its eyes, and seemed to sniff the air. But Cuiller, who was watching closely, did not see the creature's nose even twitch. Fellah's attention was focused farther back, behind his eyes, inside his skull.

"Gone," Fellah confirmed.

"How does he know that?" Sally asked Cuiller.

"Well, how does he speak Interworld?" he asked in return. "Fellah must have some kind of telepathic sense, either innate or engineered. And it would certainly be a useful quality in a singer and entertainer, to read the minds, the emotional states of his audience. His language ability had improved remarkably just from being around us."

"You're saying he senses the kzin telepathically." She didn't sound convinced.

"He found his way right to us, didn't he?"

"Okay, how 'bout it, Fellah?" she asked playfully. "Do you read minds?" The Pruntaquilun looked at her seriously. "See words. Hear words." It wiggled a shrug again.

"What is the kzin going to do next?" Cuiller asked.

"Kzin is gone."

"Gone back to its ship? Gone from the planet? Where did it go?"

"Gone."

Krater shook her head. "Jared, he doesn't know anything about the ship, remember? And he probably doesn't have much conception of planets and astronavigation."

"Gone far." Fellah said with a nod. "With prize for Admiral Lehruff. Continue his mission."

"What's that?" Cuiller said, fighting the fog of painkilling drugs in his head.

"Cat's paw . . . Mission to Margrave."

"He's reading the kzin's thoughts directly," Cuiller told Krater.

The linguist nodded. "I suppose we would, too — if we were a defenseless little dog hiding from those giant cats."

"This could prove the Navy's theories," Cuiller went on. "Cat's paw. That's probably some kind of inciting action, a deception or a fake, like a feint against a mousehole."

"I think maybe you're reading too much — "

"And what else would an interceptor-class warship be doing this far out?"

"On patrol? Like us?"

"Not with that kzin's mission so deeply ingrained in his mind that Fellah can read it this clearly."

"Kzinti are particularly dutiful," Krater pointed out.

"And this one is dutifully heading back toward Margrave. You heard that part, didn't you, Sally?"

"Yes. That much was clear."

"Then we have to stop him. Even if we can't get off this planet ourselves, we have to keep that kzin pinned here."

"Why?" she asked.

"It has the Slaver's device, doesn't it? That's the power to control human and other minds, to make them do anything a kzin would want them to. . . . Think about that for a minute."

"All right, Jared," she agreed. "But we have a problem: only two laser rifles and three kzinti to kill."

"Two," Fellah said. "Kzin the Daff fought, died soon after."

"How do you know that for sure?" Krater asked. "You were with me all the time, and I didn't see that."

"His mind . . ." The animal paused significantly. "Gone."

"And not back to his ship, either," Cuiller summed up. "That's good news, Sally. . . . Ahh-gahhh," he yawned. "It makes the odds a little more even." Cuiller finished sleepily, finally succumbing to the painkillers. His arm felt a long way away.

"Those are armed kzinti you're talking about," Sally protested. "With a functioning warship to boot."

He was already halfway down the well of sleep, but Cuiller roused. "Then the trick," he said easily, "will be to separate them from their ship . . . before they can take off." He yawned again.

The forest around him darkened as if with the fall of night, and Krater caught him as he fell into it as into a bed.

"In any human army, that would be a field piece," Cuiller observed.

After sleeping, recuperating, and moving on, he and Krater now hung inside the canopy, lost in the shadows of the curving, vaulting branches that ascended from one of the trunks. They looked down through holes in the greenery that they opened — slowly, naturally, like a riffle of wind — with their dangling toes. They were suspended above the kzinti ship, with a horizontal offset of less than fifty meters.

Cuiller studied the vessel with a pair of binoculars, working them one-handed. One of the kzinti was climbing on the outside, naked except for a beltful of tools, working with a mechanical fitting against the curve of the hull. The other, in full armor, stood watch. That one's visored helmet moved across regular arcs of the canopy surrounding the ship, and each time he panned toward them, Cuiller let the veil of leaves slide smoothly into place.

It was the kzin's massive rifle that had caught the commander's attention: some kind of pulsed energy weapon.

"Can you sense them, Fellah?" he asked the small creature snuggled into Sally Krater's arms. "How close are they to finishing repairs, hey?"

Fellah raised his head and looked gravely down, past their toes. He appeared to consider. "Repair. Soon."

Cuiller realized that the alien's exposed white hair would make an effective aiming point for that cannon. And that gave him an idea.

"I think I can improve our odds with one shot," he told Krater.

"How?"

"First, by splitting our positions and halving our vulnerabilities. I want you and Fellah to maneuver off to the west, around the ship. Put about twenty degrees of radial separation between us."

"But then what are you going to do?"

"I think I can pick off the kzin who's doing the work. Without breaking my cover."

"You'll get killed!" Sally said, alarmed. "That other one, in the armor — with the weapon he's carrying, all he has to do is bear close on you. And poof!"

"It's a big jungle."

"He can take bigger sweeps with that thing," she said.

"Sure, but I'll have time to get him with my second shot. In case he does a sweep, however, I want you in an alternate position.... You can offer a diversion or something."

"I don't want you to risk yourself — sir! Look, why not wait for a Bandersnatch to come along? That'll really keep him busy."

"Because long before then the kzinti'll be all finished up and ready to lift ship."

"All right, Jared," she said coolly. "If you won't listen to reason, we'll do it your way. But give me time to get in position."

"Ten minutes?"

"Time enough. But not a minute sooner, you hear?"

"A full ten minutes, I promise."

With a baleful look, she withdrew higher into the canopy, taking Fellah with her. Soon he could hear only the faint *whirr* of her rig's winder motor.

As he waited, Cuiller spread the leaves below him and practiced taking aim with his rifle. Holding it steady in his right hand did not work, and he could not find a point of purchase on the cloth sling covering his left arm. Then he figured out a solution.

Cuiller worked his winder and rose into the forest cover until he could get his feet under him. Paying out slack, he took a loop of the fluorescent-dyed monofilament and wrapped it around the rifle housing. He would have to control the rifle's tendency to lever up and slip the loop as he put his weight on the line, but he could do that with his right elbow. The only other danger was that the monofilament might cut into the weapon's barrel and tear it apart. A calculated risk.

Sally's time limit was still a minute short of coming up when Cuiller lowered himself back into firing position. He had no intention of letting her offer any kind of diversion and so becoming a target herself.

Cuiller moved the rifle around, holding it steady with his armpit on the stock, sighting down the pips, to the forehead of the unarmed kzin. His body was tending to pivot on the looped line, so he braced his feet against the springy branches, the same ones that made up his concealment. Then he gathered his concentration, breathed out slowly, and —

A spear of blue-white light stabbed down from twenty degrees away to his left and opened the kzin's skull. She had fired first!

The kzin on guard wheeled and sighted his field piece back in the direction from which the beam had come — toward Sally!

Bobbling slightly on his line, Cuiller shifted his aim faster, immediately found a good side-on view of the aiming figure, and fired at the breech of the kzin's rifle.

The weapon exploded.

When his weapon's energy packs discharged all at once, Nyawk-Captain was thrown backward. The eyeshield of his visor flared white but saved his vision from flying shrapnel. His whiskers were singed below the limits of its protection, however, and the insides of his arms hurt terribly. He smelled and tasted burned hair.

Only when he tried to rise did he understand how critically the blast had injured him. His upper limbs moved slowly, and some of the armor's joints worked not at all. Molten metal from the exploding weapon had locked them, dripping even as far as the knee flexor on his right side. He rolled in the dirt, trying to break out of the imprisoning bodysuit. The shell clasps up his belly line were sticking, too.

With a mammoth, flexing spasm of his back, he brought the armor upright on its knees and started to limp toward the ship's hatchway and the relative safety inside the hull. There he would also find tools to help him get free of the imprisoning suit. With every step he took, Nyawk-Captain expected more energy pulses to blast away the ablative surface and heat the steel shell over his back.

When he got his locked paws on the hatch coaming, he remembered the impossible squeeze that moving into and out of the airlock had been, even with fully functioning armor. He wasn't going to make it.

He was beating the suit's belly against hullmetal, trying to break the clasps free, when one of the humans dropped out of the trees on a thin, purple wire and put the projector of a laser rifle against his forehead. A small, fluffy white animal which curled under one of its arms jumped free and scrambled into the ship.

Nyawk-Captain, staring into the human's glaring eyes, did not dare move.

After a second, the white animal came out with the Thrintun artifact held in its jaws. Nyawk-Captain remembered leaving the device on the ship's workbench for his and Navigator's further study. As the animal emerged, a second human — this one more wounded than the first — came down on another wire and also leveled its rifle.

The first human put aside its own weapons, took the alien artifact from the Whitefluff, and aimed it at Nyawk-Captain's forehead instead.

Krater tried various settings on the Fiddle and watched with a clinical eye as the kzin twitched and went into convulsions. She settled on one which left it trembling and hypnotized inside its steel restraints.

"This process can either be painful or not," Cuiller explained to the kzin slowly in Interworld. "I don't think it understands, Sally," he said finally.

"Well, if I let up with this thing," she proposed, "he might be able to nod or something. Want to try it?"

"No thanks. You keep him under." Cuiller turned back to the kzin and said conversationally, "Now, we need to borrow your ship, Kitty. I'm going to burn you out of that armor, and you're going to cooperate — one way or another."

Cuiller studied the latches down the suit's front. They were gobbed with metal and streamers of burned plastic. He placed the projector of his laser alongside the middle one and fired a short burst. The clasp flew off into the dirt. He repeated with the other two, and the clamshell halves of the belly plate sagged apart. The commander then laid the rifle against the soft, reddish fur underneath.

"Slowly," he told the kzin.

The warrior shrugged massively, withdrawing its arms from the crabbed gauntlets, vambraces, rerebraces, and pauldrons. It divided its attention between Cuiller's aim with the rifle and Krater's hold on the Fiddle.

Krater twisted something, and the kzin's eyes crossed. Its hands moved sideways, too fast for Cuiller to react. He almost opened the massive chest with a burst before he understood that the Fiddle had prompted that sudden movement.

"Keep working on it," Cuiller told her, "I think you're getting somewhere. I hope he's either captain or navigator of this interceptor, because that's the only way he'll be able to help us."

Then inspiration struck.

"Hey, Fellah!" Cuiller called.

The tiny alien was dwarfed by the huge warcat, but he glanced up at the commander with some confidence.

"Talk to the kzin," Cuiller told him. "Get inside his mind. See words — say words. Tell him we need his ship, need him. Take us to Margrave. Tell him Margrave. He can do it the easy way or hard. But one way or another, he's going to take us to Margrave."

Fellah looked at Cuiller with his big, dark eyes gleaming out from among the white hair. The commander sensed that the alien understood what he meant. After a moment, Fellah turned to the kzin and began to growl and spit in a timbre that was no more suited to his delicate, curling tongue than Interworld was.

Through his sudden pain and the sensory confusion that the Thrintun artifact had thrust upon him, Nyawk-Captain was catching only a fraction of the humans' speech and understanding even less. Still, the gestures with the rifle were significant. He did hear the word "Margrave," which as the proper name for a human-dominated planet was common to both Interworld and his own language.

Then the Whitefluff began speaking in the Hero's Tongue.

"Thinskins take you. We-they put you . . . at disadvantage."

Nyawk-Captain stopped trying to override the nerve-scrambles that imprisoned him and listened closely.

"True enough," he growled.

"You are with . . . luck."

"Be careful how you tease me, Fluff. I might still regain enough control with just one fingerpad to squash you."

"Be silent. I-Fellah help you."

"Why should you help a kzin when you travel with the humans?"

"They prison me, too."

"True enough. So. What do you propose?"

"Human the Sally works the . . . Painstick. She does it badly, yes? You are more aware now, yes?"

Nyawk-Captain suddenly saw the opportunity before him. The alien artifact, the Painstick, impeded his actions more or less as the human woman varied the intensity and direction of its strange power. The eerie music still gave Nyawk-Captain a headache but, as the human woman fretfully twisted and fingered the device, its nerve signals were less paralyzing to him than they had been at first. Eventually he might work free of it and be able merely to simulate a body under external control. Then, if he could keep from retching, he would pretend to do what they wanted — until they were both distracted.

"I see your meaning, yes," he told the Fluff. "What do you suggest?"

"They want you take . . . ship and them. Go to place called 'Margrave.' You know this?"

"Yes, I know Margrave. My crew and I were headed there, before we landed here." And, with luck and at the human's own prompting, Nyawk-Captain told himself, *Cat's Paw* might still arrive there right on schedule.

"Play along," the Whitefluff told him. "Pretend pain. Be docile. Be watchful, too."

"Yes. Until the moment."

"I tell you when," the tiny alien advised.

The human male interrupted them with "[Something unintelligible] Margrave?"

The Fluff looked back and answered with "[More nonsense sounds] Margrave."

Nyawk-Captain nodded his head vigorously in the human gesture signaling agreement. Then, still twitching his arms in random and mechanical ways, he climbed slowly out of the armor's greaves and cuisses.

The work Navigator had been performing on the hull when he died was related only to the sensors for defensive weapons — useful but not essential systems, now. Nyawk-Captain's mission could proceed without them.

The kzin's stomach lurched and staggered with a change of balance as human the Sally tried a new twist with the artifact. The device was still making him do strange things and feel unusual sensations, some pleasant but most merely irritating. It was infuriating to occasionally lose control, but he could learn to live with that. He could even feel himself beginning to like the human female, just a little.

The other human went through the airlock first, keeping his rifle leveled on Nyawk-Captain's throat. The kzin let him. When he wanted, when the time was right, he would take away that toy before the human could fire it.

Cuiller backed the kzin into the central crash-cradle and made it sit down. While he held the rifle to its forehead, Sally used the couch's cloth straps and mechanical braces to bind the kzin. She left one forearm and paw free to work the instruments at its station. However, a brief and sweeping study of the control layout had convinced Cuiller that at least two people were needed to pilot the interceptor.

Once the kzin was secured, Krater stepped up to the main panel and fastened the Fiddle to a cleared space with a wad of stickum from her pack. She arranged it so the Fiddle's presumed working end pointed at the captive's forehead.

Cuiller inspected the arrangement. "I hope long-term exposure to that thing isn't going to render him incapacitated, or dead."

"We could do worse," she suggested.

Fellah sat quietly on the deckplates, where Cuiller hand set him down.

"Okay, Fellah, tell him we need to start the main polarizers and lift ship. He'll tell you how, and you translate for us. Or, I guess, you can just point at whatever controls we should attend to next."

The alien absorbed this and began spitting in the Hero's Tongue. Cuiller and Krater settled into the two remaining kzinti couches and tried to adapt the crash webbing to their smaller bodies.

With pantomime gestures and low growls, the kzin instructed Fellah in takeoff procedures. Then he relayed the instructions in a series that went, "Push this, pull that, turn this one until red line comes up here, do not move until this disk turns blue."

Working one-handed, Cuiller hit switches and verniers in the indicated order. The airlock closed, the board lit up, and somewhere back of them the world stiffened and shifted as the gravity polarizers kicked in.

On one of the screens, he watched the landing site and *Callisto*'s battered hull dwindle and then disappear in a wash of green. In another second the green foliage was gone, dissolving in a flutter of hazy light that turned a chlorine-tinted white as the ship, still accelerating, rose above the limb of the planet.

"Good-bye, Beanstalk," Krater called cheerfully.

"Good-bye, Daff and Hugh," Cuiller added soberly. "They were good shipmates."

"Amen to that."

As they cleared atmosphere, the kzin turned back to Cuiller directly and gestured with its free paw toward controls on the panel in front of it.

The commander studied the almost-glazed eyes and the string of dribble at the corner of the kzin's black-lipped mouth. Was he missing some procedure — landing gear, hull integrity, something important? Cuiller threw the switches that the kzin had indicated.

The cabin was immediately filled with the buzz of an open comm circuit. An anxious kzinti face peered out of the screen directly ahead. It warbled a growl at them, and its eyes grew suddenly large.

Before the kzin in the chair could respond, Krater lunged forward, grabbed the Fiddle, and began pressing all its keys. Their kzinti captive went rigid and trembled with induced catatonia.

Cuiller frantically turned all the switches on the section of control board he'd just used, scrambling them with random settings. Finally, the alien face faded out in a blaze of static.

"Our captive was faking submission," he observed.

"I'm sorry, Jared," she said apologetically. "I don't know enough about the Fiddle to make him do anything more than twitch. Can we fly this ship alone?"

"I think I could pick out the star pattern surrounding Lambda Serpentis," Cuiller said. "We can probably bend a vector in that direction. And, given a few tries with this comm system, I think we can call out those segments of the U.N. fleet stationed at Margrave."

"Who was it that he contacted?" Sally asked.

"His commanding officer?" Cuiller suggested. "Some flight dispatcher back in kzinti space?"

"The face on that comm screen appeared almost instantly, didn't it? So the relay time was virtually nil. Whoever it was is damn close, Captain. Closer than kzinti space."

"Kzin . . . self-named Lehruff," Fellah offered. "Admiral."

"I was tricked into opening a comm-circuit directly into the entire kzinti command structure," Cuiller said. "Now the entire Patriarchy is going to know something damn peculiar has happened aboard this ship."

"Damned bad," from Fellah.

"Well, not much we can do about it now," Cuiller said. "Except run like hell and call for reinforcements."

"Agreed," Krater said.

"We travel," Fellah said. "Be here 'long, long time.' In this small space," he observed thoughtfully. "Enough food here? Hey, Sally?"

"Don't worry, Fellah," she assured him. "We won't eat a sentient species."

Fellah waved a paw at the recumbent kzin. "Does he?"

"Time lies with we-us. Our side," the Whitefluff growled sternly to Nyawk-Captain. "You . . . risk. With Lehruff. Damn bad doings."

"I know it," the kzin growled in return, idly making gestures at a disused bank of controls that the Fluff could demonstrate to the humans as a pretext for making conversation. The human male cautiously worked the sliders, unaware that he was just opening and cycling the ship's atmosphere vanes. "I thought it was an opportunity worth the taking," Nyawk-Captain explained.

"Risk to be taking! Do not again."

"Why not?"

"Human the Sally will use maximum setting. Painstick cripples. It also kills."

Nyawk-Captain eyed the device where it was stuck to the main panel, aimed at him. After his trick with the comm-circuits, the woman had readjusted its settings. For a brief time, the Painstick had left him dazed and trembling.

And this had been good, Nyawk-Captain thought now. The experience had shown him the weapon's unique flaw. Continuous exposure, even at the highest settings, allowed an active brain to become acclimatized to the effect. Like a patch of skin under abrasion, his mind was developing the neural equivalent of a callus. After a span of hours he had found himself able to shape coherent thoughts and activate useful synapses around the offending signals. He still did not have much control — not enough to slip the bonds of his couch, turn upon the humans, and rend them to bloody fragments. But his head was definitely growing clearer and his limbs felt more his own.

"On this . . . heading, at this . . . velocity," Fluff groped for the navigational terms in the Hero's Tongue, "Lehruff catches us?"

"What? No, his fleet is still a day or more behind us."

"All along way to Margrave?"

"He was going there already."

"But these humans, we-they get there first," Fluff concluded. "Humans have their own fleet at Margrave?"

"Yes, there will be a battle. Not as grand as the one we kzinti had planned, but enough still to — "

"Humans have the Painstick. Soon all humans have it. Some will learn better than human the Sally." Fellah spat in a particularly suggestive manner.

Now that was a bad thought. Nyawk-Captain envisioned bands of raucous monkeys armed with copies of the Painstick. They were cutting down armed kzinti in mid-leap and marching them off as twitching zombies. He saw the males of the Patriarchy reduced to the status of shivering, voiceless females. . . . And the Fluff was right. These two humans would get to Margrave ahead of the Last Fleet and call out their Navy. They would certainly have time to turn the Painstick over to their high command, who would remove it from the battle theater for study and duplication. The Patriarchy might win this coming Battle of Margrave, and still lose their souls for eternity.

Could Nyawk-Captain stop them? Could he give these humans not just useless instructions but damaging ones? Could he dupe them into disabling *Cat's Paw*, so that Lehruff would draw even with them and take everyone aboard his flagship? That would deliver the Painstick neatly to Lehruff and then to the Patriarchy.

Or, barring that, might Nyawk-Captain trick the

humans into destroying this ship?

Unlikely. . . . His stupid (yes, it *was* stupid!) attempt with the communications switch had alerted the human male to Nyawk-Captain's potential for trickery. The humans would be doubly careful with every command he suggested now. Only those with no effect — like their current twiddling of the atmosphere vanes — would escape that scrutiny.

However, Nyawk-Captain might be able to slow them up. He could cut their lead ahead of the Last Fleet. Then Lehruff would overtake and . . . But no. Even if that one glimpse over the comm-circuits had alerted Lehruff to some kind of disturbance aboard the *Paw*, the old kzin still had his orders. He would only follow the interceptor down to Margrave and let the *Cat's Paw* make its feinting run, as planned. Lehruff knew how to do his duty, even if things he saw in a flash of broken communications might trouble his eyes.

Then Nyawk-Captain knew what he had to do.

His only worry was his failing strength. At their current speed, it would be many days before the human fleet stationed at Margrave came out to take possession of the *Paw*. Until that time, the two humans would keep him bound, physically and mentally, or so they thought. They would loosen the bonds only to feed him and take instruction in ship operations. But even then, the woman had discovered intravenous supplements among the medical supplies, and these had diagrams to guide a nonmedical kzin in an emergency. The woman had rigged drip equipment above his crash-couch and was running the tasteless liquids into the vein at Nyawk-Captain's neck.

His flesh would soon be melting away. Eventually his atrophied muscles would be as weak as the humans' own. He would be weak as a kzitten when they finally released him — but maybe that would be enough.

"Tell the human to stop his adjustments," he instructed Fluff. "We've had enough nonsense for one watch."

The little animal nodded and turned away to make his soft and useless mouthings.

Nyawk-Captain relaxed and composed his mind, exploring new pathways around the Painstick's ingrained signals. He prepared himself for a continued stream of idle days.

For twenty days Jared Cuiller had been surreptitiously monitoring the approach of the kzinti warfleet behind them and relaying his observations ahead to the human fleet that had sailed from Margrave on his alert. He had also hoped to renew with Sally the intimacy they had derived from that one long kiss among the treetops. But the quarters in the captured interceptor were too cramped, the kzin was too restless, and Fellah too keenly observant.

"Maybe later." Sally had smiled, when he first shyly proposed it. "We'll have lots of time."

But *would* they? He thought dismally of the major battle that was brewing, with a war surely to follow. As Cuiller made his observations of the kzinti fleet, he dared probe in their direction for no more than a few seconds. And still these peeks accounted for hundreds of obvious warships and other massed vessels. When the two forces came together, it was going to be a battle to remember.

Too bad, in a way, that they wouldn't be on hand to take part in it. But earlier he had arranged to rendezvous with an Empire-class supply ship somewhere on the human side of the conjectured clash point among the stars. The Navy would take this captured ship in tow and transfer off Jared and Sally's prisoner and their prizes: a new sentient life form, a working stasisbox, and — best of all — a mechanical enhancement of the Slavers' power. Rich prizes.

In the many days that the two humans and Fellah had to study the interceptor's layout, Cuiller had worked out its flight sequencers to his own satisfaction.

And now, within visual-contact distance of the globe comprising the human fleet, he shut down the gravity polarizers and let the ship drift forward at a considerable fraction of light-speed.

"Cuiller to *Sumeria*," he called, adjusting the comm panel. "Ready to match velocities."

The supply ship dropped out of the battle formation, dived below hyperspace, and showed up on one of the control board's screens.

"We'll take you with magnetic grapples, Captain Cuiller," the bridge officer informed him. And no, the rank he used was not a slip of the tongue, either: "Captain," instead of "Lieutenant Commander."

Jared and Sally began powering down nonessential systems.

"What about him?" she asked, pointing at the recumbent kzin.

At first their captive had thrashed around, testing his restraints, but as the days wore on he had become increasingly silent, spending more and more time sleeping. Krater had changed his fluid bottles regularly, taking new ones from the food generator, which she had programmed from a card in the medical supplies. Now, as they approached the englobement, the kzin's only response was an occasional yawn and whole-body shudder. She routinely wiped white drool from the fanged mouth as he lay there.

"I guess we'll have to untie him to make the transfer," Cuiller said. "We knew that sooner or later we'd have to trust your control with the Fiddle alone."

He flexed his own left arm, which had begun to heal straight and painlessly. That was probably thanks in part to his new diet of rich, red meat which seemed to be the food machine's only other setting.

Krater unstuck the Fiddle from its place on the control panel, being careful to keep it oriented on the kzin's head. Cuiller bent to undo the couch's straps and braces. One by one he released the mechanical controls over their comatose enemy.

Cuiller's head was down near the backrest when he heard the couch squeak.

"Jared! Look out!" Sally warned.

A huge paw, twenty centimeters wide, swept across over his head and snagged the Fiddle out of her hands. In the partial gravity of the control space, the device flew toward the wall, bounced off it with a *clack!*, missed Cuiller's ear by four centimeters on the rebound, ricocheted under the control panel, and skittered along the floor.

He dove for the Fiddle, but before his hands could close on it, a massive, clawed foot stamped down on the hullmetal plates. The barrel of the device exploded in a shower of fragments and sparks. Cuiller closed his eyes in reflex and felt the pieces patter against his face.

The kzin ground its foot against the floor for good measure, then kicked the mixed fragments off to one side. It had lurched out of the crash-couch to reach the Fiddle, and now the kzin collapsed against the padded armrest, gasping with the effort.

Before the kzin could move again to attack Cuiller, Sally had retrieved one of their laser rifles and slid its projector up against the prisoner's left eye. The kzin raised his paw in a warding gesture and shook his head. Then he slipped back into the chair and made to fasten the restraints again.

The kzin growled and hissed in Fellah's direction. "Better this way, he says," the alien translated, and then, speaking directly: "Thrintun power . . . Bad thing, yes? Bad in your world. Bad in his. Now, no more."

The kzin stretched his lips without baring his teeth.

Cuiller looked down at the shattered tube and glittering shards of what could be electronic circuits — or perhaps conductors of some other energy. He nodded.

"Do humans eat their prisoners?" Fellah asked, again translating. "Or do you allow an . . . honorable death . . . in hunt for sport."

"Neither," Cuiller answered. "You — " He pointed at the kzin. " — will probably be interned for the duration of the coming war."

"Kept in . . . confinement?" Fellah asked, still working through the Hero's Tongue.

"Yes, certainly."

"Worse yet. But . . ." And here the kzin thumped his paw on the couch's padding. "Better at least than this."

Magnetic grapples seized the hull. Fellah gave out a glad, barking laugh that would translate the same in both Interworld and the Hero's Tongue.

THE END

Niven • Pournelle • Flynn
FALLEN ANGELS

In 1995 Earth finally had its act together. There were two manned space stations orbiting, one from the former Soviet Union, one from the United States. Even better, the human race had finally agreed that something had to be done about the environment—and was doing it, one green law after another. By the year 2020 the Greenhouse Effect was just a bad memory, and the air was a clean green dream.

There was only one problem. All that pollution, all that CO_2—the Greenhouse Effect itself—was the only thing holding off the next, regularly scheduled ice age! With the carbon dioxide gone the glaciers came, and came down fast. In the mid-21st century, the icebergs had reached North Dakota and weren't slowing down.

But by then an alliance of the most extreme "deep ecology" Greens and the zaniest of religious fundamentalists had taken over in the winter-bound U.S.— and they weren't about to give up their power merely because they were destroying civilization. And they needed a scapegoat. So they decided that it was the "air thievery" of the folks they left stranded in the orbiting space stations that was causing the New Ice Age.

FALLEN ANGELS is the story of two spacemen. Shot down and stranded on a hostile Earth, they think there is no hope for them. But they're wrong. Help is on the way. Help from the one nationally organized pro-technology group left on Earth; the only ones who would dare fly in the face of their unforgiving authoritarian government; the only ones foolish enough to risk everything to help two strangers from space. Science fiction fandom. *Angels* down. *Fans to the rescue!*

72052-X • 384 pp. • $5.95

ROBERT A. HEINLEIN